ACROSS *the* Shores

*Four Women,
Bound by Generations,
Find Love Where
They Least Expect*

D1566886

ANGELA K. COUCH, KELLY J. GOSHORN,
CAROLYN MILLER, CARA PUTMAN

BARBOUR
PUBLISHING

More Than Gold ©2023 by Carolyn Miller
The Veil ©2023 by Kelly J. Goshorn
Running from Love ©2023 by Angela K. Couch
Love along the Shores ©2023 by Cara Putman

Print ISBN 978-1-63609-519-6
Adobe Digital Edition (.epub) 978-1-63609-520-2

All scripture quotations are taken from the King James Version of the Bible.

This book is a work of fiction. Names, characters, places, and incidents are either products of the author's imagination or used fictitiously. Any similarity to actual people, organizations, and/or events is purely coincidental.

Cover Image © Mark Owen / Trevillion Images

Published by Barbour Publishing, Inc., 1810 Barbour Drive, Uhrichsville, Ohio 44683, www.barbourbooks.com

Our mission is to inspire the world with the life-changing message of the Bible.

Member of the
Evangelical Christian
Publishers Association

Printed in the United States of America.

More Than Gold

BY CAROLYN MILLER

Chapter 1

September 1851
New South Wales

The air held the honey-mint tang of eucalypt mixed with expectancy, the dust that sought the hidden spaces of everything from her bonnet to her boots, the legacy of a thousand trudging footsteps borne of desperate greed. The cart dipped into a deep rut, jerking Josephine Wilkins against her brother's shoulder.

"Sorry about that," Elias said. "We're nearly there now."

"Wonderful." Conscious of her flat tone, she summoned up a smile. "It certainly is interesting country." Rugged ranges, lightly timbered with gray-green trees, holding the quartz outcrops that so excited her brother. Every so often the flash of a brightly colored parrot or the warbling song of a bird known as a magpie drew attention. So many different birds and animals to her native North America lived here. Why, yesterday's camp had seen a visit from a squat, four-legged, badger-like creature called a wombat, snuffling around, seeking grubs, or so one of their traveling party had said. Then, earlier today, she'd glimpsed a tall, long-legged bird called an emu, its drum-like call and man-height unlike any bird she'd seen. This land held wonders, indeed.

"Can you believe that, after all this time, we're almost there?"

Josie nodded, subtly easing her seated position, wishing she could ease the ache in her lower half, the result of too many days traveling over rough terrain on roads that should more properly be considered goat tracks. Or perhaps, given the country they were in, kangaroo tracks. Her smile faded as they passed another of the poor souls carrying all his possessions in what she'd heard called a swag. Imagine having to carry one's clothing and all provisions rolled up and strapped to one's back to walk these many miles.

"This is good country," Elias continued. "I can feel it. See those auriferous hills?" He pointed to a quartz-topped hill, something she'd come to recognize in past days. "Jardine told me of a man who simply plucked up the grass and found gold nuggets lying beneath."

One of the more preposterous-sounding stories, but one that others heading this way assured her was definitely true. And if so, well, what riches might this place hold for her too?

He coughed, the sound triggering a moment's fear. Surely this warmer climate would not allow him to succumb to influenza again? "You are well, are you not?" she asked, conscious of the anxiety in her voice.

"Of course I am." He slid her a look that suggested she was silly to worry so. But were his eyes overbright? She'd best keep on the lookout for a return of the fever.

"The size of a man's fist, Jo, nuggets the size of a man's fist," he continued, as if determined to distract her from thoughts of his ill health. "Jardine told me so himself!"

She fought the urge to roll her eyes at the mention of that man's name yet again.

"Jardine says the gold is everywhere, simply waiting to be found."

"If that truly is the case, it's surprising everyone hasn't taken advantage of such a thing."

He glanced at her. "You did not have to come."

Except she did. And Elias knew that. "You know I'm always glad to be with you." She patted his arm.

He cocked an eyebrow but said nothing more, returning his attention to the horses and the steep descent.

Josie blew out a long, quiet breath, her gaze turned to the scene below. The rock-strewn hill dipped to a gully where a profusion of river oaks suggested a winding waterway. From this vantage point, she could see a sea of tents, could faintly hear the burble and clang of the hundreds of tiny figures working so industriously below. Dread churned with anticipation as the cart shuddered and creaked down the precipitous incline, its passage veering far too close to what looked like a sheer drop to the valley. Elias leaned back, his arms straining to keep the horses in check, while she clutched the edge of the wooden seat and prayed for their safe arrival.

Memories flashed of a previous journey, treacherous and tragic, and she clamped her eyes shut, moving with the cart's bend and sway. Her heartbeat pounded in her ears. She *could* do this. They would be safe. This time.

The horses snorted, the cart jerked and juddered, and then the road finally evened out. She opened her eyes and exhaled. "Thank goodness."

Elias chuckled, a sound tinged with relief. "It got a little scary there, didn't it?"

She pressed her lips together, unwilling to admit to such a thing. Not that she should have been afraid. Not when she'd crossed an ocean and survived perilous storms; not when she'd encountered a strange seaside city filled with sights and sounds and scents most unfamiliar. Surely the adventurer she'd tried to prove herself to be wouldn't be put off by a little hill like this.

But there was an element of danger in this land of New

South Wales, a danger beyond the tales of snakes and spiders the size of a man's hand, a danger born in the recklessness that had birthed this colony just over sixty years before, when convicts had been shipped to a wild land from the other side of the world. Yet this danger also engendered a degree of daring, where one who risked could perhaps achieve despite the challenges. This seemed a land of possibilities, where the status of previous generations need have little bearing on those to come. Indeed, this seemed a land that might lead to the miraculous and do wonders for her broken spirit. And her bruised heart.

"Jardine says we need to look for the licensing hut."

Amid the plethora of dirty gray canvas tents, a hut should be easy to spot. Except the vast number of men, many of whom ceased their hurry to stare at her, made seeing much beyond the trees and rocks more of a challenge. She tucked a strand of curly brown hair behind her ear, averting her eyes from the too-interested gazes—how long since these men had seen a woman?—and turned to her brother. "So, will Mr. Jardine be here to meet us?"

"That's what he said in his letter."

Something fluttered in her midsection. Any minute now, she would finally meet this man her brother had mentioned so often and for so long. She snuck another peek at the stained and sweat-soaked miners, their dirty clothes evidence they held more care for their work than they did their appearance. Which one was he? The bearded giant with arms the size of tree trunks? The smaller man with a meticulous moustache? The one murmuring to another, while his sharp eyes remained fixed on her with a look that prickled unease down her spine? She edged closer to Elias and dropped her gaze. Somehow she knew it wasn't that man.

Apparently, this friend her brother had first encountered in California was a "stand-up fellow" and "genuinely trustworthy." She guessed him to also be kind and generous, else why would he have helped Elias in this way? Not that the news of the discovery of gold in New South Wales was a secret by any means, certainly not with the government advertising such finds far and wide. But still, she wondered what Mr. Jardine would look like, whether his voice would hold a similar clipped accent as many of the settlers here possessed, whether he'd be tall like Elias or small like her.

And what would he think of Elias's surprise when Mr. Jardine discovered that his friend had not ventured all the way out here alone.

———

The ruckus at the road drew Daniel's attention, and he rose from his squatted position by the river, shading his eyes from the sun's bright glare. Another poor soul here to try his luck, judging from the loaded cart and clean clothes and the air of enthusiasm his grinning countenance implied. And—was that a woman seated beside him?

He released a low whistle. Well, he'd learn soon enough that this was hardly the place for a lady. He could only hope the couple were without children. The men around here were hardly gentlemen, and the lack of womenfolk had led to a degradation in civility that was only exacerbated by illicit liquor, frustration, and envy. The poor woman would likely be without much variety in the way of female companionship for many a moon.

Still, it was only polite to welcome them, to see what he could do to help the new arrivals settle in. Daniel bent and tipped the remaining sediment in his pan back into the water, sluicing it clean, then collected his gear and stowed it in his tent, just a short walk away.

Wiping his hands, he made his way down to where the cart stood. He threaded his way through the men, who murmured behind cupped hands while staring at the lone occupant. He frowned. Where was her husband? What kind of man left his wife to fend off the bold eyes and hushed comments of these rash and raffish miners?

Not that she seemed too intimidated, with her chin raised, her gaze averted, studying the high ridge that rose behind the stream as if she found that the most fascinating sight in the world. Although—he glanced at her gloved fingers twisting her bonnet's dangling ribbons—maybe she wasn't as oblivious to the men's whispered remarks as she might first appear.

"Jardine?"

Daniel turned to the small mustachioed man. "Emmett."

"Any color today?"

"Not so far," he admitted. "You?"

Matthew Emmett exhaled. "I've heard rumors there's a new place, up Turon River way. I'm thinking I might try my luck there."

Daniel nodded, knowing Emmett was far more invested in finding gold than he himself would ever need to be. But then, not everyone had the noose of family duty to return to one day.

His attention returned to the cart and, more specifically, the woman, still valiantly ignoring the catcalls and ribald offers being sent her way.

"Pretty, ain't she?" Emmett said.

Daniel shrugged, but it was true. The curly dark hair seemed to crackle with energy, and her features were even, although her fair skin seemed destined to burn under the harsh sun.

"Hey, miss," one of the bolder men called, "how 'bout you get off your high horse and look at us."

His chest tightened. How could her husband leave her defenseless like this? Where was he, anyway? Still with the licensing agent? Daniel glanced at the mud and bark hut, but there was no sign of the husband's return.

John Dryson, the large, bearded fellow who seemed most intent on demanding the woman's attention, sidled closer to the cart, murmuring something beyond Daniel's hearing that caused the woman to redden and Daniel's pulse to hasten. Enough was enough.

Daniel shouldered past the onlookers and drew near the cart. "Excuse me."

Dryson turned, but the woman seemed intent on ignoring Daniel too. Very well. He would concentrate on the known troublemaker. "John, leave her be. Dinnae you see this lady's husband but a few minutes ago?"

This garnered a look of surprise from the woman and a scowl from Dryson.

"What's that got to do with you?" he growled.

"Not a great deal," Daniel admitted, "but you may find this lady simply wishes to be left in peace while she awaits her husband's return."

"But sir—"

Daniel glanced up at the woman's soft protest and was trapped in her gaze. Her eyes were a most glorious blue, luminous, sparkling like the Solway Firth he remembered from younger days. His heart thudded. A man could drown in those eyes.

He glanced away, ashamed of himself for thinking so about another man's wife. *God, forgive me.* Then he looked up in time to see Dryson's large fist swing toward his face.

Daniel stepped back, and the whoosh of air slid past, followed by the alcohol-scented stench of breath as Dryson staggered near, his movements accompanied by a hoarse cheer from the onlookers.

"Now, now," Daniel cautioned, "you dinnae really want to cause a scene, do you?"

Dryson muttered something unfit for ladies' ears, which ignited a fresh surge of protectiveness.

"I really don't think any of us need to hear such things, do you?"

The bearded man's bristles seemed to quiver with anger as

Dryson made a further comment questioning the nature of Daniel's parentage.

"I can assure you, there be proof." An oil painting displayed over the mantelpiece in a castle on the other side of the world attested to the unlikely match. "Now, tell me, how goes your search for gold?" he asked, adopting a conciliatory tone. "Someone mentioned something about Turon River."

Diversionary tactics seemed to work, as Dryson dropped his fist and muttered about the disappointing finds to be had along Summer Hill Creek, and Daniel gently encouraged him to seek his prospects at another site fifty miles away.

When Dryson had been swallowed into the crowd, whose grumbles suggested they'd been disappointed at the lack of a mill, Daniel's attention returned to the woman, whose eyes now fixed on him. He swept off his felt hat and offered a small bow. "You must forgive the lack of a fitting welcome, ma'am. I'm afraid such an environment does not lend itself to the finer points of etiquette."

She inclined her head, like he'd seen his grandmother do, and he fought a smile at the thought of this woman being anything like that grand dame.

"I trust you and your husband will find what you seek here," he said, before adding politely, "Good day to you."

He bowed again, like the gentleman he'd been raised to be, and moved away.

"Thank you," she called, her soft, sweet voice holding an American twang.

He pivoted, gaze meeting hers, his heart kicking in another moment of profound connection that both excited and drew personal loathing. To think he'd grown so immune to common decency, he still found her attractive. *God, forgive me.* He best leave and avoid her in the future, else he'd end up like Joseph in the Bible, entangled with Potiphar's wife.

"Jardine?"

He turned at the unexpected voice. A curly-headed man strode toward him, geniality pouring from his step. "Elias Wilkins?" A smile erupted from his soul. "How good of you to come!"

Wilkins pounded him on the back, grinning like a child. "How good of you to tell me."

"I had not expected to see you here so soon. When did you get here?"

"Just now." Wilkins moved to the cart and spoke to the woman, whose glance soon shifted back to Daniel.

Daniel tilted his head to her. "You came together?"

"Yes."

"Forgive me, but I did not realize you were married."

"I'm not."

"Or betrothed."

The smile Wilkins offered seemed to dim and now hold a measure of guilt. "That neither."

Truly? He'd never picked Elias Wilkins as possessing loose morals. His brows rising, Daniel faced the woman, whose confident expression had grown uncertain. "Then who are you?"

"Daniel Jardine," Elias said, "allow me to present Miss Josephine Wilkins. My sister."

Chapter 2

Josephine stiffened as the man's eyes rounded, the lightest of pink washing along the high cheekbones not speckled with rust-colored beard.

"Sister?" he muttered, glancing at Elias. "Forgive me. I did not know. I recall you once mentioned a brother, but cannae remember other family, save that your parents had passed."

"Josephine was living with my brother until recently," Elias explained.

Until life with Ethel, her sister-in-law, had become unbearable. While she was sad to leave darling baby Caroline, she knew it was best for all concerned to live with Elias instead. Who could have known the abandonment of Josephine's fiancé would have led her to such a place as this? But more she could not explain.

"Ah." Jardine slowly pivoted to face her again, and she took a moment to study him more closely. Thick-lashed dark blue eyes held intelligence and compassion, lean cheeks held a ruddiness often synonymous with chestnut hair. Yet even with his faded and stained clothes, there was an elegance about him that contrasted to the men she'd seen in the colonies thus far. That, combined with the kindness that had seen him stand up for her earlier, renewed warmth toward him, as it had in that weighty moment earlier when their gazes entwined.

He smiled, and her very soul seemed to twitch in recognition, her breath hitching, her pulse beating faster. How strange that she barely knew this man, but her senses seemed to come alive with him in a way they never had for Wilfred Elliot. "Miss Wilkins."

Oh, what was it about his voice that entranced her so? She blinked at her foolishness and straightened. "Mr. Jardine."

"I hope your travels were not too challenging."

Amusement tipped her lips. He'd said that like someone making a social call. "My travels were—"

His tawny eyebrows rose.

"—most enlightening," she said, casting a swift look at her brother. Yes, she had seen and heard things her mother—had she lived—or Ethel would have had a conniption about.

One of Mr. Jardine's brows arched higher still, begging her to elaborate.

"I did not expect to see so many diggers returning as we passed this way." Or an unlucky digger's bones under a tree, necessitating her brother and some other men to dig a shallow grave whilst she prayed for the family of this poor lost soul.

He nodded, his russet locks glinting in the sun. "This is not a place for everyone."

His glance at Elias held a wealth of meaning, a look she knew only too well. This place known as Ophir—named after the Old Testament mining region from which King Solomon received gold—was not a place for women. She had seen but a handful on their way in, and none looked the sort to take a young American woman under her wing. She lifted her chin.

Elias coughed. "You need not worry about Josie. She's stronger than she looks."

Mr. Jardine's forehead knit as if he heard the rasp in Elias's voice and was troubled by it too. "Well, best we get you sorted. If you wish to sell the horses, you should do that soon too, else you'll be paying an exorbitant amount for their upkeep. There is space between my tent and Emmett's." He pointed to the small-statured man of large mustaches. "It would be good to set that up now before the darkness hits. It's still quite cold at night."

She nodded. The cool evenings had proved a surprise, and more than one night they had awakened to see ice lace the blankets that served as their temporary overnight accommodations. They'd been told this was a warm land, yet the chill on the mountains had a way of seeping into one's bones, adding to the discomfort provided by the unfamiliar sounds and smells that drifted through the night.

Two hours later, the sun had dipped behind the tall hills, the shadows deepening into pools of black. Men's curses, murmurs, and laughter filled the fast-cooling air, and she was thankful for Mr. Jardine's assistance in helping them set up their tent next to his and allowing them to share his fire.

She stretched her hands toward the flames, wishing she'd had time to find her soft leather gloves, but all she had unpacked in the small corner partitioned off as her private space were her clothes for the morrow. Fresh clothes, the like she hadn't worn since their travels had begun three weeks ago. Now all she needed was some way to cleanse the grime and soot away.

"Miss Wilkins?"

She startled, nearly upending the tin cup being held out to her. "Oh, Mr. Jardine, sir, I did not see you."

"You don't say."

The flash of his smile tightened her chest, and she accepted the cup with murmured thanks and heat on her cheeks she was glad the darkness hid. Really, she was acting little better than a schoolgirl. Just because the man had a winsome smile did not mean she need fall under its spell. "How did the horse selling go?"

"I think your brother was satisfied with the result."

She nodded, glad for her brother, as the sale would add to their coffers. But it also signaled they would now be staying, with no easy way of return. She bit her lip, studying the flames.

"Are you all set up?"

"As best as can be expected." Their bedding was set out, an upturned crate served as their table, a tea chest as her larder, while the rest of their supplies were in great wooden drums that she would unpack in tomorrow's daylight. All of this lay under a canvas roof and surrounds, the cool breeze inching around the plenteous gaps, making her grateful for her tea. She sipped, wincing as the hot liquid burned her mouth.

"Ah, I'm sorry it's not to your taste. We don't tend to have a sufficiency of cows to provide milk."

"It's not that. 'Tis the temperature, that's all. But I am very grateful to have something warm to drink." Her gaze met his again. "And my brother and I are both very thankful for all of your assistance today."

He inclined his head. "It's how we survive out here. One cannot focus on one's self, and in order to succeed, we must often work together as a team. I've heard fellows here talk of it as caring for one's mates, which may seem indecorous talk for a young lady, but I find the sentiment most refreshing."

"We are instructed to love our neighbor, after all."

"Indeed we are." He paused, eyeing her more closely. "Am I to learn you are a believer also?"

"Yes, Mr. Jardine. I am." Even if some days her faith felt as thin and ragged as the stockings she wore. Perhaps this new land might help her learn to trust again.

A rustling from the tent soon saw Elias emerge triumphantly, holding a cast-iron skillet and several eggs. "I knew I'd find the eggs."

The gladness with which Elias had greeted their arrival had seen him insist on making their meal, something she was not averse to, especially considering the many meals she'd been responsible for these past weeks. "I am glad your eyes still work."

"I did wonder why they lay atop a barrel, like a good fairy had left them there."

"Perhaps one did," she said.

"Indeed." He grinned at her affectionately, and her heart warmed some more. Elias's brand of boyish charm had always drawn her protectiveness.

"Shall I prepare the damper?" she asked, drinking the last of her tea, welcoming its heat and the chance for momentary respite from the labors of the last hours.

Mr. Jardine glanced at her. "You know how to make damper?"

"It is not difficult." Flour and water, after all. "I've always enjoyed baking too."

He chuckled, the sound warming her like the bright coals at her feet. "I suspect our methods of baking here are not what you're used to."

She nodded and straightened her spine. "My sister-in-law would not approve of baking in hot ashes, but then, I am made of sterner stuff."

"And a good thing too," Elias added. "Ethel is the sort who can burn water." He drew nearer and wrapped an arm around Josie's shoulders. "This one might like to keep her light under a bushel, but there's no hiding it when she bakes." He squeezed lightly. "You'll have every man in twenty miles begging to marry you, Josie."

His words slipped under her defenses, stealing her breath. Wilfred might have once felt that way, but it hadn't been long before the opposite proved true and he was begging her to release him from his promise, leading her to question the word of every man. "That is not my intention," she murmured, her eyes on the fire.

"It might not be your intention, but I wager it'll be true. Now, I'll find the bacon we sourced from that last farmhouse, and we shall feast to celebrate our arrival."

"I shall leave you to it," Mr. Jardine said, pushing to his feet.

"No, you must join us," Elias said jovially. "We would not be here if it wasn't for you."

"Oh, but—"

"Indeed, Mr. Jardine, you must not leave." The words seemed to sprout and escape all by themselves. "We truly could not have gotten set up so quickly without you. Please, stay."

"Verra well. Thank ye kindly, Miss Wilkins. I'm much obliged. I have a can of golden honey syrup that might prove the perfect accompaniment, if ye don't mind my small contribution."

She smiled to herself, enjoying his lapses into brogue, and moved to prepare the damper. She might have arrived in this part of the world heartsore and filled with trepidation, but the kindness of this man made it seem as if God might not have forsaken them completely after all.

———

Daniel was in trouble. He swallowed the remaining piece of sweet deliciousness, now understanding his friend's bold claim about Miss Wilkins. The woman certainly knew her way around making damper, and if others were as blessed as he to taste this, then Elias would not have spoken rashly at all. Many a man here would delight in having a sweet wife with a talent for making sweet things. And the longer he observed and listened to Miss Wilkins, the deeper he felt his own fascination grow. Far from being the shy matron he'd once assumed, her teasing exchanges with her brother proved she had a snap and vigor about her that appealed as much as her faith did. But even though she seemed sweet and had insisted on praying over their meal—praying like she meant it, not mere rote words like so many prayers he'd heard—she was not for him. His gaze dropped. She would never meet the standard his birthright demanded. She was not English, after all.

"Jardine, you are right. This golden syrup is perfection

indeed." Elias licked his fingers. "And very tasty when added to the bacon as well."

"I have found myself most partial to that combination," Daniel admitted. He risked a glance at Miss Wilkins. "Thank you for a most delicious meal."

"You're very welcome." Her smile caught him around the heart and squeezed.

No. This was not good. He pushed to his feet and, ignoring their protests, gathered their used eating utensils and took them to his makeshift kitchen area to clean. After their long travels, brother and sister would both be tired, and there would be time enough for them to learn the ins and outs of what camping on these goldfields involved. And while his grandmother would likely have an attack of the vapors at the thought of his completing such a menial task, he had a feeling his parents would be far more understanding. Before his father's ascension to an unlooked-for inheritance, he had lived in Sydney for a time and had often spoken fondly of his years in the colonies, where he'd lived a more humble life. But appreciating his willingness to pitch in and clean was a far different matter to welcoming the fact that he was entertaining thoughts about a certain blue-eyed American lass. So he hurried to finish his job, and after checking they were settled for the night, he made his escape.

But not to bed. Instead, he felt the tug to follow his usual habit and walk around the tents scattered around the goldfields. His father might now live on the other side of the world, but it seemed something of his former profession ran through Daniel's veins too.

He passed the nearby "coffee tent," which everyone knew was really a sly grog shop, for the law prohibited the sale of alcohol out here. It didn't stop the likes of John Dryson and his cronies, sitting out the front and defiantly swilling beer from tin cups, the scent of liquor taunting the inspector were he around. Sally

Jenkins, the rotund grog-seller, had ingenious means of "skirting" the law. He'd witnessed her dispensing brandy from a tube poking from the side of her skirts and, after a question to Emmett, had learned the woman was known to strap tin containers to her waist under her clothes in order to evade detection.

He paused to say hello to Paddy and Eileen O'Leary, an Irish couple who ran the large tent that served as a boardinghouse. Many a man had hankered for a warm night under the O'Learys' roof in these past wintry months, where they could be assured three meals a day and a clean bed for ten shillings a week.

"I see you have new neighbors," Paddy said.

"Aye. Friends of mine from California. Elias and Josephine Wilkins."

"Ah. I trust she'll know to pop by and say hello," Eileen said.

"I'll be sure to let her know." Of the few women on the gold-field, Eileen was the safest, her heart as big as her girth.

"Y'might want to be telling young Wilkins to be keeping his wife away from the likes of Dryson there," Paddy said in a lowered voice. "I saw him eyeing her off earlier."

"I saw that too," Daniel said. And perhaps that was reason enough to encourage the subterfuge that brother and sister were actually husband and wife. "I'll remind them to be vigilant."

"Aye. She's a pretty lass. We don't want no trouble around here." Paddy flashed a near toothless grin. "Not any more than what we already got."

"That's for sure and for certain." Daniel gestured to the next dwelling. "Has there been any more word on Joe?"

Eileen shook her head sadly. "He don't seem to be gettin' better, no matter what I do."

"I'll stop in and see him." The German emigrant was not the friendliest of fellows, and his mystery illness had caused most people to cast him an even wider berth than normal.

"You're a good man, Daniel Jardine, as good as any parson,"

Eileen said, patting him on the shoulder. "There's a special spot in heaven for the likes of you."

"There's a special spot in heaven for all who believe, Eileen," he responded, willing her to find true salvation.

Her husband gave a guttural laugh. "Not sure if the good Lord thinks we be worthy of enterin' the pearly gates." He turned to serve a new lodger, and the moment was lost as Eileen was distracted by a call from within.

Daniel slipped away and moved next door, but his enquiry about Joe Drescher's health was met with loud snores. He was still alive then. That was something. Thanking God for the man's life, Daniel continued his rounds, offering a hello, alternately commiserating and offering what encouragement he could with those for whom gold finds remained sparse, and celebrating with those who had found. These goldfields might not have a parson, but he knew this internal tug to offer what life and light he could. This world could be very dark indeed.

He breathed through his mouth as he approached what counted as a kind of butcher shop around here. Carcasses hung from wooden supports outside the bark-covered hut, the slabs of meat covered in flies by day, the rotting meat smell announcing Callahan's wares. Lewis Callahan nodded, smoking his pipe as Daniel passed. Callahan was widely rumored to be one of the richest men out here, and it had nothing to do with the amount of gold he'd found. Some canny local squatters had discovered that sheep sold for meat instead of tallow could fetch a hefty price, and Callahan had capitalized on such transactions, earning him a reputation as a clutch-fist. But when the alternative was trapping possums or shooting parrots, it was understandable that miners might prefer a bite of mutton instead.

The Wilkinses' tent appeared dark as he approached the end of his circuit. He hoped they found the rest they needed. Elias did not appear as healthy as one should be when out in this environment, even if his bright eyes and enthusiasm pronounced otherwise.

Matthew Emmett stretched and stood from his round of tree stump he used as a seat. "I see you're a fast worker," he said, his voice dropped so the brother and sister next door could not hear.

"I beg your pardon?"

"The lass next door." He jerked a thumb at the quiet tent between this place and Daniel's.

"She holds no interest for me," he fibbed. "You have the wrong end of the stick entirely."

Emmett's chuckle held a raspy note, not unlike the one he'd heard from Elias earlier. "Now don't be hopping on that high horse of yours, my lord."

"Hush, man. How many times have I said not to say anything?" he complained.

"I still can't understand why a nobleman's son would be out here fossicking like us poor commoners."

"The world is full of mysteries."

"Och, indeed it is." Emmett gently jested at Danny's ancestry. "But to have one of near royal blood—"

"Enough of your blethering. You know it's nothing like that. And all of that social hierarchy nonsense means nothing to me."

"Aye, I do." Emmett's grin grew. "But it surely makes you fun to tease."

Daniel turned the conversation to talk of gold, and they spent a moment weighing up the prospects of Ophir compared to Turon River before finally calling it a night.

He passed the Wilkinses' tent, calling out a soft "good night," which saw Elias respond, while Miss Wilkins did not, and he was reminded to advise them—and Emmett—to maintain the illusion that they were a married couple for her safety.

And after writing of his daily dealings in his journal, he settled on the cot made of branches under his own canvas, his mind toying with possibilities of his own. How long should he stay in the colonies? He'd promised his mother he'd be home for his thirtieth birthday, and given the months-long passage to the other side of the world, he best make preparations to leave by Christmas in order to arrive by June. He'd sent his last letter from Sydney five months ago, just before he'd headed west. It would have arrived by now, and he could guarantee his mother would be champing at the bit, devouring every word describing a place she'd long expressed a wish to visit.

He drew the blanket higher, smiling in the dark. This place had certainly proved the adventure he'd imagined, the animals, birds, trees, and flowers so different to the tamed English land-scapes and Scottish lowlands of his youth. As his thoughts drifted, he wondered if Miss Josephine Wilkins was really asleep, whether she and Elias would be able to maintain their charade, and what would happen if the truth came out. His prayers ballooned to dreams as he soon fell fast asleep.

Chapter 3

Josephine woke abruptly at the raucous sound coming from high above. She exhaled, hand on her heart, as she remembered the heinous laughter was simply that of a bird. A "laughing jackass," she'd heard it called before, when she'd first encountered that startling sound, or a *kookaburra* in the native tongue.

A clank nearby drew her attention to the immediate tasks and, after completing a rushed toilette, she emerged from her blanket-screened corner of the tent to find Elias moving a pot as he encouraged the fire to life.

"Good morning, brother."

"Sorry, Josie. I did not mean to wake you."

"It was not you but the birds."

He shot her a wry grin and gestured to the pot. "I'm making tea."

"Are you? Or are you merely trying?"

He laughed at her tease, and she bent to help, and soon the water was bubbling merrily.

"Miss Wilkins."

She startled at the deeper voice and glanced up to meet Mr. Jardine's smile. Warmth fluttered inside. "Good morning, sir."

"I trust you slept well."

She wrinkled her nose. "Well" was generous. "I slept."

He chuckled. "That is something to be thankful for at least."

"Yes."

Breakfast consisted of damper and mutton, and it soon became apparent that Elias and Mr. Jardine had determined it was good to pool resources. When exactly they'd decided this, she did not know—perhaps it had been yesterday afternoon when she had been organizing their supplies in the tent, or perhaps Elias had awakened much earlier today—but she found herself agreeing that cooking to feed an extra mouth was a small price to pay for the chance to have such luxurious items as cheese and pickles. Mr. Jardine's compliments about her baking skills were not to be cast away either.

"I will take you around the camp and show you what basic stores we have," he promised, as she cleaned their utensils following their meal.

"Are the prices expensive?"

"You may have noticed there is not a lot of competition, so some charge what they like, but it behooves them to set prices that will see customers purchase and not go elsewhere." Mr. Jardine glanced at Elias then back at her. "Miss Wilkins, I fear I may have to ask you to consider something that may seem disagreeable."

"If you mean you wish me to wash your clothes—"

"No." He held up his hands. "You misunderstand. Although it is obvious it is necessary."

"I did not wish to point that out."

His lips twitched, and then he gestured for her and Elias to move a little farther away, under a great tree known as a eucalypt. "It is simply a warning, and perhaps it is wise."

"You're beginning to scare me, Mr. Jardine," she said.

"That's not my intention." He passed the brim of his battered felt hat between restless fingers then glanced at Elias. "After conversation with various people last night, I feel it best to advise that if you do not want your sister to be the object of unsolicited attention, you might be best served to pretend she is your wife."

She coughed. "Pardon me?"

"I know pretense is not what you would like, but unless you wish to be courted by every single man in sight, you may wish to hide your unwed status."

Elias nodded, facing her. "And didn't you say just yesterday that finding a husband here was not your intention?"

"Yes, but I didn't wish to lie about it."

"It seems most people believe, as I first did, that you are married," Mr. Jardine continued. "I think you'll find things easier, Miss Wilkins, if it is not known you are free."

Free. A memory panged of the letter Wilfred had sent, asking her to set him free from his promise. And now look at her, here in this mud-strewn valley in the middle of goodness-knew-where, about to be trapped by other people's expectations in a pretense of matrimony. Not that she was likely to meet anyone she might wish to marry.

"I think it's wise," Elias agreed.

Of course he did. He seemed inclined to go along with whatever Mr. Jardine said. Irritation grew, then subsided, as Mr. Jardine sent her a soft look.

"I know this is not easy, but I promise that while most of the men might have rough manners, they will not hurt you and will in fact treat you as gallantly as any fashionable man about town. But there are some who have less care, and it's only for your sake that I suggest this."

Torn between the embers of offense and wondering exactly how he knew about the conduct of fashionable men about town—which town? London?—she sighed and nodded. It seemed Elias was not the only Wilkins to go along with Mr. Jardine's schemes.

Elias coughed again, and she clutched his arm. "Are you unwell, brother?"

"I'll be fine," he muttered, shaking off her arm. "Now, Jardine, let's take that tour."

Mr. Jardine exchanged a quick look with her, one that said he was troubled by her brother's cough too, but he said nothing more about it, only encouraging her to retrieve her bonnet before their tour began.

The next hours passed in a welter of information as they threaded through the roughly plotted streets and passed the various stores. Tents, marked by flags, denoted various shops that held all manner of weird and wonderful sights: two fish strung up dripping into a bag of sugar, yellow soap, a box of raisins, saddles, blue serge shirts, shovels, a bundle of ribbons, bread, and tallow candles.

"Many of the shopkeepers will purchase for cash or in exchange of goods or gold, of course. But some of the ones who accept gold don't mind playing tricks on the unsuspecting digger," Mr. Jardine cautioned, as he drew them away from one rather less than salubrious-looking establishment. He subtly gestured to the dim tent. "That place, for example, is known to grease their pans, so when a poor digger pays in gold dust, some of it sticks to the sides."

"How outrageous!" exclaimed Elias.

Mr. Jardine nodded. "You should check out old Bentlow's fingernails too."

"Why?" Josie asked.

"As an examiner of gold dust, he'll inspect the gold and move it about, and in doing so draws some of it up."

"That's reprehensible!"

"Indeed." He gestured to another tent, where an orderly array of provisions could be seen displayed out the front. "I recommend Truman's, over there."

"A true man?" she asked.

"Honest, yes. He has been my supplier since my arrival several months ago."

He steered them past a tent that served as a doctor's then over to the creek and the bulk of where the diggings took place. Explanations followed of the various means used to extract the gold from the earth. By far the most common was tin-dish-washing, where round tin dishes, eighteen inches across the top sloping down to twelve along the bottom, were half-filled with dirt, topped with water, then gently swished and swirled until the water poured off.

"Any gold will sit at the bottom because it's the heaviest," Mr. Jardine explained for her benefit, since she was sure Elias had used similar techniques in California. He smiled, and Josie again felt that fluttering sensation in her chest. "Perhaps we shall see you take a turn."

"Perhaps you will."

"Oh, but you'll be busy making our food and gathering fire-wood, Josie," Elias said, nudging her.

She sighed. But while the pleasures of mastering cooking in what Mr. Jardine had called a "Dutch oven" awaited, she couldn't deny interest in the diggings. Yes, it was messy work, but how exciting to find the precious bright metal, to be the one who might assist her brother rather than feeling like she was the one being assisted. Yes, this was definitely something she wished to do.

⸺

Daniel glanced up to where the Wilkins siblings worked. Elias scooped up a half pail of water and gently poured it into the tin dish Miss Wilkins held. She began her swishing, while Elias moved to the "cradle," pouring water into the wooden tub where dirt from the creek lay waiting to release the promise of gold. Daniel used his spade to chop at the dirt, aiming to find the elusive metal, while his thoughts resumed contemplations on Elias's sister.

Yesterday's visit around the diggings had seen them return

Miss Wilkins to their tents with the promise they would replenish their supplies while she set to prepare their meals. Then he and Elias had gone back to the diggings.

How pleasant it had proved after a hard morning's work to return for tea and damper at noon, then again when the sun had sunk low to find his meal prepared for him, the common area between his tent and theirs tidy, and their eating utensils shining more brightly than he remembered.

"You seem to have wrought miracles," he'd said, gesturing to the neatened campsite. "I don't recall it ever looking so welcoming. Why, there are even some flowers." The tiny yellow buds poking from a glass bottle were almost as elegant as anything his grandmother might have commanded her servants to procure.

"Mr. Truman says it's called 'wattle.'" She touched the soft blooms.

"Picking flowers is all well and good, but did you collect the firewood?" Elias asked.

Her gaze snapped to her brother as a sweep of red rushed up her cheeks. "Yes, brother dear. That's what that pile of wood is," she said, pointing to a stack of twigs and small branches.

"You've been most industrious," Daniel complimented her.

"I like to feel I'm of some use," she demurred.

"Judging from the smell coming from that pot, you have done very well indeed."

And then when he tasted the stew she'd prepared, he nearly groaned aloud at the delectable taste. He could see why some men did bring their wives.

"Are you all right, Mr. Jardine?" she asked.

"Far more than all right. This meal is like manna from heaven."

"Told you she's a good cook," Elias said, mopping up the last of his sauce with his damper. "I reckon you could sell this, Josie, and supplement our income."

Daniel nodded. "That is an option. There are some places to

eat, but you could make a tidy little income by serving a few extra mouths."

"I'd be willing to pay," Matthew Emmett had said, appearing by their firelight, holding his tin plate. "Don't s'pose you've got any left, ma'am?"

"Ma'am? Oh!" Miss Wilkins shot her brother a glance then looked at Daniel before her gaze rested on their other visitor. "I'm sure we have enough." With another quick look at her brother, she scooped a generous portion into Emmett's bowl.

"Thank you, ma'am. I could feel my heart shriveling smelling that fine smell while eating my cold mutton."

"Then you'll have to join us too." Then, when Emmett tried to offer her money, she'd refused.

"Josie," Elias muttered, "we're not a charity."

"Aren't we supposed to care for our neighbors?"

"Not all of them," he'd complained, which seemed sufficient cause for Emmett to insist on paying three shillings, as per the going rate for an evening meal in Ophir.

Miss Wilkins had pocketed the coin, delight filling her face, thus drawing Daniel's amusement, and they'd sat around the campfire discussing how they could make such arrangements work.

Sure, and it was early days yet, but he was fast coming to admire her plucky attitude, such as was evidenced after lunch today when she insisted on joining them at the diggings.

"But you're a woman," Elias protested.

"Thank you for your observation. I've been aware of that for some time."

Elias rolled his eyes. "Women don't dig."

"Nonsense. I'm sure I saw several ladies yesterday."

"I didn't," Elias said bluntly. "Did you, Jardine?"

"I don't think we are too bothered here by social niceties as some are," he managed. "If she wishes to, then why stop her?

Especially as it's nice weather. It is a far less pleasant job when the rain pours down and you're working up to your knees in mud," he said, facing Miss Wilkins. "I cannot see what harm it could do, especially if you work near us."

"You are a man of intelligence, I see."

"Thank you. And you are a woman capable of surprises."

"Thank *you*."

He'd bit back a grin, but must not have been fast enough, as her gaze latched on to his, drawing her blushes. A knot of concern formed. He couldn't afford to let her think he might be enamored. But the longer he spent with her, the more she proved her ability to intrigue.

As she did even now, sluicing her way through another shovelful of dirt and hope. He leaned on his spade and watched, her brow puckered, her tongue peeking out on one side as she concentrated on the washing. Another swish, then she carefully poured off the water. Then her expression cleared, and that same radiance he'd been privileged to witness last night washed over her features. "I found some! Look!"

Elias dropped his spade and hurried to her side, peering into her dish. "That's hardly anything."

"It's better than nothing," she countered. "See, Mr. Jardine?"

He drew near and eyed the tiny bright specks. "Well done."

"Thank you." She beamed, and his heart kicked, reminding him to step away, to not stir up emotions that could not be tamped. "How much do you think it's worth?"

"I couldn't say precisely, but perhaps two pennyweights? It might be six or seven shillings."

"Which is far easier than cooking meals. We'll be rich in no time," she teased her brother.

"I don't think she quite understands," Elias complained when they returned to their cradle. "This is hard work."

"I'm sure she will know that tomorrow morning. But you

mustn't begrudge her, especially when she's trying to help."

Elias coughed again, a great racking cough that forced him to lean on the long-handled dipper.

"Are you quite well?" Daniel asked. "That cough sounds nasty."

"I've had it a while," Elias confessed. "It seemed to clear up on the ship, but the cooler temperatures seem to have brought it on again."

"You may need to visit the doctor."

"And how much does that cost?"

"Ten shillings for a consultation. But he is at least a real doctor. Fought at Waterloo then moved here to try his luck. But he knows his stuff, unlike some of the cheaper quacks."

Elias shook his head. "I'll be all right. You don't need to worry about me."

Daniel pressed his lips together and refocused on working the cradle, rocking it gently back and forth as Elias scooped a load of beaten soil and water into the hopper. Just like in the tin-dish-washing method, the gold rested on the bottom, which in this case was a wooden shelf under the hopper, as the sieve-like cradle worked.

So far they had found maybe twenty-five shillings' worth of gold, which split between them was not a bad day's return. But it seemed to cast Elias into low spirits.

"It's your first real day," Daniel encouraged later, back at their camp, as he stored their day's efforts in his "treasury"—a round matchbox of German origin that could hold eight ounces of gold.

"We heard stories of people plucking gold from the earth."

"And some have found that to be true. But most people have to work to find it."

Miss Wilkins shifted the joint of mutton in the camp oven that was suspended from three iron bars fixed in the ground in the form of a triangle, each bar a yard apart, joined at the top, above the fire. Although he'd eaten enough mutton for ten lifetimes, she seemed to have found a way to make it smell more appealing. Or maybe it was the knowledge that it was she who cooked it that drew his smile.

"Can I help?" he asked, moving to assist.

"Yes, please." She stepped back from the fire, busying herself with the plates and cups, while Daniel carefully retrieved the joint of meat.

He clasped it firmly with the tongs then hefted it into the waiting pan she held, as if this was an operation they'd done many times.

"Thank you." She smiled at him before turning to retrieve the damper from the coals.

Conscious of a warm sensation in his chest, he stepped back, turning to encounter Elias eyeing him strangely, with Emmett who had joined them again.

"Ah, Elias. How are you feeling now?"

"Well enough." This comment was belied with another of those rasping coughs that threatened to bring down the bark strips that served as roof shingles.

"That's most convincing, brother," Miss Wilkins said.

"Josie," Elias hissed, tilting his head at the man beside him.

Her eyes widened, as if she realized what she had said.

"It's quite all right," Matthew Emmett said. "I know that despite what some might say, you two are brother and sister."

Elias deflated. "How did you know?"

"It's obvious. You both look quite similar, although Miss Wilkins is far prettier than you."

Daniel joined Emmett on the log that served as their dining chair.

Emmett nudged his side. "And because of you."

"I beg your pardon?" Daniel asked, watching as Miss Wilkins continued the last of her dinner ministrations while her brother sliced up the meat. She seemed to have gotten some sun today.

Her nose and cheeks had reddened.

"From all I've learned of you in recent months, I knew you'd never look at another man's wife the way you do at Miss Josephine."

Daniel swallowed, dragging his gaze away. "I don't know what you mean."

"Oh, I think you do. And I think her brother sees it too. You'd best take a care to yourself if you don't want your reputation for good deeds being brought undone by a too-long stare."

Daniel exhaled, his gaze stealing back to the subject in question. She met his glance with a shy smile, and he knew he was in trouble indeed. It was best to put distance between them now.

Chapter 4

Water dripped its steady way down the canvas, the incessant *ping ping* as it met the iron water pot a relentless reminder of the past week of rain. Josie glanced at Mr. Jardine, but his eyes remained on the prayer book he held. Sundays were a day of rest, and while not everyone in the camp observed the Sabbath, most were glad for the chance to halt their labors at least.

She lowered her gaze to the fire they huddled around, the cool winds whipping and causing her to draw her shawl more firmly around her neck. After that initial welcome bout of fine weather, it seemed the colonies had determined to oust the weak and feeble-hearted by way of inclement weather, with rain showers and what Mr. Jardine called "drizzle" passing every day.

"Which means we can take heart and encourage ourselves to trust God and remember what the book of Philippians says, that 'I can do all things through Christ which strengtheneth me.'" Mr. Jardine closed the prayer book. "Let us pray."

She closed her eyes obediently, forcing her thoughts to still and attend to Mr. Jardine's words as he prayed for their protection, good health, and to be a blessing to their world. Such prayers suggested he could have been a parson, so sincerely did he speak.

"Amen."

"Amen." She glanced up, only to notice Mr. Jardine whip his gaze away.

Elias coughed again, and she glanced at him. His cough had worsened in past days, and yesterday he'd spent the day not working, the first—apart from Sundays—when he'd not worked at all. She'd asked him to visit the doctor, but he refused, saying it would take coin they didn't have, which she found strange, as they must still have the proceeds from the sale of the horses and cart.

"Well, this is a miserable day," Mr. Emmett said. "When shall this misery cease, do you think?"

"Never," grumbled Elias.

"Come now, brother," she forced herself to say. "One can have misery outside without it infecting one's heart too."

"Well said," Mr. Jardine agreed. But when she looked at him, he was still frowning at his prayer book as if his life depended on it.

Elias coughed again, and she inched closer. "Brother, are you sure you do not wish for the doctor to attend you?"

"We cannot afford it."

"Nonsense," she said firmly. "Why, we have enough gold just from my panning to justify the expense. Please. Let me send for him."

"No."

Mr. Emmett cleared his throat. "It is cheaper to visit than to have the doctor come here," he murmured.

But if her brother refused to go, then having the doctor come here was better than nothing at all.

"Elias, you would not wish to distress your sister, would you?" Mr. Jardine asked.

Elias coughed again, his heavy-eyed glance shifting between his friend and her. "Josie worries too much."

"I don't think she's worrying unnecessarily," Mr. Jardine persisted.

This time, when she looked at him, he met her gaze, and after the past week of appearing to avoid her as much as their close confines allowed, that fact, even more than his words, fed fear. What was he saying? That he thought Elias might die? Trepidation squeezed her throat.

Mr. Emmett glanced at her, his gaze holding sympathy, and she swallowed the wild words threatening to escape. No. Elias would be fine. Mr. Jardine's prayer meant he would be. Didn't it?

"Excuse me," Mr. Emmett said after another exchange of glances with Mr. Jardine.

He upped and departed rather abruptly, leaving their circle to the creeping rain and whistling wind. A shiver racked her body, and she drew her shawl closer.

"Well." She glanced at the other men. "I think we need a cup of tea."

She busied herself with a chore she could do, blinking away tears as every so often fear shrieked through her heart, much like the wind whipping around the canvas flaps.

"I'll see about securing the canvas on that corner," Mr. Jardine said. "No, Elias, you sit, keep your sister company." He departed too, leaving her with her brother's rasping breath, her fears, and prayers.

"*Trust God.*" Mr. Jardine's words from the service earlier wafted through her mind. She shuddered out a breath. That was right. She was trusting God. She did not need to fear. God would protect them. God *had* protected them. He'd proved so faithful in this past fortnight.

The challenges of these first two weeks—cooking by campfire in rain, cleaning the campsite from never-ending mud, laundry, let alone dealing with all manner of people and the stares as she bought her supplies—had slowly eased as Josie had established her daily routine. Mornings were taken up with preparing meals and what manner of shopping and household duties their strange little "family" of four demanded. Mr. Emmett had become part of their circle, and he, along with Mr. Jardine, proved a necessary counterweight to the gloom that seemed to have overtaken her brother. Afternoons were the time she helped by washing or panning for gold. She remained quite proud of her efforts— one afternoon, she'd situated herself next to another's man's pan dumpings and extracted nearly a pound of the precious metal simply because he'd washed too hurriedly. Perhaps it was her patience that held her in good stead or the dexterity of her fingers. Whatever it was, she was proud to be supplementing their coffers through her finds and by providing a few extra meals for other miners, even if at times her brother seemed less than thrilled.

Elias, after his initial excitement, had grown more morose, the lack of gold discovery in recent days seeming to be exacerbated by news of a large nugget in a neighboring claim worth five pounds. Envy ran thick and bilious through the goldfields, and those who were lucky enough to find gold varied between the foolish who loudly proclaimed their good fortune, thus setting themselves up as the target for thieves, and those who acted more secretively, their paranoia almost as obvious as the "new chums," as Mr. Jardine called them, who shouted of their finds.

And while Mr. Jardine assured them there was more gold to be found, he too seemed to be acting in a more subdued manner. He was polite as ever, but she'd noticed how he didn't linger near her, that his glances held nothing of the weight and depth of those first days. At times she wondered if she had done something to offend him, but, searching her conscience, she could think of nothing she had said or done save treat him in the teasing manner as she would her brother. Perhaps he did not appreciate that. But she could have sworn he was like her in being another soul who sought lightheartedness over melancholy, which was why his avoidance of her weighed on her heart so heavily.

The water boiled, and she carefully measured out the tea leaves and added them to the pot. She placed a teaspoon of sugar in her brother's cup, sure he could do with the extra energy it allowed, then added her sorry attempt at a type of biscuit—made with flour, golden syrup, and egg—on his plate as well. "Here you go, brother dear."

Elias grasped her hand. "You're a good sister."

"I know."

As hoped for, he smiled, though his laughter these days seemed at naught. Where had her bright-eyed companion gone?

Movement at the door drew their attention to Mr. Jardine, brushing off water from his hair and shoulders, shaking his boots as if the floor were not already muddied. Heaven help her try to clean her hem, stained six inches in mud that no scrubbing with the awful yellow soap here could rectify.

"There. That should hold things more steady for a time."

"You have certainly earned your cup of tea," she said, offering him a cup and another of her biscuit efforts.

"Thank you. That is most welcome." He took a bite of her creation, and a strange look crossed his face. He coughed. "What do you call this?"

"Oh. Mrs. O'Leary called it a dumpling. Is it not to your taste? I was just trying to amend our basic fare. If you don't like it, you don't need to feel obliged to eat it."

"It is unusual, but it is sustenance."

"You mean you don't like it." Disappointment stole through her. "Please, don't mince your words, sir. I much prefer honesty over dissembling."

"I like it," he said, eyes meeting hers. "Truly."

She studied him, but his eyes seemed to hold sincerity, which dared her to inch closer. "Then, will you honestly answer me this?" She glanced at her brother, who was hunched on his bed, a blanket wrapped around his shoulders. "Do you think Elias shall recover?"

He studied her, his gaze soft and compassionate. And for the first time in nearly two weeks, he touched her, stroking her hand, before clasping her fingers with his. "I think he is quite ill, and his refusal to see a doctor has not been wise."

Moisture rushed to her eyes, and she blinked it back. His hands held hers, the strength in his calloused fingers seeming to impart into hers.

"But we will continue to trust God," he continued softly. "God is sovereign, and sees all, and works all things to our good."

She nodded. She had to believe this. *Had* to. His earlier words drew into awareness. She could do this. Christ would strengthen her.

"Josie?" Her brother's wavery voice stole her attention. Mr. Jardine's hands slipped from hers, and she rushed to Elias's side. "What is it?"

"I don't feel so good."

"I know. You need to rest. Here, lie down." She wrapped an arm around his shoulders and gently eased him onto the bundle of clothes that served as a pillow, taking care to tuck the kangaroo skin that acted as an extra blanket around him with the same tenderness she remembered her mother used to have before the cruel wagon accident stole her and Father's lives.

Movement at the flap of canvas that constituted their door drew attention to the return of Mr. Emmett, who glanced at Mr. Jardine and shook his head. "He's out. A tree fell on a tent last night and squashed a man's leg."

She gasped. Mr. Jardine glanced at her and hushed his friend, but it was too late. How awful! She placed a hand on her mouth and inched closer. "The doctor?"

"Is dealing with this other incident and cannot come. I've left word, and we shall pray he attends to the other man quickly. But I'm afraid that will be some time." Mr. Emmett looked at Mr. Jardine. "It was young Henry Barton."

The newly arrived Englishman with a young wife and child? "Oh no."

"They shall be in our prayers too," Mr. Jardine said, his gaze holding her steady.

He was right. She could pray, something of far greater use than worry. She focused on making Mr. Emmett's cup of tea. God was good. They could trust Him. And she would pray for poor Mr. Barton, for his poor wife and child, and for the healing of her brother too.

———

Daniel looked up from his bedside scribblings and studied the sleeping man on the pallet whose forehead held a sheen of sweat. He recognized Elias's sickly pallor and rasping cough as a severe case of influenza—he'd seen similar things on his travels before—and the man's poor spirits and constitution were not those of one willing to fight against disappointment and disease. The doctor had murmured as much to Daniel when he'd paid the man to visit Elias three days ago, his words hushed so Miss Wilkins did not hear. "I cannot bear to crush a woman. 'Twas hard enough to tell poor Mrs. Barton her Henry had not made it." He'd shaken his gray head. "Terribly sad thing."

So Miss Josephine Wilkins still believed her brother would recover, and it felt the height of hypocrisy to suggest otherwise, especially as he exhorted her to cling to faith. But while he didn't like to destroy her hopes with the doctor's truth, neither did Daniel want her to lose hope nor lose focus on doing those things that seemed to provide some distraction. Things like tending to poor Amelia Barton, the recent widow who had gone gray overnight after her husband's tragic encounter with the fallen tree.

Focus on one more desperate than herself—Mrs. Barton had fainted, and Josephine had stayed overnight to tend to the newborn—might feel like a cheat's way to avoid speaking of what seemed inevitable, but Daniel couldn't help but hope that

God might dispense yet another miracle and see fit to restore Elias to health. Was it wrong to encourage Josie to tend to Mrs. Barton at the expense of time with her brother? Tragedy seemed to surround them—Joe Drescher too had succumbed to his malingering ways and died last night—but surely actively doing some good had to be better than standing around bemoaning things? That was what his mother always used to say, something that had often coaxed a fond smile from Daniel's father, as if he knew exactly which kind of good deed Lady Verity had got up to in her younger days. Regardless, his heart warmed to see Miss Wilkins's compassion on full display, her meals extending to provide for the Widow Barton as well.

Elias coughed and opened his eyes, requesting something to cool his parched throat. Daniel retrieved the cup of boiled water, now cooled, holding it to Elias's lips as he assisted the man to drink. "Where is Josie?"

"She's still with Mrs. Barton."

The sick man's brow wrinkled. "Who?"

"The recent widow. Her husband was crushed by a tree last week."

Elias coughed again. "How goes the hunt for gold?"

"Emmett has found some more specks, but nothing of great substance."

Elias shook his head. "Shouldn't have come. Shouldn't have brought Josie."

Guilt strummed. If Daniel had not encouraged him, they wouldn't be here. Elias might well be better, and Josephine would be safe and doing what young ladies should do.

"She is doing a good thing, caring for Mrs. Barton and her child." The words were as much reassurance for himself as for the sick man. "The poor lady has been distraught, and your sister is most generous with her time. Her being here has proved a blessing for others, so it is good that she is here."

Elias reached out and grasped his arm. "But who will care for her?"

"Why, you will," Daniel encouraged.

"How can I, stuck here ill like this?" the man complained. "No." His grip tightened, and the feverish glow that Daniel recognized from the Wilkinses' arrival blazed in his eyes again. "You must promise to care for her if I cannot."

"I will ensure your sister is taken care of," he promised.

"Good." His grip weakened, and he collapsed back onto the bed. "Good."

Elias soon fell asleep, and Daniel judged it safe to leave the sickbed and return to the diggings to see how Emmett was getting on. With much of his time taken up in caring for others, he'd barely had a chance to help his friend, and manning the cradle was hard work for a lone person.

He reached their claim along the riverside, and Emmett straightened, wiping his brow with the back of his hand, leaving a faint smear of red-brown dust behind. "You came at last."

"I was longer than I'd hoped."

"Wilkins?"

"Still too weak, but now asleep."

"And the sister?"

"Still helping Widow Barton."

"She's a good-hearted lass, isn't she?"

"Aye."

"Make someone a good wife one day, wouldn't she?" Emmett lifted a brow, his mouth twisting into tease.

Daniel ignored the smirked comment and focused on the hole Emmett had slowly been carving, pressing on the heel of the shovel with his boot. The blade arced through the soil, and he put his back into clearing it, widening the hole. Some said gold could be found deeper down, and various men had reported success in finding small golden veins in the quartz. But digging out the sand and rock and clay was back-breaking work and something he should have been helping Emmett with. No matter. He was assisting today.

"I wonder if such futile musings are why the hole is no deeper than yesterday," he said, clearing away another shovel-load of dirt.

Emmett's brown eyes widened. "Are you calling me an idle good-for-naught?"

"Me? Wonder if you prefer to spend more time wagging your tongue rather than putting in any effort? Never." He bit back a smile.

"Says the man who prefers to play nursemaid."

Daniel grinned, picking up his shovel and spraying Emmett with dirt. "You'd better have a care, else we'll soon see who is needing a nursemaid."

"Hmm, well, if that nursemaid is the fair Josie, I shan't complain."

An odd sensation squeezed Daniel's chest, and he frowned, digging the shovel edge in more deeply.

"Ah, someone does not like that idea, I see."

A quick glance up revealed Emmett's renewed smirk. "I don't know what you mean."

"I think you do."

"I think you should focus your energies on gossiping less and digging more."

Emmett chuckled. "Yes, m'lord."

That earned Emmett another shovel's-worth of dirt on his clothes, which he shook off before grasping a handful, peering at it most closely, then gasping. "Look!"

A small nugget, likely weighing about a quarter of an ounce, lay in Emmett's outstretched hand. "Well! That's a good find."

"Quick, where did you dig that from? Perhaps there is more."

Daniel struck the earth again, digging down into the ground more carefully. Within what must not have been more than half an hour, they'd found another nugget, this one weighing half an ounce, earning an exchange of grins as excitement filled Daniel's chest.

He eased into the hole, now about five feet deep, and carefully examined the layers of dirt and rock that lay there. He drew out his fossicking knife and pressed its tip to some of the darker corners. A small section held promise, and he dug around the pocket. Could it be?

Heart racing, he uncovered nugget after nugget in the dirty soil, perhaps five pounds' worth! Several times he had to fight the grin and the desire to whoop with glee—there was no need to advertise their find to would-be thieves. By the time night fell, the pocket had emptied and he and Emmett clutched their finds in disbelief. Truly?

"It feels like a miracle," Emmett whispered.

"God is very kind." For how many others chased such riches only to leave, disappointed and grumbling complaints about the colonies? "I fear it's too late to take this to the escort office to secure it for the night, but we should mark out a claim for nearby in case this proves to be a seam of gold."

Emmett nodded, and they managed to secure a nearby site before taking their equipment back to camp. There they were met with the welcome sight and smell of simmering stew, as Miss Wilkins once again worked around the fire.

She straightened at their approach, one hand on her hip as she studied them. "You have finally returned."

"As have you," he countered. "How is Mrs. Barton?"

Light drained away as her features fell. "She is not at all well and not in her right mind." She drew a hand over her hair. "I pray for her, but I wish you might come and pray for her too. She needs such comfort at this time."

His spirits sobered. "I can come after dinner, if you think that will suffice."

"Thank you."

He saw the gray wash of weariness on her features, the dark shadows under her eyes. "How are you doing? Caring for others can take a toll on oneself too."

She sighed, the sound stealing past his defenses again. "I never knew how true that was until now. Between Elias and poor Amelia and little Harry, there are so many who need our help."

"I will watch over your brother tonight," he promised.

Her upward look held gratitude, and he knew another pang in his chest. Her likeness would be worth trying to capture when he had a spare moment.

"Thank you. He stirred not too long ago and seems to have slept well. He will be pleased to see you—"

"Ah, Miss Wilkins," Emmett interrupted. "Has Jardine here told you our news?"

Another swift look at him found Daniel admitting, "I have barely had a chance."

"What news is that, sir?" she asked.

He let his smile do the talking. It seemed to communicate enough as she pressed two fingers to her lips. "Truly? You have found more?"

He nodded and drew them inside, where in hushed voices they told brother and sister about their find, showing them by the candlelight the precious nuggets of gold. Miss Wilkins examined the one offered to her. "How marvelous! I am so very pleased for you."

Her beaming smile sent shards of sunlight through his chest.

Elias, on the other hand, after initial pleasure, seemed to have fallen into another case of the sullens. "That's just my luck. I'm lying here while you find what we're looking for."

"Fortune is a fickle game," Emmett said with a roll of his eyes that Daniel hoped Miss Wilkins had not seen.

It seemed this hope was in vain, as she sighed and laid her

fingers on her brother's brow. "You should not begrudge them success, brother dear. They have both worked so very hard to make this happen. They deserve to reap what rewards may come."

The generosity of her answer again engendered warmth toward her. This kindhearted woman held qualities not unlike those he appreciated in his mother: charity, benevolence, compassion, and understanding. Such recognition heightened his determination to help her where he could. "May I be of assistance with the meal?"

"Oh! I should stir it and ensure it's not burned. Mr. Truman was kind enough to give me some root vegetables today." Her smile held forced humor. "I did not think I would ever miss potatoes until I came here."

"It is funny how we can take so much for granted until we do not have it in our possession anymore."

Like he would miss her when he departed for home.

He shook away the disquieting thought, focusing on helping prepare for their meal. After dinner he "planted" their find by burying it in the ground beneath Elias's bed, the safest spot they could think of for the gold to remain until Monday morning, when they could send it down to the secured office.

Elias had insisted, his mood as changeable as the winds. "I am not going anywhere, so if a thief should come, they'll have to get past my dead body."

"Elias!" his horrified sister exclaimed. "You should not speak so."

"Hush, Josie. It makes me think I'm of some value, even if I'll never be the owner of such a fortune."

"Why do you say such things? You will be recovered soon enough."

Elias coughed again, his glance sliding to Daniel, as if recognizing that they were men of the world and therefore not so foolish as to believe such a thing.

Cold streaked up Daniel's spine, and he shook the fear away. "Trust God," he gently encouraged.

Miss Wilkins drew her shawl around herself, her glance reminding him of his promise to visit and pray for Mrs. Barton. So with Emmett agreeing to stay and play a game of checkers with Elias, Daniel set out with Miss Wilkins through the dark streets of the tent city known as Ophir.

Chapter 5

Josephine inched nearer to Mr. Jardine as they passed the tents of miners. This being Saturday night, it was the noisiest and most riotous at the diggings, and they passed many a noisy miner, swearing, laughing, comparing notes on everything from gold discoveries to meals and accommodation, to men complaining their wives weren't here, while others complained that their wives had come. If her mission wasn't so serious, the contrast might have amused, but thoughts of Amelia and Elias weighed too heavily for such things.

Boom!

She startled, gasping. "What was that?"

"Nothing more than a discharged rifle," Mr. Jardine assured her. "It seems some men's preferred way to blow off steam."

"Blow off a leg or arm more likely," she murmured.

"I'm afraid that sometimes happens too."

Her steps paused. "Truly?"

"The doctor is a man in high demand."

She shuddered, remembering last week's trial in getting Elias seen by a medical practitioner. It was only Mr. Jardine's generosity and gentle but effective insistence that had seen the Waterloo veteran finally deign to pay them a call. Truly, she and Elias owed the Scotsman so much.

They passed a bawdy tent with a number of men drinking

outside, the scent of liquor wrinkling her nose.

"Why, Mrs. Wilkins. Where might you be traveling to at this hour of night?" a deep voice slurred. "And without your husband?"

"Ignore him," Mr. Jardine encouraged in a low voice, moving her away. "Dryson has no notion on how to treat a lady."

"Nor man," she murmured, as raised voices suggested a quarrel of Dryson's making.

Mr. Jardine chuckled, steering her around a man whose notions of chivalry included taking off his hat and bowing to her. "My lady."

If tonight's matter wasn't of such importance, she'd be tempted to laugh, but she settled for a quiet nod, which probably suited her reputation as someone of greater social status. Was this truly what others thought of her? Mrs. O'Leary was but one of many who assumed she was married, which made her wonder what they thought when she accompanied Mr. Jardine in this way.

But no matter. Tonight was not about her reputation, but about poor Amelia Barton and the hope that God would bring comfort and healing to her now.

They drew nearer the tents, where a mewling sound drew awareness of an infant's cry. The large figure of Mrs. O'Leary backed out from the tent, and she held the whimpering baby boy in her arms. "I'm afraid poor Amelia is not responding well. She can't even feed the poor child anymore. I don't know what to do."

Josephine stretched out her hands for the infant, who instantly soothed as she stroked the downy head. "There, there, precious one. You shall have something to eat soon." *Please, Lord. But what?* "Is there no place where milk can be found?"

Mrs. O'Leary frowned. "I heard Callahan mention something about a goat. Perhaps he'll know if we can source some goat's milk from a squatter nearby."

"I shall make enquiries. I'll return soon," Mr. Jardine promised.

"Thank you," Josephine said, watching him thread his way through the dark street. She pressed a kiss to the boy's forehead and cradled him closer, glancing up to see Mrs. O'Leary's smile. "What?"

"You might need to tell your husband to take care."

Her husband? Oh.

Mrs. O'Leary nodded seriously and jerked a thumb in the direction of Mr. Jardine. "That man was looking at you like you were the Madonna holding your child." She crossed herself. "If I don't mistake my eyes, that man has an interest in you."

Oh! Her heart fluttered. "No. No, he is a good, godly man. He is here to pray for poor Amelia, that is all. I'm afraid any such speculation is most unwarranted," she added more firmly. "Now, we are here for poor Amelia's sake. You said she is still not well."

"Hardly moves at all, like she's given up."

Josephine bit her lip. Sometimes she wondered if Elias was verging on the same. The thought felt so disloyal, she shoved it aside, refocusing on the infant in her arms as she touched his forehead. It seemed warm, too warm. "I think even if there's a goat handy nearby, the baby needs to drink something now. Is there no water?"

Mrs. O'Leary gestured to inside the Barton tent. "I think there's a pitcher beside the bed."

"Would you please pour me a cup? Perhaps if he takes in some water, he will settle a little."

Mrs. O'Leary disappeared inside the tent, and Josephine settled on a stump that served as a stool, shifting the baby to the crook of her arm as she stroked the soft cheeks. Cheeks that reminded her of baby Caroline's sweet looks. Cheeks that should be plumper than this.

"Here you go."

Josie thanked her then dipped her forefinger into the water and placed it in the baby's mouth. His little lips latched on to her finger as if starved, and she marveled at the instinct that such a little child knew what to do. It took some strength to draw her finger away. She dipped her finger into the water and saw the boy respond again.

"That is something at least."

"Better than nothing," Josie agreed as she resumed the activity.

This continued for some time as the sound of Saturday night revelry continued around them. Theirs was a bubble of prayer and concern until Mr. Jardine finally returned.

"I spoke to Callahan. He will make enquiries tomorrow, so hopefully we'll see a nanny goat on Monday."

"Thank you," she said, offering a quick smile. But, conscious of Mrs. O'Leary's avid interest, she ducked her head, concentrating on the task at hand.

"That's a most ingenious method," he said after watching her baby-feeding technique awhile.

"Mrs. Wilkins is very clever," her Irish supporter said.

"Indeed she is," he said kindly.

His words warmed Josie, but, given their audience, she dared not show how much. Besides, they had another job to do, something that seemed more possible as the tiny boy sighed, his heavy head sagging to the side as he finally settled into rest.

"He's asleep." She glanced up at him. "We should see how his poor mother fares."

He nodded, assisting her to stand with her small burden as Mrs. O'Leary held the tent flap open.

"Amelia?" Josie called softly. "It is Josephine Wilkins. Mr. Jardine is here. He would like to pray with you, if that's all right."

There came no sound of protest, so taking that as acquiescence, they moved inside. A lantern held a sputtering candle, and the smell of sweat and distress wrinkled Josie's nose.

"Mrs. Barton?" Mr. Jardine whispered to the figure lying on the pallet.

No response.

Josie drew beside him, the baby quiet in her arms. She reached down to touch the widow's hand. "Amelia? I have your son. He is taking some water, and we're hopeful he'll have some milk soon. I will look after him so you can rest."

Eyelids fluttered, and a glassy-eyed gaze shifted to Josie. "Th-thank you," Amelia said through cracked lips.

Something passed between them—relief, resignation, she knew not—and the space filled with a weighty sense of importance. "Until you feel better," Josie assured.

"Take care of my Harry," Amelia breathed, stretching out a hand. Josie shifted the boy to within his mother's reach, and she stroked his hair before her features eased and the thin eyelids closed.

Josie shivered. How like death she appeared.

Mr. Jardine drew closer, his coat sleeve warming Josie as it brushed her side. "Your son will be in good hands."

Why did this moment feel more significant than it was? Amelia would recover, just as Elias would. They had to. Little Harry needed his mother, just as Josie needed her brother. God wouldn't be so cruel as to let them die. Would He?

—

Daniel noticed another tremble overtake Miss Wilkins as she held the tiny boy, and thoughts of how much she looked like a painting by Raphael faded as he was reminded again of why he was here.

He refocused on the sick woman, who barely seemed to breathe. He took the moment to wrap his hand around her cold fingers. "Amelia, may I pray with you?"

There came another dip of the chin, and he squeezed gently,

wishing he could infuse strength into the frail woman who lay before them. "Heavenly Father, I ask for Your tender mercies to surround our friend Amelia. Comfort her, give her strength and courage, and help her know Your love."

He continued for a few moments longer, praying with a greater earnestness than he'd ever felt, as if this was a prayer that battled the curse of death that seemed to hover in the air.

Eventually he ceased, and he saw she was sleeping, her blanket-covered chest rising almost imperceptibly.

Mrs. O'Leary, who had stood in the corner transfixed by all that occurred, stepped forward. "I'll keep watch tonight." She pointed to a pitifully small stack of garments and baby accouterments. "Take these things for the child."

Miss Wilkins nodded, and he followed her quiet gestures in collecting what was deemed necessary.

"Should we write to her family?" she whispered. "Surely someone would wish to know about poor Henry."

"I only ever spoke to Henry once." How he wished he'd taken the chance for more. "Has she ever mentioned anything about their relatives in England?"

"No." Her eyes bent to the bed, and she pressed her lips together as if trying not to cry.

Compassion surged, and he placed a hand on her back.

"Mrs. O'Leary? Do you know of anyone to whom we might write on Amelia's behalf?"

"I'm afraid not. She's never mentioned any family."

He had reached the tent flap when Mrs. O'Leary gasped.

"What is it?" He hurried back to her side and saw the invalid's chest no longer rose.

"Amelia?" Miss Wilkins's eyes were huge. "No, she can't be."

But it seemed she was. Gone.

"No," Miss Wilkins whispered. "It can't be. We were just talking to her."

He moved to Mrs. Barton's side, searched for a pulse at her throat and wrist, but found none. "I'm sorry."

"She was never the same after her Henry died," Mrs. O'Leary said, hefting to her feet. "Well, I suppose the doctor should be called. I'll send my Paddy to do so."

Miss Wilkins sank to the floor, still clutching the little boy. "I can't believe it."

Neither could he. But perhaps this was why he'd felt the need to attend tonight, why his prayers felt weightier than normal. A life had slipped into eternity, buoyed by prayers and kindness.

Miss Wilkins wiped at the moisture on her cheeks. "This poor little boy. He's all alone."

"He has you," he said. *And me*, he could have added but refrained.

"But. . .but I don't know the first thing about caring for a child. What am I to do?"

He heard the panic edging her voice and put the garments on the bed. He drew closer, willing her to meet his gaze. "We will trust God."

"But he needs to eat! I don't know how to provide that."

"How did you know to give him water on your fingertip?"

Her gaze steadied, settling on him, and she exhaled shakily. "I don't know. I just thought it, I suppose."

"I think God, who loves this little boy as much as He loves you or me, will continue to prompt and inspire and give you wisdom and strength and all you need to be this little boy's mother."

Her chin trembled, and he was tempted to kiss the wobbling lip. Shocked at himself, he drew back, helping her to stand then moving to collect the baby's clothes.

The doctor's entry two minutes later—for once he'd been at home—soon confirmed matters, and after explaining what Amelia's wishes concerning the child were, they were advised to collect whatever belongings might be deemed suitable for the child.

"For if you don't, as soon as word spreads, I guarantee there'll not be a single item left in this tent tomorrow."

Josephine drew the little boy's head closer to her neck. "You mean people would steal from a dead woman?"

The doctor's gray whiskers lifted as he shrugged. "She's dead," he said bluntly. "And there be plenty here who ain't particular about social niceties. So, if you're looking after that boy, then I suggest you take whatever you think he'll need, because it likely won't be long until word spreads and the vultures come."

Miss Wilkins's look of horror wrenched his heart, but she soon straightened her spine and gave instructions. "I think he'll need to remember his parents with some special items." She glanced at the now-shrouded figure in the bed. "Amelia's wedding ring and her shawl. Perhaps the smell might remind young Harry of his mother," she added quietly.

He followed her instructions, and they soon had a small collection, Mrs. O'Leary and the doctor doing what they could to help pack those items deemed more valuable. Another careful search of the Barton tent showed no letters or diary that suggested an address for any family members in England.

"Perhaps we should write to see if we can find out what ship they came on," Miss Wilkins suggested.

He nodded, even as he wondered if Mrs. Barton's final words were because they had no family left.

Eventually, arms laden, they began the somber trek back to their tent, Mrs. O'Leary and the doctor bringing up the rear of their sad procession. As they passed revelers, something of the importance of the occasion seemed to waft and settle people down. All save Dryson, whose eyes glittered dangerously as he sneered at Daniel before murmuring something to a crony as Miss Wilkins passed.

They turned into the section that held Daniel's tent, entering to find Emmett holding a deck of cards in the flickering light cast by the lantern.

"What have you got there?" Emmett asked.

"It is the Barton baby," Miss Wilkins said.

"You kidnapped her?"

"Him. And no. Amelia—" Her chin wobbled again, and she shook her head.

"Amelia Barton is now with her Maker," Daniel said.

"But why do you have the baby?" her brother asked, his voice raspy.

"Because she asked me to care for him."

"At the expense of us getting sleep," her brother grumbled.

Daniel cleared his throat, and Elias had the grace to look ashamed.

"Josie, I didn't mean it," her brother muttered.

"I am pleased to see my act of charity meets with your approval," she said, turning from her brother, but not before Daniel saw her blinking rapidly, as if holding back tears.

Compassion surged within, and he touched her arm. "I shall tell Callahan that we require his goat milk tomorrow."

"Thank you," she murmured. Her movements focused on placing the infant on her bed, unwrapping him, and using a fresh cloth to gently wipe his tiny body clean.

"You are doing a good thing," he encouraged.

She nodded, gaze bent to her task, and he slipped away to find out what news he could.

Chapter 6

Exhaustion, which she knew before, seemed to have trebled, weighting her limbs, dulling her mind. In the past four days of caring for the child, she had grown so weary, between caring for tiny Harry and tending to the vagaries of her brother in addition to her usual preparations concerning meals and other duties. She'd grown better at heeding Mrs. O'Leary's advice to sleep when the baby slept, even though it seemed there was so much that remained undone. But when she couldn't even hold a conversation because her brain felt as though it had turned to sludge, she knew such practical advice was wise.

If it wasn't for such wisdom or the good services of Mrs. O'Leary and Mr. Jardine, who both took turns at caring for the child, then she might well have collapsed too. They'd managed to feed him with the makeshift teat fashioned from the finger of Josie's glove over an emptied medicine bottle filled with goat's milk. Mrs. O'Leary called it ingenious, Mr. Jardine had nodded quiet approval, and sacrificing her best glove had proved nothing compared to the great importance of keeping the baby alive.

A tear tracked down her cheek as she thought of the motherless mite currently sleeping in the tent. Panic rose again. Was she truly going to be held responsible for this child? But how else would such a tiny thing survive? The goldfields were no place for a woman, let alone a baby. But what else could she do?

Lord, help me.

The sharp edges of anxiety slowly ebbed away—her prayers had ascended far more often of late—and she inhaled slowly, taking in the aroma of today's mutton stew.

Mutton. Again. How long would they have to suffer—

No. Her nose wrinkled at her ingratitude. How dare she bemoan the tired diet when a frail mother now rested in the hillside that counted as their makeshift cemetery? How foolish, how selfish, was she?

She stirred the pot that contained their mutton stew then arched her back to a crackle of pops as her muscles' tension ebbed away. Her arms—babe-free for a few minutes at least—swung in wide circles as she sought to ease the aches and pains.

Gentle laughter came behind her, and she spun to see Mr. Jardine. "I did not expect to see a windmill here in camp."

Heat brushed her cheeks. "I was simply stretching out the kinks."

He nodded. "You have been working hard as ever. How is the child? And your brother?"

"They're both sleeping." Her lips inched up on one side. "It seems to be the first time they have both slept at the same time."

"Perhaps you should as well."

"I had a rest earlier. I fear if I sleep again now, I won't rest tonight."

He studied her a moment, his gaze searching her, seeking truth. "And are you keeping well?"

"Well enough, sir." She swallowed. "I still cannot quite believe all that has occurred in the past week or so."

Compassion washed across his face. "These have been hard days for none so much as you."

She shook her head. "I cannot but think poor Amelia would have felt far worse, knowing she was leaving her child to the care of virtual strangers."

"I think she knew that in entrusting her son to you, she was making the best choice possible. I'm sure your presence there was a godsend."

She bit her lip, her eyes welling again. She didn't feel like a godsend. More like a failure. How did new mothers manage to stay sane, with the constant crying and lack of sleep and incessant need? Little Harry was a sweet thing, but oh, how she craved rest, escape from this never-ending call of duty. She sucked in another unsteady breath, half-turned away.

"I wonder..."

His words stilled her movement. "Wonder what, Mr. Jardine?"

He shifted to see her more fully. "I wonder if perhaps you might wish to come on a small expedition with me."

"An expedition? Where to?"

He held out his hand. "I happened upon a grove of trees not too far from here and thought it most pleasant. It is not far, and you need not be long. Emmett," he said more loudly, "is nearby and could care for anyone who needs attention."

She glanced at the tent belonging to his friend, where a muffled affirmative suggested that was true. Suddenly, the idea of escape seemed more enticing than sleep. To be elsewhere, if but for a few moments, oh, that would be wonderful indeed.

Ignoring his hand—she had no wish to invite unnecessary speculation, and there'd been speculation enough with that visit she'd completed to Amelia's tent by Mr. Jardine's side—she followed as he gestured for her to join him on a path that seemed little better than a goat track. They passed the outskirts of the camp, leaving the sounds of pick and shovel and raucous cries as they entered what counted as forest.

Here the trees soared high, and there was a stillness in the air as if the world had paused. She sank onto a fallen branch and took a moment to breathe, to be still, and closed her eyes.

Her senses filled with the scent of eucalypt, the hush of

breeze in the leaves, the distant sound of a chattering magpie, the bird calls that sounded like the crack of a whip, or those that tinkled like a bell. How lovely it was to merely attend to such sounds instead of the cries and groans and moans her usual duties entailed.

"It is lovely, is it not?"

She nodded, unwilling to break the moment by speaking. Even talking required effort she was barely able to give.

"Sometimes we need to pause, to be still, and remember that God, the creator of such beauty, is here with us. Even here. Now."

She felt that. These great trees and gentle birdsong drew an intensity of wonder-filled reverence, as contemplation shifted from nature to God Almighty.

The hairs on her arms prickled with awareness, and she suddenly knew in that moment that God *was* here with her. She didn't need to be afraid. And even though her strength felt small and many challenges lay ahead, she wasn't alone. Resting here, she felt God's strength restore her spirit. It was like that verse Mr. Jardine had quoted on that Sunday not so long ago. She could do all things because Christ gave her strength.

"Here."

She opened her eyes and saw Mr. Jardine holding out a stone of bluish quartz flecked with gold. "How beautiful." She picked it up, rubbing her thumb over the smoothness.

"I found it near where we found the nuggets."

"Is it real gold?" She'd learned many prospectors were fooled by the glimmer known as mica, taking their finds to the office to learn it was worthless.

"Aye." He leaned close, his breath stirring her hair as he touched the summer-colored veins. "See how the gold contrasts to the dark blue? I'm reminded of something my mother says. That even in the darkest night, God still provides the stars."

Her vision blurred, and she blinked moisture away.

"Please don't cry, lass," he whispered.

The gentleness of his words stole inside, cramping her chest, and her breath shuddered. How could he be so kind?

A moment later, she felt his hand on her upper arm, then it slid around her back, and it seemed only natural that she curl into his chest. His other arm wrapped around her, and she felt the rasp of his cheek on her forehead, drew in his scent of something soothing and masculine, and knew she was safe, secure, and that nothing could harm her. Heaven forbid anyone see them like this, but oh, what comfort could be found in his arms.

She stayed there for a moment longer, reveling in the peace, then a snap of a twig saw his arms quickly release.

"Dryson." The tone was flatter than anything she'd heard before from Mr. Jardine. "What do you want?"

A chuckle broke from the man she now recognized as the one who had eyed her impertinently more than once. "I want what you have."

"And what is that exactly?" Had she ever heard Mr. Jardine sound so haughty before?

"A turn with the Wilkins wench. Seeing as her husband's too sickly to—"

"Do not utter another word." Mr. Jardine's voice was low, tight, cutting like a whip. "You do the lady a great disservice. She was tired, and—"

"I bet she was tired. Seems plenty tired of her husband, if you asks me."

One minute Mr. Jardine was there beside her, the next he had flung himself at the man with a roar. She stood, hands to her mouth, as Dryson's swearing notched up in volume and pitch in a manner not unlike Ethel had been inclined to do whenever she felt frustration.

"Oh, Mr. Jardine, be careful!" she called, as Dryson punched and kicked. But the Scotsman dodged and weaved, and Dryson tripped over a branch, fell backward, and tumbled down the hillside in a welter of yells and oaths.

She picked her way along the slope to reach Mr. Jardine, who was staggering to his feet. "I'm sorry you had to hear that, Miss Wilkins."

"Are you all right?" she asked, brushing dirt and twigs from his shirtsleeves.

"Better than he." He gestured with his boot to the man whose bellowing rivaled an angry bullock. Dryson was clutching his knee. "Seems he has hurt his leg."

"Something that is your own fault," she said to the bull-man. "How dare you insinuate such things?"

Mr. Jardine swiped at his brow, studying the man for a long moment before finally offering his hand to help him upright.

Another blue word darkened the air, but Dryson finally accepted, exclaiming loudly as he put weight on his leg. "You injured me," he said, smacking Mr. Jardine's hand away.

"You injured yourself." He bent to pick up a stout branch and passed it to him. "Here. Use this as a crutch, seeing as you have no liking for my company."

He did the man more justice than he ought, for Dryson eyed the branch then eyed Mr. Jardine and took a swing.

"Oh, Mr. Jardine, look out!"

As if aware of what Dryson was about, he sidestepped, and the branch swung past in a loud *whoosh*. But the shift in momentum overbalanced Dryson, who fell to the ground in another tangle of flying legs and bad language.

"Somehow I don't feel the need to help that man again," Mr. Jardine muttered as they left him, hurrying their descent down the hill.

"I cannot blame you," she said. "Are you quite all right?"

"Apart from feeling mortified about how my actions have harmed you." He slowed his pace and glanced at her, his expression rueful. "I'm so very sorry. I never dreamed people would be so quick to jump to such scandalous assumptions."

She released a shaky breath. "I am hardly a noble lady who might have cause for alarm about her reputation."

"You are a noble lady to me."

His words, simply spoken, fluttered new warmth across her heart. Why, in all of Wilfred's sweet talk, had he never made her feel treasured the way this man did? Mr. Jardine had barely said a word, but his actions, his deeds, showed he paid attention, that he noticed her, that he cared. And somehow that proved a higher compliment than anything else someone could give her.

"I am disgusted with myself for not realizing how my actions may have harmed you," he continued. "Dryson talks, and I fear neither of us will like what he has to say."

"You need not fear, Mr. Jardine. My brother will understand, and anyone else's opinion need not concern us."

He studied her, a pleat in his brow, but said nothing more, save to apologize quietly again before offering his arm as they traversed the last of the uneven ground before the tents drew into sight.

But when they finally ascertained the tent, it was to find Emmett shaking her brother's shoulder. "Wilkins? Wilkins? Wake up, man."

"Elias?" She hurried to his side, touching his brow, which was fortunately cool. "Elias, please. Stop funning. Talk to us. Open your eyes."

But he refused, and after a moment, Mr. Jardine gently moved her aside and laid his ear against her brother's chest. Then, when he slowly moved away and caught his lip with his teeth, she knew the horrible truth that his words only reinforced.

"I'm so sorry, Miss Wilkins. But it seems your brother no longer lives."

Harder words he had rarely spoken, and the harshness of them had seen Miss Wilkins pale, swaying, before he drew her into the safety of his arms. He held her trembling form for long minutes while Emmett murmured of fetching the doctor and the Barton baby began to cry.

Eventually, the child's wailing grew so persistent, she stumbled from his clasp and tended to Harry's needs. Her brother's death was not unexpected, but coming so hard on the heels of Amelia Barton, this felt even more wretchedly timed. But could any time prove a good one for a beloved family member's demise?

He drew her outside, where her brother's still form could not be seen, to a more screened place behind Emmett's tent. Here, the passing miners could not see them, and she passed the baby to him to hold as her shoulders shook and tears soaked her hands covering her face.

"I'm so sorry," he said again, knowing his words sounded so futile.

She shook her head, turning away from him, placing her hands on her hips. "I can't. . .I can't do this." She faced him, her features pink and pinched. "I can't do this anymore. There is too much sadness in this world."

"Josie." Her brother's name for her slipped from his lips. "Come here."

She hesitated, then he stepped closer and drew her near again. Her breath shuddered, and tears soon soaked his shirt, and he was grateful for the arrival of Mrs. O'Leary once again. She divested him of the baby, allowing him to wrap Josephine more securely in his arms as he prayed for her.

"Oh, my dear. Mr. Emmett told me about your. . ." Mrs. O'Leary's gaze flicked to Daniel then to the woman he held. "About your brother, dearie."

Josephine nodded, and Daniel took a moment to smooth her

hair. She pushed against his chest, and he released her. "I knew he was ill but never imagined this."

He withdrew a handkerchief from his pocket and handed it to her. She dabbed at her eyes then blew her nose as the doctor and Emmett spoke in low tones.

"Oh!"

"What is it, dearie?" Mrs. O'Leary asked.

"I wasn't here." Josephine glanced at Daniel. "I didn't get to say a last goodbye."

Because she'd been with him. Guilt writhed. "He knew you loved him."

She shuddered out a breath, rubbing her forehead. "I don't know what to do. What do I do?"

"We'll take care of things," Daniel promised. "Between Emmett, the doctor, Mrs. O'Leary, and me, you have friends who will help you."

"That's right." Mrs. O'Leary nodded.

"I'll need to write to my brother, Ambrose." Josephine's shoulders slumped some more. "I can't bear living with Ethel again."

"There'll be time enough to consider all that," Mrs. O'Leary said. "Now, you leave the little one in my care tonight. I imagine there will be much to consider, and you won't want a squalling infant disrupting your sleep."

"But I want to look after him." Her chin tilted. "Having him to focus on will help me, I'm sure."

"You've been exhausted for some time, Miss Wilkins," Daniel said. "You need to rest."

"That's right." Mrs. O'Leary eyed him. "And you will come back to stay with me. No, I don't want protest. I will not let a single lady be taken advantage of by unscrupulous men."

His chest heated. "Unscrupulous—? Madam, I must protest—"

"I'm not talking about you, sir," she said dismissively. "I'm talking about the likes of Dryson, when it becomes known that she wasn't Mrs. Wilkins and is indeed a single lady and unclaimed by any man." Her thin eyebrows shot up as if in challenge, and he swallowed.

He knew exactly what she was implying, and it was not something he'd dared entertain for longer than a minute. He had family obligations, a legacy to step into, which certainly didn't include a title-less, penniless, orphaned American bride.

The Irishwoman's gaze held steady for a long moment, then her features fell. "I trust you will come to your senses, sir. Before it's too late."

"Too late?"

Her green eyes snapped. "Before some other man claims her hand." She turned, steering her exhausted charge and wailing child toward the protection of her canvas lodging house.

They left him standing there, wondering, praying, as he dared consider a future without Josephine in it.

Chapter 7

How different this journey felt compared to the one taken not two months ago. Gone was the sense of excitement and expectation, replaced instead with a nameless dread. Yet not exactly nameless. Ethel was her name. What on earth would Ethel say when she saw the baby in Josephine's arms? Likely she would accuse Josie of scandalous actions and not believe the child was another woman's.

Josie drew little Harry closer, making sure his wrappings did not cover his face, as the dray slid on the ruts of the dirt road. It still felt unbelievable that she was heading back to Sydney Town, where she hoped to find out more about the Bartons and any remaining relatives of their poor child before boarding a ship to return to America again.

She glanced across to where Mr. Jardine walked alongside the long, low wagon that carried all of his and her possessions. They'd been lucky to join another party that was returning to Sydney, as there were whispers of bushrangers and other unscrupulous persons wishing to steal gold from returning miners. Mr. Jardine had paid handsomely for her to have the one seat on the wagon, and she'd agreed to hide his gold in the false bottom of the hastily fashioned crib that lay at her feet.

But while Mr. Jardine's actions continued to prove his consideration, she still sensed a degree of reserve in his words. Since

ACROSS *the Shores*

that moment when she'd flung herself into his arms—twice in one day!—she'd felt a renewed distance between them, where he'd speak to her kindly but never quite look her in the eye. The past few days of sorting and packing had seen Mr. Emmett the fortunate recipient of much of their equipment, in addition to his half of Mr. Jardine's find of golden nuggets, as Mr. Jardine had announced his intention to return to England. Mr. Emmett had been shocked as much as she, but Mr. Jardine had assured them this was something he had contemplated for some time. She'd accepted his reason, grateful that her journey back to Sydney, babe in arms, would be with someone she considered a friend. Even if he'd scarcely looked at her with that warmth that Mrs. O'Leary had been so sure of.

"Mark my words, that man cares for you," Mrs. O'Leary had whispered during their tearful hug goodbye.

But while he might care—even going so far as to ensure that each night her tent was pitched next to his for her protection—he still had said nothing about what would happen next. The past days of busyness had scarcely allowed time for talk and certainly no talk of private matters. Mr. Jardine would soon go to England, and she was bound for California and then back to Ethel and Ambrose again. Could she bear the wrench of saying goodbye to him?

Mr. Prout, the driver, cracked the whip, and the horses veered left, winding their slow way up the mountain pass. Several times in past days, the dray had needed to be pushed along, the deep mud of spring rains making progress slow. How strange to think it was spring here yet nearing winter at home. But then, so many things were not as she'd once believed.

"Terrible mud, this," Prout muttered.

She nodded but did not reply, having learned after the first days of travel that the man preferred his own complaints about the state of the road rather than commentary from others. She'd also learned he did not appreciate her gentle reprimand about using colorful language to ensure the horses kept going. He'd been inclined to argue, when a quiet word from Mr. Jardine had him revert to grumbling under his breath that the horses needed the cussing to keep going. She glanced across to where a ridge of hills dipped sharply, the tree cover extensive. Perfect country for masked men on horseback with nefarious intent.

She shivered and huddled closer, a sharp wind cutting past the black bombazine gown and blue woolen cloak, two of the items she'd agreed to keep from poor Amelia's small trunk of clothes. They were hardly going to fit any other woman in Ophir, and everyone had agreed that it was only right they come into her possession, especially considering her role in taking on responsibility for the Barton child. But still, she felt like an interloper, dressed in another woman's finery, even if she had seen the way Mr. Jardine seemed to approve before he'd noticed her noticing him and whisked his gaze away.

A slight moan on the wind drew her attention to behind, where dark clouds rolled across the bright blue skies.

"We're in for it now," Prout groaned. "You might wish to cover up in the back."

He yanked on the reins to slow the animals, and the lumbering procession drew to a halt. "Come on, miss. You and the lad best get under the dray unless you want a drenching."

Gathering Harry securely, she exited to join the men who were hastily constructing tents as meagre protection against the fast-approaching storm. They'd met one two days ago, and their sodden attire meant they had no desire to meet another.

As if sensing the anxiety, little Harry began to whimper, and she shushed him, the wind whipping her hair across her face.

"Get under the dray, girl," Mr. Prout shouted as the first pellets of icy rain stung her face.

She hesitated. Hiding under there seemed fraught with

potential to go wrong. What if the horses startled, and she was dragged or crushed?

Mr. Jardine finished tying down the last rope of his tent, turned, and beckoned her near. "Get in."

She obeyed just as the heavens opened and a sheet of grayness enveloped them. Those not so quick to put up their tents were caught by surprise, judging from the loud oaths she heard.

Harry's wails carried over the loud *pat pat* of rain slapping against the canvas, and she wrapped a hand around his head, wishing she'd thought to bring the glove-bottle of milk or at least thought to cover up the crib. Poor Harry's bedding would be soaked.

"Shh, little one," she murmured. "The storm will soon be over."

Mr. Jardine drew nearer; she could feel the warmth of his body filling the space between them. "Give the lad to me."

She carefully handed the child to him and took the moment to rub her upper arms to dispel the chill.

"Come here," he murmured, one arm free as he drew her close, wrapping her to his chest, as he had on that day last week.

Again, she felt that sense of security and comfort, breathing in his scent, feeling his strength permeate her weakness. She closed her eyes, allowing his strength to support her as she leaned against him. For a moment, she dared wonder what it would be like to be a family, part of his family, held in this way, supported in this way, secure, knowing her place beside him. But he'd said nothing of that, and even this moment could be ascribed to his general thoughtfulness rather than any more tender emotions.

Tears pricked, and she blinked them back, holding herself ruthlessly still so he'd not know of her distress. Oh, she must be so wearied to allow every idle thought and little thing to make her cry.

"Miss Wilkins," he murmured, his voice gentle, "please do not be concerned. The storm will be over soon."

She nodded, knowing he couldn't truly see her in the dimness but not trusting herself to speak.

"I remember some frightful storms on my travels," he continued, as if needing to reassure her. "Once, on a trip around the Cape of Good Hope, our ship encountered a storm with waves higher than the trees out there." He motioned to a tall eucalypt.

"Were you frightened?" she asked.

"Aye. Probably the most scared I've been since when I was a lad sailing a skiff, and the wind picked up and blew me halfway across the Solway."

"The Solway?"

"A stretch of sea in Scotland, near where my family lives."

"I thought you were from England."

"Aye, that too."

Her gaze lifted to meet his, and she found him looking at her as if he too was aware this was the most he'd ever divulged about his family. A dozen questions sprang to her lips, but she settled for the most innocuous one. "What happened next?"

"I was twelve and knew I shouldn't have gone out alone. My father had told me many times. I was growing quite afraid as the boat drifted farther and farther from land, until the village buildings became as specks. I was frightened, but even in the midst of that, I had this sense of peace, that it was not my time to go. I prayed and had this inkling to not panic, to make sure I stayed in the boat and not do anything that might plunge me overboard. It was not too long after that my father came and rescued me."

"How distressing for you all!"

"Aye. But my father, not a word of admonishment did he offer. When we got back to land, I kept apologizing, but all he did was say he loved me and that he never wanted me to stray again." He swallowed. "I've always thought that moment the perfect image of our heavenly Father."

God who sought to seek and save the lost. God who loved.

"I never wished to stray again either," he added softly.

"And yet you're here on the other side of the world."

He paused, as if looking for the right words to say. "That is for another reason entirely."

The question begged to be asked, but a gust of icy wind blew the tent flap up, startling Harry again. He only calmed when she took him from Mr. Jardine's arms, and he settled into the crook of her neck.

"My mother said my rebellious spirit came from her, but I don't know." Mr. Jardine's teeth glinted in the darkness. "I've never ridden my horse inside the house, at least."

Her eyes rounded. Did he mean to suggest his mother had ridden a horse inside a house? "How big was your house?"

He winced. "I believe that was the manor in Somerset."

He had a manor house? Who was this man purporting to be a poor miner?

"You have never shared about your family," she murmured. "All this time I thought you were like us, but you are not, are you?"

He studied her for a long moment, and she maintained his gaze, searching, wondering, seeking.

An enormous boom outside was immediately followed by the shriek of horses and yells and curses.

"Stay here," he said, and hurried outside.

She peered past the flap, breath catching as a nearby tree burned, the recipient of a lightning strike it seemed. The horses still pulled anxiously at their tethers, their stamping hooves shifting the dray this way and that. Her chest tightened. Imagine if she'd been hiding under it, like Mr. Prout had advised!

Memories flashed of another storm, one that had plunged a wagon down a hill and left her without parents. She blinked back emotion, focusing on the here and now. Fortunately, it seemed nobody had been injured, although the horses still tossed their heads, even as Mr. Jardine and others moved to calm them. Other men in various stages of bedraggled dress crept from their various tents and moved through the easing rain to assist with picking up various boxes and storage items that had fallen from another wagon in the height of the storm.

Oh, that the pieces of her life could be picked up so easily. If only she knew what the future held and had assurance that someone would rescue her from the seas of uncertainty. She stroked Harry's downy head, willing him to stay calm, willing her heart to be the same and face her future with confidence like Mr. Jardine did. But that would require private conversation this trip would not allow for. Would it?

The sound of songs filled the night, the flickering flames that still burned in the trunk of the tree forming the center of their group providing welcome warmth from the cool, damp air. The rain had ceased hours ago, but the condition of the tracks and restless horses meant they had all agreed to camp here for the night rather than press on.

Daniel glanced at Josephine seated beside him on the log, the tiny boy asleep in the tent. Her features held a regal quality— something about her cheekbones he'd like to try to capture in a sketch. Shadows under her eyes revealed the fatigue of caring for the Barton baby, but she did not complain, yet another quality he admired about her. Who else would have met such challenges with so much grace and poise? Admiration barely described the depths of his feelings. Feelings he could not admit to, not even when he'd been desperately tempted to in that moment of long glances before the lightning hit.

How to tell her that, as the second son of the laird of Dungally, he was in line to become the viscount of Aynsley when his grandfather died? Something that a twist of fate, being born the second of four sons, and certain legal documents had ensured was indeed true. Something that had always seemed more mirage than reality. It was little wonder his adventure-loving mother and father had not sought to tamp down his questing spirit, knowing full well just what responsibilities would be his one day: an estate in Somerset, a village possessing the family name. But with his grandfather ill and his birthday drawing near, Daniel knew he had no choice but to return to England. Something he was loath to admit to the woman whose compassion and uncomplaining spirit made her increasingly more captivating every day.

"Here you go, lads!" Prout said, hoisting a small wooden bucket into their midst. A small tin pot hung to one side. "Help yourself."

"Well deserved, I say," another man called before scooping the tin pot into the bucket and drinking the contents.

"What is it?" Josephine whispered, inching closer to him.

"I suspect it's port wine," he said, observing the effect the drink had on those who imbibed.

"From where?" she murmured.

He glanced at her, and her eyes widened.

"He stole it from the wagon's cargo?"

"It seems so."

Her mouth fell open, but it couldn't have been a surprise. Prout was scarcely a bastion of honor, as his language around a lady had proved, thus necessitating Daniel's reprimand. But still, beggars couldn't choose their method of transportation, and while this might not be his preferred mode of travel, he appreciated the protection the larger party provided. There was talk of recent bushranger activity, something he did not wish to alarm Josie with, but which marked how he spent each day, near her, ready to assist if protective measures were called for. Of course, it meant he was able to assist with young Harry as well, something he knew she was grateful for. And if it meant others looked at them and thought her his wife, such suppositions could only serve to protect her more. In his more dangerous dreams, he imagined what it would be like if she could truly be his wife instead of the society lady his family had no doubt picked out for him.

The bucket passed to him, and he passed it on to the man on Josephine's left.

"Too proud, are you, Jardine, to drink with the likes of us?"

"Not too proud." But perhaps too honorable to want to partake in ill-gotten gain. "I'm conscious some of us should not have sore heads tomorrow and may need to stay on guard tonight."

"I don't think nobody be wishin' to attack us tonight," Prout said, tipping liquid down his throat. "They all be stuck in this mud as much as we be."

Josephine shifted restlessly beside him. "Do you really fear attack?"

"No. You need not be afraid. I think Prout is right and that nobody will venture out tonight."

"But some night?" Her pupils held fear as they reflected the flickering flames.

"You will be safe. Please, trust me."

She nodded, yet licked her bottom lip nervously, and he wished he had the right to hold her hand, to show her by his constant presence that she was not to live in fear. But such actions might set up expectations even higher than they were already, and he was in no position to give promises which he could not fulfil.

Conversation around the fire turned to tall tales, "yarns" as some called them.

"Heard about the bunyip?" one man asked.

The story about a creature that lived near swamps and rivers with an eerie cry caused even Daniel's flesh to crawl, and he'd been brought up hearing Scottish tales of broonies and boggarts. He glanced at Josie, saw her expression held awed horror, and smiled to reassure her.

But that tale turned to others, and he took the chance to spin the conversation to something less eerie. "Did you hear about the man who plucked gold nuggets from a clump of grass?"

"What is the point in telling us now, when we are heading back to Sydney Town?" one man groused. "Surely that kind of yarn is best kept for those who need to be going to the gold-fields. No, tell us something else."

But the other stories the men shared held a more macabre tone, and guessing Josephine had no wish for more stories of death, he was glad when a wail from the tent drew her attention. "I should go."

He nodded, standing to assist her to rise from the log. "I'll come with you." She glanced at him quickly. "Just to make sure you're all right."

They traversed the long grass as they moved to the tent he'd erected earlier during the storm. His tent was now propped nearby, and he wouldn't mind the chance to write something of today's observations, perhaps trying to sketch something of what he'd seen. Falling into his bedroll soon held appeal also. Little Harry's restless nights didn't just eat into Josie's sleep.

"Do you think it's made up?" she asked.

"What is?"

"The story of the nuggets from a clump of grass. I. . .I remember Elias being excited, telling me about it as we came to the camp."

"No. It's not made up."

"How can you be so sure?" she asked as he held the tent flap open for her. "And why are you smiling like that?"

"Because," he said slowly, "I know the man who found them."

"You do? Who?"

He paused, knowing he could trust her, and finally admitted the truth. "Me."

Chapter 8

The recent storm and days of rain meant their passage up the mountain range was slow, the weight of the wagon requiring men to haul and push by turns. She'd descended from her perch several times in order to lighten the load, but Mr. Jardine assured her that her weight was negligible by comparison. Still, she was prepared to do what she could to assist, to prove that having her here was not the burden so many of them grumbled about.

She snuck another look at Mr. Jardine, his muscles highlighted by his rolled-up shirtsleeves as he joined the other men in tugging the dray from yet another muddy embrace. Such a broad back, such a strong man, someone she was admiring more and more each day.

With a heave, the wagon shuddered from the mud's hold and, as the men cheered, Mr. Jardine smiled at her and helped her ascend again. They soon continued their weary path, but Josephine barely noticed, her mind returning to ponder the news Mr. Jardine had shared last night.

He was the finder of the nuggets? It seemed too remarkable to be true. But then, how else would Elias have known? And, as she was fast learning, Mr. Jardine was a man of secrets, and much of what she thought she knew about him obviously proved she barely knew him at all. She'd been so tempted yesterday to ask more about his family, but the moment had not proved right. She could only hope that such a moment would present itself very soon, especially as each day took them closer to Sydney.

Mr. Prout snapped the whip to motivate the horses to a slightly faster pace. She clutched the edge of the wagon side, hoping the jostling would not wake Harry in his crib. He'd slept poorly again last night, and when she'd appeared at the campfire to break her fast with something Prout called porridge, she'd overheard complaints about broken sleep from several of the men this morning. She smiled to herself. It was somewhat amusing that the smallest member of the party could have the biggest impact.

She wondered how long it would be until they reached their next destination, a bark hut that rather grandly pronounced itself as an inn high on the mountain ridge. Still, the hope of a proper bed and warm water kept her spirits up.

Around them, tall peaks dived into deep ravines while flocks of brightly colored birds swept through the air in great swathes of color. It seemed remarkable how they knew just where to go, moving like a twirling ribbon through the sky.

"See the cockatoos?" Mr. Jardine called, pointing to the white birds with yellow crests whose raucous cries filled the morning air.

She nodded, her heart glowing as he smiled at her in return.

Oh, she loved his smile. She loved his enthusiasm and awareness. He always seemed to know the moment her spirits needed boosting. She wished she could be that for him too.

The wagon shuddered over another sodden stretch, but this time the wheels did not bog, turning sluggishly as they inched their way upward. The hills were steep here, rocks tumbled precariously atop one another, and the plentiful tree cover held an abundance of wildlife. Already today she'd spotted two kangaroos, one with a baby in its pouch.

A whistle drew attention to a nearby clump of trees. Her heartbeat stalled when she saw a rider. He eyed them but made no move, one hand at the edge of his hat, shading his face against the sun.

"Mr. Prout?"

"Haven't I told you not to talk, lass?"

"Yes, but who is that man?" she asked, pointing.

An oath slid under his breath, and he yelled at the men to be ready.

She glanced at Mr. Jardine, saw he'd drawn nearer. "Josie, you'll be all right."

"Is that a bushranger?" she asked, her pulse hammering.

"It's possible."

"Why hasn't he approached us yet?"

"Maybe he thinks we're too numerous a party," he suggested.

"Or maybe he's a scout for a gang," their driver said.

"Prout, that's enough! Do not scare the lady."

She kept her eyes on Mr. Jardine's face. "Do you think he will attack?"

"I pray not."

A swift exchange between the two men saw Mr. Jardine hoist himself onto the dray and reach forward to collect the rifle Mr. Prout handed to him. She shivered, watching as he positioned it to where the man had disappeared.

"No other reason for why a man would be over there and not on the road," Prout muttered.

"What happens if they attack?"

"Then we do what they ask."

They passed along the track for several more minutes, each second loaded with fear. Her mouth was dry, her limbs stiff, as she prayed for the safety of all.

"How much farther to the next settlement?" she asked.

"Ten miles or so. There's a farm two miles ahead."

She remembered now how she and Elias had spent the night camping on the meagre homestead of a farmer and his wife and wondering at how a woman could be brave enough to live out here. Doing their best to survive, the threat of robbery or illness or accident requiring constant vigilance. But perhaps love made such things bearable, made a woman willing to forget the past and seek a future with her husband. Like Amelia Barton had done, like Eileen O'Leary chose. Like perhaps she. . .

She glanced back at Mr. Jardine. He winked at her, and she found a corresponding smile before fixing her attention on the baby again.

A shout swung her attention to the west, where three masked horsemen raced toward them, their guns held high. Bushrangers! *Lord, protect us!*

"Mr. Jardine!" she called, peering over her shoulder to see him scramble atop the barrels and crates, taking careful aim as he fired.

The crack of the rifle woke Harry, who began to scream. "Shh, little one," she said, bending to soothe him.

Another rifle fired, this from one of the other men in their party. A sharp return of fire drew yells as the three men drew nearer still. Mr. Prout slapped the reins, urging the horses forward, and she slid to the small space between the seat and buckboard, lifting Harry to her chest as he continued to scream.

"Halt!" The tallest of the horsemen pointed a pistol at Mr. Prout. "Stop now."

Fear traveled up her spine, and she clenched her teeth to keep from chattering as Mr. Prout obeyed.

"Give us your gold," another voice said. She ducked her head, unable to look at the black, black eyes.

Mr. Prout gave an audible gulp. "We have none," he said bravely.

She froze, her hand on the crib. That was untrue. There was

gold lining the bottom of the crib. But perhaps Mr. Jardine had never spoken of his finds, so Mr. Prout believed it to be true.

"Woman, stop the child screaming, else I'll put a bullet in you too."

She reached in to quench Harry's crying, but his tears had escalated into hysteria, and nothing would stop his wailing save milk. "P-please sir, he needs milk."

"Then feed him."

"I need his bottle."

"Then get it," he snapped.

She bent and noticed movement behind her. Was that Mr. Jardine? Oh, she hoped they would not see him.

But her attention was snagged by the bushrangers' commentary, the men incredulous that nobody in the dozen or so in this party had found gold.

Anger burned. What right had these men to steal the reward of others' hard work? She retrieved the bottle, shoved it haphazardly at Harry, who latched on, his screams cutting away to offer blessed silence, save for the nickering and hooves of horses and creaks from the wagon.

"You, woman."

Her attention returned to the man who seemed to be their leader. "What?"

His eyebrows rose. "Not exactly polite, are you?"

"Says the man pointing a gun," she muttered.

"Feisty, aren't you?"

When she needed to be. She kept this thought behind her teeth, certain it wasn't wise to provoke the men. But surely the fact there had been an exchange of gunshots but nothing more boded well. She'd heard awful tales of bushrangers who'd shot before speech. And worse. A shudder crawled across her skin. Perhaps there was a way to talk themselves out of this situation.

His gaze narrowed. "Then tell me. Who here has gold?

Tell me, or I'll shoot." He cocked the trigger, aiming at Mr. Prout's neck.

She swallowed, praying desperately for the right words to say. If she admitted to the gold in the crib, what would stop these men from shooting them all? What would make them leave?

"Why do you doubt us?" she asked. "My brother died"—she plucked at her black sleeve—"without finding more than an ounce of gold, which went to feeding us and helping us return to Sydney."

All true. Yet judging from his expression, he was unimpressed. What could she say to convince him?

"Don't you think we would still be there if we'd had success?" Heat surged across her chest. How dare these men steal? "I cannot speak for others, but I know for myself and my child that we are poor and have nothing you might want. Please, leave us alone."

The men glanced at each other.

"Please, let us pass. The child is innocent and doesn't deserve violence."

The wagon creaked behind her, and she fought not to turn around. Mr. Jardine must still be there.

"You." The pistol waved in her face. "Do you cook?"

"Who cares as long as she does other things," the black-eyed man muttered, his gaze roving over her figure.

Her stomach tensed, her mouth falling open. "How dare you?"

He shifted his pistol until it faced her. "I dare because of this."
Bang!

The horseman's shoulder jerked before one of his cronies took aim and shot behind her.

A cry met her ears, and she shifted in her seat to see Mr. Jardine slumped on the back, blood pouring from his head. No. No!

"Speak woman," the bushranger called above Harry's renewed

screams. "Else the next one dead will be you."

She covered her mouth with her hands, her chest heaving, her lungs desperate for air. Mr. Jardine couldn't be dead. He couldn't. *God, help us!* What could she do?

Sobs threatening to rip from her lungs, she returned the child to his crib and shakily pushed to her feet.

"Sit down!" one of the men called.

"No." Desperation propelled her to clamber up on the seat, searching for a handhold to hoist her into the back to reach Mr. Jardine. "You might as well shoot me too. What is the point if the man I love is dead?"

"Your husband?"

She needed a weapon, something, anything she might throw and release some of the wild rage pent up inside. "Go away! Leave us alone!" She stamped her foot. "Can't you see we don't have what you want? Haven't you done enough damage already?" She tugged off her boot and threw it at the man, and when it fell short, she screamed.

The piercing wail halted Harry's own, and she turned and finally climbed up from the wagon seat onto the nearest barrel. Here she could see Daniel's prone figure, broken and bleeding. No. No! It was not meant to end this way!

She inched forward to reach him, waiting for the bullet that would end her torment, but instead heard the sound of hooves. Her heart hitched. There were more of them? Well, she had no dignity left to lose. She peeked back, dull eyes searching for the new arrivals, and realized the trio were retreating.

"Miss?" A tug came on her booted foot. "They've gone."

And so had Daniel. Harry's screams had resumed, but she didn't care. Her insides ached with trying to hold back more of her own. "Mr. Jardine—" She couldn't finish the sentence.

"Your husband?" one of their traveling companions asked.

She'd wanted him to be. And now he never would.

"You were so brave, miss," another man called.

She barely heard. What cared she for the compliments of men who had cowered, saying nothing, while she had dared speak her mind to the thieves?

Harry's persistent crying layered misery upon her heart, and she pointed to Mr. Prout. "Hold him."

He said not a word, nodding as if scared, and she resumed her careful crawl across unsteady crates and wooden chests into the back. She gulped down emotion as she neared Daniel's slumped body, not caring that her movements sent packages tumbling from the wagon to the ground.

"Mr. Jardine?" She lowered herself beside him, caressing his hair as if he were alive. "I'm so sorry," she whispered.

Tears spilled from her eyes as she touched his hand, like he'd clasped hers. Was this all this country was good for? Killing brothers, mothers, old men, and those in their prime?

A shaky sob escaped. How could she go on? What would become of them now? These other men might be good sorts, but none of them cared about what happened to her. None of them cared about the Barton baby.

Another sob erupted from her chest. Poor Daniel. If only she'd had the chance to share her heart. If only she had known his. Or at least known something of his family. Who should she contact? Apparently, there were people who needed to know. A man's family could not be in possession of a manor house without being of some importance. What should she do? How would she get on?

The questions swirled around her, trapping her into indecision and pain. She barely knew which way to turn.

She grasped his hand, wishing he knew of her regard. Smearing tears from her eyes, she studied him, tracing his beloved features in her mind.

The blood beside his ear had dried. Did that mean his heart

had stopped so quickly? She reached out a hand to touch it, then noticed his eyelid twitched. Then opened.

And with a shriek, she tumbled from the wagon and fell into blackness.

Chapter 9

"M"r. Jardine?" Josephine gently wiped his brow against the surprising November heat.

No response.

She suppressed a sigh, taking the moment to trace his forearms and gently caress his calloused fingers. Elegant fingers, she'd often thought them. Long, brown, and lean, like the man himself. How she longed for the day when he'd wrap those fingers around hers again. "Lord, heal him."

From beyond the wattle-and-daub walls, she heard the bleat of the nanny goat and the restless stomping of horses' hooves.

Here in the farm high in the mountains, the hours passed into days that slid ever closer to summer as she passed her time waiting, praying for a miracle. Daniel had not yet awakened from the traumatic events of last week, his flicker of consciousness lapsing as he succumbed to the clutches of his illness.

Thank heavens for Mr. Aitkens and his wife, who had generously allowed them to take over their bedroom with the house's sole bed. God bless them for sacrificing their sleep so that Daniel's could continue. She'd slept on a chair since their arrival and known Mary Aitkens as akin to an angel when she agreed to care for little Harry, leaving Josie free to tend Daniel.

She swallowed. The discovery of a farm whose willing owners had instantly provided shelter and comfort had proved solace even as Mr. Prout remained eager to continue the journey east. She dared not think of what would happen should they be forced to remain behind.

"Miss?" a voice called through the bedroom's makeshift door.

She stood gingerly, her body still a mass of black and blue. No broken bones, fortunately, but the rest of her felt every inch of her fall. She moved to open the door. "Yes, Mr. Prout?"

He winced, as if her appearance repulsed, but she paid no mind to that. Not when something of far greater import hovered between them. His gaze dropped to the battered felt hat he held, passing the brim between his fingers. "We be fixin' to leave today."

"Today? I thought you said tomorrow at the earliest."

He glanced away, out the open door, where shafts of sunlight stole in. "They say there be another series of storms approaching, and the men be restless. We don't want to be crossin' the Nepean if she's in flood."

She pressed her lips together, holding back the protest. It was understandable, and she couldn't blame them. But what was she to do? The doctor, retrieved from the nearest settlement ten miles away, had said the bullet that had scored Mr. Jardine's temple had done no permanent injury greater than an awful scar, advising that he needed to be kept quiet and still. That was before Daniel had fallen into a fever, through which she had nursed him as best as she could. She couldn't allow him to be moved, and to further trespass on the generous hospitality of the farmer and his wife seemed rude.

"Miss? I, er, could pass on a letter if you think that might help."

A letter, of course! Surely his family would wish to know. But how was she to contact people when she didn't know where they lived?

"Miss?"

She glanced at the injured man in the bed. His loved ones

needed to know. She straightened her shoulders as she faced Mr. Prout. "Will you leave our trunks and things here?"

He nodded. "It'll take but a few minutes to unload."

"Then I will compose a letter. But please do not leave until I have given you that."

"Yes, miss."

She hurried to the small satchel and searched through it, seeking the leather-bound journal she'd often seen him write in. Perhaps there was a clue there.

She opened the journal, thumbing to the front, but no word of an address in England or Scotland could be found. She flicked to the back and found a series of sketches. Her stomach swooped. Sketches of a woman. A beautiful woman with curly brown hair, smiling as if she had no cares in the world. Sketches coupled with her name.

When had he sketched these? Why?

Temptation grew to read through his jottings, which perhaps she ought to do, as there might be further clues regarding his address. A quick skim of the dirt-stained pages found nothing more, although she did see her name mentioned several times. But more she wouldn't read. Even if she might have noticed her name paired with a phrase of "lovely lass." She couldn't read more, not when the thuds outside suggested their possessions were being unloaded with more haste than care.

She lifted the journal, and a small white engraved card fluttered from a pocket in the leather. She picked it up. Aynsley Manor, Somerset, England.

Who lived there? Her heart stabbed. A sweetheart? Someone he obviously cared for deeply, seeing as this was the only address he'd kept in the whole of his journal. And Aynsley Manor? That sounded very grand. Surely this person had to be someone of means, someone who Daniel must esteem greatly. Were they betrothed?

Her chest stung, but there was no time for disappointment or envy. She inched to the bed and grasped his hand. "Mr. Jardine?"

No response, although she thought she saw movement flicker beneath his closed eyelids.

"Daniel?" Oh, how she loved to say his name. She glanced at the card again. "Do you know someone who lives at Aynsley Manor? It's in Somerset, England."

This time there was no mistaking the way his lips tried to form words. *Oh, thank You, Lord!* She shifted closer, bending her ear to his mouth as he tried to speak.

"I'm sorry, sir," she said, failing to hear what sounded like more breath than word. "Could you please repeat that?"

Something thick and viscous squeezed through her chest. Who was this person whom Mr. Jardine cared for?

He coughed, and she realized he'd speak more clearly with a sip of water, so she helped him draw a taste, tilting the tin cup against his lips before settling him on the bed again. "Sir? Are you able to speak more clearly? Who lives at Aynsley Manor in Somerset?"

His eyelids flickered and then finally opened, his blue eyes staring into hers. "My grandfather."

His grandfather? "I will write to him, let him know that you are here."

His eyelids closed, but she sensed he was agreeable. Time was of the utmost importance anyway.

Carefully ripping a page from his journal, she used the pencil found in another pocket and inscribed a note explaining about Mr. Jardine's illness. She addressed it to "Daniel Jardine's Grandfather, Care of Aynsley Manor, Somerset, England," and folded it. She tipped a blob of candle grease to seal the paper closed, then blew on it to cool it before rushing outside to where Mr. Prout was maneuvering the wagon and horses to depart.

"Sir." She held the letter high as she drew near. "You said you wouldn't leave yet."

"And I haven't. I'm still here, ain't I?"

She placed the letter in his hand. "You will make sure it gets sent, won't you?"

"I will if you have coin enough for postage."

Coin enough? She'd barely found enough of Elias's savings to contribute to their upkeep here at the farmer's. *Lord?* A thought flashed. "I think you have forgotten, sir, that Mr. Jardine paid for my seat and for our expenses all the way to Sydney Town. I am sure our stopping here means you have been more than amply recompensed for the cost of posting a letter, would you not agree?"

His perpetual scowl deepened. "You drive a hard bargain, miss."

"Please, for the sake of Mr. Jardine's family, please ensure this letter gets delivered as soon as possible."

"Very well."

With a snap of his whip, he encouraged the horses on their way, and she raised a hand in farewell to the other members of their party.

Leaving her here, the questions about her future seemed to grow each day as she wondered what God's plans were for her, for Mr. Jardine, and the child.

———

Light met his eyes when his eyelids lifted before he quickly closed them again. His head ached, his thoughts remained slippery, clarity like an elusive speck of gold swirling through mud layers. Heat followed cold, sweat sliding into shivers. He felt lost, like a twig in the midst of the sea, memories blurring with the present. But something remained, a constant presence, two. A voice he was fast coming to love, and the sense that just as before, when he'd been drifting out to sea, God was here too and hadn't finished with him yet.

"Mr. Jardine?"

He remembered those words. His mother used to tease his father with the same. How long ago that seemed now. He hoped his parents were well. It had been too long. Wasn't he planning to return to see them? Or was that another part of this dream?

"Mr. Jardine, I have some broth here that Mrs. Aitkens made. I'm sure you'll never guess what it is. Mutton, that's right."

He heard a smile in her voice, more of that tease he enjoyed.

"Come on. Let me help you so you can eat, else I'll be forced to tip this down your throat, and if it's anything like the last time, you'll be wearing more on your neck than I can clean."

His eyelids inched up to meet a curly-haired lass with blue eyes. She smiled, and the sight triggered an echoed response. He allowed himself to be helped up, then obeyed as she gently encouraged him to eat from the food spooned into his mouth like a child.

"You're doing very well."

He vaguely remembered a tutor saying something similar. Or perhaps it was the nanny from when he was a wee lad.

"Now, one more mouthful, then you can be done."

Who was this woman? Something about her was familiar, but he couldn't quite recall.

"Who are you?" he asked.

Her face fell as if he'd disappointed her, and he suddenly knew he did not want to upset this woman. She was something good in his life, someone good in his life. It was evident in her cheerfulness, her smile, her consideration.

"I am Miss Wilkins," she said softly, collecting the spoon and dish before turning away.

Wilkins. Wilkins. He remembered a Wilkins. "Elias?"

Her gaze met his again. "He was my brother."

"Was?"

Her lips twisted in a grimace of pain. "He died not so long ago."

"I'm sorry." That was the correct response, wasn't it? From the way she nodded, her eyes sober, it would seem yes.

"And you're his sister?"

Another nod. "Yes. I'm Josephine."

"From America."

Her lips lifted, but her gaze remained watchful. "Yes. You remember?"

He shut his eyes to blessed darkness again. "Remembering" was less the cause than something he'd put down to instinct. He had a sense of what was more right than not, and the fact she came from America seemed to make sense in his fuzzy brain. "Every so often I get these glimpses, but things still seem vague."

He heard a scuffling sound, then a baby's cry, then, "Excuse me. I best check on little Harry."

Harry? Who was Harry?

His ears strained for more clues as he listened, trying to put the scattered pieces together to make sense, like a dissected map. Eventually, he heard her return. He guessed it was her, from the familiar scent. He might not remember all, but he did like this scent.

"Are you asleep, sir?"

"No," he admitted. Although more rest might soothe his eyes, his brain still teased to know what was happening. "Please tell me, what are you doing here?"

A beat. "Caring for you."

He'd asked the wrong question, judging from the stiffness in that reply. Perhaps a better question would be "Where are we?"

"In a farmer's homestead on the mountain range. Mr. and Mrs. Aitkens have kindly agreed to look after us while the rest of our party returned to Sydney."

Sydney. He opened his eyes. "My father lived in Sydney."

"I beg your pardon? I thought you were from England."

"I was. I am." Wasn't he? He drew up an aching arm, rubbed his forehead, and encountered—"Bandages? Why is my head wrapped?"

"You were shot by bushrangers."

He blinked, and suddenly the memories flooded in. Horses. Gunshots. A baby's screams. A calm voice. Fear like nothing he'd known before. Searing pain.

"You. You saved us."

She caught her bottom lip between her teeth and gently shook her head. "That was your own doing, Mr. Jardine. You shot one of the bushrangers, and he raced away for dear life after shooting you." Her voice wavered.

"I remember someone screaming." His hand reached to clasp hers. "You were not harmed, were you?"

She eyed their entwined fingers, and after giving them a gentle squeeze, slowly released. "I was frightened, but that was all."

"I'm glad no harm befell you."

She studied him worriedly, and he wasn't sure if that was indeed true.

"You are unharmed, aren't you?"

"Yes. It's just, I'm not certain that you will think so when you know our predicament."

"Which is?"

"Do you remember Mr. Prout, the wagon driver?"

"Fussy man, swears too much."

She nodded. "He left here five days ago. I have been caring for you, and the doctor has visited, but when you are more fully on the mend, then we shall have to see how we can arrange transportation to Sydney."

He winced. "Does he still have our things?"

"I asked him to leave them here. I wasn't certain how much

would be needed." She drew closer. "The gold is still safe. I checked."

The gold? Oh. "Then we shall be all right. That will provide nicely for us."

"Us?" she whispered.

"Yes. For us to return to Sydney."

"Sydney," she echoed, her gaze falling.

His head throbbed so, he barely understood. What was wrong with going back to Sydney?

"And then, sir?" she asked.

"Then what?" He winced as another aching buzz encircled his head.

"I'm sorry, sir. Here. Have some of this drink. The doctor said it will help ease your pain."

He obeyed, unable to forgo noticing how good her arm felt around his shoulders as she helped him sit upright, unable to not appreciate her sweet scent or how her warm breath brushed his cheek or the delicate tendril of curled hair that drew desire to loop around his finger.

And then, mere moments later, after sipping the foul-tasting concoction promised to ease his pain, he couldn't help but drift off to dreamless sleep.

Chapter 10

The Nepean River swelled wide and important. Josephine glanced around Emu Ferry, the approach busy with drays and carts even at half-past two in the afternoon.

"The ferry boat only takes three carts at a time," Mr. Waters, their wagon driver said, pushing his gray hair off his forehead. "I'm sorry, miss, but seems we'll be here for some time."

No matter. Josie clutched Harry closer, taking care to wrap the muslin carefully so he could breathe. Since leaving Mount Victoria three days ago, their trip had proved most smooth, their wagon one of many returning from the goldfields, though some passed the other way still, their carts overloaded with sieves and kettles and cradles as they ventured to try their luck. The biggest challenge on their trip across the mountains had been the lack of fresh water, but after paying for some at a public house, they felt more refreshed.

She glanced across to where Daniel sat, his health such that he'd been granted the chance to ride in the cart also. He offered a wan smile, something he'd often done as if to reassure her. The decision to risk traveling to Sydney she'd left up to him, and she hoped he'd not been exaggerating when he'd said he felt fit enough to try. Finding Mr. Waters had been another of the godsends she'd prayed for; his willingness to cart them and their belongings on easy stretches had bolstered her hopes this wouldn't prove too taxing. But still, she couldn't help the impression that Daniel was being generous in his estimation of his health.

Harry wriggled, his face screwing into displeasure, and she took the time to change him. He hadn't seemed to suffer too much from their fortnight-long stay at the Aitkens' farm. Indeed, he and Mrs. Aitkens seemed to derive much pleasure with each other's company, to the point that she'd wondered if the farmer's wife was becoming so attached to the baby that it might prove traumatic to leave. Would leaving the Barton child in the hands of a capable wife prove to be kinder? But still, the thought that Amelia had asked Josie to care for the child kept her mouth closed. That and careful observation of the farmer's wife's less than svelte waistline that suggested she would bear her own child in the new year, something she confirmed herself, admitting to the anticipation of an autumn arrival.

She finished swaddling Harry, glancing up to see Daniel's eyes rested on her. She lifted the boy to her shoulder. "How are you feeling, Mr. Jardine?"

"I'm enjoying the sun. It feels good to simply sit here, doesn't it?"

"It seems a long time since we've had the chance to feel warm."

"I'm sure Ophir is feeling warmer now. Hard to believe a place can get snow and still bake in the sun."

"This is an unusual country, is it not?"

"A good country. One teeming with possibilities."

The words strummed an echo in her mind, reminding her of something Elias had once said, or so she had thought. No matter, it was true. This land might prove harsh at times, but it could also prove a blessing, as the gold hidden in the crib had proved.

A restive horse in the cart ahead nickered, drawing the cart owner's loud cries to stand still and grumbles from others whose own animals grew restless. Mr. Waters hopped from his perch, going to his own horses' heads, talking to them softly.

She saw Daniel's gaze had fallen on them, and she wondered again at his story. Was he a rider? Did his grandfather's estate boast many horses? Was this Aynsley Manor the house where someone had ridden a horse inside? How bizarre that seemed, and how she longed to know. Yet the opportunity to ask him about his past, about his future, had remained problematic, any potential opportunity for conversation always within hearing of the ears of others.

"Miss Wilkins?" Her attention returned to him. "You look lost in thought."

Perhaps now was the chance to ask him. "I'm just remembering something you once said. About someone riding a horse inside."

His countenance lightened as he chuckled. "I believe that was my mother."

"Your mother? I thought your family was very grand."

"Not as grand as some," he said.

"Hmm. I have a feeling that is something only the rather grand will admit to."

"You may be right." He eased himself up against the side of the cart that served as his backrest. "Let's see. I have never really confessed to much about my family, have I?"

"It does make one question whether you have something to hide."

A flash of his grin hinted at appreciation for her tease. "I suppose it does. Well, what is it you wish to know?"

"Where, exactly, are you from? Why are you here? Elias mentioned you often, but I don't think even he knew who you truly are."

"Who I truly am? You make me sound far more mysterious than I am." He tilted his hat to shade his face, then clasped his hands over his flat stomach. "Let's see. I suppose I should start by telling you that my father was once a curate here in Sydney Town."

Well. No wonder he seemed born to the role of comfort and compassion.

"He learned of an inheritance in Scotland and returned to his homeland, where he met my mother, an English lass and a viscount's daughter."

"Truly?"

He nodded, stretching out his legs. "I don't quite know this part, but it seems within the legalities of their marriage was a provision that the second son would take on the Aynsley name and viscount role." He held up a hand. "Meet the second son."

Her jaw sagged. "You're a viscount?"

"Not yet. My grandfather is alive still, I hope. But one day I will be."

She stared at him, feeling her futile hopes slipping away on the gentle breeze. She was not this man's equal, not in any way. Her throat grew tight, and she wrapped a hand over Harry's head to protect him from the sun's relentless heat.

"I was born with something of my mother's adventurous spirit and, knowing I had responsibility awaiting me and two younger brothers who could take the role if necessary, it was agreed that I could take some time to explore the world, which is what I've done. I met your brother in California and then came here, something I've thoroughly enjoyed."

Josephine nodded, her gaze shifting to the bright sparkle of river.

"And as I promised to return to England for my thirtieth birthday next year, I expect this will be the last of my adventures before the responsibilities begin."

She swallowed, still not daring to look at him. This was the crux of the matter. "So you return to England soon."

"As soon as I can secure passage, yes."

And she'd return to California. She hid the burn of disappointment by pressing a kiss to Harry's neck.

Fortunately, further distraction was provided by the shout of Mr. Waters that they would be next, and further contemplation was lost as around them the movement of animals, men, and carts demanded full attention.

Their cart inched forward, taking the third place on the punt alongside a wide dray and a team of six bullocks and a carriage being driven by a fussily dressed man. He did not appear impressed as Mr. Waters shifted their cart near, complaining about raffish people, with a long look at Mr. Jardine as he said this.

Amusement spurted that this man would take exception to a viscount's grandson, something Daniel seemed to appreciate too, taking the man's ill humor in good stead.

"Pardon me, sir," Daniel said in an affected tone she'd never heard before. "I found myself traveling without my valet, and this is the best I can manage."

As Josie smothered her amusement behind a hand, the man stared at Mr. Jardine hard before muttering about the nerve of some people.

Daniel's amused eyes caught hers, his grin causing her heart to trip before her pleasure faded. He was leaving and had said nothing about her going too. It was folly to think someone of his privileged heritage would give her more than a moment's thought, let alone a future. Perhaps in years to come, he'd feel a momentary sense of gratitude for her help in nursing him to health, but anything more she could not hope for. *Would* not hope for, she told herself fiercely. Theirs was a friendship that would soon end in Sydney Town.

And suddenly she didn't want them to arrive at all.

Sandstone buildings lined wide streets, the cream structures holding a clean orderliness a far cry from the mud-splattered tents of the goldfields one hundred and fifty miles west. Truly, it seemed as far a leap as when he'd first arrived, and he couldn't help contrast the mellow heritage of green and gracious Aynsley with the bustling newness of this land.

Mr. Waters encouraged the horses past a park, a welcome spot of greenery in this land. Daniel knew his father had long tried to grow some of the plants from this region. Perhaps taking him some more samples might prove a manner of appeasing him for Daniel's absence these four years.

He glanced across to where Miss Wilkins sat, holding the baby tight, her expression devoid of delight. Funny. He thought she'd be happier about leaving the colony and returning home, not looking stoic, as if she were heading into battle instead of enjoying the beauty of Circular Quay's sparkling water with its many ships boasting flags from around the world.

"Here you go, sir," Mr. Waters said as they drew up outside the Hit or Miss Hotel.

Daniel quickly shifted to assist Miss Wilkins to descend, smiling at her as he hoped for the light to illuminate her features once again. But she barely spared him a glance, thanking him in her polite manner, before moving to the rear of the cart and instructing their driver about which belongings needed extra consideration.

Daniel quietly assisted, taking care to possess himself of the gold-laden crib. He nearly staggered with the weight, but as he neither wished to worry Miss Wilkins about his health nor evoke suspicion from their driver about the unusual weight, he forced himself to straighten as they entered the hotel.

A request for two rooms soon saw their possessions deposited upstairs, and he was grateful for the opportunity to finally close the door and breathe a sigh of relief.

He needed space to think, to contemplate what could come next, what should come next. He had gold to weigh and exchange, ship tickets to purchase, mail to check, and letters to write, as well as a myriad of other things to consider about his future. Back in this bastion of civilization, he grew only too aware of what responsibilities lay ahead. And while some things might be what he wished to do, others remained forever out of reach.

"Lord, what do You want me to do?"

He closed his eyes, stilling the rush of confusion in his mind and heart, trying to get back to that moment of perfect peace he'd found in the tall forest near Ophir. In that moment with Miss Wilkins, he'd held her in his arms and felt all could be right with the world.

Miss Wilkins. Could anyone be more admirable? Mr. Aitkens had told how she'd barely left Daniel's side in those moments of fever. How her compassion and kindness and faithfulness were such that even the doctor had gruffly admitted he'd been impressed also.

But more than that, more than any work ethic, he found her faith as sweet as her looks. Had he ever found any woman as desirable?

But was this what God wanted for him? He needed to let God speak to his heart.

He spent much of the next hour praying, trying to listen, seeking those senses that had led him so many times into what later proved to be God's paths. He'd learned over the years that sometimes a stray thought could be God-inspired, the impulse to speak to a man leading to a conversation about eternal things, just as other times he had felt the compulsion to visit men needing practical help, like he had with Mr. Drescher.

His thoughts slowed, the energy demanded from the past days of travel having taken its toll. He might have slept for a time, for he woke when a knock came on the door.

What? He shoved a hand over his face. This mattress was the softest he'd slept on in six months, so no wonder he'd fallen asleep. He moved to the door and opened it. Josephine. Holding the Barton baby. Compassion surged at the look of exhaustion in her eyes. "Miss Wilkins. How have you found your lodgings? Is your room to your satisfaction?"

"It is very fine, thank you, sir. But I confess to some concern, as I suspect it might be expensive."

"You need not worry about the cost," he began. "I—"

"I do not wish to take advantage of your generous nature, sir."

"Like I took advantage of yours, caring for me, when I was sick?"

She shook her head. "That was different, sir. You needed me, and now I think on it, the whole situation would not have happened if I had simply told the bushrangers about the gold. Truly, I'm very sorry. I could. . .I could not have lived with myself if anything bad had happened to you. Especially now that I know you're to become a viscount one day. So please forgive me for not mentioning the gold."

"Mentioning the—? Oh, my dear Miss Wilkins, please do not trouble yourself about that anymore. I could have owned up to the gold as much as you. Indeed, it was my own foolish actions that drew their line of fire. You are not to blame at all."

"Regardless, I have no wish to be beholden to you." Her eyelids lowered, the sweep of dark lashes something he wished she'd raise so he could see her beautiful eyes again. "I know this accommodation is more than what I could afford, and knowing that I need to purchase a ticket for passage to California, I do not wish to be further obliged to you."

"A ship ticket? Miss Wilkins, I feel it only right to stand in as your brother would and see you safe that way. You need not trouble yourself about such things."

She swallowed. "My brother?"

These feelings he had were anything but brotherly. But of that he could not speak. "Yes," he rasped.

Her lips pressed together, then she jerked a nod. "Thank you." Her eyes lifted, still not quite meeting his, then as if remembering, she jiggled the baby higher in her arms. "That reminds me, sir. When you go to the shipping office, will you please make enquiry about the Barton family and see if there is a way of finding where they came from? I should like to think we have done all that is possible to track down any family Harry may have."

"Of course."

He was half-tempted to ask if perhaps she'd like to accompany him, when her eyes lifted to meet his, stealing the words away. For a long moment, he felt that sense of deep connection again, as he searched for what she wasn't saying. Did she care for him? She'd rarely expressed anything of her feelings, even though her actions had suggested that was the case. But was it presumptuous of him to think so? Sometimes he had the vaguest thought she'd once confessed her love, declared him as the man she loved. Or was that wishful thinking? What if these feelings were nothing more than too much emotion splashed about during a particularly fraught period of their lives? Was there enough to build a life on? *Lord?*

She dropped her gaze, her head. "So you will purchase my ticket?"

"I will."

"And you do not require any funds from me?"

"No. Miss Wilkins—"

But his enquiry about whether she truly wished to return to America or whether she might prefer to join him in England was cut short by the wailing of the baby, and with an apologetic look, she murmured her farewell.

She left him wondering how he would accomplish all he needed to do. And, more importantly, what her answer would be. Clearly, he needed to spend more time on his knees.

Chapter 11

L ight sparkled across the blue waters of Sydney Cove, the trees providing some shade from the December sun. Josie wore fresh freckles now, the southern sun harsher than what she was used to, and while many things had been tamed, it seemed her skin was not one, rebelling in tiny dots of honey brown.

Not that it mattered. Her looks were inconsequential. She was returning soon to California, and beyond that, she scarcely knew what she would do. This, a chance to sit in the park by the water like a grand lady with little Harry lying on a blanket on the grass beside her, was one of the last chances she'd have before her ship left on the morrow.

Daniel had taken care of all the arrangements, as he had with many other things in these past five days. All she had to do was take care of little Harry, and the two of them had visited what counted as local attractions, parks, the docks, and a place by the point known as Mrs. Macquarie's Chair. The seat, carved from sandstone and originally built for a governor's wife, afforded a most excellent view of the harbor. Now she sat, watching the gulls dive and squawk, searching for food. Across from her, the shoreline curved, a few fishing huts and more substantial buildings alongside coves and cliffs of stone topped with trees.

Turning her head, she could see the lighthouse on the

southern cliff known as the South Head of the harbor. The other way saw the point named after Jack the Miller, swampland stretching into the sea. This was a restful place, reminding her a little of that moment in the bush with its cathedral-like awe. She traced the gold-flecked stone in her pocket and felt her agitation ease. At least she'd have something to remember him by.

"Ah, here you are."

She glanced up, forced a smile. Was it wicked that she still greedily gazed upon Daniel, admiring his even features and the way his smile lit his countenance? Perhaps it was, knowing she would not be part of his future. Her chest ached with the hollowness sure to be hers when they parted. "Did you have success, sir?"

He inclined his head and moved closer. "The tickets are purchased, yes."

The tickets that would send them in opposite directions. Pain clutched her chest, stealing her words, forcing her to simply nod.

"Do you mind if I sit?" he asked.

"Please do. It is a most pleasant, soothing view."

A faint frown shadowed his eyes. "Are you needing to be soothed?"

"Oh no," she lied. But Daniel's intense gaze said he did not believe her. She needed to change the subject. "Have you got your mail?"

"Yes. I wrote to my family too."

She nodded, wondering when the letter she'd sent to Aynsley Manor would arrive. "They will be very pleased to see you."

"I hope so." His smile was edged with wryness.

How could he doubt their delight at his return? Why, she would give nearly anything to be someone he wished to return to. But that was not to be, she told herself fiercely. She needed to just get through today without tears. There'd be time enough for tears on the ship tomorrow. And all the days to come.

"I have something for you."

Her heart skipped as if she hadn't just told it to behave. "Really? You did not need to."

"I felt I did." He handed her a paper-wrapped package, something that was heavier than it looked. "Please, open it."

She undid the sleek cream ribbon and carefully opened the paper. Breath suspended. "Oh, how beautiful."

The gold cross was quite plain, unadorned save for some tiny inscribed words and numbers. She held it up but could not quite read it. "What does it say?"

"It is my favorite verse, something I thought you might appreciate in days to come." He slid a finger under the inscription. *Phil. 4.13.* "It's a reference to the book of Philippians, chapter four, verse thirteen. 'I can do all things—'"

" '—through Christ which strengtheneth me.' "

The words rushed through her soul, a reminder of what she'd faced time and time again. God had been faithful, He had given her strength, and from what she knew now, He would continue to give courage, wisdom, and all she needed to face the coming days. When she'd be alone. But not *quite* alone, she reminded herself. This cross was a reminder that Christ Himself would be with her.

"Thank you, sir." Her voice caught, and she swallowed to clear the gravel in her throat. "It's beautiful."

"I had it made from one of the gold nuggets we found."

She nodded, emotion darting to the back of her eyes and nose forbidding further speech. Oh, if only she could stay.

"I wanted you to have something to remember our time here, when we're away across the shores."

Tears burned, but this time she could not blink them away. One trailed her cheek, forcing her to turn and face away, toward the lighthouse on the heads, to where their ships would leave on the morrow and they'd be separated forever. She drew in brine-laden air, but her breath caught.

"Josephine?" His voice was gentle as his hand wrapped around hers. "Please do not cry."

"I can't help it," she whispered.

"All will be well, you'll see."

How could it be? Not if they were parted. But how could she ask for what she truly wanted? How could she beg this man born for nobility to consider someone so far beneath him?

He wrapped an arm around her, drawing her close, then his lips were on her forehead, her cheek, and she had to fight the urge to tilt her head so his lips would find hers.

"Please don't cry," he begged. "I thought you'd be happy."

She shook her head, all desire to pretend forsaking her. Courage—the courage that cross symbolized—demanded she finally speak the truth. "I don't want to go," she murmured.

"You want to stay here?"

She shook her head, swiping at her cheeks with the heel of her hand. "I don't want to go to America."

Gulls cawed, and the sea continued its relentless purr as she wondered if he was calculating how much he'd wasted on her ticket.

"Where do you want to go?" he asked, his voice low.

"England." She finally dared meet his face. "Perhaps I can find the Barton family and give the sweet boy to his relatives."

He nodded slowly, his gaze deep. "Is that the only reason you'd want to go there?"

She swallowed, then shook her head.

"Why else would you wish to go there?" he whispered.

Love demanded honesty, demanded no more hedging about the truth. "Because that's where you'll be."

A smile glimmered on his lips. "You want to be with me?"

"More than anything."

His gaze lightened until the depths of his eyes resembled the sparkling harbor. "Truly?"

She nodded, heart wondering, as his face lowered and drew closer, closer, until his mouth met hers.

He kissed her, his lips warm and firm and delicious against hers. Her hand slipped up to touch his face, and he sighed and tugged her closer, his hand smoothing her hair as he murmured of his love, his desire to have her near.

Was this a dream? She pulled back, searching his face, but no. His warm smile seemed as real as little Harry gurgling happily on the blanket at her feet.

"What is it?" he asked.

"I cannot believe it."

His expression was tender. "You did not think I could send you away to America, did you? Not when I've finally found someone I treasure more than gold."

Her heart might explode from all the fluttering within. "So, my ticket tomorrow?"

"Is on the same ship as mine." He tilted his head. "I hope that's all right with you."

"All right? I hoped but scarcely dared dream of this."

His smile lit a candle inside her chest. "I wonder though."

"Wonder what?"

"Perhaps I should see if I can change it."

"To what?"

His lips found hers again, and after a flurry of silent, passionate promises, he murmured, "I think four months is an awfully long time. I might have to see if I can change it to married quarters."

Breath caught. "But then we'd need to be married."

"Indeed we would." His lips curled on one side. "Have you any objection to marrying me today?"

"Of course not." Marry him? Today? The happiness soaring within stumbled at a new thought.

"What is it, my dear?" he asked, tracing a finger down her

cheek.

"Perhaps your family will object," she said with great reluctance.

His arm tightened around her shoulder. "I've been praying about this for many days now. And I feel a great sense of peace that my family will be so overjoyed at my return, they won't mind where my wife is from. And then, when they discover you are the one who saved my life, I think they will be on their knees in gratitude."

Was he serious?

His gaze grew soft. "I have met many people across the world, but nobody with your character, your courage, and your faith. Josephine, I love you, and I know that my family will come to love you too. Please say you'll be mine?"

Her heart soared sea-eagle high, swelling with affection for this man. How many times had he helped and nurtured her, protected and blessed her? "I love you. Of course I will."

He laughed, the sound drawing a chuckle from the baby at their feet. He pressed his lips to Josie's hand as delight shimmered within and around them with promises for the future. Love. Hope. A place to belong.

God was good. And so, so faithful. And she knew that each day could be trusted to the one who would always love, strengthen, and guide them, wherever they might be in the world.

Author's Note

While small traces of gold had been found in Australia for many years, it wasn't until 1851 that the first payable goldfield was discovered in Ophir, New South Wales. This soon led to thousands of "diggers" from all over the world coming to seek their fortune in the goldfields, dramatically boosting Australia's population and forging the concept of "mateship," which helped shape Australia's identity as a nation. The resources at the State Library of New South Wales helped flavor some of the scenes here. For a woman's perspective on colonial life in the goldfields, I found the article "A Lady's Visit to the Gold Diggings of Australia" by Mrs. Charles Clacy invaluable. For more information about behind-the-scenes details and to sign up for my newsletter, please visit my website www.carolynmillerauthor.com.

Carolyn Miller is an inspirational Regency and contemporary romance author who lives in the beautiful Southern Highlands of New South Wales, Australia, with her husband and four children. Together with her husband, she has pastored a church for ten years and worked as a public high school English and Learning and Support teacher.

A longtime lover of romance, especially that of Jane Austen and Georgette Heyer's Regency era, Carolyn holds a BA in English Literature and loves drawing readers into fictional worlds that show the truth of God's grace in our lives.

Carolyn's bestselling historical novels include the award winning *The Elusive Miss Ellison, Misleading Miss Verity,* and *Dawn's Untrodden Green.*

The Veil

BY KELLY J. GOSHORN

DEDICATION

To my father, Harold Joseph Criste. Thank you for modeling that hard work, sacrifice, and character matter. Like Franz, my story's hero, you were a man of honor and I cherish the brief time we had together on this earth.

ACKNOWLEDGMENTS

Writing a book may seem like a solitary endeavor, but I assure you that is not the case. First and foremost, I thank my Father in heaven for allowing me the privilege of co-creating with Him. A joy I never anticipated in this life. And to my real-life hero, Michael Goshorn, Sr., for patiently loving me through my first contracted deadline. To Angela K. Couch, my dear writing friend, for inviting me to be a part of this novella collection. And to Linda Glaz, Linda Glaz Literary Agency, for representing me on this project. To my critique partner, Debb "The Slasher" Hackett. Thank you for working so diligently to help me bring Franz and Caroline's story to life. You always challenge me to be a better writer and I wouldn't want to be on this crazy writing journey without you. To my Darling sisters who were always willing to Zoom-write, trouble shoot, and brainstorm this project with me – Debb Hackett, Lisa Kelley, Dani Pettrey, Crystal, Sandow, and Stephanne Smith. Thank you for cheering me across the finish line, ladies. I love you all. Dankeschön to friend and neighbor, Teresa Breitenthaler, for editing the German dialogue and phrases used in The Veil. To Beth Fleming and Lisa Kelley for your invaluable feedback. And to Cynthia Ruchti for your guidance and encouragement throughout this project. Your insights and suggestions are greatly appreciated. Many thanks to Rebecca Germany, Barbour Publishing, for believing in this project, to Ellen Tarver for seeing me through several rounds of edits and whipping my German speakers into shape, and for all those working behind the scenes at Barbour to bring the Across the Shores novella collection to readers.

And, behold, the veil of the temple was
rent in twain from the top to the bottom.
MATTHEW 27:51

Chapter 1

Near Camden Depot
Baltimore, Maryland
July 16, 1877

Caroline Wilkins's heart trumpeted in her ears. *Now what?* Alone and in a strange city, she found questions swirling about in her mind. How long would she be stranded? What would become of the belongings she'd been forced to leave behind? And most importantly, where would she sleep tonight?

"Keep moving," the attendant shouted, motioning for the displaced passengers to exit the train.

She redoubled the effort to ignore her trembling knees, slid her gloved hand along the wrought iron rail, and stepped from the train. Before ordering them to disembark, the conductor had assured the disgruntled travelers they should be able to resume their journey on the morrow. But without a guarantee of lodgings or transportation, the morrow might as well be a fortnight away.

A gang of men loitered on the tracks, shouting angry epithets. Several held cudgels wrapped in white cloth. Darkened whiskers lined their cheeks, and red kerchiefs looped around their necks above soiled shirts. The hair lifted on her nape, sending a chill rippling over her spine. *Strikers.* The people responsible for preventing the train from reaching Camden Depot.

The brilliant afternoon sun beat down on her as she tried to recall the directions the attendant had hastily given. Perspiration beaded on her brow. Large flowers and vines stitched onto the black silk tulle clung to her skin. However, Caroline refused to remove the veil that stretched from the comb affixing the fabric to her hair to the monogrammed pin on her right shoulder, concealing her left cheek.

She prayed the densely embroidered lace shielded her from curiosity seekers. Whether they gawked at the large white bandage protruding above her collar or the unusual way she wore her veil, like an old woman's winter scarf, she didn't know. In spite of their stares, the covering provided a measure of ironic comfort since the fire, and she was unwilling to part with it—suffocating heat or not.

Women lined the right side of the street. Some held fast to the wrists of children while others clutched rocks and yelled foul words Caroline had never heard from the men of her acquaintance, let alone a member of the fairer sex. Tension hung in the air like humidity after a summer rain. Instinctively, she adjusted her grip on her purse strings. She dared not lose her bag, or she'd have no money and no ticket to reboard the train once service resumed.

To her left, several wagons queued near a warehouse. Would she find a cab there? Hopeful, Caroline lifted her skirts and headed that direction.

Three men rounded the corner as she neared the wagons. A brawny, clean-shaven man with meaty hands and a thick neck tipped his hat and smiled. She froze. Not so long ago, she would have been flattered by such attention. Not anymore. Though his eyes seemed kind, his powerful build intimidated her, especially after Charles had nearly—

Her insides clenched. Although she'd kept him from his wicked intentions, Charles was nowhere near the size of this man. She shoved the memory aside. The safest course would be to rejoin the group of marooned travelers. She draped the dark fabric snug against her cheek, making sure to obscure her nose and mouth, then secured the scarf pin and backed away.

Once at a safe distance, Caroline stretched her diminutive frame onto the tips of her toes and resumed searching for a carriage. There. She spied several a few yards ahead.

So had everyone else, it appeared.

The crowd surged toward the conveyances, sandwiching her between strangers in a most immodest fashion. She wedged her hands against the back of the woman in front of her, but failed to create any reasonable distance or slow her forward progression.

Men poured into already congested streets from nearby buildings. With fists raised in protest, their voices united in booming chants for better wages. Women joined the fray, dragging their children with them. Caroline's pulse somersaulted through her veins. She and her fellow passengers were surrounded.

Though she hated to be rude, this was no time for the genteel manners she'd been taught at Miss Lillian's School for Young Ladies. She ducked beneath a man's arm and shimmied herself into the gap in front of him. For once her petite stature worked in her favor. Only a few feet more and she could squeeze into a carriage and escape the madness descending on the city.

When she finally emerged on the other side of the throng, one cab remained. The horse snorted and jerked its head. The driver yanked on the reins. "One more," he yelled. "Got room for one more."

As she lifted her boot to the carriage, tears pricked her eyes. What might've happened had she not found transportation?

A hand gripped her shoulder and spun her about, pulling her veil taut. She winced as the comb's teeth dug into her scalp. She stared into the eyes of a man she'd met on the train. The one whose wife had shared their sandwiches with her.

"What are you doing?" Her voice warbled, revealing the turmoil churning inside her. "I'll miss my carriage."

His forearm pinned her against the side of the conveyance. "Sorry, miss. I truly am." He angled his head toward the cab while his wife climbed inside, clutching their infant. Once his family was safely aboard, he released Caroline, and the hansom pulled away, taking her hope of escape with it.

Alarm bells sounded in the distance. Her breath quickened. She lifted a trembling palm to her chest in a vain attempt to ease the ache in her lungs. Was help on the way? Would the demonstration be quelled? She squeezed her eyes closed and willed herself to ignore the chaos erupting around her.

Police wagons maneuvered into the swell, parting the demonstrators like the Red Sea. Whistles blew. Baton-wielding officers leapt into the crowd, splintering off a small segment of rioters while the majority continued their advance toward the locomotive.

Helpless to oppose the burgeoning tide, Caroline surged forward with them. Dozens of men stood atop the train, some with fiery torches. Others rammed blazing sticks through the railcar's windows, setting cabins alight.

Smoke billowed from the burning train, stinging her eyes. Memories flashed like images from a nightmare—burning flesh and searing pain. Her chest tightened. Not again. Though her feet touched the ground, the swarm crushed her, dragging her closer to the flaming rail cars. Her strength was no match against the advancing mob.

The face of the man with kind eyes came to mind. If she could find him, would he rally to her assistance? Should she dare risk relying on a stranger's help? Especially one as large as the man by the wagon? What if a wretched heart lay behind that gentle façade? But what choice did she have? If she didn't do something soon, she'd be trampled.

As unseemly as the behavior was for a young lady, Caroline jumped as high as she could above the sea of people and waved her arms. Her purse swung wildly as she scanned the row of wagons blocking a side street. Seeing him only a few feet away, she called out, unsure her tenuous voice could be heard over the pandemonium.

The heel of her boot landed in a rut, and her ankle twisted. Grimacing, she shifted her weight to the opposite foot only to be tossed like a ship on an angry ocean. The drawstrings tore loose from her wrist and pitched her reticule forward. "My bag!"

She bent to retrieve it and was knocked down from behind. Boots kicked her ribs. She flinched as pain ripped through her side. She curled into a ball and wrapped her arms around her veiled head.

The tears she'd been holding back leaked from her eyes unbidden. Father had no idea where she was. She'd fled without leaving word. Would her bruised and trodden body even be recognizable?

She grasped the heirloom cross dangling from her neck, a gift from an aunt she'd never met. The same aunt with whom she'd hoped to find protection from her father.

God, please send an angel to rescue me.

———

Franz Köhler searched the crowd. Where was she? Though their gazes had met for the briefest moment before the curious woman retreated into the crowd, she'd awakened something inside him—something warm and strangely familiar.

He rubbed his palm along his whiskered jaw. Why had she backed away from him? What could he have done to frighten her? Maybe it wasn't him at all but the growing number of protesters in the streets.

"What are you looking at, *kumpel?*" Heinrich Müeller asked in his native German tongue.

"No one." His friend's eyes narrowed, and Franz cleared his throat. "Nothing, I mean."

Heinrich pointed to the men gathering on the tracks. "Are you coming?"

Franz craned his neck and continued searching for the mysterious woman among the stranded travelers. *"Ja."*

"Come then. *Herr* Winkler expects us to join the march. We must all stand together against another cut in our wages."

Franz nodded. "Ja, Heinrich, in a minute."

He hopped onto a nearby freight wagon, ignoring the rebuke from its owner. His gaze roamed the crowd. The woman's black veil should be much easier to locate from this vantage point, but what if he couldn't find her in the chaos? What if he never saw her again?

He spotted a figure in black attempting to board one of the carriages and watched in horror as a man restrained her. The breath left his lungs. An unexplainable need to protect her coursed through him. Franz jumped from the wagon and waded into the maelstrom. His broad chest and strong legs allowed him to move through the swarm rather than be swept along, but her small stature made it difficult for him to follow her progression.

The influx of demonstrators forced the crowd toward one of the flaming rail cars. Alarm bells sounded nearby followed by thunderous hoofbeats. Whistle-blowing police jumped from their wagons, blocking his view of the woman. Brandishing clubs, they attempted to curtail the mob's advance.

Her veiled head popped above the crowd a few feet away. This time when their gazes met, she called out, but her voice was no match above the din.

Smoke from the burning train clawed at his throat. He lifted the red kerchief over his mouth and nose. A rock pelted his shoulder. Despite the sting, Franz remained undeterred.

With one more powerful stride, he reached her, but not

before her outstretched hand disappeared inside the melee. Her shrieks filled his ears. His gut twisted at the sight of her curled form being kicked and stomped beneath the protesters' feet.

Bending low, Franz shielded her with his body. His knuckles scraped cobblestones as he slid his hands beneath her and scooped her into his arms. "You are safe, *Fräulein*."

Men knocked into him, jarring his balance. He angled her body against his chest, tightened his grip, and muscled his way through the throng. When he emerged from the crowd, he spied an alley to his right. He quickened his pace, turned into the narrow passageway, and gently lowered her to the ground.

Franz nudged her shoulder. "Fräulein." No response. He jostled her again. "Fräulein, where are you hurt?"

This time her head rolled away from him. The floral lace hid most of her face and a single dark ringlet escaped her peculiar shroud. A white bandage circled her neck, protruding above the collar of her black shirtwaist. He glanced at her hand, so dainty it nearly fit in the palm of his own. Pinkish-white scars trimmed the edge of an additional bandage peeking beyond the cuff of her glove. What had happened to her? And who did she mourn?

The young woman's lips parted. She murmured something about a bag before her voice faded and her eyes fluttered open.

"Franz Köhler," he said, pointing to himself. Her focus darted from his face to the tall buildings lining the alley then back to him. He kept his tone soft so as not to frighten her. "You need *Doktor*?"

The young woman winced and clutched her side then scrambled away from him. Eyes wide, she crawled backward until she rested against a large wooden crate. With her attention trained on him, she clambered to her feet and grimaced when her weight landed on her left foot.

Franz lifted his hands, palms out, as he rose to his full height. Her gaze traveled the length of his torso. "Not again. Please,

God, not again." She clasped her pendant and swayed.

Franz lunged forward as she crumpled into his arms. This time he didn't plan to let her go until he learned who this intriguing woman was and why she had unexpectedly captured his imagination.

Chapter 2

Shots rang out from the direction of Camden Street, and Franz tensed. Were the police firing into the crowd, or had a roughneck striker brought a weapon to the rally?

Protesters stampeded into the alley. *Beeil dich! Polizei!* a woman yelled, warning him to hurry.

He scooped the injured woman into his arms and fled the narrow passageway toward Montgomery Street. Holding her tight against him, Franz maneuvered his way through back streets and alleyways. He glanced at the young woman he carried. How had the day gone so horribly wrong?

The workers had organized a peaceful demonstration, a simple strike for better wages. However, when news spread among the workers that Baltimore and Ohio dividend holders had received a 10 percent payout while the employees received the same in pay cuts—the second one in eight months—the workers had had enough.

Their plan to occupy the tracks and disrupt rail traffic until their grievances were heard had disintegrated into a melee. No one should have been hurt. Especially not an innocent woman who'd been forced to disembark a train on which she'd purchased a ticket.

His arms ached as he neared his home in the German district. Adjusting his grip on the wounded stranger, he climbed the stairs to his family's meager home above the clockworks. His lungs begged for more air than his shallow breaths provided. Unable to grasp the latch, he kicked the door with his boot.

The lock clicked. *Mutter* swung the door open and gasped at the sight of an unconscious woman cradled in her son's arms. Without offering an explanation, he ducked inside then whizzed by her.

His brother, Lukas, shot to his feet, nearly knocking his chair into Franz's path.

Questions loomed in their eyes, but Franz had no time to explain himself or that he didn't even know the name of the woman he held.

"To Margaretha's room," Mutter directed, trailing after him.

His arms ached to relieve himself of the precious burden he'd carried nearly ten blocks from the train depot. He bent forward and gently laid her on his sister's bed.

The afternoon sunlight gleamed through the window. Mutter pulled the shutters closed. Her worried gaze drifted to the young woman. "Where is she hurt?"

"I do not know." Franz gulped in another breath. "Protesters jam the streets. I had no other place to take her."

Mutter examined the young woman's abdomen. When her probing fingers touched the stranger's ribs, she flinched, and her eyes shot open. The grimace she wore spoke to her pain, silently answering Mutter's question.

Although most of her face remained hidden behind her veil, the portion he could see appeared ashen. He narrowed his gaze and attempted to peer through the dark lace, but the large embroidered roses obscured his view.

Franz stepped forward and patted her arm. "Shh, is safe here, Fräulein," he assured her in his broken English.

She yanked her arm away. Her gaze flitted between him and Lukas before landing on Mutter.

"What have you done, Franz?" Lukas lounged against the doorway, steaming mug in hand.

"*Nichts*. She is frightened, that is all." He glared at his brother. "The demonstration turned violent. The crowd nearly crushed her. I rescued her."

"*Nein*," Lukas scoffed. "You probably trampled her with your big feet."

Franz ignored the barb. Lukas always assumed the worst about him—always needled him about his size. Where Franz enjoyed peace and harmony, Lukas favored strife, debate, and criticism—especially where his older brother was concerned.

"We have no time for your provocations now," Mutter said. "I think her ribs are bruised, and her ankle is swollen." She stuffed a folded blanket beneath the injured woman's foot. "Lukas, fetch den Doktor!"

"Me?" He shoved himself off the door frame. "Nein. Franz stomped on her. Let him go. *Frau* Henderson expects her clock repaired by four o'clock, and one of the gears does not cooperate."

Margaretha's blond head peeked into the room. "I'll go."

Franz nodded. *"Danke."* Margaretha smiled then disappeared.

"Willkommen." Mutter's palm lay against her chest. "Welcome to our home. I am Berta Köhler." She waved him closer. "And this is my son Franz."

He bowed his head. "Fräulein."

Her eyes flashed in recognition. Although he'd only shown her kindness, apprehension resided in her gaze—he was sure of it. His heart pinched. She'd been through a great ordeal, so her fright was understandable, but that did nothing to repel the rising sadness inside him. Why did it matter if she feared him? That was nothing new. He'd become accustomed to people assuming he'd use his brawn to get whatever he wanted.

She shoved herself upright and grimaced then slid her hand over her side. "I'm Caroline Wilkins," she said, her voice raspy.

"Nein. Nein," Mutter gently cooed as she reclined their guest against the pillows again. "My daughter, Margaretha, has gone for den Doktor. Until then, you lie still, ja?"

"Mutter," Franz said, "she doesn't understand our German. You must speak English."

She waved off his suggestion and reached to unpin Caroline's head covering, but the young woman gripped Mutter's arm with her gloved hand, revealing the scarred flesh.

"No. Please, leave it on," she begged.

"It is stuffy in here," Mutter said, continuing in her native tongue. "You will be more comfortable without it."

Again, with the German. Perhaps it made Mutter feel better to talk to Caroline and encourage her to rest. However, using their English, flawed though it may be, was the only way he knew to put the frightened woman at ease.

"Please."

Caroline's pleading gaze matched her tone and wrenched Franz's heart. The inexplicable need to protect her surged through him again, just as it had during the protest. "Let us do as she asks, Mutter. We want her to trust us."

"Very well." Mutter nodded and stepped back.

Caroline's reluctance to remove her veil piqued Franz's curiosity. While the majority of her left cheek lay hidden, the visible portion of her right cheek was blemish-free. He surmised that if her gloves were worn to conceal injuries, her shroud must be intended to obscure the same. What must she have endured to fear him and his family seeing what lay beneath her veil or to cover herself in such a manner during the heat of summer?

"Is gut Franz bring here," Mutter said in imperfect English. She patted Caroline's hand. "Rest. Doktor come."

Caroline gave a tight nod of her head, assuring Mutter she'd understood. However, as her fingers stroked the gold cross hanging from her neck, Franz doubted her anxiety had lessened. All he could do was pray that *Gott* would calm her fear and allow her to see his true character. Otherwise, Caroline may flee their home before he discovered why he'd been so compelled to rescue her.

———

Caroline's side ached, but her throbbing ankle hurt even more. She glanced at the woman tending her. Berta had the same kind blue eyes as her son.

A twinge of guilt pricked her conscience. Should she let them know she understood their native tongue? German was only one of many languages she spoke fluently. French had been a required subject in her boarding school. When Miss Lillian discovered Caroline's aptitude for languages, she'd set her star pupil on a course to learn German, Italian, and Latin as well.

The deception wasn't designed to harm the Köhlers, but only to allow her to evaluate whether or not the family could be trusted, especially Franz. Should she lend her confidence to the mammoth of a man lurking near the door? Since his size intimidated her, and he had been one of the men participating in the riot, perhaps she shouldn't reveal her knowledge of German just yet. Keeping her fluency a secret might help her assess if she was in any immediate danger.

"May I have a glass of water?" she asked, motioning as if bringing a cup to her mouth.

"Ja." Berta rose and fled the room, leaving Caroline alone with Franz. The giant moved closer. She blinked rapidly, and the muscles in her neck tensed. She'd mistakenly assumed Franz would fetch the drink, since he was in the doorway.

Surely he wouldn't hurt her—not with his mother only steps away. Could she even trust her own judgment? After all, she'd mistakenly believed Charles, as her fiancé, would protect her before he'd isolated her in the library and then. . .

Caroline scooted to the opposite side of the bed and bit back a grimace.

Franz lifted his palms, a frown now dwelling where a smile resided moments earlier. He raised the sash beside her headboard a few inches. A delightful cross-breeze swished by her.

"*Besser?*" he asked, then shook his head. "Better. American now and speak English. Not always so gut. But Mutter and *Vater* they like speak German."

Conversing with him in his native language would be easy, natural even. Would that be the better course of action? Perhaps she could glean more about him and his family, get a better sense of his character. He seemed kind, but she couldn't excuse the fact that he'd been present at the riot.

But why would a man prone to violence follow after her and rescue her—a complete stranger? Either he had nefarious designs, like Charles, and when she'd awakened in the alley she'd spoiled his plan, or his kindness was genuine and hid no ulterior motive. But which was it?

He glanced at her again, his gaze lingering a bit too long on her face. No doubt wondering what atrocity lay secret beneath her shroud. Then his attention shifted to the bandages her gloves couldn't completely conceal. She crossed her arms over her chest, tucking her hands snuggly against herself and away from his scrutiny.

Ogles and stares from men weren't strange to her. She'd endured them long before she'd ever donned her black veil—but for a vastly different reason. Men unfailingly found her stunning, something most women envied, but Caroline believed a curse. Primarily because the marriage prospects Father trotted in front of her gawked at her appearance even more than they did his purse strings. Those who spoke in rapturous tones had nothing to say in appreciation of her intellect or accomplishments. After a while, every conversation that extolled her beauty grew monotonously tedious, just paired with a different face and last name.

However, Franz ducked his chin when he'd apologized for

his clumsy English—something only a humble man would do. She'd not once known the pairing of the two words. Certainly none in her acquaintance, especially not her father or brothers.

She studied Franz as he adjusted the pine cone weights on a handsomely carved wall clock. He'd shown her nothing but compassion, and she'd returned that kindness with fear and skepticism.

Would she ever know the pleasure of being courted by a man who didn't know who Caroline Wilkins really was? Who wasn't after her father's fortune? Someone who merely enjoyed her company? Someone who saw *her*.

Chapter 3

"All of Caroline's things are gone." Franz raked his fingers through his hair. "Nearly all of the passengers' belongings were looted or destroyed during the riot."

Mutter tsked. "Did you give them the description Herr Doktor Berger translated for us?"

"Ja. Nothing resembled the bag she described."

She sighed. "There is nothing to be done about that now. You can tell her after *dem Abendessen*. Have a seat."

Supper smelled delicious. His stomach groaned for the *Jägerschnitzel* Mutter had prepared for their dinner. He yanked a chair from the table and sat beside *Opa*. His grandfather had made the journey with them from Bavaria several years earlier. "Where is Margaretha?"

"She eats with Caroline."

A twinge of disappointment knotted his stomach. Although he would have enjoyed that assignment, he didn't look forward to telling Caroline she'd lost all of her possessions.

Fingers steepled, Opa bowed his head and blessed the meal.

After a hearty "Amen," Vater jabbed a piece of fried pork then passed the platter to Lukas. "What about compensation?" he asked. "Did they give her a new ticket?"

Franz cut the tender schnitzel with his fork then swished the breaded meat in the mushroom gravy and savored the taste as he chewed. "I put her name on the Remuneration List. When she is besser, she must complete paperwork at the station office. Then they make the decision."

Lukas gulped his coffee then wiped his mouth against his sleeve. "What is to be done about Caroline? She cannot remain here much longer."

"Why not? Your life has seen little disruption," Franz retorted.

"I do not want her here. She is running from someone or something."

"Why do you say that?" Franz asked before stuffing a generous piece of Jägerschnitzel into his mouth.

"Look at her dress." Lukas rolled his eyes. "She is from money. Women like that do not travel alone."

His brother spoke the truth about Caroline's mourning dress. It was much nicer than anything Mutter or Margaretha owned. But only a fool would debate such things. She'd lost everything. "Nein. She wears widow's clothes. There is no one, or Caroline would have asked us to send word of her whereabouts."

Lukas shook his head. "Listen to my words. Someone will come for her, and trouble is certain to follow."

"We cannot put her out," Mutter countered. "What would become of her?"

"Berta is right," Opa said. "If she had not lost her money, we could arrange for her to stay at the Weimar's boardinghouse, but she has no way to pay."

"Oh, she has money," Lukas said. "You can be certain of that. If we pressed her, there would be someone who could wire funds." He scoffed. "Or even besser, come take her off our hands."

Franz's jaw clenched. "Why must you always oppose me? If I say the grass is green, you argue it is blue just to vex me." The vehemence in his tone rivaled that of his younger brother, and Franz regretted his harsh manner. He prided himself on his ability to keep his emotions in check.

"Enough discussion." Vater's voice sliced the tension.

Franz glanced at his parents. With their gazes locked on one another, Vater's brow arched. A slight dip of Mutter's chin was her only response to Vater's unspoken question. Franz admired the way his parents silently communicated on just about any topic. While Mutter would defer to Vater when they disagreed, Franz could only remember a few times they weren't of one mind.

Vater helped himself to another serving of Jägerschnitzel. "Caroline may stay until she makes a plan for herself."

His brother shoved his plate toward the center of the table. "We are trying to launch our business. This woman will be a distraction."

"I am the head of this house, and the decision has been made."

Lukas grabbed his mug and stormed out of the kitchen.

Mutter flinched when the shop door slammed behind her youngest son. "I know he worries for all of us, but I do not think Caroline's presence will be a problem. If someone comes for her, they will be happy we tended her." She cleared Lukas's plate. "For now, I am happy to have another woman in the house. She and Margaretha are of the same age. It will be nice for your sister to have a companion."

Franz sipped his *Kaffee*. "I am glad she can stay. I think Gott sent her to us for a reason."

"*Vorsehung*," Opa chimed in. "How else could you find her in such a crowd?"

Franz shrugged. Opa believed in divine providence, that everything happened for a reason, and that, in time, Gott's plan would make itself known. Like his grandfather, Franz trusted in Gott's plan for his life and was curious to learn if Caroline might play a significant role in his own.

However, he couldn't ignore that she hadn't asked them to inform anyone about her injuries or her whereabouts. He massaged his beard. Lukas was correct. Someone should be looking for her.

Franz suspected there was much more to Caroline Wilkins's story than she'd disclosed.

———

Four days had passed since the riot, and Caroline had only been out of bed to use the necessary. According to Doctor Berger, her ribs were bruised, not cracked, but he'd been firm regarding little or no weight on her left foot for several days. Then she could begin gradually increasing her activity.

Margaretha perched on the edge of the bed, sipping from her coffee cup. Eager to practice her English, the young woman had chatted happily with Caroline about their upbringing in Bavaria and the journey to America less than five years prior.

Caroline hated deceiving the young woman, but how could she explain that she'd misled them about her understanding of German because she'd been frightened by her older brother? The same older brother, who, after careful scrutiny, appeared more a lamb than a lion.

Knuckles rapped against the door. "I come?"

Margaretha nodded toward the door. "Franz, ja?"

"Yes," Caroline answered, tugging the covers higher over the night dress Margaretha had loaned her.

"*Komm doch rein!*" Margaretha called, inviting Franz to enter.

A hesitant smile parted his lips when his gaze landed on her, and Caroline's pulse quickened.

"I wind clock." Franz grasped two gold chains that hung below the chalet, one in each hand. He gently tugged each, one at a time, until the two pine cone weights rose from mere inches above the ground to their stopping place beneath the house.

The timepiece featured large oak leaves and a deer head with multiple points on its antlers. Her favorite feature was the darling green bird that popped from behind a door above the clock's face on the hour. Admittedly, the little fellow's chirping had played havoc with her sleep, but his charm surpassed any annoyance.

Shoulders back, Franz faced her again. "Cuckoo keep time for you."

He unleashed a broader grin, one that made his eyes shine as if keeping the clock running on time was a sacred duty—one he was honored to perform. Between the family's broken English and the German she'd overheard, she'd gathered the Köhlers repaired clocks.

He dragged the chair from the corner beside her bed and hesitated, a frown replacing the glorious smile he'd displayed moments earlier. Was he searching for the right words?

"Everything gone," he said, his eyes softening. "All things burn when trains have fire."

Caroline inhaled a sharp breath. *Everything. . .gone?* Her ticket and traveling money, her only letter from Aunt Josephine—all gone? Acid churned in her stomach, and she clutched the heirloom pendant at her neck. How would she notify her aunt or buy passage to her home in Scotland?

Contacting Father was *not* an option. No doubt he'd be furious with her for disappearing, and he'd insist she marry Charles upon her return. That, she was unwilling to consider.

She sank into her pillows and clamped her eyes closed. "What about a ticket, Mr. Köhler? Will they give me another?"

"Ja, I think so." He leaned forward, elbows resting on his knees. "Your name on list. When better, you make claim."

Make a claim? She pinched the bridge of her nose. While not a definite no, neither was it a guarantee of any assistance or remuneration for her losses.

Margaretha patted her hand. "Vater say you stay until besser."

"Ja, Mutter and Vater agree." Franz's eyebrows squished together, causing faint lines to crease his forehead. Was he worried about *her*? A complete stranger? Moisture pooled in her eyes as her gaze flitted between the siblings. "Thank you."

While the tension had eased in her neck, she barely knew the Köhlers and could not impose on their generosity for too long, especially with no certainty she could ever repay them. There was only one thing to be done. She'd have to summon all of her courage and persuade the Baltimore & Ohio officials to give her a new ticket.

Otherwise, her plan to escape Father's clutches and avoid marriage to Charles would be over before it began—derailed by a railmen's strike.

Chapter 4

Caroline blinked at the bright morning sun gleaming through the bedroom window. A light breeze ruffled the curtains, and the clopping of horse hooves against packed earth drifted through the open sash. How long had she slept? Rest had alluded her ever since she'd learned of her financial predicament a few days prior. Apparently, she'd finally given in and let slumber consume her.

She tossed back the covers and swung her legs over the side of the bed. Cool, polished wood shone beneath her feet, and the scent of Berta's lemon polish tickled her nose. No matter the difficulty, Caroline resolved that today she would ask Margaretha or Opa to accompany her to the Baltimore & Ohio management office and make her claim for damages against the railroad. If she received proper compensation, she should be able to sail for Scotland within a fortnight.

Although she preferred a long soak in hot water, she'd make do with a quick washing at the basin. She winced as she stepped into her freshly laundered black gown and made a mental note to thank Berta or Margaretha for washing the garment. Using Margaretha's looking glass, she unpinned her veil, then unwound the petroleum jelly–coated bandage on her neck.

She stared at her reflection, barely recognizing the young woman who'd once been the most sought-after debutante in

Philadelphia society. Several small blisters hopscotched a dotted path toward a singular large, fluid-filled sack bordered by angry pink skin. She sighed. That blister would likely leave a scar. She doubted the disingenuous men of Father's acquaintance would pursue her now.

Both Berta and Margaretha had offered to help Caroline keep her wounds clean, but she'd refused, preferring no one see the hideous blisters marring her skin. She dipped the edge of her washrag into the basin, squeezed out the excess water, and carefully dabbed the edges of the wound. Satisfied, she smoothed a generous glob of petroleum jelly over her skin and applied fresh bandages.

She removed her gloves and repeated the process of unwrapping and cleaning the blisters on her hands. Unfortunately, her wrist sported an even larger burn sack than her neck, and clear fluid seeped from the rim. Fresh air made the wound sting, and she grimaced. This injury didn't appear nearly as grave, but it too had a high probability of leaving a blemish.

After combing her hair, she did her best to pin her locks into a loose chignon then secured her veil. She glanced at the black crocheted gloves on Margaretha's dresser. Wearing her veil proved challenging at times, but keeping her fingers gloved applied too much pressure to the blister, and she wanted to avoid a rupture.

Caroline stared at her bare toes. Donning stockings and shoes would prove too difficult with bandaged hands. Did she dare leave the bedroom in such a manner? What would Father say if he knew she strolled about the house in her bare feet? She shook off the notion. What was the point of fleeing her father's home if she allowed his voice to live in her head and dictate her actions?

With nothing to be done about the matter, she reached for the doorknob and entered the kitchen. She could only hope that, without her boots, the hem of her dress would hide the infraction until she could ask for Margaretha's assistance.

"Guten Morgen." Franz's sober expression wrinkled his brow.

Berta tapped an empty chair. "Sit. I get plate."

"No, thank you. I just needed to ask Margaretha's help with—"

"Nein," she said, her mouth spreading into a grin. "Is hot." With hands on Caroline's shoulders, the older woman guided her to a chair across from Franz and gently tucked her onto the seat.

She'd be lying if she denied the smell of Berta's potato pancakes and gravy hadn't awakened her appetite. Berta dished up a serving of what had become a staple breakfast while staying with the Köhlers. Caroline bowed her head, thanked God, then listened while the family continued their conversation.

"I do not plan to return to my job at the rail yard until the strike is over."

Was she mistaken, or had Franz's voice wavered? Caroline's gaze darted from Mr. Köhler to Franz before finally settling on Mr. Köhler.

Silence consumed the room. Her stomach roiled, and suddenly the potato pancakes and gravy lost their appeal. She was eavesdropping—again. How would they feel if they knew she understood their conversation? *Lord, help them to understand why I wasn't honest at first about—*

Mr. Köhler's fork clanked against his plate. His steely gaze targeted his eldest son. "I do not think I heard you correctly."

Tension hovered in the air like the smoke from Opa's pipe, choking out the warmth and cordiality Caroline had usually found in the Köhlers' home. She'd thought to confess her fluency moments ago, but a knot tightening in her belly begged her silence, at least for the moment.

Franz scrubbed a hand over his whiskered cheeks. Was he uncertain how to respond? Or did he know exactly what he wanted to say but feared his father's reaction?

For Caroline, it had always been the latter. As a woman, she understood being under the thumb of an overbearing parent. She'd been raised that a woman was to be seen and not heard. To smile and nod and never, above all else, offer an opinion on anything. Could a man feel invisible too?

Her heart drummed quicker, and Caroline leaned a little closer to Franz, wishing she could somehow encourage him to find his voice. But if he did, how would his father respond?

Franz glanced at Caroline. Had she encouraged him with a slight nod of her head? How could that be, considering they spoke different languages? He supposed she didn't need to understand German to comprehend the friction sparking between Vater and son. Unsure why it mattered, Franz wished this skirmish about his job would not unfold before her eyes. Would she find him cantankerous and disrespectful? He didn't like to disagree with Vater, but if he didn't push for his rightful place in the family, things would never change. Then what kind of man would he be?

Franz cleared his throat. "I agree with the strikers. The money we earn is not enough for the long hours and hard work."

Lukas scoffed. "They will just replace you with other men who will work for less money."

Again, Lukas argued against him. With each adversarial engagement, Franz sensed distance growing between them. Despite Franz's repeated prayers for God to heal Lukas's heart after the loss of his wife and daughter, he found it increasingly more difficult to extend his brother grace.

"Nein. The cost to hire and train unskilled workers will convince management to give us a raise. We will stand together and fight for better wages."

"You are not unwise like the others." Vater shook his head, punctuating his words. "Only a fool walks away from a gut job because their pride gets in the way."

Vater buttered a thick slice of bread as if the matter had been settled. Maybe for Vater it had, but not for Franz. "You are wrong. The strike is not about our pride, but to stand up for what is right."

Caroline's eyes widened. Had the sharpness of his tone frightened her? He inhaled deeply then slowly eased the breath from his lungs before continuing. "Our wages should not be cut so wealthy investors get a larger dividend."

Vater pointed the butter knife at Franz. "You are to keep the position."

"Allow me to work on the clocks with you and Lukas. The shop is my *Geburtsrecht*, and I choose to claim my birthright."

"You were not made for fine craftsmanship," Lukas snickered. "Your hands are too big for that."

That argument again. He gritted his teeth against the unkind remarks threatening to spew from his lips. *Eins, zwei, drei. . .* Perhaps counting to ten would ease the tension in his spirit.

He did not wish to bear a grudge against his brother. His family did not know the hours he spent making adaptations so that he could carve beautiful clocks alongside them in the shop. Someday he would show them, but not until his own creation far surpassed even his brother's handiwork.

"We have discussed this before," Vater said. He finished the last swig of his Kaffee. "Your salary pays for the wood we import from the Black Forest. You carve the body of the clock and put the gears and bellows inside, ja? Leave the design to your brother and me."

Franz balled his fist. Why did Vater never see eye-to-eye with him? Why wasn't he able to persuade Vater to his opinion the way Lukas could? He was the eldest son, yet the family business, the craft that had been the trade of the Köhler clan in Bavaria for over a century, would be handed to his younger brother simply because Franz was a burly man.

"We are still new to this country. I do not want you or this family mixed up in this labor strike. You cross the picket line, keep your mouth closed, and earn your salary." Vater put his hand on Franz's shoulder. "We all have a part to play, son." His stern voice had softened. "You find another job if you like, but until then, you must tell Herr Winkler that you will return next week when the line resumes service."

Franz's pulse throbbed in his ears. He fought the instinct to blurt a series of protests, but past experience told him it would do no good to belabor the point. "Ja, I will speak with him." However, what he would tell Herr Winkler might not be exactly what Vater had in mind.

Chapter 5

Caroline's gut twisted tighter than one of Berta's wrung-out dishcloths. She didn't know any of the Köhlers well, but the light she'd already become accustomed to seeing in Franz's eyes had dimmed. And when he'd spoken of his birthright, his sad tone, combined with the craving in his voice to be heard, had nearly undone her.

She was confident Franz had already known his request to join the family clockworks would be denied, yet he'd been compelled to ask. Who would have guessed that this large, strapping man shared the same struggle she'd endured her entire life—to be valued for who she was. Not limited by others' false assumptions based on her outward appearance.

Yet how did she reconcile this with a man willing to participate in a violent labor strike? One that blocked her train and derailed her plans to escape to Scotland, where she could remain out of her father's reach forever? A man who, by his own words, still wanted to join the protestors and not return to work?

Mr. Köhler stood and removed a folded sheet of paper from his pocket and handed it to Franz. "This is the list of items we need from the hardware store. Tell Gunther I will come down and pay him later in the week."

Franz's shoulders drooped, and with them, her resolve. Seeing this intelligent, capable man reduced to nothing more than an errand boy made it increasingly difficult to keep him at arm's length. Conflicting emotions swirled inside her, and she wanted to scream. But properly bred young ladies didn't do that either.

Margaretha dried her hands on her apron. "I want to come too, Franz. We need several things from the market. I'll get my bag, and then I am ready to leave."

He shifted a somewhat defeated-looking gaze in Caroline's direction. "Is ankle besser to come with us?" he asked, switching to English when he spoke to her. "I take you depot and file claim."

She'd nearly forgotten about her plan to seek a ride to accomplish that very same thing, yet God had made a way without her even having to ask. Caroline lifted a quick prayer of thanks. "Yes, thank you. I'm anxious to see about a new ticket."

"We have gut plan." He mustered a smile, even if Caroline believed it a half-hearted one. "I get wagon. Station too far to walk on bad foot."

"Thank you." A bit of joy had returned to his voice. She admired his effort to make the best of his circumstances.

Lukas jutted his chin toward her. "You go to depot?"

The younger brother's curt tone surprised her. "I think so." Her gaze bounced to Franz then Margaretha before settling on Lukas again. "I will just need to be careful."

He wiped his mouth and excused himself from the table. "Gut. If can go depot with Franz"—his arm swung wide over the kitchen floor—"can help Mutter and Margaretha in *der Küche*."

"Lukas, Caroline is guest," Mutter chided in German.

His lips flattened into a thin line, and a chill swept over Caroline. What had she done to make him dislike her so?

"I am sorry, Mutter, but we do not know her. She is not our guest. She is a boarder who is capable of earning her keep."

Lukas's words stung, but he did have a point. Fleeing her father's household and her fiancé meant she must earn her own way. Besides, assisting Berta and Margaretha with meals would help pass the time while she waited for remuneration from the railroad.

Keeping her tone even, as she'd been bred to do when difficult people or circumstances presented themselves, she responded, "Lukas is right." She shifted her attention to Berta, with whom she'd formed a bond of sorts. "I am happy to help."

Berta hesitated then nodded.

Caroline looked forward to spending time with Berta and Margaretha, but she had no doubt Lukas would come to regret the arrangement when he discovered the family's new helper knew as much about cooking as she did the politics of Franz's labor strike.

⸻

Franz offered his hand to assist Caroline into the wagon. His pulse intensified at her touch, and for a brief moment, he allowed himself to imagine the pleasure of stroking her skin with his thumb. All too soon, her palm slid from his, leaving an ache in his chest and a longing to touch her again.

Franz climbed aboard and seated himself next to her before easing the wagon away from Camden Depot. He maneuvered the conveyance through the gap his coworkers made in the picket line but couldn't help notice Caroline's white-knuckled grip on the bench when one of the strikers approached.

"Is safe, Fräulein. I know this man."

"Guten Morgen, Franz. Did you tell Herr Winkler you will speak for us at the strike talks?"

Heinrich's narrowed gaze focused on the woman swathed in black beside him. Franz wanted to tell him not to stare, but acknowledging his rudeness would only make Caroline more uncomfortable. Better to answer him and be on their way.

"Ja. I come tonight."

"Gut," he said, rubbing his hands together. "We are counting on you to get this sorted out in our favor."

"I'll do my best. Pray for wisdom. That is what both sides need."

With a gentle slap of the reins, Franz guided the horse farther from the station. Their trip had been relatively unsuccessful. Still unable to locate Caroline's possessions or receive an affirmative answer as to whether the railroad intended to reimburse travelers for their losses, they'd only succeeded in confirming that her name appeared on a growing list of disgruntled passengers seeking compensation.

Sitting rigid on the seat beside him, Caroline fidgeted with a thread from her bandage. She'd born the disappointment well. Now alone with her thoughts, he wondered if she ruminated on her circumstances. He searched his mind for something to say to ease her concern, but he doubted his limited English could accurately express what he'd hope to convey. *Gott, make a way for us to communicate, that I might lighten her burden.*

The telegraph office came into view. Caroline had been living with his family for several days, and she'd not once asked to contact any family or friends.

He pointed toward the brick building that also housed the post office. "Fräulein?" She turned her head, giving him just a glimpse of her face, as the majority remained hidden beneath the veil she wore in a manner more befitting his Oma Gertrud than a grieving young woman. "Send word to family? Tell them you safe?"

The tip of her tongue glided over her lips before she pressed them together and looked away.

Her lack of a verbal response left Franz in a quandary. Had his thick accent made his question undecipherable? Or worse, had he overstepped his bounds and upset her?

Black fabric brushed his leg when they turned onto Lexington Street, and an idea formulated in his mind. What if she had no one to apprise? There'd been a thin sheen of moisture in her eyes.

Her garments suggested she was mourning someone, but it had never occurred to him that her loss might've left her completely alone in this world. His throat constricted. Why else would a young woman of supposed means be traveling by herself?

Unsure what to say, Franz decided he would remain quiet and allow her to—

"There is no one."

He kept his tone even so his question would appear less intrusive. "No family?"

"None I wish to remain in contact with. I'm hoping to sail to Scotland and live with my aunt. It's just. . ." Hands placid in her lap, her voice cracked, and a piece of Franz's heart cracked along with it. She tucked her chin against her chest. "I've never met her, and she has no idea I wish to come and. . ."

She dabbed her nose with an embroidered handkerchief she'd fished from a pocket hidden somewhere in the folds of her skirt. Her shoulders straightened, and she lifted her head abruptly, as if she suddenly remembered who and where she was.

"Pardon my outburst, Mr. Köhler. I've not been myself for several weeks." She cleared her throat. "What I meant to say is that after I receive compensation from the railroad, I will write my aunt Josephine to ask if I may come and live with her in Scotland. Then wait till I receive word so I can purchase my passage."

"Call me Franz, *bitte*." He gathered the reins in his left hand then wiped his right against his pants. "May I say Caroline?"

She nodded. "I suppose that wouldn't be too indecorous."

Franz wrinkled his brow. "What means in-de-crous?" He shrugged his shoulders and smiled.

"Improper."

"Oh." He rubbed his jaw. "And what means im-pro-per?"

Caroline bit back a smile. "Impolite manners."

"Ah, that I know." He lifted his chin, pleased he finally understood. "I use gut manners with many ladies."

Caroline's lips parted as her eyes rounded. "You keep company with many ladies?"

Franz mulled over Caroline's question. Heat flashed up his neck, warming the tips of his ears. "Nein," he answered crisply. "Only Mutter and Margaretha."

Caroline chuckled. He enjoyed the sound of her laughter, but silence once again filled the empty space between them. He imagined it could be quite pleasing to sit in mutual solitude with someone whose soul thrummed in unison with his own. Nonetheless, he found it disarming to be so attracted to Caroline and know only that she'd been stranded in Baltimore and had family in Scotland.

Would she open up to him if he tried to learn more about her? He didn't have much experience with women. While he could offer his future bride a heart and body untouched by another, he also had little knowledge how to make conversation with a lady. Why did his hands feel so clammy? And worse, why did his mouth feel as dry as a loaf of week-old bread?

He searched his mind for a topic that would entice her to share more about herself. "Tell me about *Tante* Josephine?"

She faced him again. At this angle, one of her blue eyes lay concealed behind the floral lace of her veil, but he could tell Caroline weighed his question. Would she trust him? He would not press her. One question showed his interest in learning more about her. If she did not answer, he would—

"The truth is, I don't really know my aunt." Franz strained to hear Caroline's soft voice over the din of streetside conversations, clomping hooves, and nickering horses. "I'm told my father's sister visited when I was very young. She was to live with us and help Mother care for me, but in the end, she opted for an adventure to the Australian goldfields with her brother, Elias. Poor Uncle Elias perished there, but Aunt Josephine met a Scotsman named Daniel Jardine and eventually returned to Europe."

"You not see or hear from her?"

"Only once." Caroline wrapped her fingers around the gold cross dangling from her neck before opening her palm so Franz could see it. "Aunt Josephine sent me this necklace for my sixteenth birthday. She said Daniel had it made from one of the gold nuggets they'd found."

"May I?"

She nodded and lifted the pendant away from her bodice. His fingers slid beneath it.

"That is fine craftsmanship," he said, releasing the medallion to her care.

"It's even inscribed with a reference to their favorite verse, Philippians 4:13. " 'I can do all things—' "

" '—through Christ which strengtheneth me,' " Franz said with her in unison. "That scripture is *mein Favorit*."

Caroline's gaze latched onto Franz. "Mine as well," she whispered.

Perhaps this notion that he and Caroline were destined to be together wasn't as ridiculous as it sounded. Die Vorsehung had brought Opa and Oma Gertrud together. Maybe it wasn't too much to hope that God would intervene and repeat the pattern two generations later.

Franz shoved a heavy breath from his lungs. Somehow, he doubted it would be that simple.

Chapter 6

Caroline swiped a match on the strike plate above the stove, opened the cast-iron door, and tossed the matchstick inside. Before long, she'd have the fire hot enough to reheat the coffee. Though she'd been with the Köhlers for several days, she couldn't help feeling a tad bit uncomfortable alone in their home for the first time. However, the outing earlier that day inquiring after compensation for her ill-fated belongings had made her foot swell, and she'd opted to remain home while they attended the midweek service. Her solitude also afforded her the opportunity to unpin her veil and allow herself respite from the summer heat.

When the rich aroma of coffee filled the kitchen, she poured a cup then strolled into the parlor and examined the books inside an old walnut bookcase. With nearly two hours to spend alone, she might as well read. She lifted the glass pane and slid the door over a track above the leatherbound volumes. Her fingers skimmed the spines until she happened on one of her favorites, *Immensee*. Her German tutor had assigned her this title when she was but a romantic young girl of thirteen. Reinhard and Elisabeth's portentous love story had stayed with her ever since.

As she settled into the wingback chair nearest the open window, the folds of her dress brushed a stack of papers and sent the documents fluttering to the floor. She bent to retrieve them, and the word *free* leapt off the page. She scanned the notice—an advertisement of some sort for the Köhlers' store.

Had Franz written it? More likely his mother or sister had penned the document, for she couldn't imagine a man writing this legibly. Her father's penmanship resembled the bird tracks she'd observed scratched in the dirt below the feeders in their garden. Yet the lines appeared bold, confident even—very unlike a lady's delicate hand. Even though the notice was not written in German, the strokes showed little hesitancy on the writer's part. She liked that.

SALE

Fine Bavarian cuckoo clocks
Hand-carved German timepieces for your mantel,
wall, or hallway.
All sizes 20 percent reduced.

OR

Have our artisans create a custom-designed
clock for free.

Caroline blinked. That couldn't be correct. She glanced over the advertisement a second time. "Have our artisans create a custom-designed clock for free," she whispered.

She slumped against the back of the cushioned chair. If the Köhlers had already advertised this sale in the newspapers, they would go out of business. What could they have been trying to say? She riffled through the pile of papers she'd knocked to the floor and found the same advertisement written in German. After skimming the original, she found their mistake. They'd meant to say there would be no additional costs for made-to-order purchases, not that the clock itself would be free.

If she edited the notice, she could kindly point out their mistake and determine if any of the bulletins had already been distributed before the shop opened in the morning. She could suggest the Köhlers offer a coupon the customer would bring to the shop to waive the design fee.

Her stomach tightened. In order to explain the mistake to the Köhlers, she'd need to divulge her knowledge of German. How would they react when they learned of her deceit? Would they forgive her or send her packing immediately?

No matter the cost, she wouldn't repay their kindness with any further deception.

She rummaged through various drawers in the sitting room for a charcoal pencil or pen and ink. Finding nothing, she searched similar repositories in the kitchen. She yanked open a drawer in the corner cupboard. The contents of a metal box rattled. Believing it big enough for a writing implement, she placed the hinged container on the counter and opened the lid.

Coins jiggled beneath a folded wad of greenbacks. Mouth agape, she stared at the paper currency. She'd not seen a mass of bills this thick since Charles had insisted on accompanying her while shopping for her trousseau. She shuddered at the memory of him eyeing her figure in each outfit then bestowing his approval or disapproval with the slightest motion of his head. Caroline fisted the folded bills. When would thoughts of that dreadful man leave her and never return?

The door latch clicked, and her gaze snapped toward the entryway. She dropped the money and hastily lifted her veil from her shoulders, draped the floral lace around her head, and secured the pin.

Steely blue eyes bounced from the open box to the greenbacks scattered beside her feet before narrowing into thin slits. "What is meaning of this, Fräulein?"

⸻

Franz hurried down the alley and rounded the corner toward the clockworks. If he hustled, he might be able to beat his family home, check on Caroline, and retire for the night without needing to explain why he'd not attended midweek services with the others. He didn't like keeping secrets from his family, but he believed trying to negotiate a fair end to the strike for all parties was the right thing to do. Unfortunately, with a hardheaded, set-in-his-ways Vater, Franz had determined long ago that, on rare occasions, the course that yielded the least friction was his best option.

He skidded to a halt at the sight of lights in the upstairs windows. So much for dodging explanations. Probably for the best anyhow. At least now his conscience would be at peace even if he'd have to endure Vater's and Lukas's disapproving glares for weeks to come.

Vater's angry voice carried through the open window, bidding him to pause his ascent of the stairs. *"Sie ist nict mehr willkommen."*

He tensed. Why would Vater want Caroline to leave? Why would she no longer be welcome in their home? He ascended the last few stairs by twos and joined the family in the kitchen.

"Ja. We feed her, give her a bed to sleep in, and she steals from us." Lukas's livid tone matched Vater's.

Franz's gaze darted to Opa seated at the table, the metal box that stored their savings hinged open beside him as he sorted the money into piles according to their denominations. Why was he counting their reserves? Did they suspect Caroline had stolen from them? And what had they done with her?

Soft cries spilled beneath Margaretha's door. Franz moved toward the bedroom. Lukas stepped in front of him. "Out of my way."

"Nein."

"She is crying."

Lukas folded his arms over his chest. "Gut. We caught her taking money from the family savings. Margaretha is with her while Opa determines how much is missing. We do not want her to escape out the window before we alert the authorities."

"You think Caroline would crawl out a second-story window and make her way through a strange city at night with a sprained ankle?" He scoffed. "You are a bigger simpleton than I suspected."

"Simmer down, Franz." Vater's stern voice barked, alerting Franz that no objections would be tolerated.

His heart hammered in his chest. He didn't want to simmer down. He wanted to throttle the entire lot of them.

Franz pivoted toward his grandfather. "Surely you don't agree with this fool." He jerked his thumb over his shoulder at Lukas. "You think Caroline would steal from us?"

Opa suspended his counting and looked over the rim of his spectacles. "Nein, but they will not listen to an old man." He shrugged. "So, the only way to prove her innocence is to do the counting."

"No one has asked Caroline her side of the story?"

"Nein," Mutter said, planting closed fists on her rounded hips. "She is a sweet girl. I do not understand what I saw, but I know there is an explanation we must hear before we malign her character to the police."

Vater opened his mouth, but before he could protest, Mutter raised her palm. "Wilhelm, we are no longer in Bavaria. In this country, a person is not guilty unless proven so."

Opa cleared his throat. "The money is all here. Sixty-seven dollars and nineteen cents, just like the ledger indicates."

"There." Shoulders back and chin high, Franz scolded his Vater and Lukas. "She did not steal from us."

"If we'd not come home when we did, she would have taken every penny," Lukas griped as Franz shoved him aside.

Franz raised his hand to knock then hesitated. Caroline's muffled cries wrenched his heart. *She must be so frightened, Gott.*

Give me the right words to calm her fears. He tapped his knuckles against the door. "Fräulein?"

Margaretha opened the door.

Perched on the side of the bed, Caroline cradled her head in her hands, her shoulders quaking with every sniffle-filled gasp for air. Everything inside him wanted to take her in his arms, stroke her hair, and whisper that all would be fine. But he did not have permission for such intimate contact. Instead, he kept his voice low and measured.

"Fräulein, I not think you steal the money. Come, please. Let us talk."

Skin red and blotchy, she plodded past him into the kitchen. Her shoulders sagged, and the heavy breath she exhaled sounded to Franz as if she might buckle under the weight of her burdens.

He tugged the bench from beneath the table and motioned for her to sit down. She obliged him and scooted closer to Opa.

"I make the Kaffee," Mutter said. "Perhaps it will ease the tension."

Vater shook his head. "No Kaffee. Fräulein Wilkins needs to explain herself before we send for die Polizei."

"Polizei?" Caroline's head snapped toward Vater. "*Keine Polizei, bitte.*"

Franz's jaw slackened as he slumped into the chair opposite Caroline. Her voice trembled, but her flawless German didn't go unnoticed as she begged Vater not to send for the police. Brows crimped, Franz shook his head. "*Sprechen sie Deutsch,* Fräulein?"

She averted her gaze, choosing to concentrate instead on a loose thread on her dress. "Ja."

He scrubbed a hand over his whiskers. Caroline had known German all along.

———

"I never intended to deceive you. I just—" Caroline wasn't sure if demonstrating her deception by speaking German helped or hurt the situation, but it was important the family understood her part of the conversation.

"Never your intent?" She flinched at Lukas's booming voice as he paced around the kitchen. "Nein. You decide to withhold your knowledge of German, all the while listening to our conversations, and you expect us to believe that was not an intentional choice, Fräulein?"

Before she could respond, Lukas continued his accusations. "Is that how you knew where we hid the cash box? Were you planning to take the money and buy a train ticket?"

Although he had enough indirect evidence to support his false assumptions, she did not appreciate the assault on her character. But that was beside the point. She'd severed their trust, and she had no idea how to repair the damage.

Hoping to find a smidge of lingering faith in her nature, she risked a glance at Franz. Perched across the table from her, he leaned forward with his elbows on his knees, staring at his folded hands. Did he doubt her integrity as well? Her stomach roiled. If Franz had misgivings, she had little hope of convincing the others.

She swallowed repeatedly, but nothing alleviated the sharp, pinching pain at the back of her throat. Why hadn't she told them the truth from the beginning? She'd been scared, that's why. Miss Lillian's admonition sprang to mind. *Fear is not a good basis on which a young lady should make decisions.* She couldn't argue with that wisdom, but it would have been exceedingly more beneficial to her current circumstances had she remembered the sage advice days ago.

Mr. Köhler's gruff tone interrupted her thoughts. "Do you have nothing to say?"

Believing her apology would fall on fertile soil, she inhaled deeply and mustered every ounce of heartfelt sincerity she possessed. "I am sorry. I was alone in an unfamiliar city and frightened after being swept up in the riot." She hated the fact her chin quivered as she spoke. "It's true Franz rescued me from the fray, but he'd also been participating in the protest."

She paused when Franz glanced her direction. His stony gaze mimicked his dour expression. "I didn't know then what I know now—that I can trust you, Franz." She pursed her lips in a vain effort to control the emotion in her voice. "Someone I once mistakenly believed I could depend on took advantage of my naiveté. I'm afraid I don't trust easily any longer."

Lukas quit his pacing. With both hands, he gripped the ladderback chair beside Franz and leaned over the table. "None of this explains why you were snooping in our things. What were you planning to do with the money?"

He pushed away from the chair, and it wobbled before righting itself. "What are you hiding? We don't even know if you are truly injured beneath your bandages. Maybe you wear that veil to disguise your appearance. For all we know, the authorities will swoop down on us in pursuit of you."

Franz shot to his feet. "That is enough. Let her speak."

Caroline squirmed on her chair. She was thankful that Franz had ended Lukas's inquisition, but his tone remained flat. Was he reserving judgment until after she answered their questions, or did it signal a lack of interest in the outcome?

She clamped her eyelids closed briefly then laced her fingers together in her lap. "Perhaps I should I start at the beginning."

Chapter 7

Caroline's knee bounced beneath the Köhlers' pine table. Where exactly was the beginning? Was it her father's autocratic nature, his favoritism toward her brothers, or the endless barrage of marriage prospects who would advance his business connections but cared little for Caroline herself?

She supposed the event that triggered her abrupt departure from Philadelphia, her arrival in Baltimore, and her insertion into the Köhlers' lives was the most appropriate place to start. But she had no intention of telling anyone about Charles's unwanted advances. She did, however, owe this family who'd been so kind to her, who'd tended her wounds and welcomed her into their home, the truth.

Hopefully, she could find the balance between what they might want to know and what she believed they needed to know. She inhaled a fortifying breath and squared her shoulders. "Let me begin by saying it is possible the authorities are looking for me. But not for breaking any laws."

"But someone is looking for you, Fräulein, ja?" Lukas asked.

She shuddered at his demanding tone. "Mein Vater."

"And he is a man of means?" Mr. Köhler asked.

"Ja, and substantial political influence as well."

Lukas tossed his hands in the air. "*Wunderbar*. Your Vater will think we are keeping you here to extort money from him."

He turned to his father. "I say first thing tomorrow she wires her Vater and asks for a ticket so she can go home."

"Nein!" Caroline's staunch reaction drew the attention of everyone but Franz, who appeared to be listening, yet he'd barely spoken a word and had only once glanced her way. She hadn't meant to betray him. How would she make him or any of the Köhlers understand?

"I'm grateful for all you've done for me, and I don't wish to bring trouble upon any of you," she said, keeping her emotions in check, "but I have no intention of returning home."

Berta stooped beside her and slid a hand over hers. "I think your Vater will be worried where you are. Do not let him suffer."

Caroline's chin quivered. *She would not cry.* "To my Vater I am *nur eine Tochter*—only a daughter." How many times had he invoked that phrase to justify ignoring her, as if each syllable wouldn't carve away a piece of her self-worth?

"As a daughter, I have no purpose except to marry well. The man Vater expects me to marry. . ." She cringed at the memory of Charles's hands groping her. "He is disreputable, and I will not be bound to such a man."

"I am sorry for your troubles, Fräulein, but this changes nothing," Mr. Köhler said. "Your refusal to contact your Vater is no reason to hide your knowledge of German, to listen to our conversations, or to steal from us."

Caroline bristled under the weight of his misguided accusation, but seeing as the family was already cross with her, she held her tongue in check. "I wasn't stealing. I was searching for a pencil. I wanted to help you."

"Help yourself to our profits," Lukas mumbled.

Fists clenched at his side, Franz broadened his stance. "Why must you be so antagonistic? Why do you believe the worst about Caroline?"

"Why are you so willing to believe the good in everyone and everything?"

"Nein, nein," Opa interrupted. "Bickering gets us nowhere." His sympathetic expression soothed Caroline's frazzled nerves. "Let her finish."

Franz leaned against the wall, feet crossed at the ankles, and folded his arms. "Fräulein," he said, his gentle tone putting her at ease, "why did you keep your knowledge of German a secret from us?"

Caroline's gaze locked with his, her thoughts a swirl in the sea of blue staring back at her. Plain and simple, she'd been leery of his size—at first.

Her chest tightened. She'd assumed the worst about him. Size didn't equate to mean or violent any more than her beauty equated to shallow or unintelligent. Didn't he deserve better than to have her believe false assumptions about him? Isn't that what others had done to her most of her life?

Although it may have been understandable at the time due to her encounter with Charles, she couldn't justify the ruse going on as long as it had. Franz and all the Köhlers, with the exception of Lukas, had invited her into their lives, and she'd repaid them in a most unkind fashion. Her gaze snagged on his, and she knew before she ever spoke that her answer would cost him. "I was afraid. . .of you."

As soon as the words escaped her, she regretted them. She didn't know Franz Köhler well, but the look of disappointment in his eyes nearly undid her. Why did his good opinion matter so much?

———

Franz scrubbed his chin. None of this made any sense. He doubted Caroline would steal from them, but discovering her with all their life savings jarred him as much as learning she spoke German.

He'd sensed Caroline had been frightened of him when they first met, but he'd hoped his actions had shown his concern for her, his desire to protect her. Discovering she harbored lingering doubts about his nature due to his size stung like the prick of a German *Bremse*. He wouldn't wish the bite of that nasty horsefly on anyone.

Knowing a man she should've been able to rely on for protection had taken advantage of her trust made Caroline's skittishness understandable. But she was just one more person in a long line who made assumptions about his character based on his unusual height and breadth. Most assumed he would use his brawn to intimidate people, while others, like his brother, questioned his abilities. Their narrow vision saw him fit only to use his strength for manual labor. Their effort to label him was frustrating, to say the least.

"Afraid of Franz?" Margaretha asked, a grin stretching her lips wide. She looped her arm in his. "Franz is the kindest man I know."

"Time has shown me the same," Caroline said before looking away. "I'm ashamed of my earlier opinion of him."

He pushed from against the wall. Did he detect a swath of pink coloring her cheeks?

She glanced around the room. "I'm very sorry for listening to your conversations, for not letting you know I understood German. It was unconscionable, and you deserve much better. Please, forgive me."

Mutter and Margaretha showered her with smiles and hugs, while he, Vater, and Opa nodded their acceptance of her apology.

"Danke."

"I know you distrust me most of all, Lukas, and your distrust is not unfounded, especially after coming home to find me in such an awkward moment. Alone in the house, I'd removed my veil. When I heard the latch, I panicked to cover my face again and dropped the money."

Vater's brows pinched together. "And you said you had the cash box open because you were looking for something?"

Her breath hitched. "I'd nearly forgotten about the mistake." Rising from her seat, she grabbed some papers from the counter. "I accidentally knocked these on the floor, and when I picked them up, I spotted an error in this advertisement," she said, pointing to the top sheet.

A mistake? Lukas had conceived the idea, but Franz had written the bulletin. He'd reviewed the wording several times on his own. Both Vater and Lukas had agreed to the discounted pricing, and Margaretha had checked the spelling in her German-English Dictionary.

Vater hooked his reading glasses over his ears one at a time. "Let me see, bitte."

Caroline handed Vater the paper. "Here it is," she said, once again pointing to the text.

Franz and Lukas read along over Vater's shoulder. "We offer 20 percent discount on the clocks in stock, or the customer can design a clock at no extra charge. This is gut, ja?"

"Nein. Written this way, it means that customers can place an order for a *free* custom-designed cuckoo clock."

Lukas leaned closer. His jaw slackened as he reread the document.

"I believe what you intended to say is that you are not charging extra to design made-to-order clocks."

"And you say if we had placed this advertisement in the newspapers, our customers could expect a clock at no cost?" Lukas asked.

She nodded.

He shoved his hands into his pockets. "*Dankeschön*, Fräulein." He gave her a tight nod and slipped from the kitchen.

Franz shook his head. He couldn't remember the last time his brother apologized. He bent low beside Caroline's chair and slipped his large hand over hers. "Danke." A ripple of warmth shot through him, and he stepped away. Why had he touched her? Doing so only intensified his longing for her.

Vater removed his glasses "My dear Fräulein, it appears I have misjudged you. How can we ever repay you?"

"That's not necessary. I'm happy I found the mistake before it went to print."

Mutter gently squeezed Vater's shoulder. "Perhaps we can reassure Caroline that she is welcome to stay with us as long as she needs."

"Ja, that is a gut plan," Vater said.

Caroline laid her palm against her chest. What would she have done had they not believed her? *Thank You, God.* "Hopefully, I will not trouble you too long. Once the railroad reimburses me for my ticket and lost possessions, I plan to sail to Scotland and live with my aunt. While I'm waiting, I'm happy to assist Berta and Margaretha in the kitchen. I'm not much of a cook, but I'm willing to learn."

For the first time that evening, the tension in Franz's neck and shoulders eased. While he was glad Vater had agreed to let Caroline stay, her mention of sailing to Scotland left him hollow inside. With each passing day, Franz was more convinced that Caroline belonged here, with him and his family. Not only until her compensation came but forever.

But how would he persuade her to stay?

Chapter 8

Franz climbed the stairs to his attic workshop. He couldn't have predicted the evening's events if he'd been offered a hundred dollars. Caroline was fluent in German and several other languages, and her discovery of their incorrectly worded advertisement had saved the family a lot of money, perhaps even their business.

Even more astonishing—Caroline was, by rights, betrothed, since her father would force her to marry against her will if she returned home. His heart ached when he thought of her wedded to a man who was so undeserving of her. Despite all of her troubles, Franz could not help but marvel that God himself had orchestrated such an elaborate series of events to bring her here—to him. *Vorsehung.*

He leaned against the open window sash and stared at the night sky. "Vater in heaven, if Caroline is the *one* I have been waiting for, let her see me as an honorable man. Remove any fear of me that lingers in her spirit. If I am wrong, and Caroline is not the woman You have for me, then I beg You to take this longing to protect her—to cherish her—away. It is too much for my soul to bear."

The door creaked, and light footsteps padded the measured gait of someone taking the steps one at a time. *Caroline?* He turned to see her standing at the top of the staircase, a steaming mug of Kaffee in each hand.

"*Darf ich?*"

Caroline's polite request to join him spoke to both her elegance and education, leaving Franz questioning why his stubborn heart was drawn to a woman from such a vastly different background. "Ja. *Komm doch rein!*" he said, welcoming her to his attic workshop. He reached for the cup she offered. "Danke."

"I wanted to see where you disappear to in the evenings, and Berta suggested I look up here."

With her bottom lip tugged between her teeth, she glanced around the dimly lit room. Did being alone with him in the shadowy garret frighten her? He turned the knob on each of the three lanterns hanging above his workspace, brightening their illumination. If he was honest, it hadn't been just to ease her fears. Now he could see her lovely face—at least the portion not hidden beneath her veil.

"*Bitte setzen.*" He pointed to a stool beside his workbench.

"Why do you work here instead of in the shop with the others?" she asked, making herself comfortable on the seat.

He shrugged. "I prefer the solitude. It allows time to think and pray."

She arched a brow. "And perhaps affords some distance from Lukas?"

He chuckled. "Ja, that too. But he's not *all* bad."

"I'm sure he has many fine qualities, but sometimes he can be a little—"

"Harsh?"

"Direct."

"You are kinder than you should be toward him." He positioned a large piece of Lindenwood over a pair of sawbucks, aligned the paper template, and used a charcoal pencil to trace the pattern.

"Lukas was a very different man before his wife, Johanna,

died on the voyage to America. She was heavy with child, and as is the way of things sometimes, she lost the baby and her own life." He shook his head. "There was nothing to be done, but the joy left mein *Bruder* that night and has not returned."

"How awful," she said. Her eyebrows drew closer together, forming tiny creases in her skin. "I can't imagine how painful that must be. His anger, no. . .bitterness, makes much more sense."

Franz straightened and tucked the charcoal pencil behind his ear. "How does it make sense that Lukas treats you poorly because he blames himself for their death?"

"When people are hurting, they lash out. My guess is it temporarily removes the pain. I don't think Lukas is really angry with me, or you for that matter. He is angry with himself and probably Gott too. Until he allows Gott to heal the hurt places inside his soul, he won't know peace or joy."

Jaw slack, he stared at Caroline. Not only did she hold no grudge against Lukas, she sympathized with him. Franz admired her ability to see the good in others, especially when it involved someone who didn't look too hard to find the good in her. His chest swelled. She was a woman of virtue.

"Lukas has been difficult to live with the last few years, but the best way to minister to him is to love him in spite of his sharp edges of late."

She nodded. "It's more than enough. It's everything."

Her words settled into his soul, giving him hope that his brother would one day find peace and joy again.

He removed the saw from the hook on the wall. With a smooth, practiced rhythm, he cut along the charcoal markings. He enjoyed this—having Caroline sit with him in the quiet of the attic, an occasional conversation when something interesting came to mind.

Their gazes met. "You never married?" she asked, before sipping her Kaffee.

"Nein." Heat warmed his neck. "But I should like to someday."

There were so many things he wanted to know about Caroline. Would she trust him with her past or keep him at arm's length? "The man your Vater chose for you. . . do you not love him?"

"No. But at one time I believed I'd learn to love him."

Learn to love him? What an odd expression. He would never marry a woman solely to gain from the union. Then again, he was a man and could provide for himself. "You would marry a man you do not love?"

She glanced away. Had he embarrassed her?

"I apologize, Fräulein. It is not for me to say who you should marry. I am glad you discovered his true nature before you exchanged vows."

"So am I." She moistened her lips. "Actually, Franz, Charles is the reason I was afraid of you at first."

They'd already been over this. His size had intimidated her, as it did many people until they knew him better. Must they revisit the topic?

"Several nights before I left Philadelphia, my fiancé. . ." Chin tucked low to her chest, she shoved a heavy breath from her lungs. His stomach twisted. Whatever she was about to say would cost her something. He laid his tool down and stooped beside her.

"Charles accosted me," she said, reverting to English.

Franz searched his memory. He didn't know this word and so desperately wanted to understand what she was going to tell him. "Auf Deutsch, bitte."

"Er legte seine Hände auf mich."

Her words pierced Franz's heart. The man who should treasure her had laid his hands on her? He gritted his teeth and bit back a dozen questions burning in his soul, but he would not ask them. Only listen to whatever she wanted to share.

Her gaze shifted to her hands, fingers interlaced, resting in her lap. "During the struggle, we landed on the floor near the fireplace." Her lips quivered when she sucked in a breath. "Desperate to stop his advances, I grabbed a burning log and shoved it in his face." She lifted her bandaged hands. "While it did have the desired effect of halting his assault, we were both injured."

Bile rose in the back of his throat. What kind of man treated a woman in such a way? Especially one he was supposed to cherish for the rest of his life.

"The next day, I told mein Vater and insisted he confront Charles and break the engagement, but he refused, saying Charles's actions were of little consequence since we were to be wed soon. I would besmirch our family's reputation if I didn't honor my betrothal commitment. I protested, saying I wouldn't marry a man of such low character." She paused, fisting the black fabric in her lap. "But Vater blamed me for the attack. He said, 'Proper young ladies would never entice a man to behave in such a manner by accompanying them unchaperoned.'"

Franz brought his fist to his mouth. He didn't know who he wanted to pummel more, her beast of a fiancé or her pernicious Vater.

She glanced at him, shoulders shaking. "Mein Vater said I should consider myself lucky that he would still marry me after I'd attacked him with a piece of burning wood."

Caroline stood and limped several feet away. "*I* attacked *him?*" She lifted her bandaged hand then tugged at the high collar of her dress, revealing the length and breadth of her bandage. "*I* attacked *him?*" she repeated.

A compelling need to console her rose from deep within. He moved beside her. "May I?" he asked, arms extended.

She nodded, and he tenderly wrapped his arms around her and pulled her close. "Shh," he whispered. "*Es ist nicht deine Schuld.*"

She lifted her head from his chest, and stray tears coursed over her cheeks. "Do you really believe it wasn't my fault?"

He cradled her lace-swathed cheeks in his palms. "Ja, Caroline. A man of honor behaves the same in the dark as he does in the light."

———

Afraid to break the spell, Caroline dared not breathe. She should be afraid to be alone with him in the secluded attic, but she wasn't. Something inside her drew her to him like a lamb to its shepherd.

Franz's heart beat wildly beneath her palm. His gaze shifted to her mouth, and his lips parted. Would he kiss her? Heaven help her, she wanted him to. Not the lustful variety of her dreadful encounter with Charles, but tender and sweet, as if kissing her was his sole ambition in life.

"Caroline." His husky voice sent gooseflesh rippling over her skin. "I. . ." His hands slid to her shoulders. He lowered his forehead to hers for a brief moment, then he kissed her temple and stepped away. "*Vergib mir,*" he said, backing into his workbench.

"There is nothing to apologize for, Franz," she said, inching toward him.

"Nein. I wish for you to see my heart—to see me as *ein Ehrenman.* A gentleman of honor would not have taken such liberties."

"You have taken no liberties—at least none that I didn't willingly allow. The events of the last few weeks have tormented me, but your words are a great comfort. That is another kindness I don't know how to repay."

"There is nothing to repay." He returned the saw to its hook on the wall then grabbed a sheet of abrasive paper and vigorously scratched the rough edge of the freshly cut Lindenwood.

"I don't agree. You rescued me from the mob and defended me to your family, and I repaid you by letting my fear get the best of me. Surely there must be something I can do to show my appreciation."

"You owe me nothing. But if you like, in the evenings you can bring me Kaffee and sit with me while I work. If you are comfortable alone with me in the attic, that is."

"I won't disturb you?"

"Not at all."

"All right," she said, sensing the awkward tension between them easing.

He blew the wood dust from the board he'd been sanding. "It is a gut plan."

"It's been such a long day. I should turn in." She pointed to his mug. "If you're finished, I'll take your cup to the kitchen."

He handed her the mug. When their fingers brushed, she tensed and glanced away.

"*Gute Nacht*, Caroline."

"Good night, Franz." She limped toward the stairs. Had she heard a hint of sorrow in his voice? Did he regret his affections a few minutes prior, or like her, did he lament the passing of such an intimate moment without his lips finding hers?

"Caroline." Her heart skipped a beat at the sound of her name, and she turned to face him again.

He lifted one of the lanterns from the hook above his work-table and moved beside her. "Actually, if you are willing, there is something you could help me with."

"Anything."

"Herr Winkler has designated me as a representative for the Trainmen's Union because my Englisch is better than many others. But it is not as good as I want it to be. If I give you some specific words and phrases, would you write them in Englisch for me?"

"You would go against your Vater's wishes?"

"On this matter, ja. I am no longer a child and must do what I think best."

Was representing such men the right thing to do? She'd witnessed firsthand their lack of respect for private property and little concern for the physical safety of innocent bystanders. Yet according to Franz, they were good men, like him, who had momentarily allowed their emotions to seize them.

"This is important to you?"

"Ja. The protests have spread along the rails to Pittsburgh and Chicago and grown more violent. I desire to be a voice of reason between the warring sides—at least here in Baltimore. The men count on me to negotiate a fair end to the strike—better wages, shorter days, and fixed schedules."

His gaze hadn't waivered while she considered his request. Finding a peaceful end to the strike was in everyone's best interest, wasn't it? "I'd be honored to help you."

"Dankeschön."

There was a wholesomeness about Franz Köhler, a lack of pretension that was utterly absent in the men of her acquaintance—until now. And while she'd been raised to admire men who wielded power and strength, who made others bow to their whims, she was becoming increasingly aware that her heart belonged to a humble German immigrant with the soul of a gentleman.

Chapter 9

Franz tapped his pencil against the ledger before tallying the figures in the deposit column a third time. He stared at the paltry sum. Business for the clockworks had been bleak at best in the days immediately following the strike. The riots had not only shut down the railroad but depressed business across the city as many were afraid to travel, especially in the neighborhoods surrounding Camden Depot. Most ventured out only for essentials, which apparently didn't include purchasing or repairing wall clocks.

He'd been in a foul mood for the last hour, ever since Caroline had joined him at the table with pen and paper, determined to finish her letter to her aunt in Scotland. He blew out a breath, and she looked up from her script, eyebrows peaked. "Something wrong?"

How did he tell her nothing would be right again if she boarded a steamer for Europe? If he found the courage, would she be willing to receive his words—be willing to postpone her trip to discover what might grow between them? Had she given their "almost" kiss the night before another thought?

Franz could think of little else.

"Ja," he said, tapping his pencil against the ledger again. "Business no gut."

"I'm sorry." She offered a sympathetic nod. "I'm sure things will turn around as soon as the protests quiet down."

You're such a coward, Franz. Are you going to allow her to post that letter without telling her how you feel—without even asking her to stay? His chest tightened. Why did it feel like his heart was shrinking alongside his fortitude?

Gott, if this is Your will, give me the right words and prepare Caroline's heart to hear what I have to say. He slid his arm over the pine knots. If he could hold her hand, he'd find the courage to relay what was on his heart. "Caroline, I—"

Margaretha burst into the kitchen exuberantly prattling about the ladies' meeting at Zion Lutheran Church. Franz jerked his arm beneath the table like an errant boy caught with his finger in Oma Gertrud's cake batter.

His sister plopped on the bench beside Caroline, hands fluttering about, unaware of the opportunity she'd just squashed for him. Franz closed the ledger and shoved his chair from the table. If he was honest, it was his own fault for dallying, but his foul mood was about to tick up a notch—or four.

"Gut news," Margaretha said, her face beaming. Like Franz, Margaretha wanted to use her English as often as possible. "The church plans a. . ." She paused, as if searching her memory for the right words. "Basket auction on Saturday night at the German Social Club. All the monies help protestors who not work."

"A basket auction?" Caroline asked.

"Ja, ladies make supper and men bid on them. Winner eat supper and dance with the lady."

Franz straightened, his bad mood improving by the second. A dinner and dance? He glanced at Caroline, and their gazes met briefly before she looked away. Would she want him to win her basket?

"Marta Werner and Elise Neumann say they make paper to pass to churches and markets."

When Mutter and Margaretha said they were attending a

meeting at Zion Lutheran Church to find a way to help the
families of the striking men, he assumed they would plan a food
collection drive. Leave it to the women to find a way to bring
the whole community together and do a little matchmaking too.

"Mutter and I clean and decorate social club." She glanced at
Caroline. "If ankle is besser, you help too? And—"

"Slow down, *Liebling*," Mutter encouraged, placing a gentle kiss on Margaretha's head. "Caroline won't understand a
thing you say."

Lost in the prospect of dancing with Caroline, Franz hadn't
noticed Mutter join them. Margaretha continued her rapid pace,
undeterred by Mutter's playful admonishment. He'd not seen his
sister this excited in quite a while. Franz suspected her enthusiasm might have something to do with the young man he'd
introduced to her after church a few months earlier. Maximillian
Schneider had worked with Franz in the railyards, but, like himself, Max had chosen not to participate in the strike after the
protests turned violent.

Perhaps Franz was not the only Köhler looking for love.

⁓

Caroline's cheeks heated. Franz had caught her staring. If she
made a basket for the social, would he bid on it? He'd been about
to tell her something before Margaretha had come home, and
from his demeanor, she'd gathered it was important.

She'd laid awake a good portion of the night thinking about
Franz. When he'd comforted her, it felt like coming home or
what coming home *should* feel like—safe, warm, protected—
like she finally belonged somewhere. Or to someone.

The mere thought sent her pulse skittering through her veins.
This was insane. How could she be so attracted to a man she'd
only just met? Could she trust her instincts when they'd been
entirely flawed concerning Charles? Then again, she'd not had
much say regarding their betrothal.

Because Charles was her father's business partner, she'd known him since she was a girl. She'd been fond of him then, as he tended to lavish her with sweets and gifts, including a pony. Their engagement, however, was hastily announced to Philadelphia society before he'd even asked for her hand. She'd been nothing more than a quid pro quo for his continued investment in Father's business.

Fists pounded against the Köhlers' door, snapping Caroline's thoughts to the present.

"Franz, öffne die Tür!"

Franz opened the door, and a frantic-looking young man about six inches shorter than him entered the kitchen, a crumpled cap clenched in his fist.

"Max, what is the matter?" The alarm in Franz's voice made the tiny hairs on Caroline's arms bristle.

Perspiration beaded on Max's brow as he gasped for breath. "You must come and talk the men down," he pleaded in German. "B&O President Garrett requested Governor Carroll send the National Guard to Cumberland to quell the uprising there. Our men will not allow the soldiers to board the trains. They are armed and have cornered the guardsmen in their own armory."

Caroline's knee bobbed beneath the table as she recalled the turmoil of her first day in Baltimore. At breakfast, Lukas had read a newspaper report about the president of the Pennsylvania Railroad threatening to give the protestors "a rifle diet in their gullet" if they did not end the violence and come back to work.

"Is it only our people?"

"Nein, the unrest has spread to other workers. Factory men, box-makers, and sawyers have walked out. Women and children have lined the streets to watch the soldiers march to Camden Depot." He gulped more air into his lungs. "You must come with me now. The men respect you. I know they will listen to you."

"Ja. I will come." He turned to Caroline. "Before I go, can you help me with the list of words we spoke of last night?"

Her pulse throbbed as memories of the frenzied riot flashed in her mind—burning torches, the pressing throng, the fear of being trampled. She didn't want Franz to go, but it wasn't her place to ask him to stay. However, she could help him be prepared to negotiate a peaceful outcome.

She nodded and grabbed a new sheet of stationery, dipped the nib of her pen into the ink bottle, then drew a line down the center of the paper. As Franz spoke, she wrote the word or expression in German in the first column then translated to English in the second.

"We have no time for this," Max said, yanking on Franz's arm. "We need to hurry. More soldiers are on their way."

He waved off his friend's petition. "She is almost done. It does us no gut if the soldiers do not understand us, nor we them."

"All done," she said, fanning the paper to dry the ink. She had Franz read through the list twice to check his pronunciation. Satisfied he was ready, she folded the slip and handed it to him. "You'll do fine."

"Dankeschön, Fräulein."

"I'm glad I could help."

He stuffed the paper into the front pocket of his pants then hugged his mother and sister goodbye. Without seeking permission, he tugged her into a tender embrace that ended all too soon for Caroline's liking then stepped over the threshold and disappeared outside, taking a piece of her heart with him.

Chapter 10

Dust particles danced in the sunlight streaming through the large attic windows. Caroline hadn't been in the family's loft without Franz. Despite Berta's proximity, the garret seemed cold and lonely without his presence. Just one more reminder that he hadn't returned home last night after leaving with Max to try and convince his fellow strikers to keep their wits about them and not fire on armed National Guardsmen.

"Komm!" Berta said, motioning for Caroline to follow her.

The older woman knelt in front of a steamer trunk and lifted its domed lid. Delicate rose-patterned fabric lined the interior. She removed a stack of garments, each sandwiched between a layer of thin paper, and set them aside.

Linen, wool, and poplin, in a variety of shades, peeked from their thin sheaths. Tired of wearing her black gown, Caroline itched to glide her fingers over the colorful cloth.

"Ah, here it is." Paper crinkled beneath Berta's fingertips, revealing a blue dress, azure, like the sky. "Johanna's favorite." Her eyes glistened as she clutched the gown to her chest.

Caroline's heart pinched at the longing in Berta's voice for the daughter-in-law she'd not see again this side of heaven. Did Caroline's own father miss her like that or merely the financial security her marriage to Charles would have afforded?

Shoving a deep breath from her lungs, Berta offered the dress to Caroline. "For you to wear to *der Tanz*. You will look striking when you dance with Franz."

Caroline lifted her palm in protest. "I couldn't. It's too special."

"Nein." Berta wagged her head. "No joy comes from it sleeping in this old trunk." She reached for Caroline's hand and placed the dress in her open palm then cupped her cheek. "Wear it, Liebling. Give it life again."

"Dankeschön."

Berta smiled, revealing tiny lines around the corners of her mouth. "Wunderbar." Her eyebrows peaked. "Franz favors the blue."

That was Berta's second mention of Franz. Was she playing matchmaker? Did she suspect her son might have feelings for Caroline, or was she simply fishing for a reaction from her?

"Let's see how it fits."

Brown paper tucked inside the remaining folds of blue sateen glided to the floor. Caroline held the dress to her shoulders while Berta smoothed her hand down the length of the gown. "*Zu lang*," she tsked. "We will need to hem the skirt about two inches."

Franz's mother pressed the garment against Caroline's abdomen. "Ja, and at the waist also," she said, holding her index finger a smidge above her thumb. "*Ein bisschen.* Komm! Let us take our work downstairs. The attic is too dusty."

"I'll put these away first." Caroline folded the garment over her arm and pointed to the small pile of dresses Berta had removed from the trunk. "Then I'll be down."

"Danke." The floorboards creaked beneath Berta's shoes as she descended the stairs. "I will get my sewing basket then make the Kaffee."

After returning the garments to the trunk, Caroline held the blue frock against her body. A tingle raced the length of her spine. Would Franz win her basket supper and not only be her dinner companion, but her dance partner for the evening as well? If so, would it be because he wanted to be courteous or because the attraction she sensed was mutual?

One thing she knew for certain, her father wouldn't approve of a man who worked in the rail yards and whose prospects wouldn't improve his own. Franz Köhler may not have the refined manners of Charles Stuart or much of an earthly inheritance, but he had everything she wanted in a man—a gentle spirit and a heart devoted to God. And, in the weeks she'd been staying with his family, he'd not once asked her to reveal what lay beneath her veil. The fact her stomach fluttered with imaginary butterflies in his presence was an added bonus.

Envisioning herself lined up for a waltz, Caroline practiced a gentle curtsy while her fictitious partner bowed. Gazing down at the fabric pressed against her bodice, she twirled several times, accidentally spinning into a rickety table.

A hidden object wobbled then shed its cotton cloak. Caroline gasped. The most intricately carved clock she'd ever seen greeted her. She leaned closer and inspected the delicate chalet with flower boxes displayed below the upper windows. A man stood outside the house wearing traditional Bavarian lederhosen, hands clasped behind his back. A small feather protruded from his hat, and a bird perched upon his shoulder.

Why was this exquisite clock hidden away in the attic? Was it an heirloom? If so, why wouldn't the Köhlers display such splendid artisanship in their home? If not, why didn't they advertise it in their shop? Certainly, such marvelous handiwork would bring a fine price.

Was it flawed?

Caroline gathered the dress in one hand, draped it over her shoulder, and gently lifted the clock for closer examination. The details on the man's face were impeccable as were the tiny rosebuds carved into the window boxes. The clock itself had white roman numerals painted in the appropriate position with two hands that easily glided as she rotated them. A tabby cat curled beneath snow-laden fir trees standing at attention on either side of the chalet. The man, however, appeared off-center, lonely even. Is that why the clock had been banished to the garret? Surely Lukas or his father could reposition him and make the clock worth selling.

The latch clicked on the attic door. "Caroline, Kaffee is ready."

"I'll be right down."

Caroline returned the clock to its home atop the wobbly table. Who would squirrel away such incredible artistry? She'd only seen Franz use large tools when creating the hollow case of the clock. Hadn't he said he worked in the rail yards because his family believed his hands were too thick to use the compact tools necessary for such precise work? The clock didn't resemble any of the designs in the family's shop. While expert craftsmen, his father, brother, and Opa favored more masculine features—rams' horns and bears' heads. None of their work had this level of precision.

"Caroline," Berta called from the bottom of the stairs, "are you coming?"

"Coming." Caroline concealed the ornate clock beneath the sheet. She shook her head. Somehow, it just didn't feel right to hide such beautiful craftsmanship from the world.

The artisan had a keen eye and took extraordinary pride in chiseling the tiniest details, like the bird's feathers. He also possessed a romantic spirit, one favoring hearth and home. Someone who found immense gratification in his work but remained too humble, or possibly too vulnerable, to share his creation.

Warmth spread through Caroline along with a growing surety she knew exactly which Köhler fit that description.

Franz lifted the magnifying glass and examined the small wooden figurine in the soft glow of the kerosene lamp. Something wasn't right. But what? He inspected the arms, head, even the angle of its back.

The attic door squawked on rusty hinges. "Franz, are you ready for your lessons?"

Caroline. His pulse quickened at the sound of her voice. Though he'd only known her a few weeks, he'd come to cherish this time together with her in the evenings. He carved the hollow body of a future clock, and Caroline wrote lists of words that she would soon have him practice while he worked. Although he loved Mutter and Margaretha deeply, neither woman would have the ability to sit with him and enjoy the solitude.

He shoved the carving into his pocket and cleared a space at the end of his worktable. "Ja, come sit with me, bitte." Grabbing the lantern by its metal handle, he moved to the stairwell and illuminated her path.

She thanked him for his kindness, then tugged a stool beside his. Instead of sitting down, however, she pressed her lips firmly together and fidgeted with a loose thread at her cuff.

"You wish to ask me something, Caroline?"

"It's really none of my business."

He chuckled. "Ask your question. It is for me to decide whether or not to answer you."

On the heels of that remark, she moved near the large attic window. "You've mentioned you work in the rail yard because your family believes your large hands prohibit you from carving intricate designs or fine tuning a clock's gears and bellows..."

His brows furrowed. Where was she going with this question? "Ja, is true."

She crossed the garret and stood near the large steamer trunk. "Have you ever showed your family this clock you work on here in the attic?" she asked, uncovering his secret passion.

His chest tightened. How had she discovered his project? And what had convinced her that he had crafted the clock instead of Lukas or Vater? "Nein."

"It's stunning. Why do you stash your talent in the attic when your design would bring a nice price in the shop?"

"Nein. Nein. Nein." She flinched as he strode toward her, and he regretted his harsh tone. He hadn't meant to startle her, but there was no room for negotiation where *this* clock was concerned. "Clock not for sale." He reached for the dustcloth, but Caroline's light touch on his arm interrupted him. Rivers of gooseflesh rippled over his skin.

"Please, don't," she said, her tone wistful. "I'm captivated by it." She locked her blue-eyed gaze with his. "It's like I've found a window into your soul."

His pulse hammered in his ears. How did she see into the very places most people, including his own family, didn't bother to look? He inhaled deeply and counted to five before easing the air from his lungs. *Just because she admires the clock does not mean she fancies you.*

"The attention to detail. . . I've never seen anything like it, not even in your father's shop."

Franz straightened his shoulders. "Ja, you like? You think is gut?"

"It's exquisite." She leaned closer, her attention lingering on the solitary figure. "I'm curious why the man isn't centered in front of the chalet? He's leaning forward as if he's looking for something, but nothing is there."

Ah, Caroline had a fine eye for detail. He scratched his beard. How much should he reveal? Could he trust her with his secret? "If I answer, you promise not tell others about clock?"

Her head bobbed enthusiastically beneath her black lace covering, and Franz bit back a grin. Everything about this woman enchanted him. Charming or not, he hadn't planned to share his creation with anyone—at least not yet. He swallowed the knot in his throat and lifted a silent prayer that she wouldn't think him foolish.

"This is my *Meisterwerk*." He shook his head and searched for the English words. "The masterpiece I make for my bride on our wedding day."

Caroline stilled, arms slack at her sides. "You're. . .engaged?"

His eyes narrowed. "What means 'engaged'?"

"It means you have asked a woman to marry you, and she has accepted."

"Nein," he said, chuckling at his miscommunication.

She clutched the pendant dangling from her neck and slumped onto the steamer trunk. "So, you're not engaged?"

Did her surprise indicate disappointment that he had not yet found his bride? Or relief that he had not indicated an attraction to her? How would he answer her question without risking his heart too soon?

"Nein," he repeated. "I explain in German." Franz pointed to the solitary figure in front of the chalet. "Like me, the man remains alone until Gott reveals his bride. Only then can I carve her likeness and place his companion beside him, ending his solitude. My Meisterwerk represents my heart—all the good things I hope for our marriage and my commitment to stand by her side through life's hardships."

Caroline's eyes glistened. "That is the most beautiful thing I've ever heard. Whoever you choose will be a very blessed woman, Franz." She held his gaze. "I'll pray she is deserving of you."

He could look into those blue eyes for a lifetime. Did he have any chance with Caroline, or should he give up on such a senseless notion? The thought of her leaving Baltimore made his gut twist. How would he live without her sweet presence?

"Caroline, I. . ."

She stepped away, then tugged a handkerchief from her cuff and dabbed her eyes. "I suppose we should begin our lessons."

"Ja, that is gut idea."

He thumbed the figure he'd shoved into his pocket. The woman still needed a good deal of work, and carving her veil would be challenging, but Franz had no doubt Caroline, and her likeness, were worth the effort.

Chapter 11

Caroline crimped the edge of the *Bierocks*, sealing the potatoes, carrots, and gravy inside. She seasoned the crust and slid the tray into the cookstove. There was nothing to be done now but offer a quick prayer and hope her supper for the basket auction turned out well enough.

Exhaling, she wiped her forearm across her brow and plopped onto the kitchen chair. The oven heated the house, and no breeze fluttered the curtains, tempting Caroline to retreat to her room, where she could remove the oppressive veil clinging to the perspiration on her neck.

She glanced at the clock. The respite sounded wonderful, but her comfort would have to wait. She needed to choose a recipe for dessert and have her dish ready to bake when the meat pies finished cooking.

Caroline thumbed through Berta's notebook of handwritten receipts. A yellowed slip of paper drew her attention. Rice pudding. No, that wouldn't work. She needed something that would transport easily in a basket.

Turning a few more pages, she found a recipe for *Springerle*. She skimmed the list of ingredients and directions. Too complicated. Unfortunately for the recipient of her culinary efforts, the curriculum at Miss Lillian's School for Young Ladies had prepared her for a life of cotillions and meaningless conversation.

Assuming the girls would marry into the finest circles, they'd spent little time on domestic skills like cooking.

Her shoulders slumped. Surely there must be one dessert in Berta's receipt book that Caroline could manage with halfway decent results.

Paper crinkled at the opposite end of the large kitchen table. "He likes *Gugelhupf.*"

Caroline glanced at Opa, who peered at her over his newspaper. Like Berta and Wilhelm, Opa preferred to speak to her in German. "Pardon?"

"Franz. Though more of a breakfast cake, he has a fondness for the dessert."

"Mmm. I can't be certain if Franz will bid on my meal, let alone win it. I just need a recipe that won't crumble en route and is easy to prepare."

Opa's silver-tinted eyebrows tented before his gaze returned to the article in the paper. "Gugelhupf."

Caroline flipped through the receipt book a second time.

"You will not find the directions in Berta's cookbook." He folded his newspaper and pointed to his temple. "The steps are in here."

She narrowed her gaze. "You know how to bake?"

Opa's hearty chuckle warmed Caroline's heart, and she couldn't resist laughing along with him. She enjoyed being part of this family, if only for a little while.

"Ja. When Gertrud was alive, she did the baking, but who do you think taught her?"

"I thought the Köhlers were clockmakers?"

"We have been many things—bakers, tailors, and for the last hundred years, we are clockmakers."

"Today, I will teach you to make Gugelhupf." He stood and rolled his sleeves then retrieved an unusual copper pan from the cupboard. "Grease this well with butter and make sure the cone is coated well," he said, pointing to the chimney protruding from the center.

She narrowed her gaze. "Opa, the cake will have a hole in the middle if we use this pan."

He grinned. "Ja. That is the way of it."

Although she didn't understand the point of a cake missing its center, she had no reason to doubt Opa, who appeared much more adept in the kitchen than she.

After she slathered fat on the cone and the ridges embellishing the sides of the deep pan, Opa sprinkled flour inside. "Pat the dish over the sink and coat the butter with the flour so the cake does not stick."

He raised his index finger. "I almost forgot the raisins. They are Franz's favorite." He dug through the pantry. "They must soak in rum for an hour."

Caroline tapped the pan, spreading the flour evenly across the surface. "That's the second time you've hinted that Franz will be eating this dessert, Opa. Only the auctioneer and I will know which basket is mine."

He poured a small amount of alcohol into a bowl and added the dried fruit. "Nein. Ladies always find a way to let their preferred gentleman know which dinner is theirs." He lifted his palms in question. "How else can their favorite know for certain on which meal to bid?"

Her mouth fell open. "That's cheating."

Opa's mischievous smile lighted his eyes. "That is how the game is played, Fräulein. Besides, all the money will go to help the families struggling since the strike, ja?"

He shuffled to the china cupboard and tugged open a drawer, rattling the glass panels. "Here," he said, handing her an embroidered cloth napkin, "Franz will recognize this."

Her fingers traced the intricately stitched blue and green floral border. "It's beautiful."

"My Gertrud stitched it for our first home in Bavaria."

Caroline gnawed her lower lip. If she adorned her basket with something Franz would recognize, would he try to win it? And if he did, would it be because he wanted to spend the evening with her? Or because he was a kind man and wouldn't want her to be embarrassed if her efforts fetched a low price?

Opa shrugged his shoulders. "What harm can be done by it unless you prefer *not* to let Franz know you made his favorite dishes?"

"Surely there must be some young lady whose basket Franz would prefer to bid on."

"Ja, there is."

Caroline's stomach churned. Why had she asked? She could have lived in blissful ignorance had she not pressed the matter.

"Yours," he said. "Even more so since you make the Gugelhupf."

She planted her fists firmly on her hips. "Be honest. What if I wasn't here? Then whose basket would Franz purchase?"

"He wouldn't."

"He wouldn't bid?"

"He would not attend, Fräulein."

"Surely a kind man with steady employment, like Franz, would have his eye on at least one young woman."

"Franz is not a man to pursue the ladies." Opa returned to the table and measured flour into a large mixing bowl. "Franz wants die Vorsehung."

"Destiny?"

"Nein. Divine providence. He waits for Gott to bring him the right woman." His voice softened, and his gaze locked on hers. "The one to make his heart sing." Opa's eyes misted. "It was the same for me and Gertrud. Franz desires nothing less."

Divine providence. Her heart pumped a little faster. Could that be true? Franz hadn't spoken of any particular affection for her. Did Opa see something blossoming between them, or was it merely the wishful thinking of a romantic soul hoping his grandson would soon find a wife?

Either way, Gertrud Köhler had been a fortunate woman to be loved by a man like Opa. And Franz was so very much like him. Slow to anger, gentle-spirited, good-humored. And they shared the same kind eyes—eyes that gave Caroline hope she could be loved for who she was, sight unseen.

She eyed the hand-stitched napkin. Why not? If Opa was right, and Franz would recognize his grandmother's table linen, then for better or worse, she'd have her answer.

———

Franz trudged up the stairs to his family's home above the clock-works. His leaden feet, bearing the weight of the stalled discussions with management, made each step more daunting than its predecessor. Unsure if anyone remained awake at the late hour, he wriggled his key in the lock and quietly slipped inside. A lone kerosene lamp flickered on the table. The welcoming scent of fresh baked goods lingered in the air, tantalizing his taste buds. Gugelhupf?

His gaze bounced from one kitchen surface to the next. Mutter usually left a serving of dessert for him when he worked late. He opened one cupboard after another to no avail. Had they neglected to save him any? That didn't seem right. Knowing the sweet raisin bread was his favorite, Mutter often tucked the last piece away for his lunch the next day.

He rolled his achy muscles. Nothing seemed to be going right. He extended his hand close to the pot on the stove. At least the coffee was hot.

Floorboards creaked behind him. *Please, Gott, don't let it be Lukas. I'm in no mood to spar at this hour.* He glanced over his shoulder. Opa's silhouette filled the darkened entryway. His eyes glanced heavenward. *Thank You, Vater.*

"Any progress?"

"Nein. Stubborn men like Heinrich Müeller refuse to release the National Guardsmen, and management says they will not negotiate until the men are freed." He lifted a mug from the hook beneath the shelf. "Kaffee?"

"Ja." Opa tugged a chair from the head of the table where he usually sat opposite his son.

Franz grabbed the steaming drinks and joined Opa. "So many people are counting on me."

"I understand you worry about letting the men down, but if you persist, I know you will be successful."

Franz swiped a hand over his face.

"You don't believe me?"

He shrugged. "Common ground must be found between the stockholders and the workers, but when I suggest the slightest compromise, the labor leaders stir the men up and insist they not give in an inch." Elbows on the table, he dragged his fingers through his hair. "If the strikers do not release the soldiers, the board plans to hire men to replace them and fire all those who participated in the protest, including me."

"Ahh, that is a Herculean task. I do not envy you. You are in my prayers." Opa squeezed Franz's shoulder. "At least you have the basket auction to look forward to."

Franz smiled. "Ja, it will be nice to enjoy an evening where I am not trying to convince a bunch of hotheads to compromise."

"An evening with Caroline, talking and dancing, should lift your spirits."

Opa's deep brown eyes examined him. A surge of heat raced up his neck, warming his ears. He'd not spoken to anyone of his feelings for Caroline, but Opa had always been able to read his soul, always been able to discern what Franz was thinking and feeling. "That depends on which basket I win."

"Ja, but I might have information that could help you."

"Nein. We are to bid blindly."

Opa swatted the air. "You sound like Caroline."

Franz's head snapped to attention. "What did she say?"

"She thinks, like you, that it is cheating if I give you a hint what her basket looks like."

"She is right."

"I suppose you are right," Opa said, wrinkling his nose. "Gertrud's first Gugelhupf was no gut either."

Franz's brows peaked. "Caroline made Gugelhupf?"

Opa nodded.

"And you believe she wants me to bid on her basket?"

"I may be an old man now, but I was once a young buck like you. I see how you two look at each other."

"There is no *way* that Caroline and I look at each other."

"Ja, there is. It was the same with me and Gertrud. You cannot fight die Vorsehung, Franz. You know this to be true." He took a generous swig of Kaffee and continued. "Besides, she beams like moonlight on a cloudless night whenever you come near."

"Listen to yourself," Franz chided. "Vater says you are foolish when you speak of such things."

"I am certain," Opa said, pointing at his chest. "It is die Vorsehung."

Deep in his soul, Franz sensed Opa was right. His heart had leapt at the first sight of Caroline—as if it had been asleep and finally awoke to the one it had been created to love.

Vater had encouraged Franz to take a wife before the family left Bavaria, but he didn't want just any woman. He wanted *the* woman—the one God Himself would choose. The only one who would make his heart sing, like Opa's did for Oma Gertrud. Franz shook his head. He sounded as ridiculous as his grandfather.

"She is a gut woman, Franz. The kind that stays at a man's side through all of life's trials."

"We are too different. Caroline went to boarding schools, and I am an immigrant just learning English. The men in her social circles wear fine suits and come from wealthy families. She was raised with servants. . ." He glanced at his thick, calloused hands. "While I labor in the rail yards." Shoulders sagging, he looked at his grandfather. "She deserves much better than I can give her."

"If Caroline wanted those things, she would not be here with us hiding from her Vater." He pushed away from the table and placed his mug near the dishpan. "Gute Nacht, Franz."

He shuffled toward the hallway then turned and faced his grandson again. "She chose one of Oma Gertrud's embroidered napkins to line her basket. Now that you know, what will you do?"

Franz slouched in his chair. That was an excellent question. Thankfully, Opa had not waited for the answer.

Did Caroline truly feel the same way about him? And if she did, why did she insist on wearing her veil? Didn't she trust him? Did she think her appearance would alter his growing affection for her? Or was her hesitancy the result of a deeper scar, one invisible to the eye?

Unfortunately, he had none of the answers he sought, but if Caroline truly wished him to bid on her supper, he would oblige her—Gugelhupf or not.

Chapter 12

Caroline froze in the entryway of the large room. Men in fine suits and ladies donning the latest baubles and frippery filled the German Social Club. Caroline pressed a gloved hand against her veiled cheek and double-checked that her scarf pin was fastened securely. Even though the dress Berta had altered for her was a fine weight for summer, a few beads of perspiration on her neck sent a shiver coursing down her spine.

Why had she agreed to come? It seemed every pair of eyes in the large hall stared her direction. Did she imagine it, or were people whispering about her, wondering what hideousness lay behind the lace?

"Breathe," Margaretha whispered. "All is gut." She tugged Caroline's hand. "Turn in baskets?"

Caroline nodded, inhaled deeply, and followed after Margaretha, hoping her weak legs would sustain her.

At the auctioneer's table, they were directed to add their names and a description of their meal to the growing list of ladies in attendance. "Take zis," a rotund woman with a dour expression said, handing them each a small piece of paper. She attached a similar slip to their hampers then gave the baskets to a young girl, who disappeared behind a burgundy curtain.

"When zis number called, men vill bid. You meet your vinner here. He pays, zen gets dinner wis you. Dance two times wis him, including first. Zen you may dance wis others."

"Danke." Eyes beaming, Margaretha looped her arm inside Caroline's. "Now find Franz and Max, ja?"

During the time she'd spent with the Köhlers, Caroline had come to think of the younger woman as the sister she'd never had. Margaretha had confided her attraction to Max, and Caroline knew her friend was as excited to dance with him as she herself was to spend time with Franz.

Arm in arm, they strolled into the main gathering. Where would they find Franz and Max in the packed room? Her heart raced. Flashes of the protest invaded her mind. The hair on her arms prickled as Margaretha tugged Caroline deeper into the room.

Caroline locked her knees and pointed to a less crowded area near the stage. "I. . .I prefer to wait over there."

Margaretha's gaze tracked the direction Caroline had indicated. "Ja, we meet you there."

Chest tightening, Caroline pivoted on her heels and wove through the crowd. The lace veil clung to her moist lips when she inhaled, nearly suffocating her. She shoved the tulle below her chin. If only she could yank the comb from her temple and be free of the stifling head wrap, but that would mean exposing her cheek. Something she wasn't prepared to do.

Arriving at their rendezvous spot, Caroline leaned against the wall and fought the nausea roiling in her stomach.

A man cupped her elbow, and Caroline snapped her gaze to the stranger's face. "Are you ill, Fräulein?"

She pressed her palm to her chest and stared into the face of Franz's coworker, the one who'd spoken with Franz when he'd taken her to the train depot. "I don't think so. It's just warm in here."

He pointed to his chest. "Heinrich Müeller. I know Franz—"

"From the rail yard."

"Ja." He glanced around. "Many people come." He narrowed his eyes. "Your veil make it vorse. You should part wis it?"

"I'll be fine." Her shaky voice betrayed her doubt.

"*Das Wasser* help?"

She reached for the cup of water Heinrich offered. Her basket number slipped from her hand and floated to the floor beside his shoe, numeral side up.

"I get zat for you." He stooped, retrieved the paper, then tucked it into her gloved hand. "Vant me tell Franz your number?"

Heinrich smirked then leaned closer. If not for her veil, Caroline was certain she'd feel his breath on her cheek. "Or leave it be *our* secret?" he asked, brows tented in question.

She blinked rapidly. "I. . .I—" Where were her words? Her thick tongue failed to produce a single syllable.

"Gut." He lifted her gloved hand to his lips and pressed a gentle kiss against her knuckles. "As you vish, Fräulein."

"Caroline? Heinrich?"

Heinrich flinched at the sound of Franz's deep voice, but for Caroline, his presence eased the tension in her muscles, and the ache in her chest abated.

"I bring these," he said, glancing to the lemonade and cookies in his hands before returning his focus on the pair. "But you have Wasser."

Franz's expression turned grim, with steely eyes and a frown replacing his usually pleasant disposition. "You know him, Caroline?"

"Nein," Heinrich said. "She vas alone and ve talk. Now ve gut friends."

Why had he said that? She didn't know anything about Heinrich. "We don't—I mean, we aren't—" Her tongue seemed to twist on every syllable she uttered.

Franz handed the refreshments to Margaretha then thrust his burly arm between her and Heinrich, forcing the man to step backward. "I think you go now."

At first, Franz's brawny physique had frightened her, but not anymore. She'd come to know his gentle, protective nature. The hands that had once frightened her now made her feel safe. Actually, it was more than safe—he made her feel special.

"Vhy you so serious all the time, Franz?" Heinrich asked. "You like old man."

"C'mon," Max said, yanking Heinrich away from his friend. "Go find other voman to pester."

Heinrich shrugged free from Max's grasp and confronted Franz again. "Because you are friend, I give advice."

"Ja, what is that?"

Heinrich glanced at Caroline, his gaze traveling the length of her form before returning his attention to Franz. "Be careful, Franz, or I snatch your veiled flower away."

Franz balled his fists. "Nein. Caroline is with me, and that all you need know."

Heinrich bowed in Caroline's direction. "Fräulein."

Caroline offered a tight nod of her head, but her thoughts were mulling over Franz's words. She was *with* him? What on earth had Franz meant by that? Was he merely being protective, or was he implying that he alone was escorting her this evening? The implications sent a dozen butterflies swooping and fluttering in her stomach.

Even *if* Franz was attracted to her, wouldn't he insist on seeing her entire face before courting her? So far, the large embroidered rose design on her veil had obstructed his view of her cheek. Would any man take a woman for his bride without first laying eyes on her?

But after the extensive list of men who'd feigned an emotional connection with her just to escort one of the season's most eligible debutantes, Caroline needed to stand her ground. Never again would she allow a man to prance her about in front of his peers like a fine Arabian, disregard her virtue, or pursue her only to secure their own fortune.

In her heart, Caroline didn't think Franz Köhler was such a man, but she couldn't risk it. No matter how deep her affections, if he wanted to win her hand, he'd need to take a leap of faith—to take her sight unseen or not at all.

———

"Nummer Dreizehn." The auctioneer pounded the gavel. "Number Thirteen," he proclaimed, easily switching between German and English. "Sold for seventy-five cents to Max Schneider."

Franz chuckled as Margaretha beamed and hurried off to meet Max by the auctioneer's table. Not only did Franz suspect a romance budding between the pair, but that Opa had encouraged Margaretha to give Max a hint about which hamper belonged to her. By the smiles they exchanged, both Margaretha and Max appeared pleased with the outcome.

He glanced at Caroline waiting with the other ladies yet to have their numbers called. When their gazes met, the corner of her mouth tipped into a slow smile that made his body heat rise.

He'd not known her long, but his heart had sprung to life the moment he'd laid eyes on her, giving him hope he wouldn't spend his life alone. If things went well for them tonight, he planned to ask for her father's address in Philadelphia so he could declare his intentions and officially ask permission to court her.

But tonight was for—what did his American friends call it—wooing? He would risk his heart, and his pride, to make certain Caroline understood how special she was to him.

"Vierzehn," the auctioneer shouted. "Fourteen," he repeated in English, holding up a basket draped in one of Oma Gertrud's embroidered napkins, just like Opa had said. The man pulled back the cloth and ventured a look inside. "Bierocks and Gugelhupf."

The minimum starting price for every basket was fifteen cents, but Franz wouldn't insult Caroline's effort with such a paltry sum. Instead, he would offer fifty cents as soon as the caller opened the bid, demonstrating his commitment to winning her basket.

The mallet banged against the upside-down crate serving as the caller's lectern. Franz raised his hand and shouted "Fifty—"

"One dollar."

A hushed murmur rumbled through the room as men craned their necks to see who had started the bid with such a generous sum. Franz, however, didn't need to look to confirm what he already knew. Heinrich, his coworker turned rival, had made the lucrative offer. Had Lukas put him up to this to make Franz spend all of his money?

"One dollar," the caller repeated. "Do I hear one dollar plus five?"

"One dollar plus five," Franz responded.

"The bid is one dollar and five." The auctioneer scanned the room. "Will anyone give five cents more? Looking for one dollar and ten cents."

"One dollar, twenty-five."

Blast. How serious was Heinrich's intention, and how had he known on which basket to spend his money? Had Caroline told him? Was more going on between them than he was aware? "One dollar, thirty cents."

The crowd sniggered at his meager increase.

"One dollar fifty," Heinrich countered, not waiting for the auctioneer.

Franz had made a fool of himself upping the bid by only a nickel. At this rate, he wouldn't be able to buy a rose for Caroline, let alone any additional refreshments. "One dollar, seventy-five cents."

"Two dollars," Heinrich countered, waving multiple bills above his head. His stony gaze locked on Franz. "Final offer."

A collective gasp filled the social hall.

Ahh, so there was a limit to what Heinrich would spend. Franz, on the other hand, would spend every penny he had to win Caroline's basket.

He dug into his pocket and retrieved all of his coins and quickly tallied their value. How could this be? He trawled his fingers through his hair then added the sum a second time. Why had he been so foolish with his money? If he hadn't purchased the refreshments earlier to impress Caroline, he could have matched Heinrich's bid and then it would have been lady's choice.

"The bid is two dollars," the auctioneer shouted. "Do I hear more?"

The room fell silent. Franz's cheeks burned under the crowd's scrutiny. There was nothing to be done. He couldn't make money appear from nowhere. Chin tucked low, he glanced at Caroline and gave her a tight shake of his head.

Her mouth fell slack, and she clutched the heirloom pendant dangling from her neck as the auctioneer's gavel pounded Franz's defeat for all to hear.

"Sold to Heinrich Müeller."

Chapter 13

*S*old to Heinrich Müeller? How could this be? Why did this man she barely knew make such a big fuss to earn her basket? She suspected his dramatic purchase had less to do with enjoying her company than it did outshining Franz.

The room swayed, and Caroline massaged her temple. *Breathe, Caroline. In. Out.* The last thing she needed was to faint in front of all in attendance. *It's just dinner and a couple of dances. Then you can find Franz.* She clamped her eyes closed and mentally repeated the instructions several more times. *In. Out.*

"Fräulein," the auctioneer called. "Meet your vinner by the table in the entryvay."

She scanned the crowd for Franz as she exited the stage. Since he'd towered above the others in attendance, he should have been easy to spot. Had he left when she shut her eyes?

"Caroline," Franz's soft voice called to her. "Are you ill? You not look so gut."

"I'm fine. I was—"

"Hallo, Caroline." Heinrich glared at Franz. "I von the bid, fair *und* square. Caroline share supper wis me vithout trouble from you."

Franz narrowed his gaze. "Ja, I know rules. Caroline not look well, so I check on her."

Heinrich offered his arm. "Oh, zen allow me, Fräulein."

201

Caroline swallowed hard then looped her hand through the gap. She winced when he tugged their intertwined forearms close against his side. "Please be careful, my wrist is sore," she said, glancing at Franz over her shoulder as Heinrich guided her toward the auctioneer's table.

"I vill be careful, Caroline," Heinrich said.

"I prefer Miss Wilkins."

His lips curled upward in what Caroline determined to be a forced smile. "As you vish, Fräulein Vilkins. However, I should like you to call me Heinrich."

She had no intention of addressing this man as anything but Mr. Müeller.

The auctioneer banged the gavel in the large open room to their right, marking the sale of another basket. Since Franz hadn't won her hamper, would he bid on another? That was a dismal thought. How had the whole evening ended so topsy-turvy?

Heinrich handed the young girl the paper with Caroline's basket number. She slipped through the large burgundy curtains and returned with the correct hamper sporting Oma Gertrud's hand-embroidered dish towel.

The buxom woman at the auctioneer's table levied a pointed glare at Heinrich. "You eat together, and she dances two dances wis you. One is the first. Zen she is free to dance wis who she vants."

"Ja, I understand."

Heinrich grasped their dinner basket with one hand and her elbow with the other. He snaked his way through the crowd to the back of the large room where couples were enjoying their suppers. Each table sported a red and white checkered cloth, a candle, and a blue canning jar filled with black-eyed Susans.

"*Perfekt*," Heinrich said, setting their basket on a table in a secluded corner of the room.

Caroline scanned the isolated area. Most of the partygoers

were sitting closer to the dance floor. "I'd prefer to sit more toward the front so I can see the couples dancing, wouldn't you?"

"Nein," he said, tugging a chair from the table and motioning for her to sit. "Is quiet here."

Once seated, Heinrich scooted her closer to the table. He positioned himself across from her, then rolled his sleeves to his elbows. "Varm in here, ja?" he asked, unfastening the top button of his shirt.

Ignoring his question lest he ask her to remove her veil again, she opened the wicker hamper and removed the plates, silverware, and meat pies she'd wrapped against a warming stone inside a dish towel. "I made Bieroks. I hope they are to your liking." She handed him a dish. "I'm not a very experienced cook, but I did my best."

"Danke, Fräulein. Zese are a favorit. Meine Mutter made zese ven I vas boy." He lifted the meat pie to his mouth.

"Ahem." She cleared her throat. "Shouldn't we thank the Lord for our meal first?"

His cheeks flushed. "Ja." Food in hand, Heinrich said a quick blessing, but before she could say "Amen," he bit into the warm fare. He swiped at the gravy dribbling on his chin with his finger then wiped it on his pants.

Caroline handed him one of Oma Gertrud's hand-sewn napkins that matched the dish towel lining the basket.

"Danke," he said, dabbing at the portion that remained in his bushy moustache.

She cut into her meat pie with the side of her fork. The aroma of warm beef and onion beckoned her courage to sample her first homemade dish. How bad could it be? Heinrich was already devouring his second one.

Her companion belched then wiped his mouth with the napkin. "Good appetite, ja?"

Suddenly soured on the idea of finishing her portion, she

rested her fork against her plate. Heinrich's appetite may be healthy, but Caroline's had most definitely disappeared.

"Very gut, Fräulein Vilkins. Seasonings is not like meine Mutter's, but is gut."

"It's probably the caraway seed. The recipe called for fennel, but Frau Köhler did not have any. Opa Friedreich suggested the substitution."

Using a toothpick, Heinrich extracted shreds of meat from between his teeth then wiped the bits on Oma's lovely napkins. He rocked his chair back on its hind legs. "Vhy you hide behind zat veil? From vhat little I see, you are pretty voman."

She might've been flattered by his words if his table manners didn't rival a pig at a feeding trough. A shudder coursed through her. *Just two dances and you're done.* "I'll answer your question, Mr. Müeller, if you'll answer one for me?"

"Vhy not. Have no secrets," he said, scratching his neck. "You go first."

"Why did you outbid Franz in such a brash manner?"

He sniggered. "Franz says he vant besser vages but vill not stand und fight wis us. Talk, talk, talk. Time for talking over." He tapped his chest with his thumb. "I besser man for you, Fräulein. I strong, not veak like Franz."

She gritted her teeth and swallowed her desire to let Heinrich Müeller know exactly who she thought was the *besser* man of the two.

He vigorously scraped his nails beneath his chin. "Now you. Tell me vhy you vear zis scarf like meine Oma."

"I was injured in a fire." She lifted her hand and pulled back the edge of her glove, revealing her bandage. "I've worn the veil ever since."

"It must be bad, ja, if you vear that shroud all the time?"

"Quite garish."

His eyebrows squished together, and if Caroline had any

money, she'd bet it all that he didn't understand the word or the sarcasm in her tone. The tiny creases beside Heinrich's eyes paired with his salt-and-pepper hair led Caroline to believe him to be in his midthirties. She didn't know if he'd ever been married and didn't care enough to find out, but his manners tonight certainly spoke to why he wasn't attached at the moment.

Musicians donning lederhosen and felt Alpine hats took center stage, carrying brass horns of varying sizes including a trumpet, trombone, and flügelhorn. The men formed an arc behind a guitarist seated on a stool. Off to their left stood a gentleman with an accordion strapped to his chest, and when his fingers started bringing the keys to life, the assembly shot to their feet, clapping along with the traditional German *Volksmusik*.

Heinrich eased the front chair legs onto the floor then pointed to Caroline's dish. "You eat zat?" he asked, raising his pitch to be heard over the band.

"You may have it." She slid the plate toward him, watching as he gulped the last of the meat turnovers. Though impolite, she couldn't help but stare at his mouth. Was it her imagination, or did his lips appear swollen?

He scratched his chest then reached over his shoulder in what appeared to be a futile effort to do the same on his back. "Should ve dance?"

Caroline accepted his hand. Splotchy red welts dotted his forearm. "Mr. Müeller, your skin."

———

Franz had spent the last hour trying not to mope and ruin Margaretha's evening with Max. The couple had welcomed him to their table even though he didn't have a companion for supper. His sister had shared her portion with him, however, watching Heinrich dining with Caroline across the room had squelched his appetite.

As the musicians started playing, Franz's sour mood

worsened. Caroline may be obligated to only two dances with Heinrich, but Franz didn't think he could stomach watching their hands touch and their bodies sway in time with the music.

"Stop punishing yourself," Margaretha said. "What is in the past should stay there. If you stay in low spirits, Caroline may avoid dancing with you when she is able."

His sister departed with Max to join the other couples dancing the traditional *Steiregger* and headed for the lobby. Margaretha was right. Perhaps a walk outside and a chat with Gott would improve his disposition. Help him focus on his blessings rather than the disappointment the evening had been so far.

A man exiting the building ahead of him caught his eye. Was that Heinrich? But that couldn't be. Did he have no desire to actually spend time with Caroline? His fingers curled into a fist. Had Heinrich only bid on her basket to embarrass him?

"Heinrich?"

The man pivoted to face him. "Ah, Franz, gut. Go to Caroline. She's in the back—"

"Are you walking out on her?"

"Ja. Look at me." He shoved his welt-ridden arms forward for Franz to inspect. "Something in the meal she prepared did this to me," he said, scratching his chest. "You can have her."

Hardly believing his good fortune, Franz whirled around and hurried back to the main room. With most of the assembly on the dance floor, he was able to maneuver quickly along the rear wall. The sight of her empty table made his already rapid pulse double-time through his veins. He surveyed the dance floor but couldn't see her. Where could she be? *Lord, help me find her.*

Something brushed his shoulder. "Can I help you find someone?"

The tension drained from the stiff muscles in his neck and shoulders at the sweet sound of Caroline's voice. He spun around. *Thank You, Gott.* On a whim, he wrapped her in his arms and lifted her off the ground. She gasped, and a tinge of pink splashed over her nose and the portion of her face not concealed by her veil. "Nein. I have found what I have been looking for," he said, planting her feet on the hardwood floor.

He intertwined his fingers with hers. "Come, let's dance. We have much to celebrate."

"Franz, wait. I. . .I cannot dance with you."

His gaze darted to her boots. "Did you reinjure your ankle?"

"No." Her broad smile from moments ago now turned upside down. Did she not want to dance with *him*?

Caroline shifted her weight from one foot to the other. "I. . .I only know how to waltz," she said, peering around him at the couples promenading on the dance floor.

Uh. He was a complete *Dummkopf*. Of course she wouldn't know the complicated steps to their traditional German folk dances. Why hadn't he thought to teach her a few before tonight?

He scraped his hand along his beard. Now what? While he could dance a clunky waltz and would happily sacrifice his pride to please Caroline, the musicians did not have the correct instruments for him to request Strauss or Schubert. But he might just know an alternative that could work.

He offered his arm. "Come with me?"

"Franz, I—"

He pressed a finger to her mouth, halting her protest. "Trust me, Caroline."

She responded by sliding her arm through the crook of his elbow, making his heart pound a bit harder. He escorted her to Margaretha's table. "Wait here, bitte."

Franz spoke to one of the musicians. When he returned a few minutes later, Caroline's feet tapped along with the accordion's lively beat. "You like *die Musik*?"

"It's hard *not* to like it. Does it have a name?"

"Ja, the polka. Is very popular dance in my country and all Europe."

She opened her mouth as if to ask a question then pursed her lips in a flat line. Franz suspected Caroline's heart wanted to join him, but her head reminded her she didn't know the steps. Perhaps a little good-natured prodding was in order.

"If you can dance *der Walzer*, Fräulein, you can polka."

Her eyes narrowed as she contemplated his statement.

"If you promise not to laugh, I will show you how."

She crossed her finger over her heart. "I promise."

"First der Walzer." He bowed then held his hands in position around an invisible woman. As he moved, he counted aloud. "One, two, three. One, two, three, ja?"

She bit back a grin and nodded.

He mustered what he hoped was a stern gaze and held up his finger. "You promise not laugh, Fräulein."

She straightened her posture. "Go ahead with your lessons, Herr Köhler," she said, a hint of humor in her tone.

"The polka has half-step, that is more hop and is bit faster than der Walzer." He grasped his imaginary partner for a second time. "Like this—one und two, three und four." He counted again, bouncing on the "und" and this time adding in a turn. "One und two, three und four."

Caroline hid her mouth behind her gloved hand, but her amusement sparkled in her eyes. He waggled his hands in front of her. "Try with me."

Her fingers glided over his palms, sending Franz's pulse thrumming in his ears. Did his touch cause the same reaction in Caroline?

"Now, step back with right foot and follow me. One und two, three und four. One und two, three und four."

Before long, Caroline's feet moved in quick step with the music. With his hand on her shoulder blade, Franz steered her toward the rear of the dance floor where the crowd had thinned. A few curls escaped her veil and bobbed along in time with the mellow tones of the flügelhorn.

Caroline had come from a world of confinement where decisions about her life were made without her input or consent, and she'd not been encouraged to depart from those expectations. While it was only one polka, she'd overcome her fear by placing her trust in him.

Warmth spread through his chest as he held her in his arms. Without reservation, Franz knew that if he lived a hundred years or danced a hundred dances, this one would remain his favorite.

Chapter 14

F ranz rocked back on his heels as Margaretha's door closed with Caroline sheltered on the other side. Although the evening hadn't begun the way he'd envisioned, not one issue did he have with the way it had ended. Not only had they danced several polkas together, but he'd enjoyed the Gugelhupf Heinrich had abandoned in his haste to get home and find relief for his hives.

The clock on the wall sprang to life, and the little green bird popped from his hiding spot and cuckooed eleven times. Franz should be exhausted, but the evening's events had left him exhilarated instead.

He whistled while he stoked the fire in the cast-iron stove. A cup of Kaffee would be good company while he mulled over how to approach Caroline about a courtship. Unsure whether or not her father deserved such respect, if she wished it, Franz would make the trip to Philadelphia, introduce himself, and properly declare his intentions to marry Caroline.

Lukas leaned against the entryway dividing the kitchen from the sitting room. "I take it your evening with Caroline was a success, since you are fluttering about like a lovesick bird in spring."

"Ja, it was a fine night. What has you up so late?"

"I am waiting for Margaretha. I assume she did not come home with you?"

"Nein, Max asked to escort her. They cannot be far behind." Franz reached for a mug hanging from the hooks above the counter. "Kaffee?"

"Why not." Lukas tugged a bench from beneath the table. "Perhaps I can persuade you to tell me more about why you are grinning like a schoolboy."

Franz poured the steaming beverage into two mugs, handed one to Lukas, and then seated himself opposite his brother. Would sharing his feelings for Caroline drudge up memories of Johanna that would be painful for Lukas?

"Go ahead," his brother prodded. "I don't think you will sleep if you do not tell someone."

The latch clicked open, and Margaretha and Max walked inside, saving Franz from a conversation he'd rather avoid.

Lukas glanced at the clock—ten minutes after eleven. "She is late," he barked. He stood and folded his arms over his chest. "Is this how you show respect for our sister?"

"Nein, nein," Max said, palms raised in surrender. "We stayed to help clean the social hall then came straight here."

Franz coughed into his hand to thwart his smile. Listening to Lukas play the protective older brother was gut. Something had changed in him the last few weeks. His rough edges seemed a little softer to Franz, though Max Schneider would probably disagree.

Margaretha set her basket on the table then swatted Lukas's shoulder. "Leave him be." She faced Max. "Will I see you at church tomorrow?"

"Ja," he said, giving her a peck on the cheek before making a hasty exit.

She locked the door behind him. With hands on her hips, she pivoted to address Lukas. "You are incorrigible," she scolded. "You'll have him too frightened to come calling again."

"If that is all it takes to dissuade his pursuit, then he is not worthy of you."

She sighed and tossed them a hasty Gute Nacht before leaving the room.

Franz waited for the bedroom door to close behind her. "Don't be too hard on him. Max is a gut man."

"I know that, and you know that," Lukas said, seating himself at the table again. "But it is too early for Max to think he has nothing to prove." Something mischievous glinted in his brother's eyes. "We keep him on his toes a bit longer, ja?"

"Ja, it is a gut plan." Now *this* was the brother he remembered—lighthearted, strong of character, and thinking of someone other than himself. *Thank You, Gott, for answering my prayers. Keep softening his heart, Lord.*

Lukas swigged his Kaffee. "Enough about that youngster. Let's get back to why you look like a lovesick pup."

So much for distracting Lukas from this line of questioning. How much should he say? He swiped his clammy palms on his pant legs. Speaking his thoughts aloud somehow made him feel foolish, yet if he hoped to fully restore his relationship with Lukas, he would need to risk his pride.

"I know Caroline has only been part of my life for a few weeks, but tomorrow I plan to ask her if I may court her properly."

Cup halfway to his mouth, Lukas jerked, sloshing Kaffee over the side of his mug. He stared at Franz, Kaffee droplets trickling from his fingers. "Have you—never mind."

"I thought you liked Caroline?"

"Ja, ever since she showed us our mistake on the advertisement, I have a new appreciation for her. She is a fine woman and not at all what I'd assumed someone of her birth would be."

It was hardly an outright apology for misjudging her, but Franz decided it better to accept the spirit of Lukas's words and not belabor the issue. "But you don't think I should pursue her?"

Lukas shook his head. "Nein. I think it is a gut match."

"Then what?"

Lukas drummed his fingers against the pine table. "Have you...seen her?"

"Seen her?"

"Ja. You know, beneath her veil?"

"Nein. I don't need to see what I already know. She is a beautiful woman."

"I agree that she has a kind heart, but what if she is..." Lukas leaned across the table and lowered his voice. "Disfigured? What if it sickens you to look upon her marred face?"

Franz scoffed. "That is not likely."

Lukas's brows peaked high above his blue eyes. "Why else would a young woman shroud herself beneath black lace? Margaretha says she even sleeps with it on."

His brother posed a fair question, but did the answer make a difference? While he was curious, deep in his soul he believed Gott had chosen Caroline for him. If that was true, wouldn't Gott also grant him the ability to look past her scars and see her heart just as He did?

"Is it fair of her to expect a suitor to take her sight unseen?"

Franz cringed at his brother's choice of words.

Lukas stood and patted Franz on the shoulder. "Remember, trust works both ways."

His brother's footsteps faded down the hall, leaving Franz alone to ruminate on their conversation. He hated to admit it, but Lukas's questions had exposed a truth Franz had been trying to deny—he did want Caroline to remove her veil before he proposed. Not because he believed it might change his feelings for her, but because he wanted to know she trusted him.

The men in her life thus far had done little to inspire her

confidence. By all accounts, they'd viewed her as a commodity to leverage for their own personal gain. He understood she needed time to heal, but he needed assurance that she saw the difference between him and the men who had hurt her so deeply—that he was not like her father or Charles. That to him, she was priceless.

Removing her veil was a sign that she would not keep any part of herself from him in marriage. Was that too much to ask from one's future wife?

———

Pulse thrumming in her ears, Caroline leaned against Margaretha's closed door—her entire body weightless. If she didn't know better, she'd believe it possible for her to float out the window and drift clear to the stars.

Over and over, she replayed the warm sensation of Franz's breathy voice whispering in her ear, "Gute Nacht, *Schatzi.*" He considered her his treasure—something rare and precious. A pleasurable chill swept over her skin, leaving a trail of gooseflesh in its wake.

For the first time in her life, someone valued *her*. Not for what she could offer them—money, prestige, or bragging rights for claiming the most sought-after debutante of the season—but for who God had made her to be.

Shoving off the door, her feet moved in time to the imaginary polka playing in her mind. *One und two, three und four. One und two, three und four.* She sighed. Franz Köhler was the kind of man who could repair the damage the wrong sort had left in their wake.

Caroline danced to the dresser then propped Margaretha's looking glass at an angle against the wall. She removed her monogrammed pin and let the folds of her veil hang loose over her shoulders then wiggled the comb from her scalp. Her fingers trailed her cheekbone as she examined her appearance in the mirror.

Not once had he asked what lay beneath the black lace. What would Franz think if she was brave enough to stop hiding behind her veil—brave enough to allow him to see her entire face? Would he be angry she'd waited until after he'd grown attached to her before revealing the truth of her injuries?

Lost in her own thoughts, she'd not heard the rap against the bedroom door before Margaretha burst in. "Gut, you not asleep. I want hear about—"

Scrambling for her veil, Caroline knocked the lace shroud to the floor, but Margaretha's slack jaw and wide eyes told her there was little use retrieving it.

"Caroline?" With one hand covering her mouth, Margaretha shook her head. Eyes narrowing, she stepped closer. "Your face."

Caroline grabbed her veil from the floor and hastily wrapped herself inside her black cocoon. After securing the fabric with her scarf pin, she tugged Margaretha onto the bed beside her. "You mustn't say a word—not to anyone."

"Not even Franz?"

"Especially Franz."

Margaretha continued her examination of Caroline's cheek. "Franz has right to know. He loves you."

"And I love him too, very much."

"Then why—"

"Just promise me, Margaretha," she pressed in a firm tone. "You won't tell him."

"Ja, I promise."

She closed her eyes and squeezed Margaretha's hand. "Thank you."

The thought of Franz asking her to marry him filled her with equal parts dread and delight. She wanted him to ask for her hand, and she intended to accept his proposal if offered. However, when she'd fled her father's house, she'd made a promise to herself not to marry unless the man would take her without seeing the entirety of her face. She knew no other way to protect herself from men like Charles.

Even if it meant losing Franz.

Chapter 15

Franz glanced at his pocket watch. Only a few minutes until Caroline should arrive for their picnic luncheon. He'd asked her to bring the remaining Gugelhupf, and he'd supply the rest. Only light fare, but cheese, fresh bread, and strawberries should do nicely.

With Margaretha's help, he'd transformed a corner of the attic into a romantic picnic nook. At her direction, he'd swept the floors then covered the wooden boards with a quilt. Two bed pillows propped against Johanna's old steamer trunk provided a comfortable place for him and Caroline to sit and, if all went the way he hoped, make plans for their future.

Footsteps padded up the stairs, prompting a last-minute prayer. *Prepare her heart to hear what I'm about to say. May Thy perfect will be done.* He smoothed his hands over his best shirt and trousers. They were a little wrinkled from the night before, but there had been no time to launder them.

As Caroline climbed the last few steps, Franz was once again reminded of her grace and elegance. Her veil shielded much of the left side of her face. He already knew she was a beautiful woman—both inside and out—but today there was a sparkle in her eyes and her skin glowed. If this was what love did to a woman, he would not complain.

"You are more beautiful than ever, Schatzi," he said, relying on his native tongue to reveal the depth of his feeling for her.

A twinge of pink dusted her cheeks. She smiled and slipped her arm into the crook of his elbow. "Dankeschön."

When he tucked her close against him, warmth spread through his chest. This was where she belonged, beside him for the remainder of their lives. He didn't doubt their mutual attraction, but was she ready to commit to him—ready to bare her scars to him?

He escorted her to their picnic spot near the open attic window so they could enjoy the breeze. Her fingers covered her parted lips. "Franz, it's lovely. I cannot believe you went to all this trouble for me."

"I could not have done this without Margaretha's help. She was horrified when she learned of my plan for a romantic luncheon in the garret, but I think it turned out well." Taking her hand, he guided her onto the blanket. "Sit with me, bitte."

Caroline sat beside him on the quilt and tucked her legs under her, making sure her dress covered her ankles, then leaned back against the trunk.

Franz offered her refreshments, and before he knew it, hours had passed lost in conversation about the poor outcome of the strike and the likelihood he and his coworkers would be unemployed soon. They even had a good laugh at Franz's expense when they recalled him dancing with his imaginary partner. Despite having no formal plans for the remainder of the day, when the kitchen clock cuckooed four times, he determined he should get to the heart of his invitation to their attic rendezvous.

"Caroline." She looked at him, and Franz knew beyond all doubt, beyond all reason, that he loved this woman. A knot formed in his throat. What would he do if she refused him?

He shoved that thought from his mind, concentrating instead on the same errant curl that always seemed to escape her veil. Unable to resist the temptation, he reached for the twist and slowly slid his fingers down the coil, extending the spiral at least an inch before he released it to spring back into a corkscrew.

"I've wanted to do that for a long time," he said, easing his forehead against hers. His thumb grazed the bandages on her hand. "How are your burns healing?"

"Very well, no infections." Her smile shrank into a frown. "But they will leave scars."

He slid his palm beneath hers. "May I?" he asked, tapping the bandage encasing her right hand.

She tugged her bottom lip between her teeth and considered his question a moment then nodded her consent.

He untucked the end of her bandage and gently unwound the white cloth. With his fingertip, he outlined the pattern of pinkish-white skin that half-mooned her wrist below the thumb then fanned over the back of her hand. She shivered beneath his touch. "Does it hurt?"

"No," she whispered. "Not anymore."

Her breathy response stoked a simmering fire inside Franz. "Gut." He grinned then raised her hand to his mouth, retracing the same markings with his lips.

Her breath hitched, and Franz couldn't help but notice the rapid rise and fall of her chest. His was not the only pulse careening out of control.

He captured her gaze with his. "This doesn't matter, Schatzi," he said, bringing her scarred hand to his chest. "Nor does this." He trailed his finger from the top of the bandage on her neck to the ruffle of her high-collared dress.

The soft sigh that escaped her parted lips only made his desire to hold her, to kiss her, increase tenfold. He cradled her lace-covered cheek in his palm. "And neither does whatever you hide beneath your veil."

She blinked back the tears welling in her eyes. "Franz, I—"

He cupped her hand against his chest. "My heart came alive

the moment I saw you, Caroline. No blemish, mark, or scar could ever change that."

———

Caroline's heart pounded so fiercely, if she wasn't leaning against the old steamer trunk, she'd keel over from exertion. Every fiber of her being longed to kiss this man, to feel his lips nuzzle hers. Despite the lovely breeze tickling the gooseflesh on her neck, she was sure her body temperature would set her blood to boiling inside her veins.

How on earth was she to resist such heartfelt professions of love and adoration? Did she even want to try?

"I need to know you feel the same way—that you will not conceal any part of yourself from me if we are to marry," he said, looping the end of her veil around his index finger. "Trust me, *Schatzi*. Do not put a barrier between us any longer. Let me look upon the woman I love. The woman I wish to marry."

His declarations filled every nook and cranny of her parched soul. He loved *her*. Not anything he could gain from marrying the daughter of a rich and powerful man. With him, she wasn't a possession to prop up a weak man's ego or a business deal to ensure financial stability. She was a woman, desired by a man who simply wanted to cherish *her*.

Caroline searched his eyes and found nothing but devotion staring back at her. Then why did her stomach feel like it was tying itself into knots at the thought of breaking the promise she'd made to herself? If she unpinned her veil right now, if she gave in to his request, would he still want to marry her, or would the knowledge of all she'd kept hidden from him make him withdraw his offer?

How could she make him understand a lifetime of only being valued for what her alleged beauty and familial connection could offer men? She walked away from that world when she left her father's home, and she was determined to find her way in this new one on her own terms.

God, prepare his heart for what I am about to say, and give me the words to help him understand.

She untangled his finger from her shroud then nestled their hands in her lap. "Not yet, Liebling."

A sultry smile inched over his lips at the use of the endearment. "Then when?" he asked, caressing her scarred wrist with his thumb.

"After we marry."

"After we marry?" His brows furrowed. "Are you—"

She raised a palm. "Since the time I was a child, I have been groomed for one thing—to marry a rich and powerful man. Before the fire, many suitors professed undying love for me. None of them, however, wanted *me*. Instead, they wanted my father's money and the hope of possessing a woman some considered the most beautiful in Philadelphia society.

"When Father tired of me rejecting man after man, he insisted I marry Charles. After that horrid debacle and my hasty retreat, I made a promise to myself that I would never marry unless the gentleman would consent to say his vows without seeing beneath my veil. If a man could love me enough to marry me sight unseen, I'd know he was a man I could trust forever."

Franz stood to his full height, his breadth blocking much of the light from the garret window. Hands clasped behind his back, he paced the width of the attic. With each step, the knots in Caroline's belly tightened, nauseating her. Would she lose him?

He ended his ruminations and extended his hand to her, helping her to her feet. "Schatzi." His thumbs brushed her unbandaged skin, sending rivulets of delight surging through her. "I know these men have hurt you, and your soul bears wounds that take much longer to heal than those on the outside, but I am *not* those men. To love someone is to trust them with your hopes and dreams as well as your fears. To truly love, you must put aside all barriers and risk the most tender places of your heart to another's safekeeping."

She folded her arms over her chest and turned away from him. "That's not fair, Franz. I've shared my entire past with you."

"Ja, and was that trust not well placed? Have you not found safety and acceptance in my love for you? Has it not drawn us closer?"

She nodded. "Yet you want more from me."

"Ja, I do. I want all of you, Caroline—even the part you hide behind lace."

He stepped in front of her and, with a gentle nudge of his finger, lifted her chin until their eyes met. "I am ready to share my life with you, both the good and the bad. I am ready to promise to protect and cherish you as long as I have breath in my lungs—no matter what scars you may have inside or out. But I need to know you see me as a man of honor who is worthy of your trust. Can you do that much for me, Caroline? Can you remove your veil for me now as a sign you will not hide any part of yourself from me after we marry?"

"Franz, I..."

He fished a small object from his pocket and placed it in her open palm. "This is my Oma Gertrud's ring. It is not fancy, but it represents the best love I know, apart from Gott, and the kind I offer you, Caroline."

A sheen of moisture glistened in his eyes as he wrapped her fingers around the worn silver band. "When you are ready, Schatzi, come to me."

Chapter 16

Caroline stared at the wedding band in her palm, one side worn thin from a lifetime of love. Her shoulders shook as tears streamed unbidden from her eyes. What had she done?

Franz strode down the stairs, the sound fading as he neared the kitchen door. Should she stop him? Did she have anything different to say? Why couldn't she let the past remain there and embrace the plan God was unfolding for her life right now?

She plopped down on the steamer trunk and revisited the events of her afternoon with Franz—the tingling sensation of his thumb caressing her hand, his earnest pledge to love her, scars and all, and the disappointment in his eyes when she insisted on waiting until after they married to remove her veil.

More than an hour passed while Caroline sat in the dimming attic light rehashing their conversation but not finding any different conclusions. Only God could help Franz understand why this meant so much to her. *Grant me Your wisdom, Lord.*

The steps groaned under the weight of someone's shoes. Was it Franz? Had he come back? Had he reconsidered his opinion?

She swiped at the tears on her cheeks. "Franz," she called, her breath quivering.

"Nein. It. . .is me, Opa. The stairs have stolen the wind from my lungs."

Caroline sniffled and patted the space beside her. "I'm afraid

I'm not much company."

"Ja, I hear your weeping, and my heart aches." Bible in hand, he lowered himself onto the trunk. "I come to check on you."

"Dankeschön." She kissed his cheek. "I've made a mess of everything, Opa."

"That is life. We make a mess, and we clean it up. None of us escapes this life without a few scars, but you cannot hide from my grandson any more than you can hide from Gott."

She bristled at the suggestion she hid from anyone, let alone the God she loved. "What makes you think I avoid God?"

"Ja, you talk to Him and go to the service with us each week, but I suspect, in here"—he tapped her temple—"you think because your earthly Vater rejects you, because he fails to see your unique value, that your heavenly Vater will do the same."

She opened her mouth to protest, but Opa continued, determined to make his point. "But He knows you, Caroline. You hide yourself behind the veil because you are afraid that you'll never be good enough. I suspect you shroud yourself in lace because you don't want others to see you, not even Gott."

Was that true? Had the veil meant to protect her from the deceitful heart of men kept her from embracing her true identity as a child of God?

He flipped his Bible to the Gospel of Matthew and read from the twenty-seventh chapter. "And behold, the veil of the temple was rent in twain from the top to the bottom. . ."

Caroline remembered this passage from her years in Sunday school, but what she didn't understand was how it related to her current predicament with Franz.

"Before our Lord sacrificed Himself on the cross, the veil in the temple separated the people from Gott. Only the High Priest was permitted to enter the Holy of Holies. When Christ died on the cross and the veil was torn in two, for the first time, Gott's people could bring their praises, confessions, and burdens to Him directly. With no barrier between man and Gott, anyone who chooses may commune with the Almighty, receive forgiveness, and discover His will for their lives with no need of an intercessor."

"Yes, I'm familiar," she said, regretting the hint of exasperation in her voice.

"Do you love my grandson?"

"Very much."

"Then I urge you to take down this veil, Caroline. Allow the man Gott chose for you to see beyond your head covering. With Gott's help, allow Franz to aid you in healing the wounds on the inside—the ones that hurt the most."

He handed her the Bible and tapped the words he'd just read from verse fifty-one. "I hope you will think on this for a bit and see what the Holy Spirit has to say, ja?" He stood and kissed her forehead. "Gute Nacht."

Opa shuffled toward the stairs. "Franz hopes you choose to remove your shroud and open your heart and soul freely to him. However, if this veil is that important to you, I believe he will marry you with it on. But he shouldn't have to."

Caroline stared at Opa's Bible. Its worn leather cover and ragged edges spoke of a man who walked with God, and she'd be wise to heed his counsel. She read the German words printed on the book's thin onionskin pages until the light from the attic window grew too dim to continue.

Where would she be if God had not sent His Son to take on her sin, to tear down the curtain keeping God and man at a distance? She could not fathom having the kind of relationship with God like the Jews of the Old Testament.

Wasn't that the point of Opa's Bible lesson—to choose the type of relationship she would have with Franz before they married? If she made him wait until they said their vows, she might have the assurance of knowing he'd chosen her sight unseen, but

Franz may always doubt the depth of her trust in him. Could she really remove the veil and all the protections it afforded? Could she make herself vulnerable *before* she wore Oma Gertrud's ring?

She wanted to more than anything else, but what if her earlier reluctance had hurt him too much?

There was only one way forward, and for both their sakes, Caroline prayed it wasn't too late.

———

Franz strummed his fingers on the kitchen table. What was taking so long? Mutter had agreed to take Caroline to the market so he could put the finishing touches on his gift for her.

Although Gott had revealed with certainty Caroline was the woman He had chosen for Franz, had Gott given Caroline the same assurance? After all, they'd known each other less than a month. As soon as she had a response from her aunt in Scotland, Caroline would have the means to leave.

Franz dragged his fingers over his beard. He'd been a complete idiot to press Caroline for more than she was ready to give. Her request to keep her face concealed from him until after they said their vows was unusual at best, but hadn't he also hidden part of himself away from others? Didn't his fear of ridicule from his father and Lukas spur him to conceal his knack for intricate carving?

Caroline's praise and affirmation of his skill had helped Franz realize God had given him a gift and he would no longer hide it. No more stashing his talent in the attic or denying it by working as a menial laborer. If his family would not make room for him in their business, then he would strike out on his own, hopefully with Caroline by his side.

———

Caroline scurried up the back stairs to the Köhlers' residence above the clockworks. When Berta told her Franz would be waiting to speak with her when they arrived home, it had taken every bit of ladylike decorum she'd learned from Miss Lillian not to lift her skirts and run the last few blocks.

She paused with her right hand on the latch and inhaled deeply, willing her pounding heart to calm. With her left, she stroked the cross pendant and recited the verse whose inscription it bore. "I can do all things through Christ Jesus which strengtheneth me."

The house was unusually quiet for midmorning when she stepped inside. The men, of course, would be in the shop, but shouldn't Margaretha be bustling about with meal preparations? Odd. Franz was nowhere to be seen. Her heart, so near exploding moments ago, now seemed to shrink painfully tight inside her chest. Had Berta misunderstood?

An envelope bearing her name leaned against a large, yellow hatbox in the center of the kitchen table. She tilted her head and examined the package. What was Franz up to? She lifted the flap and slipped a small card from within.

> *Schatzi,*
> *I know now this has always been for you.*
> *You are the one that makes my heart sing.*
> *Franz*

As her gaze fell over the words, any residual doubt she had about shedding her veil disappeared. She tucked the card back into the envelope and stared at the package. Of all the things he could give her, why on earth would Franz buy her a hat?

With no answer to that question, she opened the lid and gasped. Nestled in a bed of straw lay Franz's clock—his Meisterwerk.

Carefully, she lifted his magnum opus from the box, marveling once again at the minute details he'd so lovingly carved. But now, the man in lederhosen, so off-center when she'd first discovered the beautiful timepiece, no longer stood in solitude. She blinked back tears. His lips now touched another's—a woman wearing a black head covering.

"Like me, he's no longer alone."

Warmth spread through her at the rich baritone of Franz's voice, and Caroline spun to face him.

"The clock is beautiful, Franz. I'll cherish it always. Has your family seen it?"

"Nein. It is first for your eyes. Then I hope to persuade Vater to let me share in my heritage and join him and Lukas in the shop."

She returned the clock to its straw nest inside the hatbox. "Never doubt you are a master craftsman."

His eyes searched hers. "I am glad you are pleased with it."

Was that longing in his gaze? Merciful heavens, this man could make her temperature rise. *Stay focused on the task at hand, Caroline.*

"I have some gifts for you too. Wait here." She dashed into Margaretha's room, removed the bandage from her neck, and returned moments later with the items she wanted to share hidden behind her back. "Choose a hand."

"Right."

Following his lead, she offered him a white envelope of her own. "My inquiry to Aunt Josephine."

His brows peaked in question. "You never posted your letter?"

"No. With or without compensation from the railroad, I've known for a long time that I belong here—with you."

His lips parted in the same sultry grin he'd given her the day before. If marriage to Franz would afford her more of those, she'd never regret what she was about to do.

"Hold out your hand for your next gift."

As soon as he complied, she placed Oma Gertrud's ring in his palm then covered it with her own. "You said to give this to you when I was ready."

He waggled his brows and inched his way closer. "Caroline."

His husky voice made her knees want to buckle beneath her. Somehow, she managed to step away. If things turned out the way she hoped, she'd never need to move away from him again.

"I owe you my heartfelt apology, Franz." She swallowed down the fear clawing at her throat, desperately trying to convince her to play it safe. *I can do all things through Christ which strengtheneth me*, she reminded herself as she fingered the heirloom cross pendant.

"You were right, Franz. I've been hiding—hiding behind the veil and the mourning clothes, behind the hurts of the past and the scars of the present," she said, untangling the monogrammed scarf pin from her veil.

His eyes widened as black lace dangled along the side of her face. "Schatzi, you do not need to—"

The breathy endearment had nearly undone her. She lifted a finger to her lips. "Please, let me finish."

He swallowed hard. "Ja, go ahead."

"I hid because I didn't want to be seen—to be admired for my outward appearance or familial connections, but you saw *me*. You saw through the lace to the anguish and pain and just loved *me*. In fact, you seemed to love me before you even knew me. And what did I do? I repaid you by withholding my trust when you so clearly deserved it."

She stepped closer. "You are the most honorable man I know, Franz, and worthy of my trust. So, this is my last gift for you."

His gaze tracked her fingers as she worked the comb free that secured her shroud to her hairline. "I will never withhold any part of myself from you again."

His jaw slackened at the sight of her face, and he sank onto the bench. "I. . .I don't understand, Caroline. Where are the bandages?" he asked, shaking his head. "Where are the scars?"

She knelt beside him, cradling his palm against her cheek.

"There never were any. Leastwise, not on my face. Only a few bruises that healed within a week or so."

He needed no encouragement as his fingertips immediately explored her face, gingerly tracing her cheekbones, eyebrows, nose, and chin. Gooseflesh slid down her neck and fanned over her shoulders. She tilted her head back, granting him full access to the ugly scar on her throat.

"You're so beautiful, Caroline," he said, as his lips showered the disfiguring mark with a trail of kisses.

Although removing her veil and opening her wounded heart to Franz had been the hardest thing she'd ever done, she could trust his words, knowing with certainty that he loved and accepted her, blemishes and all. As he lowered his mouth to hers, she received his kiss, knowing nothing would ever come between them again.

Kelly J. Goshorn weaves her affinity for history and her passion for God into uplifting stories of love, faith, and family set in nineteenth-century America. Her debut novel, *A Love Restored*, won the Director's Choice Award for Adult/YA fiction at the Blue Ridge Mountain Christian Writers Conference in 2019 and earned recognition as both a Selah Award finalist in the Historical Romance category and as a Maggie Award Finalist for Inspirational Fiction. When she is not writing, Kelly enjoys spending time with her young adult children, binge-watching BBC period dramas, board gaming with her husband, and spoiling her Welsh corgi, Levi.

Running from Love

by Angela K. Couch

DEDICATION

To Jonathan. I might seem able to handle things by myself, but I do need you. I cannot do this alone.

ACKNOWLEDGMENTS

I cannot express enough gratitude for the help and support that made this story possible. To Jonathan, for daily support and filling in the gaps. To the kids for being patient with mommy. To my critique partners, beta readers, and editors – for making my offering better. To God, for more than I have room to express.

Chapter 1

Anna Köhler choked on a scream—and the rank odor that shattered any relief or hope that had flitted through her at the sight of the small cabin. Rest. A place to lay down and sleep. Was it too much to ask?

Obviously. Because mice droppings covered everything. Every square inch of the small cabin. In the otherwise bare cupboards, in the corners of the room, and scattered over the loft that would serve as a bedroom. Maybe her brother's bedroom—spiders had also left their mark, lacy webs laden with dust. She shuddered and cast a glance at Ernest, who had already deposited her bags in the middle of the ramshackle cabin.

He looked the single room up and down. "This will do."

He must have read the disgust in her expression—not that she could hide it—for he ducked his head and turned back to the door. "Maybe you should have stayed in Montana," he threw over his shoulder.

Maybe I should have. Teeth gritted, Anna swallowed against the tightening in her throat and the hurt sending a spasm through her chest. She'd left friends and home behind because of him. He was the one who'd gotten involved with a group of no-accounts that had led him to break the law. He was the one who'd returned home in the middle of the night with a sheriff hot on his heels. What other choice had there been in that moment? He'd not only ruined his name and life but hers as well.

She slipped her fingers around the simple gold cross hanging from her neck. "Please, Lord, give me patience." Closing her eyes, she pictured her mother when she'd given her the pendant. Anna grasped the image of home. Maybe she should have returned to her family instead, but she'd promised to look out for her brother.

"Need anything in town?"

Anna spun to Ernest. "It'll be dark in a few hours. We have to clean this place if we're sleeping here."

"There's a broom in that corner, and I was told the well's been maintained. What else do you need?"

Frustration surged. She sputtered, trying to find the right words to describe what she felt and what she needed from him.

He was already headed out the door, his large frame momentarily blocking the sunlight. The door wobbled on leather hinges. "I need to go for a ride. Clear my brain."

"Clear your brain?" She followed, her stomach plummeting. She'd seen his gaze linger on what had looked like a tavern in Caylee. He had no intention of coming home—if that was what this place was going to be—with a clear brain. "Promise me you won't come home drunk."

Ernest glanced at her. "Trust me, Sis." He flashed an easy smile, almost making him resemble the boy he had once been, blond hair shaggy across his brow and blue eyes bright. "I told you, things will be different here."

Yes, plenty was already different, including their family name, apparently. He'd introduced them as Anna and Frank Wilkins— Mother's maiden name—to everyone they'd met. At least she kept her Christian name. She had no idea how he'd come up with *Frank*. He didn't even look like a Frank.

Ernest winked. "Just scoping the area. I'll be back in a couple of hours."

Enough time for her to get the cabin inhabitable on her own. He ran from responsibility, as he always did. Would anything really be different here? Anna didn't watch him go. Instead, she grabbed at the door and flung it closed. It banged, then creaked, then crashed to the floor with a swoosh of air and dust. Cobwebs danced.

She released a gust of breath. If she had something to throw, it would have already smashed into the far wall. But breaking things wouldn't give her a clean place to sleep. Anna grabbed the broom and attacked the floor, sweeping until she gagged on the air. She stepped outside and filled her lungs. Mama's voice echoed from her memory, a gentle reminder to sweep with care. She'd do well to heed.

Anna raised her eyes to the eastern horizon and the flat wasteland of this country. They had come through the mountains a week ago and continued through the foothills, watching as the prairie flattened. In the west, the mountains stood against the horizon, the sun sinking toward them.

She turned back into the house and eyed the broken door. The old leather hinges had weakened and split. They would need to be replaced, but she had nothing for that tonight. She finished breaking the door free, leaned it against the outside wall, and resumed sweeping—both the floor and the cobwebs—and then washed down every surface until the sunlight faded too much to be able to work.

Still no sign of Ernest.

A warbling howl rose from just over the rise, sending a chill through Anna. She hurried back into the cabin. The door fit into place well enough, and she slid the small table across the floor to keep it upright. Again, the howl taunted as though mocking her efforts. She'd lived in Baltimore most of her life and then in a couple western towns, but never this far from everyone. The emptiness of the cabin sank into her.

"Probably just a coyote." She'd be fine, and Ernest would be home soon. She lit a fire in the small cast-iron stove with the wood left in the bin and returned to washing down the open shelves on which she would store the dishes and food they had purchased that morning. Not that she would eat anything tonight. The taste of mouse still saturated the air and chased away her appetite.

The howl grew nearer.

Anna glanced out the tiny glass window to blackness. How had it gotten so dark so quickly? A horse whinnied, and her mare replied. Anna's heart leapt. Finally, Ernest had returned. She took a breath. "Patience." Though never one of her strong suits, her brother needed that much from her. He'd made mistakes, but he had a good heart. He simply needed a second chance.

After filling the kettle she'd purchased in town with water from a canteen, Anna set it on the stove for hot cocoa. Ernest preferred coffee, but so long as he didn't *require* it, she intended to treat herself. A yap right outside the door jerked her upright. And footsteps. A knock at the door.

Please be Ernest. "Hello?"

She only heard part of the muffled reply, something about. . .police? She jolted across the floor and yanked back on the table. The door followed. A gray beast jumped through the widening crack.

Wolf!

Anna yelped and twisted away, but her foot caught on her hem. She fell. Her palms rammed against the rough floor, and pain shot up her arms.

"Hannibal, here!" a man barked.

The wolf whimpered and lunged out the door, disappearing into the blackness. Anna scampered to her feet as a scarlet-coated man stepped into the cabin, his flat-brimmed Stetson coming to his hands and his expression pensive.

"I'm so sorry for the fright, miss." He extended a hand. "Are you injured?"

She made it to her feet on her own, while trying not to make a show of avoiding his hand. She carefully folded her arms across her stomach and compelled her pulse to slow. Unsuccessfully. It continued to race as she looked up into the dark eyes and striking features of a mounted policeman.

Wait. Where was Ernest? He couldn't be in trouble with the law already. They'd only been in the area a few days!

"Maybe you should sit down," his voice rumbled. "You're whiter than the day after a blizzard."

She pulled her arm away from his supportive grip and shook her head to clear her thoughts. "I'm fine. But my brother isn't here."

His eyebrow cocked. "I see. Will he be home soon? I assume you are the folks renting this place from Hal?"

"The man at the livery? Yes. That's right." But why was he beating around the bush? "Can I ask what you want with my brother?"

The scarlet-clad policeman raised one of his dark eyebrows. "Not a thing."

"Then why did you ask about him?"

"I didn't."

"Wha—" Anna reviewed their brief exchange, and heat infused her face. "Why are you here?" Her words came out far more clipped than intended. The way she was going on, he'd start investigating them just because of how she acted. She forced her lips to curve upward. "I mean, I wasn't expecting a visitor tonight. I was a little startled. Why—I mean, is there anything I can do for you?"

A smile sparked in his eyes before pulling the corners of his mouth. "Just wanted to check in on you and your brother to be neighborly."

Her heart did a strange sort of twist. She could hardly argue about having an attractive and upright neighbor, but given Ernest's past trouble with the law... "How *neighborly*, exactly—I mean, where do you live?"

He chuckled. "I should have introduced myself."

Like she'd given him an opportunity. She forced a laugh as well, but it came out like a flapjack—short and flat.

"Constable Benjamin Cole. The North-West Mounted Police officer assigned over this area. I keep house for some friends, a homestead farther up that'a ways." He motioned to the...south? She was still getting her bearings. "I heard someone moved in here and thought to drop in and see if they—*you*—needed anything." He smiled, and the tension began to ease from her chest. He wasn't here for Ernest.

Not yet.

"Thank you for the consideration, but..." She glanced at the dimly lit disaster surrounding her. Her eyes burned to match her cheeks. Now was not the time to fall apart into a puddle of tears. "I'll manage." She set her hand on the table and winced at the stab of pain. Her hand felt full of slivers from her fall. "My brother should be ho— back soon." She'd almost said home, but this hovel was definitely not that.

Constable Cole again arched a brow at her as though questioning her sanity—as well he should. From just outside, the wolf-dog, or whatever the beast was, howled and then whined. It peeked its head around the offset door.

"Don't mind him. He's harmless. Just a big mutt eager for attention." The constable lifted the door and slid it aside. Beyond, Anna could make out the dark coat of his horse tied at the hitching post. The wolf-dog lingered just beyond the threshold, head down on his paws, eyes begging.

"What is he, exactly?"

"Mix of a few breeds, the main being a Greenland sled dog."

"From Greenland!" She couldn't imagine such a foreign place.

The constable chuckled. "Not for generations. The breed was brought over long before my time, and this fellow was born and raised in the North. Like I said, sled dogs."

Until now, Anna had considered *this* north. "I suppose if you get lots of snow up here, that could be useful." Though she wasn't sure why horses and a sleigh wouldn't be more practical.

"Hannibal here is retired." He tapped his leg and whistled. The dog bounded to him with a happy yip. On three legs. How had she not noticed that when the animal had first pushed in? His thick coat was a beautiful mix of white and gold with only traces of black. She stepped near and extended her hand. The dog pushed his head into her palm.

"What happened to his leg?"

"Bear trap."

Anna cringed and crouched to rub the dog's neck. "Poor fellow."

The door scraped against the floor, and she glanced up to see that the constable was inspecting the worn leather that had once kept it in place. He hummed. "I wish there was something I could do for this tonight, but I'd need at least a hammer."

He glanced at her, and she shook her head. His eyes took in the rest of the cabin. "I'll fetch you some more wood from the stack at the side of the cabin and make sure you are set up for the night before I head out."

Anna gave the dog a final pat and straightened. She should protest, say she was fine and could manage on her own, but the thought of being left alone. . . Her heart still raced from the last fright. "Thank you, Constable."

Chapter 2

Trying to ignore the mousy odor that clung to every square inch of the cabin, Benjamin piled wood beside the rusty stove and took a minute to examine the pipe acting as chimney. Solid but worn and probably in dire need of a cleaning, if the rest of this cabin was anything to go by. He could see the effort Miss Wilkins had gone to in contrast to the areas she hadn't yet reached—namely, the corner behind the stove. The kettle sang, and he used his glove to lift it from the heat.

"Where would you like this?"

Large blue eyes raised to his, and she paused, rummaging through a small crate with CAYLEE MERCANTILE stamped across the side. "The table is fine." She approached with two porcelain cups as dainty and fragile as the flowers depicted on them. "Please join me for a cup of cocoa." Her nose scrunched. "Unless you prefer coffee."

The hope in her gaze urged him to nod. "Cocoa is fine." Not that he could remember the last he'd had any. Usually, he ingested chocolate in the form of cakes and other desserts. A moth fluttered past his nose. "Let me get this door back in place first so the lantern doesn't attract more bugs." He hurried with the task, wedging the door into place with a length of post he'd found near the woodpile, though very aware of the woman's movements behind him. Probably wasn't appropriate being alone like this, but he'd feel worse abandoning her. Besides, he was still in uniform, so he had a duty to protect—even if only from her fear of encroaching shadows. Hard not to watch as her long skirts swept across the floor, her movements gentle as she poured dark liquid into the cups. Memories surged, images of his mother—though he cringed at the thought of her in a place like this. What was Miss Wilkins doing in a frontier hovel? Alberta may have been named an official province the year before, but it was far from civilization in both concept and vicinity.

"Please, have a seat and make yourself comfortable." She set a cup with painted bluebells in front of him and then pulled the second chair, one with a board missing in its back, to the table for her own use.

"This one's sturdier." He hurried to switch chairs.

"I don't—" Her protest died as he sat.

"I shouldn't stay long."

"Please, don't go." She spoke a little too quickly, desperation tinging her voice. Her lips pressed into a thin smile. "I mean, enjoy your cocoa first. I wish I had something sweet to go with it." She sent a nervous glance to the miniscule window.

"You mentioned your brother. Is he due back soon?"

She shrugged and studied the contents of her cup. "He wasn't clear on a time. But I'm sure he'll be along shortly." She didn't sound convinced.

Benjamin nodded. First night in a place like this with a broken door and no one to keep a body company—couldn't fault the woman for her nerves. "Where are you from?"

A flicker of surprise battled with uncertainty as her gaze flitted over his uniform. "Um, Baltimore. A city in Maryland."

"Yes, I've heard of Baltimore. I'm from the East."

She nodded and took a ladylike sip. "That's where our family still lives."

Something told him there had been other stops she'd rather

not mention. "What brought you all this way?" He smiled to help his interrogation seem less official. Judging from her sudden fidgeting and refusal to fully look at him, the uniform seemed to be winning out. A knot formed in his stomach. Most law-abiding folks took comfort in the scarlet coat he wore.

She shrugged, again staring into her teacup. "Adventure. An attempt to make something of my life."

Hannibal seemed to hear the same ache in her tone and laid his head on her lap. The shadow of a smile touched her lips as she smoothed her hand over his dense coat.

"And what is your dream, Miss Wilkins?"

Her head jerked up. "You—you've already learned that name?"

That name? A strange way to put it, but Benjamin offered a relaxed smile. "I keep abreast of most everything that goes on in this area, including newcomers. Mr. Rogers, who rented this cabin to your brother, told me your name. Well, your family's name. I haven't had the pleasure of your Christian one."

She looked at him with what he interpreted as mistrust, though he was hopefully mistaken. "Anna," she squeaked.

Anna. The name suited her with her blond hair pulled back in a haphazard bun, a hundred strands flying free. "But as to my first question?"

"My dream?" Even in the low light, he could see the red rise to her cheeks. She was no longer looking at his uniform, but his face. She lowered her attention to his lucky mutt. "Nothing of consequence. And God knows best."

"I suppose." Benjamin really hadn't given God much thought the past few years. He believed and all, but life was busy, and he had plenty on his plate.

"I hold to that with all my heart, Constable Cole. I trust Him."

"Just not at night with a broken door." He meant it in jest, but her eyes widened.

Her chin jutted. "Even then."

"I'm sorry, I didn't mean to imply—"

She lifted a hand to the pendant hanging from her neck. A small cross. "I admit that I am not always as brave as I should be, but I wouldn't be in this forsaken little shack if I didn't believe God had a purpose for me here. And, for your information, I was doing quite well until your wolf-like dog bounded into my home unannounced. And when you leave, I shall be well enough on my own." She drank her cocoa in a couple of gulps and stood.

Benjamin followed suit, enjoying the strong chocolate concoction—something he had not expected. He set the dainty teacup on its saucer and rose to his feet. "I didn't mean to offend you or question your faith. You are a very brave woman, and it has been a pleasure to meet you."

Her expression softened, and her mouth hinted at a smile. "You as well."

The air between them drew out in an awkward manner. He searched for something more to say, but after the day he'd had, it eluded him. He'd be wise to sleep on it and stop by tomorrow to make sure her brother found his way home and to make amends. "I'll be off."

Anna followed as far as the threshold. "I. . .thank you for pausing to introduce yourself. And Hannibal." She provided the latter with a dose of affection behind the ears. She might be ready for him to leave, but she did not look as eager to say goodbye to his dog.

"Why don't I leave Hann here for the night, give you some company until your brother gets home?"

Her eyes lit as they lifted to his. "I couldn't ask you to do that."

"It's nothing. He seems to be enjoying the attention." Benjamin felt a smile pulling at his mouth as something warm sifted into his chest. He didn't want to admit it, even to himself, but he was glad to have a reason to come back.

Anna buried her face in the thick fur and groaned. Sun streamed through every crack in the walls and around the door, but her head ached from lack of sleep. She had tried to wait up for Ernest, Hannibal sleeping at her feet. *Things will be different here.* She'd repeated the lie over and over until even she didn't believe it anymore, only to crawl into her sleeping roll at some ungodly hour of the morning. Hadn't taken long for the dog to cuddle up to her side.

"Good boy, Hanny," she murmured, then stifled another yawn. "Guess we better get up and get something done." More than listen to the wind howl outside.

A strong gust shook the small cabin and was joined by the *tat, tat, tat* of something falling around her. Tiny, elongated, black pellets rained from between the boards over her head. A gag rising in her throat, Anna tossed off her blankets and scampered out from under the loft and the shower of mouse poop.

Hannibal trotted after her, not minding that his coat had gathered its fair share of the offensive specks.

"Let's go, boy." Anna dusted herself off on the way to the door. She shook her head, swinging her hair forward and back to dislodge the pellets. All she wanted was a long warm bath far away from this horrid little mouse hole!

Outside, the wind snatched at her skirts and hair—hopefully cleaning it—and the morning sunshine warmed her. A friendly nicker drew her attention to the corrals. Two horses munched on the overgrown grass, leaving weeds tall in their wake. A low growl rolled in Hannibal's throat. Anna spun as a form staggered from the outhouse.

"What's with the dog?" Ernest murmured.

"Where have you been all night?"

He gave a grunt and moved toward the cabin. "Got back hours ago, but the door was locked. I didn't want to wake you."

She so wanted to believe him. "The door is broken. Fell right off its hinges."

"Hmm." He lifted the door from its place and leaned it against the outside of the cabin. "We'll have to fix that."

She moved to follow and so did Hannibal. He paced beside her, the hair standing up on his neck as they neared Ernest. Again, a growl rumbled in the dog's throat.

"Easy, boy," Anna soothed, bending to scratch his head. "Ernest is friendly." Though he smelled a little rancid—like cheap whisky. His eyes were hooded and red.

"Where did you get a dog anyways? Why's he only got three legs?"

"He was caught in a bear trap."

Ernest massaged his temples, shaking his head. "You found him in a trap? No blood?"

"No, that's how he lost his leg who knows how long ago." Anna wet her lips. "The local mounted police left him with me since I was alone."

Her brother's face hardened. "A Mountie was here? What did he want?"

Anna patted Hannibal's neck, and he seemed to accept that, despite the man's size, Ernest was not a threat. They followed him into the cabin. She slid the table farther out of the way of the door and set the length of post just outside. She had cleaning, breakfast, and a mountain of washing—there was no way she was climbing back into her mousy bedroll.

Ernest stood in place, and it was hard to tell if he was squinting at the brightness of the day or glaring at her. "Anna, you never answered me."

She sighed. "Constable Cole dropped in to welcome us to the area and see if we needed anything. With the door broken and night upon us, he was kind enough to leave Hanny here as my guard." She couldn't help the smile at the image of him crouching to give the dog instructions to stay with her and keep her safe—words that had not been meant for the animal's ears, she was sure. Constable Cole had lingered in the doorway, almost as though regretting his need to leave. Not that he could have found her attractive in the least last night with her hair falling from its pins and her work clothes stained from the day's labors. Maybe she could clean up and put on a good dress before he returned this morning.

"What were you thinking? Anna, we don't want him poking his nose around here."

"Who, the dog?" She bit the inside of her cheek to keep from chuckling. "I'm sure Hanny won't do much more than scare away pests with that nose of his."

Hannibal's ears perked, and he darted out the door with a happy yip. Anna followed as far as the doorway, where her brother also stood. He swore under his breath. A red-clad form stood out on the horizon, tall in the saddle of his black horse. Anna felt a smile on her lips, then a shot of panic at the realization that she looked even more bedraggled than yesterday.

Chapter 3

B enjamin reined in his horse and nodded to Miss Wilkins and the man at her side, presumably—*hopefully*—her brother. Same blond hair and light eyes, but the brother stood well over six feet tall and was built like a buffalo, making his sister appear petite beside him. They looked to be similar in age, but the young man wore a haggard look while his sister radiated sunshine. Her light hair hung loose over her shoulders like a wavy shawl. Her eyes reflected the dawn behind him.

"Morning." Anna smiled, but now he could sense an uneasiness about her. She glanced at her brother, who stuffed his hands into his pockets, before returning her attention to Benjamin. "You're out early."

"I have a long day ahead of me, but I wanted to make sure your brother made it home all right."

"As you see, I made it back just fine." Wilkins's voice held an edge. Either he wasn't much on mornings or much on Mounties.

Not one to be intimidated—even if he wouldn't stand a chance in a fistfight with the man—Benjamin swung from his horse and extended his hand. "Glad to see it. I'm Constable Cole."

"Constable, huh?" His hands stayed in his pockets.

Anna cleared her throat. "This is my brother—"

"Frank. Frank Wilkins." He gave a tight smile.

Anna glanced between them, a crease forming in her brow.

"I imagine Hannibal is anxious to be off, but I feel bad. I haven't had time to feed him anything yet."

The dog bounded around his legs. "I brought along some jerky, and there's breakfast waiting for him at the jail."

A humph rose from the brother. "Caylee's big enough for one of those? Get much business around here?" There was almost a challenge in the way he said it, but it was probably just a reflection of his foul mood. Anna scowled at her brother's comment.

"More than I'd like." Benjamin offered a smile but would keep his eyes open and maybe send out some inquiries into the young man's past. "I'd happily leave those cells empty and spend my days lending a hand to folks in the area. Speaking of which." He nodded to the door of the cabin and flipped open the flap of his saddlebag. "I found these and figure they might as well be put to good use." Would be easy enough to replace the iron hinges he had removed from one of the unused rooms upstairs. No one would know in the meanwhile. He set them in Anna's hands and watched her smile bloom.

"You didn't have to do this. We'll probably have to make a supply run again this afternoon."

"Bugs are out in force this time of year. Best not leave the door off for too long." And the reward warmed him more than it should.

"Thank you." She glanced at her brother. "Wasn't that kind?"

Suspicion was the only thing Benjamin saw on the man's face. "Sure was. Thanks, Constable. Let us know when we can return the favor." Frank took the hinges from his sister and started toward the cabin.

Anna sighed. "I'm sorry. He's tired."

"Imagine so." But it would be interesting to find out what else lurked behind Wilkins's dour mood. "I'll be off, but don't hesitate to call on me if you need anything." He was about to turn, but a small black speck in her hair caught his eye. Was that

a. . . ? He pinched the mouse poop from her locks and dropped it to the grass.

Her mouth fell open. "So disgusting!" She shuddered and swatted at her hair, shaking the golden waves over her shoulder. "I hate that cabin," she murmured under her breath.

"Been sitting most of a year." But from what he'd seen last night, she was well on her way to making it a fine little home. He wished he could offer her more, though. Like the three-bedroom house he rented from Corporal Bryce, built for a family, not a lone bachelor.

His thoughts jogged sideways until an image of Miss Wilkins skidded him to a stop. While he admittedly found her attractive, he wasn't in a position to court or woo a woman. "I should be on my way. Best of luck." He tipped his hat and hurried back into the saddle. With a whistle, Hannibal was at his side, and Benjamin touched the brim of his hat with a nod to Anna. Guilt pestered as he rode away. He wished he could do more, but he knew little to nothing about the sibling pair, and something sour stirred his gut when he considered the brother. All the more reason to keep a professional distance. It was one thing to be neighborly, another thing to start imagining a future with a woman he'd just met.

Even if her eyes sparked with determination.

Even if she wasn't one to turn away from a difficult situation and hard work.

Even if her hair had felt like silk between his fingers.

He rode straight to town and unlocked the door to his office, which also served as the jail. There was a cot set up across from his desk, but he was sure grateful he didn't need to sleep there anymore. He hung his hat on its peg and lowered into the ladder-backed chair. He'd start with paperwork—a true villain if there was one—and then slip over to the boardinghouse for breakfast.

Benjamin only made it as far as the envelope he had set aside the afternoon before. He rested his elbows on the desk and fortified himself with a breath. This letter came too close after the last a week ago. It couldn't bring good news.

But how long could he hide behind work and pretend he didn't have the time?

He tore the corner and poked his pencil in the hole. The paper tore along the seam, the truth opening to his grasp. A single page instead of the small novel his mother usually wrote monthly.

Dear Benjamin,

Foreboding struck with the opening. Usually just his name. Never so formal.

Your father's condition has worsened, and Doctor Foster fears he does not have long. Please don't let this hurt remain between you until it is too late for any reconciliation. Please come home as soon as possible.

Benjamin lowered the paper and stared. If it were only his father, he would stay away. But his mother rarely asked anything of him. Could he not do this one thing for her? He didn't have to forgive the man or even like him. He could just say a few words and pretend that the air had been cleared between them.

And hold his tongue against anything the old man had to say in return.

Teeth gritted, he took up a paper and penned a request for a short leave of absence from his post. Just enough time to travel east for a goodbye.

———

Anna looked to the door where her brother worked to attach the new hinges while she finished sweeping the last of the mouse droppings. She'd had Ernest clean the loft first while she made breakfast, so hopefully this would be the last of those horrid things she saw in here.

"There's your door," Ernest announced, opening and closing

it with an easy hand. Not even a peep from the hinges. They'd likely been oiled before being delivered. "What are you grinning like a fool about?"

"That was hardly a smile. I was only thinking how kind it was of Constable Cole."

Ernest grunted and slapped the door closed. "Nice indeed. I don't trust your friendly Constable."

"*You* don't trust *him*?" She raised her brow at that bit of irony. "What right do we have to mistrust him when we're the ones lying? Isn't the reason we came all this way so we don't have to hide? You promised me things would be different."

"I haven't done anything wrong since crossing that border."

Anna threw up her hands. "Except lying about who we are."

He huffed out a laugh. "In the day and age of telegrams, and even telephones in some places? Motorized machines? How hard would it be for word of what I've done to be sent up here if someone had an itch to know? Men have been extradited before."

She groaned. "Maybe for murder. Not theft."

"Leave it alone, Anna."

She held her ground. "I don't want to lie to Constable Cole."

He faced her squarely, his jaw tight. "You wouldn't have to if you'd just stay away from him. I don't care how he flatters you or looks at you. No good can come of him poking his nose around our business."

Anna's heart stuttered. "What do you mean, how he looks at me?"

Ernest shook his head and swung the door back open. "Leave it alone." He pointed one last look at her. "And keep away from that man. That's all I ask. Please."

Anna turned away from her brother, listening to his footsteps trail away. He was right, of course. Maybe not about going by the wrong name, but about how foolhardy it would be to be friends...or anything else...with a mounted police officer.

Chapter 4

The short logs shifted under Anna's weight as she scaled the dwindling stack of firewood at the edge of the crib that had been built to contain a much larger supply. The old wood planks of the structure bowed, and she hurried to push the bundle of shingles she scavenged onto the roof to free her hands. Next, she placed her foot on the window ledge while grabbing the edge of the roof. She clung to the side of the cabin and tried to garner more strength. . .and courage.

Maybe this is a bad idea.

Not knowing how to reverse her path, Anna levered herself over the ledge of the roof and gulped a breath but didn't allow herself a glance down. The cabin might be small, but the height was far beyond her comfort. A fall would easily crack bone.

How are you getting down?

She pushed aside the pesty voice in her head—she talked far too much to herself these days anyway. The route down was not the most prevalent need. First, as a drizzle of rain last night had made apparent, she had shingles to replace.

On hands and knees, Anna crawled—or tried to, with her skirts and the bundle of shingles hindering her progress—over the peak to where she'd tossed the hammer. She deposited the shingles near the chimney and then looked about for the small sack of nails that teetered far too close to the drop-off. She should have planned this better, but there was nothing for that now. She sat and, inch by inch, slid toward the nails. The shingles still held moisture, making them slick, and it was impossible not to reconsider the consequences of falling.

"Lord, please keep me on this roof."

She glanced downward. If she did fall and sustain an injury, Ernest would not find her until evening. If she was conscious, she might be able to crawl into the cabin and tend any minor hurts. But what if she broke a bone?

What if she broke her neck?

Anna's breath came in quick, short bursts, making her head light. Not helpful. She forced her lungs to slow. Deep breaths. And extended her hand to the pouch of nails. A scooch closer, and she snagged the tie between two fingers.

Success!

She was pushing backward up the slope of the roof when a high-pitched whinny sounded from the road. Her horse answered, and a dog yipped. Her gaze traveled to the horizon and the man seated tall in his saddle, red coat like a banner announcing his arrival.

What a time for him to arrive! How must she look, perched on the roof, her skirts up around her knees? Anna tugged the hem lower. Her foot slipped with the motion, and she started to slip. A scream scratched her throat as her foot extended beyond the roof and she tossed herself backward, the nails flying from her fingers as she attempted to grab moist shingles.

The thunder of hooves suggested the Mountie had seen it all. Flat on her back and arms extended, heat infused her face. At least from this position, he couldn't see her blush—only her feet and ankles protruding past the edge of the roof.

"Miss Wilkins? Are you all right?" At least he had the courtesy of sounding panicked.

"No," she squeaked. What a horrid sound! She would remind

herself later to feel mortified at what he must think of her.

"Don't move."

Not if she could help it, but she had the sinking sensation that she was sliding downward, over the edge. She clamped her eyes shut and imagined the scream that would no doubt accompany her fall. Then her broken body laid out on the ground, Constable Cole's handsome face peering down at her, seeking any sign of life.

The thud of boots on the roof above her jerked her back to reality. She ever-so-slowly cocked her head to see him breach the ridge.

"How did you get up here without a ladder?" he demanded.

"How did you?"

"From the saddle."

Oh, that was clever. Though she doubted her mare would stand steady long enough. "I climbed the woodpile."

He sat and slid toward her much like she had done, arm extended. She reached one hand up, and he wrapped her fingers with his. "I've got you." He leaned back and dragged her away from the ledge, the wood shingles scraping her spine.

As soon as her feet were on solid wood, she rolled to her stomach and scrambled to the peak. Knees tucked under her chin and heart thudding wildly, Anna closed her eyes a moment to catch her breath. Unfortunately, along with safety came the presence of mind to be embarrassed. Heat surged to her face, likely accompanied by an infusion of red to match his coat.

Warmth encompassed her shoulder, Constable Cole's grip firm as he crouched beside her. "Are you all right? What are you doing up here?"

She compelled her gaze to meet his. "I am fine, thank you. At least, I was until you distracted me."

"I'm sorry." His lips pressed thin. "But what are you doing up here?"

Anna waved to the bundle of shingles she had deposited near the chimney. "The roof leaks."

"Where is your brother? Surely, he would be—"

"Better suited for this task?" She shrugged his hand away. "He has work elsewhere." Her face heated at the thought of the constable thinking her a fool for being up here, for thinking her incapable of so simple a task. "Really, a hammer is not that difficult to wield." So what if she hated heights and skirts were completely unsuitable for climbing around on a roof? Pants were the answer. Next time, she would don a pair of her brother's.

Constable Cole sat back on his haunches, a smile touching his mouth. "I have no doubts as to your abilities to use a hammer, Miss Wilkins. But—"

"Please, call me Anna." She hated the misuse of her mother's maiden name, despite understanding Ernest's fears.

"All right, Anna." He paused, a light rising in his eyes and his expression softening. He drew off his flat-brimmed Stetson. "Benjamin."

Oh! This wasn't at all what she'd planned. Not after the lecture Ernest had given her several times since their first meetings. She had to keep Constable *Benjamin* Cole at a distance. Definitely imprudent to think of him by his given name or sit close enough to notice the warmth of his chocolate eyes and the subtle curve of his mouth. She redirected her gaze and cleared her throat. "I'm not sure that would be proper."

"Proper? Because I'm a North-West Mounted Police officer?"

"Exactly." She couldn't forget who he was—which shouldn't be hard with that uniform he wore. . .only he wore it oh so well. Snug across the shoulders and chest. Tapered at the waist. Her lips felt incredibly dry, and she wet them as discreetly as possible.

"I'm also your neighbor." He smiled easily and sent her heart back to racing, his gaze studying her face far too keenly.

"Very well." It wouldn't do to argue with a police officer, right? It might raise his suspicions that not all was perfectly proper and within the law. She didn't have to admit how much she liked his name or how well it fit a man so stalwart and good.

Benjamin abruptly stood and made his way across the roof to collect the shingles, hammer, and pouch of nails. He moved nimbly, never once slipping or losing his balance. She decided to credit his boots—which hugged his calves to his knees— and lack of skirts. It only took him a moment to focus on the main problem areas and kneel near a patch of missing shingles to begin staging the replacements. "We get some incredibly strong chinook winds. It can be hard to keep a roof intact."

"Chinook?" She had never heard the term before and hoped she'd spoken it correctly.

He nodded. "The Blackfoot have a better title for them. *Snow Eater.*"

"The wind eats the snow?" She raised a brow at that one while moving to help. A better occupation than sitting on the peak enjoying the view of a certain mounted policeman backdropped with the Rocky Mountains. Not as pleasant, but safer somehow.

"Sure does. A good chinook will give you a week of spring in the middle of winter. The wind is strong and takes some getting used to, but it's a nice break from the cold."

She picked up the pouch and handed him a nail.

"You never did say where your brother is off to instead of helping patch the roof."

What was it with lawmen and their obsession with information? "If you must know, he's working. He found a job with a large ranch near here."

"Mackenzie's?"

She could hear Ernest in her head, telling her not to say any more than she had to, but what harm could come of it so long as he was doing honest work? She nodded.

Benjamin positioned a shingle, tapped the nails in, and reached for another. "Mackenzie is a fair man. Treats his hands right."

"Glad to hear it." She passed him two nails, trying not to focus on their hands touching. He had nice hands, long fingers and broad palms that showed callouses but not roughness. Anna snapped her hand away. She was much too aware of this man— probably because she was trying so hard not to be! And now she overthought everything concerning him.

"Does that mean you'll be settling here?" He repeated the process, only two strikes sinking the nail out of sight.

"For the time being."

They continued, moving carefully from one patch of missing shingles to the next. "And the rest of your family? Or is it just you and your brother?"

Surely no harm could come of sharing a little more. "Both my parents are still alive. And there are seven of us children— though hardly children anymore. Most of our family is back in Maryland." Where Ernest had not garnered the interest of the law. They should never have come west.

The Mountie continued working, hardly looking up before putting forth the next question. "Why so far from home?"

"I think it's my turn, Constable." She gave him a stern look, hoping he'd not press. "What of your family?" Her chest tightened as she considered the possibility of a wife and children. He was likely a couple years her senior, and Mounties could marry, could they not?

"Back east as well. Guelph. A small town in Ontario."

"Your parents?" she pressed, trying not to overthink how he might interpret her interest. "Or. . . ?"

A laugh—or something similar but less happy—broke from him. "Only my parents. I do have two younger sisters, but both have married."

"But not you?" It was strangely easier to breathe now.

His lips twitched, and he glanced up at her. "No. Not me."

———

Benjamin paused with his hammer raised over a nail and stole a glance at the woman with light in her eyes. Her gentle smile held him in place. He should clarify that he had no intentions of taking a wife at this time. His duty to his country and keeping the peace came first, leaving little time or energy for keeping a woman happy. Not that men in the force didn't marry. Some did. Corporal Bryce, in whose house he stayed, had married in the early years of the NWMP and now had grown children, the oldest of whom had entered the academy to follow in his father's footsteps.

Sourness turned Benjamin's stomach.

His father had always expected the same of him—to follow the plan laid out for him from his infancy. Benjamin had been braced for resistance, but not the rage, when he'd announced his plans of joining the North-West Mounted Police.

He'd left that night and not looked back.

Why start now? Why not wait until after his father passed? The man's funeral might be easier to attend.

"Constable?"

Benjamin blinked away his train of thought before it plummeted into an abyss into which he'd rather not sink.

"Is something wrong?"

He shook his head and focused on the nail. He'd almost forgotten the hammer in his hand. A sure sign something was wrong, but with him. Proof that his father's course was all wrong for him—or him for it. He'd make a horrible preacher.

Though as a preacher, he'd be able to better appreciate a good woman like the one perched on the roof with him, the sun glinting on the golden cross hanging from her neck. His gaze lingered on her neck longer than it should, appreciating the length and divot where it met the angles of her collarbones.

"Forgive me for prying."

What had they been talking about? Family. Sisters. Marriage. He sent the nail into the shingle with a single strike. "It wasn't that."

"Oh." She gave a shallow laugh that hardly made it out of her throat. "Please don't think I was asking because of my own interest. . .in such a thing."

"Of course not." And yet he had.

"I assure you, I have no—I mean, we've only just met, and you are an officer of the law—"

He raised a brow. "So you wouldn't consider marrying a Mountie?"

Red rose to her cheeks. "No. I'm not so particular about who I'll marry."

"Oh?" He sat back to watch her. Making her blush was far too easy and enjoyable.

She batted the air with her hand. "Of course, I'm particular about important things, like if he's a kind man and law abiding—"

"Mounties generally are."

"Huh, well, he'd also need to be good with children and—and some education would be a benefit."

"Understandably."

"And he'd need to be a believer, a good Christian."

Benjamin motioned to her pendant. "I figured as much." But would he measure up to her standards? He believed in Christ and tried to do what was just, but in his family that had never been enough.

"I'm merely not too particular about his occupation." She made as though to stand but wobbled and again sat.

"Maybe you should be." Benjamin moved to the last area in dire need of new shingles. "A Mountie, for example, can be called upon to move quite regularly, going where he's needed. Not every location is suitable for women and children to follow. He works long hours and often into the night. And it's not the safest occupation, to be sure."

Anna straightened. "But it's not as though the West, even this far north, is so wild anymore. And even if it were, to know that your husband was doing his duty, protecting people and bringing some civility to the wilds, would be worth it. Besides, life and death are in God's hands, and we have little control over them."

Benjamin started. How could he not? Nor could he press down the affection rising through him. What manner of woman was this? Perhaps not a great beauty, but attractive with her vibrant eyes and the glow in her cheeks—very capable of making his mind and heart travel in a direction few women had been able to make them go.

Chapter 5

Benjamin encouraged his horse to a gallop across the rolling hills but was unable to outrun thoughts of Anna. Three days since the incident on the roof, and he couldn't put her and their conversation from his mind. Nor the feel of her in his arms.

A steep drop into the coulee that marked the edge of Mackenzie land forced him to slow. He directed the horse down to the river. While attempting to assist Anna from the roof, she'd fallen into his embrace. Even now, he could hear her gasp of surprise, see the strands of hair fallen over her face begging to be brushed away only to reveal the fullness of her lips.

The light spray of water kicked up by his horse did nothing to cool the sudden warmth rushing through him. Not unusual when in full uniform on a summer day, right? He pushed hard the last few miles to Lawrence Mackenzie's homestead—if it could be called that. The large, two-and-a-half-story brick home, shutters framing large windows, and grand porch welcoming guests stood out on the frontier.

One of the ranch hands hollered out to the house as Benjamin rode up, and Mackenzie met him on the front veranda, a scowl on his face. "Thank you for making it out, Constable Cole. Join me inside."

Benjamin followed past the grand foyer, serenaded by the tinkling of piano music. He caught the glimpse of the twelve-year-old girl in the parlor to the left while her father led him to the right.

"Your daughter is very talented."

Mackenzie motioned to a tall-backed leather chair. "Cora loves that thing as much as she loves the horses. With the other children, you practically have to put the branding irons to them to get them to practice."

Benjamin chuckled. That's how he'd been, despite his mother's insistence that he learn. Now, he craved putting his fingers to ivory. There was one occasion about a year ago in Major MacLeod's home, but generally there was not much opportunity for a Mountie to play piano.

"As to why I asked you here."

"Have you been having trouble?" Cattle rustling wasn't so common anymore. And the wolf population dwindled each year.

"Nothing we haven't been able to handle. On the contrary, things have been going well. In fact, I have plans to expand." The larger man sat behind his desk and smiled for the first time since Benjamin's arrival. "I've struck a deal with Charles Wade, the ranch to the north. Twelve hundred acres of grazing."

Benjamin leaned forward. He'd met Wade on several occasions. The man was well set up. "I didn't realize Wade had intentions of selling."

Mackenzie shrugged. "His wife has failing health. With the profit, he'll find a comfortable house in Calgary. That's where you come in."

Now he was lost. "Pardon?"

"He was quite adamant that he wanted cash for the land, and only cash."

The hair prickled on the back of Benjamin's neck. "That'd be a lot of money."

"I won't muddy the waters with an amount, but yes." Mackenzie glanced to the closed door. Only the faint tinkle of the piano sifted through the thick oak. "I don't have a man I can trust with it."

"You want me to guard your money." Benjamin didn't have to ask, but how to turn the man down? He was an officer of the law, not a hired guard. He worked for the government, not a civilian, no matter how wealthy he was.

"You are an honest man, Constable. I have watched you closely the past year since you were stationed here, and I know I can trust you. And no one would dare rob a Mountie."

Not usually, no, but if anyone did, the uniform made him a surer target.

"Only as far as the Bank in Nanton to Caylee. A few hours. And I'll make it well worth your time." He reached in his desk and withdrew a fold of bills.

Benjamin pushed to his feet. "I'm not for hire."

Mackenzie sighed and motioned him back down. "Please, I don't mean to insult you, only to be certain of my judgment of your character. I do need your help as an officer of the law. Is it not better to stop a theft before it happens than after? Much of what you do, dressed in scarlet and keeping your presence in this province, is to prevent crime. How is this any different?"

Benjamin opened his mouth with an argument but couldn't find one. The request wasn't completely unusual. "When?"

"We are still drawing up the paperwork and making arrangements. Probably three weeks."

Benjamin nodded. "I'll see what I can do."

They concluded their meeting, and Benjamin bid the man goodbye. His horse tried to reach the short grass at the base of the hitching post, lips extended with hopes of a nibble. "Come on, boy." Benjamin allowed for a mouthful before bringing the gelding's head up and climbing into the saddle.

"Don't mention what we discussed to anyone," Mackenzie said from behind him.

Benjamin nodded with a glance around at the men who had paused their work to watch. "We'll be in touch." He touched his hat and pulled his horse around to ride out past the main stable. Two men stood out front. Anna's brother—Frank Wilkins—with a pitchfork in hand and a slightly older man with a smoking cigarette between two fingers. Something about the latter's face drew a memory, but from where? He pondered it as he rode back to town, growing more certain with each mile.

Benjamin rode straight to his office instead of picking Hannibal up from where he hung out with Hal at the livery most days due to his leg. The first order of business was to shuffle through the "Wanted" bulletins. Benjamin kept two piles, one for the province and one from south of the border. Out of his jurisdiction, but useful because Alberta was so close to Montana. He lifted the paper he'd sought, studying the charcoal likeness with renewed interest. If it wasn't the man himself, it had to be at least close family. Norman Drake. Wanted for multiple robberies and possible manslaughter.

Benjamin leaned back in the hard chair and blew out his breath. The heavy feeling in his gut said Norman Drake was in Canada hiding out on Mackenzie's ranch. But he had no proof, and the man hadn't committed known crimes north of the border.

Yet.

Mackenzie was right to be nervous moving that much cash and right not to trust anyone.

The mewing at the door barely breached his thoughts. The stray calico was hoping Benjamin had lunch to share. Honestly, he'd lost his appetite. He didn't like Anna's brother becoming friends with a man like Drake. But how to intercede?

Chapter 6

Sunday morning, Anna tucked her hat on her head and pinned it in place. The embellishments hadn't survived their flight very well, so she had replaced them with a wide blue ribbon from the mercantile, making a simple bow on the rim. The pale tone almost matched her dress, though that was trimmed in white lace at the bodice. She pinched her cheeks,then questioned why, since Benjamin Cole was quite talented at bringing color to her face. Not that she hoped to see him. On the contrary, she had given herself a good talking-to and locked her heart quite securely from the good constable.

But who knew who else she might meet? A lawman was out of the question, but perhaps there were other good Christians of the single male variety to distract her from—

Anna shook her head, ridding her thoughts of a particular someone. She honestly didn't want another man in her life right now. Ernest needed her. But other female friends would be wonderful. It was getting rather lonely out here.

Not knowing what time church began, Anna headed out to saddle Cocoa or to see if Ernest would so she could keep her outfit cleaner.

The strength of the wind caught her by surprise and threatened to snatch her hat from her head, pin and all. She set a hand on top and looked around. No sign of her brother. His horse was missing from the corral. He hadn't told her he had plans to leave, only that he had no interest in going to church with her. Not a surprise, as he'd stopped attending months ago. But riding off without a word?

She bit her lip and set her Bible and gloves on the wooden lid covering the well. Ernest had left the bridle and other tack in a small shed near the corral, so she headed that way, carefully avoiding the evil-looking bushes and the browned spiny burs untouched from last year. The last thing she wanted was the tiny hooks to snag on her best dress.

Thankfully, the bridle already hung from the saddle horn, and it wouldn't be too difficult to haul them to where her horse waited. She had no intention of missing church. Then, partway out of the brush, the bridle slipped from the saddle. She grabbed for it and felt a tug on her hair. Then a release. Everything was fine—she'd simply come too close to one of the bur bushes. Bridle in hand, she set about catching Cocoa and saddling her.

Gloves tucked into her sash to keep them clean and Bible in the saddlebag, Anna started toward town. She'd seen the small log church on the edge of the settlement, and anticipation spurred her forward. Would the community be welcoming? Would the other women be open to friendships? Would they be here long enough to really build relationships before Ernest compelled another move?

Anna shook the thought from her head. Her brother was doing better and seemed not to mind his work at the ranch. Maybe he would mature over the next few months, maybe even find a good woman to keep him on the right track so Anna could make plans of her own.

Dark brown eyes and an easy smile teased her thoughts. Maybe someday falling for a Mountie wouldn't be so bad.

Except the one you want doesn't even know your real name. What will he think when he learns the truth?

Better to avoid him altogether.

The small cluster of buildings and houses sat rather quiet and still, with all the businesses closed and shuttered for the Sabbath. The only person working was the constable, or at least it appeared so with his black gelding tied in front of his office and Hannibal stretched out in a spot of shade under cover of the eaves. There was no sign of the man himself.

She directed Cocoa toward the church. She might not have recognized it as such if the mercantile owner, Mr. Smith, hadn't pointed it out when they had first arrived in town. Log walls and no steeple. A cluster of hitching posts suggested a gathering place, though this early in the morning, they all sat vacant.

At least she wasn't late for the meeting.

Leaving Cocoa tied near the front of the church, Anna walked to the building, curious about the inside. The door swung easily, no lock in place, and she let herself in. Rows of benches were lit by rays of morning sun through the two windows on either side, the wood bracing the four small panes of glass of each window forming a cross, as though a reminder of the reason for attendance. To worship. To seek Christ.

She breathed deeply, an attempt to fill her soul with the small church's peaceful state. Yes, it was humble and rustic. . .but so was the stable and the cross.

Her heart did a happy skip at the sight of a piano nestled in the front corner of the room. A glance around suggested she was completely alone and would be for a while. Surely no one would mind as long as she played softly. She closed the door and sank onto the stool. Her eyes slipped closed as she laid her fingers on the cool keys. One of the notes rang slightly sour, but that was easily ignored. Music fed her, and soon her fingers, though stiff from lack of practice, glided over the keys, bringing both feelings and thoughts out of obscurity.

Frustration.

Sorrow.

And a growing hope.

As the final note rang through the building, Anna opened her eyes to the dancing dust motes in the rays of light and the man who stood near the door. She steadied herself on the edge of the piano and winced as her forearm bumped a B-flat.

Benjamin smiled.

"Mor—" Her voice squeaked, so she cleared her throat and tried again. "Morning, Constable Cole." Dare she ask how long he'd been there?

"Good morning to you. I was just investigating who had broken into the church."

She started before catching the humor in his eye. "Can you make arrests when not in uniform?" She stood.

"Of course." He started up the aisle.

"And what is the punishment for such an offense?"

"In the case of a church, I think it would depend on the intentions of the perpetrator."

She held her position and the frown on her face. "Obviously, only the vilest of intents." She waved her hands at their peaceful surroundings.

"Obviously." He paused as he reached the piano. "The punishment for such a crime should be an encore."

A grimace wasn't difficult to feign. "That seems a rather harsh punishment, Constable."

He leaned into the instrument, looking at her far too intently. It was hard not to return the stare. His cotton shirt loose at the collar, a tan coat open at the front. Blue denim pants hid his black boots, but she recognized them easily enough. "Though it seems it won't be the first punishment you've received this morning," he said after a moment, his mouth turning up. "Or rather, battle lost."

"What?" She failed to follow what he alluded to.

He chuckled. "We don't have much burdock here"—he circled around her—"but Hal does seem to have let it run amuck out at your place."

Anna was still not certain what he was talking about. Her brain was a little busy tracking his course to her side. His hand reached to her hair but paused. "May I?"

"Please." Maybe then— "Ow!"

"Sorry," he murmured, his attention focused on the side of her head. "You have a cluster of burs in your hair that seems quite content to stay put."

"I have what?" Oh, no, she hadn't gotten away clean from the bur patch. She reached up to feel for the intruders, but he caught her hand.

"You might only tangle them worse. Let me try." He pulled a chair up beside her and slid the pin from her hat. Off came the hat itself. Then, ever so slowly, he began to pull at her hair—at least that was what it felt like. He probably worked very carefully to pry the burs and their hundreds of miniscule hooks from her tresses. Soon her neat bun was all but undone, random strands of hair a mess around her shoulders. Oh, that she could bury her cheeks in her hands to cool the heat infusing them!

⸻

Warnings sounded in Benjamin's brain to step away and find the woman a mirror or someone else to untangle her hair—long strands of spun cornsilk slipping between his fingers and doing strange things to his gut. Despite the bristly offenders, the moment seemed far too intimate with them alone and morning light warming the room.

"Last one." He dropped the final bur to the pile of four others and pushed to his feet. His brain wasn't nearly as clear as he needed when this close to her.

A soft groan escaped her lips, and a becoming blush rose to her cheeks. "I can't believe I didn't feel them there." She combed her fingers through her hair, taming it. "Wouldn't that have made a wonderful first impression on the community?"

He chuckled, but only because he was at a loss of what else to say.

She twisted her hair into a bun and pinned it in place. "What time does church begin?"

"Um. . ." He wracked his brain, having seen the town and folks from the area gather, but never having attended. "Around ten, I think."

Her brows arched in surprise. "You don't know?"

Shame struck him with surprising force. She imagined him a good Christian who attended church every Sunday with penitent heart. The thought of shattering her opinion soured his stomach.

"That would explain why you're so early." She slipped a time-piece from a pocket in her skirts and gave a low whistle. "It's only eight thirty. I hadn't realized."

"Yes, we have some time before anyone else arrives."

She pinned her hat back in place. "So, you are attending?"

"Of course." Was it wrong to hide the truth from her, that he had been running from both religion and God? That he had been in this building plenty of times but for town meetings, not worship?

A smile pulled up the corners of her mouth, and thoughts of confession fled. As did the opportunity when Anna focused again on the ivory keys and began to plunk out an easy tune, one he remembered as a hymn. He lowered into the chair and hovered his fingers above the keys.

Waiting.

For the perfect moment to join in.

Wonder lit her smile when he did. "You are a man of surprises."

"Trying to keep up," he replied, continuing the tune as well as he could remember. Resolve settled into his chest. He would try to be more worthy of a woman like Anna Wilkins. Even if it turned his plan for his life on its head.

Chapter 7

*C*rack!

Anna picked the largest piece of splintered wood from the ground and centered it back on the scarred stump. The weight of the axe burned her muscles as she raised it over her head and then brought it down with all her strength.

Snap!

Setting the axe aside, she gathered the handful of split pieces and carried them to the side of the house. Mostly, she just needed a few minutes to catch her breath and rest her arms. She was used to working hard and had learned her fair share of skills since coming west, but Ernest usually took care of chopping firewood. Now he spent long hours at the Mackenzie ranch, sometimes through the night. She missed his company, but at least his time was spent constructively. He'd been out of work when he'd gotten involved with the wrong men in Montana.

She smiled to herself and sent a thank-you heavenward. Ernest seemed more even-tempered lately and had put away part of his first paycheck as savings. He had a future here and could make something of himself. Maybe soon she'd make plans of her own. She missed Baltimore and the family. As much as she liked the Rockies, going home held plenty of appeal.

Anna returned to the axe and again took aim at a foot-high length of log. She brought the axe down and sank it deep. Only, the wood didn't split. And her axe wouldn't let go.

At least in Baltimore she wouldn't have to chop firewood anymore. Or deal with quite so many mice.

Biting her tongue to keep it tame, she lifted the full weight of log and axe and brought them down together. The blade wedged deeper, and her arms screamed for rest, but she wouldn't let this piece of wood win. She slammed it down again but with little progress. Likely a knot she'd missed seeing, but she was determined.

A familiar yip made her let the axe fall prematurely. The log hit on its side, flung the blade out, and then fell in two at her feet.

"Hello there," Benjamin called as he appeared around the corner of the cabin. Oh, why couldn't she think of him as *Constable* anymore? After their encounter in the church a few days ago, it had been almost impossible to keep her thoughts in check. Thankfully, Hannibal met her first, his nose nuzzling her hands, begging for pats. Just the distraction she needed.

"You're back." Her words came out much more breathless than she'd intended, much too full of hope. She was simply eager for company—any company besides her own. Church had been wonderful, but most of the other women were older, married, and with children. They were too busy to build much of a relationship with. Not that that had anything to do with the up-kick of her heart or the flutters in her stomach. Or how good this man looked despite his lack of uniform.

"I am." He swung down from his horse, a somewhat awkward motion given the large basket draped over his arm. He must have noticed her curiosity, for he smiled and held out the basket. She could have sworn she heard a meow, but it must have been carried on the wind.

She took the handle, and the weight shifted within. "What. . . ?" Anna reached for the flap lid, but Benjamin stayed her hand.

"Might want to take her inside first. She's tame enough but might run for it after the ride she had."

Another meow answered all other inquiries. "You brought me a cat?"

His mouth crept higher on one side. "Thought she might help with your mouse situation."

His kindness warred with her embarrassment at having a *situation* in the first place, though she was hardly responsible for the previous inhabitants of the cabin. "That was thoughtful of you."

He shrugged and turned back toward the cabin, horse in tow. "Just being neighborly. Besides, she's been hanging around the jail since spring. I made the mistake of feeding her, and she's a regular now."

So perhaps it was less thoughtfulness and more desire to solve his own problems. That bode better than having him over here, trying to take care of her—she could get far too used to being looked after for once.

"It'd be good for her to have a warm home before winter." At the front of the house, he handed her the basket and tied his horse to the nearby fence. "Keep a hold on that top."

The lid of the basket lifted as he spoke, and Anna threw her hand over it. Too late. A flash of orange, gray, and white flew from the basket and raced around the side of the cabin. Hannibal barked and raced after her.

"Oh no!" Anna tossed the basket aside. "Will he hurt her?"

"He's never bothered her before." But Benjamin still sprinted past her to where Hannibal stood by the woodpile, looking up.

"I'm not going up there again," Anna said before feeling heat rush through her. From the subtle curve of Benjamin's mouth, he was also remembering the fool she'd made of herself last time.

"We might be able to entice her down."

Anna had no lack of faith in his abilities to entice, but the cat was probably not as susceptible to his charms—the charms she *really* needed to stop thinking about. "I have some leftover bacon in the cabin." At his nod, she hurried inside but couldn't refrain from glancing in the small mirror she'd mounted over the washstand. The braid she'd wrapped into a bun that morning had all but come apart, and strands of frizz stood in every direction from the day's activities. Her face was blotched with dirt and still glistened from perspiration. One glance at her yellow-print skirt, and she shuddered. But what could she do with the good constable standing out there waiting for cat bait? Besides, a man given to detail would notice her efforts and assume she held an interest in him.

Shoulders back and teeth gritted, she pivoted from the mirror and fetched the bacon from the cold box she'd put together from an old crate. Well, maybe she had time to wash her face and hands. A natural response after working outdoors. And throwing her hair in a fresh braid would hardly be a noticeable change. At least she'd appear a little civilized.

Benjamin met her at the door, cat in hand. "When I called her, she must've assumed I already had a treat."

"Oh." She managed a laugh, but obviously she'd taken far too long for such a little errand. Anna took the small feline from his hands, and he closed the door behind them. It was not the first time they'd been shut in this cabin together, but for some reason the room seemed smaller. Or he seemed to take up more space. Perhaps it was just her awareness of him.

She sat at the table, the cat cuddled to her chest, and held the strip of bacon for her to eat. "She's such a pretty girl."

"Yes, she is."

Anna glanced up and found his gaze on her. "Um, a name. Does she have a name?"

He made a face and sat on the corner of the table. "Afraid I've only ever called her *Cat*. I hadn't planned on a permanent relationship."

"Whether her home here is permanent or not, she'll need a name." Anna made a study of the cat, wishing she could again do a thorough study of the man looming over her. White covered the cat's face and three of the legs, with orange and gray marbling her back and tail. "How about Marble?"

Benjamin smiled, and something shifted within Anna. The strangest feeling of rightness, that this was where she belonged. The longing for permanency.

"Then that's settled." But really nothing was. Ernest would have a conniption if he saw her now. She'd agreed to avoid this man, to keep him at arm's length. It was better for everyone that she did. "Thank you. . .Constable."

Something flickered in his face, and he found his feet. "I'll leave you two to get acquainted, then, and be on my way."

Good, she told herself, but didn't feel it. The bigger dilemma was how to keep him away?

———

Seated on the old rocker, tucked safely in the cabin, Marble's rolling purr soothed the agitation in Anna's chest. After she'd washed away the day's grime and dressed for bed, Anna spent the evening writing a letter to her parents, updating them on the recent move without fully disclosing the reason. Ernest was well and had work on a ranch, and that was all that mattered. Why worry them over his past behavior?

Because he needs their prayers.

The whisper of her thoughts broke the stillness of the evening.

But they will be praying. Just not for anything specific. That was why Ernest had her.

And what of you?

An ache arose within. How she wished to curl up like this kitty in her mother's embrace and spill her heart. She'd share her frustration and worries over Ernest and his past choices, her fears of what might happen to him if his intentions to stay on the right path fell apart as they had before. She'd cry on her mother's shoulder over her crazy attraction to a man she couldn't have and how unfair that was.

The lifting of the latch and the sigh of the opening door jerked her upright, and she swiped at the moisture in her eyes. "You're home."

"Sorry it's so late. Got chatting with one of the other hands after we finished up at Mackenzie's."

She pushed up but kept the small cat tucked under her arm. Most of the afternoon had been spent befriending the thing and getting her to relax, but Anna wasn't confident the animal was completely comfortable in her new home.

Ernest tossed his jacket and work gloves on the table and walked to the stove, where she kept his dinner warm. She met him there with a motion to the basin of fresh water she always had ready.

"Wash, and I'll set this on the table."

"Thanks." He took a step and then eyed her companion. "Where'd you get a cat?"

Anna had hoped to delay the conversation but refused to lie. "Constable Cole dropped her off. I guess she was a stray, and he figured we'd have use of her with all the mice here."

She could feel her brother's gaze scorch her back as she gathered his dinner and laid it out on the table. "He was being neighborly." Her attempted smile was met by a dark glower.

"I asked you to not go near him."

Anna met his stance, reminding herself she hadn't done anything wrong. "I didn't *go* anywhere. He came here."

"But we both know why."

"I have no idea what you're talking about. I have been civil, but nothing more."

"Nothing more?" He raised a brow. "I've seen you look at him. A blind man would notice your interest."

Her jaw dropped, but no words came. Was she really such an open book? Maybe to Ernest—he was her brother, after all, but surely not to Benjamin—*Constable Cole*. She'd so fully let her guard down and her heart wide open.

Her brother eyed her. "We can't afford to attract the attention of the law—any attention."

"You mean, *you* can't afford it." She had no reason to hide except for him. There was no other reason not to entertain the attentions of a Mountie but her brother's past. A bitter sensation climbed through her. She set her jaw against all the words, all the accusations and frustrations she wanted to spew at him.

The hardness in Ernest's expression melted, and he sank into his chair. "I didn't ask you to come with me. You shouldn't be here."

Her own anger ebbed. "Don't say that. I want to help. I do."

"I can tell." His sarcasm broke with a groan.

She'd left her home and employment for him. She'd made this cabin inhabitable and made sure he had a hearty dinner to come home to at night. She washed his clothes and cleaned up after him. Couldn't he see how hard she tried? She hadn't solicited the constable's attention. She had tried to discourage it despite her own feelings. How much did her brother expect of her?

"I'm sorry, Sis. I'm tired and have a lot on my mind right now. The way that Mountie keeps showing up here..." He shook his head. "I don't like it. Maybe he already knows everything and is just hanging around to get more information from you."

Anna's core cooled. Could that be so? Could Benjamin be using her to get to her brother, all his attention a deception?

"Please, Anna, like I said before, I am glad that you are here, but please stay away from that man."

"Of course." She'd not be played a fool.

Marble shifted in her arms, and Anna rubbed the cat's head, retreating from Ernest. "It's late. I'm going to turn in." So much for the discussion she'd considered having with her brother about helping out a little around the homestead. She'd not made any more progress on the woodpile, and one of the boards on the corral had broken when she tried to climb over it. She'd tied a rope to hold the horses in for now, but a new plank would be needed soon.

"Good night, Anna."

She mumbled her reply and crawled between the quilts on her pallet. Sleep. After she'd gotten some sleep, she'd figure out what do.

Unfortunately, despite the exhausting day and her burning eyes, her brain refused to rest as she listened to her brother's movements through the cabin. He disappeared outside for close to an hour before finally blowing out the lamp. His rumbling snore finally lulled her to sleep.

———

Anna awoke with a jerk to the *thwack thwack* of what sounded like an axe. Morning light glowed in the small window. She yawned and shifted under the weight on her chest. Then looked to the closed eyes of the feline curled in a ball on top of her quilts. That brought a small smile. That and the steady chopping from outside. Ernest must have seen the need and taken time to help. He really could be thoughtful sometimes.

She ran her hand down the cat's soft fur, a moment of weakness tugging her thoughts back to Benjamin as he'd presented her with the gift.

Not a gift. He was just being neighborly while trying to rid himself of a stray cat.

Something in her rebelled. Marble was hardly a nuisance, and there had been more depth to Benjamin's gaze.

Don't think it!

She gently rolled the cat off her, making a nest in the quilts so Marble could continue her slumber. Anna found her feet and trudged to the washbasin, her arms and back stiff from yesterday's labors. She hadn't been born to this kind of life, to dirt under her nails and calloused palms. What would Mama think of what she'd become?

"She'd be pleased you're doing what needs doing," Anna muttered to herself. She stared down at the washbasin, any hope she'd felt a moment earlier sinking like the dirt through water, coating the white porcelain in black. She wrapped her shoulders with her shawl and headed out the door to dump the water and clean the basin as should have been done last night.

Morning air tinged her skin with a cool touch as she strode across the yard to splash the water on the rhubarb and mint plants she had discovered at the edge of a weed patch—likely a neglected garden from years past. She had plans to clear away the weeds a little each day to see if any other perennials survived.

At the well, she drew up the pail with clear water and filled the basin. She scooped a little into her hand to wash the grittiness from her eyes. Her cool palms soothed the ache in her eyes, and she held them in place for a long moment, willing herself to fully awaken. She should thank her brother for tackling the woodpile and then hurry to fix him a good breakfast before he left for work.

Anna only made it partway around the cabin before her feet stalled. An all-too-familiar scarlet coat hung over the saddle on a handsome black gelding. She crept forward enough to see Benjamin wielding the axe, a growing pile of kindling at his feet.

She blinked at the sudden moisture in her eyes. Why must he keep returning and being so. . .

No. It was just her tired brain and the frustration of Ernest's absence and neglect. Sucking a deep breath, she squared her shoulders and stepped forward.

"What are you doing here?"

He looked up, a hint of a smile lifting one side of his mouth. "Good morning to you too."

She cleared the sudden tightness from her throat. "I didn't mean to sound accusing. I'm just surprised. I thought Ernest was out here." Anna didn't dare glance down and bring attention to her lack of proper attire, but the mere thought of her nightgown heated her face.

He cocked his head. "Ernest? I thought your brother's name was Frank."

Anna stared, the state of her appearance suddenly the least of her concerns. She'd forgotten the name Ernest had given. Oh, how she hated lies! But how to proceed without betraying her brother? "I've. . .I've never called him that. But you know how some are, don't want to be known by their childhood names out in the world."

A smile returned, but suspicion lingered in his gaze. "And have you always gone by Anna?"

"Always."

"Anna Wilkins."

The blood seemed to drain from her head, leaving her dizzy. She needed to move this conversation away from names before a whole can of worms dumped from the sky. But first, "Did you go by Ben or Benjamin as a child? Or some other endearment?"

He chuckled and seemed to relax. "Benji, actually."

Tension slipped from her along with a chuckle. "Benji?"

He waved her off, though his face seemed a little redder than moments ago. "Just to my mother." He raised the axe and sent it down into another log, hacking it into splinters. His sleeves were rolled to his elbows, and perspiration glistened on his brow.

"I'm sure you have a busy day. I can do that."

"I have some time. It's not like you don't have enough on your own plate, trying to get this place livable."

"It's not as though I'm on my own." She had to dissuade him and get him on his way before Ernest wakened. His horse was still in the corral, so he likely remained asleep in the loft but how much longer, with the crack of the axe against wood? "I have my brother."

"Which explains why you were shingling your roof alone and chopping logs yesterday. Obviously, your brother is very involved."

Anna stared, not sure what to do with his heated observation. "He works long hours for Mackenzie. And I am a very capable woman, Constable."

Benjamin's expression gentled. "Yes. Yes, you are, Miss Wilkins. But you shouldn't have to do all this on your own." He leaned the axe against the chopping block and took a step toward her. "I apologize if I've overstepped."

"It's not that. I'm very grateful for every time you have ridden to the rescue, but I need to do this on my own." Not because she wanted to but for Ernest's sake. And the lies he'd told.

She felt his presence behind her before he spoke.

Chapter 8

M orning, Anna. Constable."

Benjamin blew out the air from his lungs, disappointed more than he should have been at the interruption. He turned and faced Frank—or was it *Ernest*? The cold glare from Anna's brother urged him to glance to his horse, where he'd left his coat and gun belt hanging over the saddle. Benjamin kept his gaze passive and locked on the behemoth of a man. "Just being neighborly. When I was here yesterday, I couldn't help but notice this pile of logs your sister was trying to work through. Figured *someone* ought to lend a hand."

"I'd have gotten to it," Frank or Ernest grumbled. The latter seemed to suit the man better. And there was something about that name. He'd read it or one similar recently, though he couldn't place where. "Besides, it's summer. Not like we're needing much kindling yet."

"I need it for cooking," Anna said softly.

Her brother didn't so much as look at her, his gaze boring into Benjamin. "You probably mean well, but I'd appreciate it if you left my sister alone, Constable."

Benjamin held his hands out, not liking the man's tone or insinuation. "I've only been trying to help her."

"Really. Just that?"

He usually had a quick answer, but the words caught on his

tongue. What was the proper response? That he had no interest in the man's sister? He wasn't sure that was completely honest anymore. But to admit to this man, or even himself, that his initial attraction to Anna Wilkins was becoming much more than that?

"I'd like you to leave, Constable. Nothing against you personally, but we're fine here on our own."

He glanced to Anna to see what she thought of her brother's demands, but she stood stock-still, eyes closed, jaw tight. Maybe she shared the sentiments and wanted him gone. He'd heard it in her tone more than once, pushing him away even though she was grateful for his help. Representing the law, he'd gotten used to being unwelcome, but this time the cut burned deeper.

He stepped to Anna's brother and shoved the axe into his hand. The last thing the young man needed was a weapon, but at least it would keep him from throwing a punch. Maybe he'd put the axe to work. Benjamin walked to his horse, donned his coat and belt, and swung into the saddle. He reined close to Ernest, pausing only a few feet away. "If I were you, I'd be more concerned about who I was keeping company with." Benjamin nudged his horse forward before a reply could be made. Hopefully, the young man would take the warning to heart.

Benjamin whistled for Hannibal, who chased ground squirrels near the corral, and headed toward town. Ernest or Frank, or whoever he was, was easy enough to push to the back of his mind. But Anna. . . Did she share her brother's sentiments? Did she want him to stay away? Why did it matter so much to him?

He rode straight to the NWMP post, avoiding any detours and offering no more than a nod and "morning" to those he passed. He pushed into his office and dropped his hat on the desk as he sank into the chair. His weekly report was due, and the letter from his mother remained in the drawer, unanswered. Maybe he did need to go home for his mother's sake. He reached for the letter and spread it open on his desk only to stare at the words as the clock on the wall ticked away the minutes. Again and again, he pushed thoughts of Anna from his head. Two more weeks until he transported Mackenzie's funds, but after that. . .

A tap at the door brought his head up. No one ever knocked. If they needed to speak with him, the townsfolk knew they could walk right in. He stepped to the door and pulled it open to reveal the woman he'd just ridden away from.

"Anna."

She stepped in, a sigh on her lips. "You're probably thinking, 'What are you doing here?'" Her voice dropped half an octave as though to mimic his. "That would be fair," she said in her own voice. Her chin was up, but she only briefly brushed his gaze with her own. "I'm sorry about my brother. He can be. . .protective. But he shouldn't have run you off."

"I didn't consider myself 'run off,' per se." Though his pride still smarted.

"I just wanted to make sure you didn't think me ungrateful for all you've done. I love Miss Marble —"

"*Miss* Marble?"

She flashed a shy smile that was far too charming. "The cat. She's a sweetheart, though I'm still accustoming myself to her hunting habits." A cringe wrinkled her nose. "But back to what I was trying to say. Miss Marble has been a huge blessing as have the hinges. You've saved me from more than one bump and bruise and even a large dose of embarrassment." She stood close enough that he could smell a hint of lemon. Perhaps in her hair, which fell in a braid over her back. She had changed into a blue calico dress, but otherwise her appearance was unaltered from when she had stepped out of the cabin less than an hour ago, the early sunlight highlighting golden rays in her hair.

"I'm glad I was there, but I'll keep my distance, if that's what you want. You are a very capable woman." Capable. Strong.

Determined. Beautiful. Everything he desired in a woman, a partner...

Benjamin closed the door—though perhaps not the best move. That was probably all she had come to say, and the motion brought him so much nearer.

"I don't agree with what my brother said." The words came rushed, and her blue eyes flickered to his face.

His throat tightened. "That I should stay away from you?" A feat becoming more difficult by the moment.

Red bloomed in her cheeks, and she inhaled sharply. "Maybe I shouldn't have come."

"But you did." He lowered his arm from the door but didn't retreat. Wasn't sure if he could. "Why did you?"

"My brother was rude. I wanted to apologize." Her hand rose as though she would touch the wool of his coat.

"Maybe he was right." Benjamin leaned in. A little. Just to better breathe her in.

"About?" Barely a whisper on those shapely lips.

A dozen alarms sounded in his brain, warning that he wouldn't be able to reverse after crossing this line, but for the first time in his life, he let them ring and pressed his mouth against her soft cheek, catching only the corner of her lips. His fingers stole to the line of her jaw, catching a loose strand of her hair. That was all he'd intended, but he couldn't pull back. A breath away, barely touching, a growing need for more, a sudden thirst he'd never felt with such intensity.

Her head turned toward him, and their lips brushed, stayed, and moved oh so slowly, exploring, discovering, igniting the coals of affection that had been simmering deep inside. His hand slipped behind her head while the other stole behind her back. Sweetness. The taste, the sensation of touch, and blood surging through his veins. Life, stirring him awake.

Her lips moved, hesitant against his, but wanting. Enough to leave little doubt that she regarded him the same. Her brother was out of luck. There was no way he could keep his distance now.

Oh, such a feeling! As she'd never experienced before! The feel of his mouth against hers, slowly caressing, but somehow touching deeper. The aroma of leather and wool and soap teased her senses as more than just air seeped into her lungs. Hope. Awakening a hundred dreams she'd tucked away into the "someday." To be held, cherished. . .loved?

No, no, no. Too soon for that. Really, what did they know about each other? They'd barely met but a couple of weeks ago. And he was an officer of the law.

Keep your distance!

Oh, but the taste of him was so fulfilling, and the sensation of his embrace set her nerves alight. She didn't want this kiss to end.

As though in tune with her thoughts, Benjamin drew a breath away. She glanced up to see his eyes still closed, his lips still parted.

"I'm sorry," he whispered.

"Are you?" She wasn't sure where the question came from, but it would be nice to know if he did regret such a glorious moment. Had she done it poorly? This was the first time she'd allowed a man to kiss her—despite a couple of attempts made by less worthy fellows. Even if she never saw Benjamin Cole again, she wouldn't regret that kiss. Though how regretful it would be not to see him again. She waited for his answer, the ticking of a clock becoming more pronounced with each second.

He withdrew, releasing Anna and turning away. Uncertainty skittered through her.

Pulse pounding in her ears, Anna backed away as well. Against the door. Maybe now was a good time to escape, save him from an answer. She pulled on the latch and slipped into the sunshine, much brighter than when she'd entered the build-ing only minutes ago. The streets seemed busier as well, folks rushing to and fro to start their morning. Now removed from the intimacy of moments ago, her brain cleared. She should have stayed home and let Ernest's words stand. Nothing could come of falling for a lawman who didn't even know her real name.

Ernest needs to learn from the consequences due him.

Not the first time she'd heard the voice, but again she pushed it deep. He was her younger brother, and she loved him. He had a chance to change, to turn over a new leaf. How could she threaten that?

"Anna."

The call reached her as she put her foot in the stirrup. Ben-jamin's voice held an apology, but she wasn't sure she wanted to hear it. How rude to ride off without letting him speak, though. What to do, what to do? She couldn't very well continue to hang here.

"Anna, please wait." He was almost to her.

She glanced over her shoulder, and the look in his eyes dropped her back to the ground. "Yes, Constable?" Keep things proper between them. Keep her distance.

"I don't want to stay away, despite your brother's request."

She turned completely.

"I want to help you in any way I can." He continued toward her, closing the distance. "I want to know more about you. To learn your likes, dislikes, your hopes and dreams." He stopped toe to toe with her. "And someday soon, I'd like to kiss you again."

Oh, please. She closed her eyes, needing to block him out for one moment, to regain her bearings, and think straight. How could this ever work? He knew her mother's maiden name and believed it to be her own, her brother was wanted by the law just south of the border, and. . . "I'd like that too."

Chapter 9

Anna smiled at the sound of hooves and Hannibal's happy yip. She hurried out of the cabin. Benjamin sat high in his saddle, a blue-flowered handkerchief in hand. "I believe this is yours, miss."

"Thank you." She took it from him, a smile already making her cheeks ache from its breadth. She tucked it into her pocket for another day. A simple handkerchief in the lone pine at the edge of the property. What could be more clandestine? A simple signal to let him know she could use a hand with something around the homestead and that Ernest was away. Wood that needed chopping. A fence in need of a new rail. A gate broken loose from its top hinge. Simple rules were in place to keep things proper—no entering the cabin, as they had no chaperone; no lingering after the work was done; and no more than the simplest peck on the cheek to show the growing affection between them.

Life had never been sweeter—but oh, how she longed for more. Longer conversations, unfettered by time or secrets still between them. To truly kiss him again. To be held in his arms and forget about everything else for a good long while.

"Did that rope not hold?" Benjamin asked, dismounting. He had tied a broken fence rail in place with hopes of keeping her adventuresome mare in place.

"No, it's done its job. And if you have anywhere else you need to be, I will make do well enough on my own." Mostly, she had been looking for an excuse to see him.

"I can stay a short while." He tied his horse and moved to her. "I do have some important business this afternoon though." He grasped her arms and pressed a gentle kiss to her forehead. "Until then, I am at your service."

"It's just the garden. I found an old plow buried under some briers, and I think we have the harness, but I must admit that's a little out of my expertise." Not that she couldn't have figured it out, but he would make the task easier and more enjoyable.

"Probably beyond mine as well, but let's see what we can figure out together." Benjamin slid his fingers between hers, and they walked to the edge of the garden where she'd left the plow, cleaned and with harnessing lying close.

"I've tried to mark out any plants I want to keep, but the rest needs to go." She had pulled enough weeds by hand to build a hut.

They worked to hitch Cocoa and began the slow plod down the length of the garden, the three blades turning up neat furrows—at least they would have been neat if not for the tall weeds piling in their wake.

"You should rake up all these weeds and burn them away from the garden. The last thing you want is the seeds sprouting for the next seven years to haunt you."

Seven years? She could almost imagine still being here after all that time. Maybe not in this cabin, but in this country, near this man.

She walked beside him as he directed the plow, their conversation ebbing and flowing easily. Because he hadn't asked her anything more about her brother. Her family, yes. She'd shared about life back in Baltimore with lots of siblings and the best parents a girl could hope for. His family, though, he hadn't shared much about.

"Is your mother much of a gardener?" She crossed her fingers that this segue would encourage him to more than the few non-descriptive grunts she usually got from him on this subject.

"A little. She enjoys flowers."

Encouraged, Anna continued. "What are her favorites?"

"Last time I was home, she had planted a row of daisies along the front of the house. Quite impressive when they bloom for such a small flower."

"Like little bursts of sun, yellow with brilliant white rays."

A smile turned up the corners of his mouth, but his eyes remained solemn.

"Did she do much with berries or vegetables? I must say, I am quite excited about those raspberry canes I found." Not much fruit setting this year, but next year, with the grass cleared away from their roots, there might be a decent harvest.

"No." Benjamin's tone had changed, turned monotone. "My father was the vegetable gardener."

"Was?" Not the present tense like when he spoke of his mother. She felt the pain seep off him and settle in her own heart. She laid her hand on his arm.

"He's not well."

"I'm sorry. Is he—"

"They don't expect him to live much longer."

"Oh, Benjamin. . ." Anna's steps faltered. She could only imagine hearing that news about her father, a bear of a man with endless strength. The thought of someday losing him. . . "Can't you get away? Surely your superiors would understand and let you go long enough to see him again. What are you still doing here?"

Benjamin kept moving. "I'm needed here right now. Too much is happening."

Did he mean with her or work? She hurried to keep pace. "Didn't you tell me your family lived in Ontario? That's, what, straight north of Ohio? A couple of days on the train, and you would be home. The total trip would take less than a week, two with more time to visit."

"About that."

"So leave. Go be with your father."

"I don't know that I want to."

The words were spoken so softly, Anna questioned if she'd heard them right. "Why?"

"Whoa." Benjamin stopped the horse but didn't look at her. "We didn't part on the best of terms." He gave a low grunt that reminded her of her brother. "Despite what my mother says, I find it hard to believe he really wants me to come."

"I doubt that very much," she whispered and reached for his hand. It still gripped the worn handles of the plow, so she set hers over his. "He's your father."

He glanced at her out of the corner of his eye. "Not according to him."

"What?"

"He disowned me. I chose the law over the church and, according to him, there couldn't be a much greater sin. To turn from my calling, what I had been raised to."

Understanding dawned. "Instead of becoming a preacher, you joined the Mounted Police."

"I was so tired of being forced into a role I didn't fit. By the time I was old enough to head to the seminary, I didn't care if I never read another scripture again. Everything was too confining. When I read the bulletin asking for young men to serve in the West, all I could think of was adventure and freedom."

She could hear Ernest's argument with their own parents only a couple of years earlier. Adventure and freedom. But Benjamin had taken a very different path. "While still doing some good."

"I think I was hoping to prove that to him."

"How long has it been since you last saw your father?"

Benjamin blew out a breath. "A little more than seven years."

Anna tightened her hold on his hand. "That's too long. Surely he's softened by now."

"My mother seems to think so. She's been begging me to return, and I probably should for her sake."

"I think you should too." Though the thought of him leaving. . . How she wished she was bold enough to offer to go with him, to be at his side and support him. But their relationship was still in its infancy, despite already questioning how she would get by without him.

———

Later that day, Benjamin stalked away from the telegraph office. He'd finally sent his request for leave, something he'd planned to do—should have done—weeks ago, and if approval was given, he would leave as soon as this business with Mackenzie was finished. He shook his head as he pushed into the jail, Hannibal at his side. He had been out to the Mackenzie ranch earlier that afternoon to solidify the details and plans for Friday—two days from now. An uneasiness soured his stomach.

Benjamin dropped his hat on the desk and lowered into his chair. Sweat moistened his spine. This July weather was much too hot for full uniform, but he only loosened the top button of his coat. Plenty else might have led to the unsettled feeling. He hated sneaking around behind Anna's brother's back. It was what she wanted, but not the way he did things. Better to face conflict head on—even if it included coming fist to fist with the man. How long did she want to keep their relationship from her family? Or did she plan to sneak away with him to get married when the time came?

Married?

Benjamin sat upright. There was no longer an if or maybe in his head when it came to sharing his life with Anna. If she would have him, he wanted her as his wife.

He almost laughed out loud at the thought, and Hannibal's

head jerked up before resting back on his front legs. Benjamin never expected himself to marry while still serving in the force, but now he couldn't imagine remaining alone. Not while Anna Wilkins walked the earth.

He stood and started to pace. First the job for Mackenzie, then the trip home, and after that he could focus on his plans with Anna. For the first time since leaving her home that morning, a smile teased his mouth. And for the first time in years, he glanced heavenward and acknowledged that maybe God was smiling down on him after all.

The creak of hinges turned him toward the door and Mackenzie's fourteen-year-old son. Panting, the boy held out a folded paper. "Father sent this."

Benjamin hurried to open the note and scan the page. A change in plans. He'd ride today.

Chapter 10

Anna was pulling weeds from the raspberry patch when Ernest arrived home, his horse frothy and breathing heavily. She hurried across the yard. "What's wrong?"

He swung down, shaking his head. "Nothing. Just in a hurry."

She narrowed her eyes at him. "Why are you so early?" He didn't usually arrive until evening—never midday.

He shoved the stirrup out of the way and loosened the cinch. "My shift got changed. I need to go back this evening."

"Oh." She fetched the curry brush and began working the length of the animal's neck. It wasn't the first time his shift had changed due to one of the other hands becoming ill or getting hurt, but tension drew tight the muscles of her brother's neck. "Nothing else?"

He glared at her and hung the saddle over the fence. "Leave it alone." He led the horse to the corral without letting her finish. She dropped the brush back in the pail and turned to the cabin. Best fix him dinner. Hopefully, a hungry stomach was the worst of what was going on.

She had barely reached the door when the pound of hooves again pulled her attention to the road. She didn't recognize the horse or its rider. But she didn't like the hardness of the gaze he turned her way. Nor anything about him, really. She ducked inside the cabin. The last thing she wanted was a conversation with the dark stranger. She'd let Ernest send him on his way.

From the cabin, she listened for the horse's retreat to the main road, but all she heard was the murmur of voices. She peeked out the window. The stranger and Ernest stood by the shed in deep conversation. Neither seemed pleased. What was going on? Stomach knotted, Anna slipped out the front of the cabin. Both men faced mostly away, so she hurried around the corner and crouched to listen. Only snippets of words until Ernest looked to the cabin, his face somber. "I don't like that Mackenzie changed his plans. Or how much he's been talking to that Mountie."

"Won't matter. I know the route, and it'll only be one man. And the cash, Ernest. More than enough to get your sister out of this cabin and set yourselves up on your own ranch like you want. Freedom. It's all sitting there in Nanton, and soon it'll be on its way to us."

Ernest frowned but nodded.

No! He couldn't possibly be considering holding up someone carrying cash back from Nanton. Her chest constricted, making air scant and her head light. Everything she'd given up—her home, employment—all to help her brother change, and for nothing? He was about to throw everything they had built here away for a few dollars.

Including her relationship with Benjamin.

Sourness crept up the back of her throat. What to do, what to do? She couldn't talk him out of it. She'd failed in the past. He would tell her she'd misunderstood and there was nothing going on. The only one who would listen to her was Benjamin. . .but then he'd know. Everything. Every ounce of information she'd held back, all their dark secrets. And Ernest would no longer be safe. He'd be locked away for his crimes because of her.

It's not your fault.

Why did it feel like it was?

It's not your fault.

The whisper in her head, the one she'd pushed aside for so long, returned with force. She couldn't protect her brother from the consequences of what he did, and she had to stop trying. Anna gripped the cross hanging from her neck. "Lord, help me do what I must. And please, help Ernest, keep him safe, and don't let him do this thing. Please."

She remained crouched behind the cabin until the stranger rode off, then loaded her arms with firewood, something to explain her presence should Ernest see her. Thankfully, he stood across the pasture, shoulders stiff, head bent forward. What was going through his mind? How could he go through with robbery from his own employer?

Inside the cabin, she hurried with dinner, frying a can of beans to go with the leftover biscuits from breakfast. Her mind spun with her brother's conversation and the one she must have with Benjamin. What would he think of her for not telling him the truth from the start? Would he want anything to do with her once he knew that her brother was a villain?

Tears beaded in her eyes. The problem was, Ernest wasn't a villain. Not long ago, he had been one of the kindest, gentlest boys she'd known, before a streak of rebellion had sneaked in. She'd give anything to bring that little boy back again.

His shadow filled the door. He said nothing as he washed his hands and seated himself at the table. She loaded his plate, and he ate slowly, chewing each bite much longer than usual.

When he finished, he met her gaze only briefly. "I need to head back to Mackenzie's. I'll see you in the morning." He started toward the door.

"Ernest."

He paused.

Don't do this. Please, it's not too late, her heart screamed, but instead, Anna swallowed her protest and whispered, "I love you."

He stood in place a long time. Not moving forward or back.

Finally, his head dipped in a nod, and he jogged to the corrals.

Anna held herself in place, listening to his every move. The creak of the saddle as he mounted. The pounding of hooves on the too-dry path. Still, she waited, her pulse pounding just as loudly. One more minute, then a sprint to saddle Cocoa. She rode hard to Caylee, not letting herself think of what awaited her. She would confess all she knew to Benjamin and try to trust God with the rest. Her thoughts still buzzed and her lungs burned when she reined Cocoa in front of the jail. She lunged up the two steps, across the short length of boardwalk, and thudded her fist against the door.

Across the street, a horse whinnied, and she glanced behind. A man was loading a wagon with sacks from the mercantile.

She focused back on the door and knocked again. "Benjamin?"

Nothing from within. She tried the latch, but it didn't give. Could he have gone home already, or was he out on his rounds? She leaned her forehead against the door and clamped her eyes closed against the helplessness welling.

"You looking for the constable?"

She spun to the man who had been loading the wagon, now halfway across the street. "Have you seen him?"

"Rode out toward the south not two hours ago."

"Do you know where he was going?"

"Not for sure, but my guess would be Nanton. That's the route he was on."

Anna sucked a breath. Not Nanton. He couldn't be the one Ernest and his friend were gunning for. He'd be riding into an ambush set by her own brother. "How do I get to Nanton?"

Benjamin shoved the pouch stuffed with cash into his saddlebag and tightened the straps. The tension in his shoulders spiked pain through his head. He climbed into his saddle then offered a brief nod to the bank clerk who had followed him out, no doubt fighting the same misgivings as he. Nothing for it now. Benjamin tightened his grasp on the reins and directed his horse out of town. As soon as he breached the edge of the bustling community, he gave the animal his head and encouraged him to a lope, a pace they could keep for a while and still put miles under them. He wanted to make Nanton within an hour and lock the cash up nice and tight in the jail until the exchange tomorrow.

A few miles outside of Nanton, the ground sloped toward Willow Creek. He slowed his pace as he approached the bridge and searched the ridges on the other side. The murmur of voices rose with the rush of water. . .or was he imagining it? Imagination or not, the hair bristled on the back of his neck. He itched to take his revolver to hand, but that wasn't how he was trained. Mounties only drew a weapon as a last resort. Not when they jumped at shadows.

Halfway across the bridge, a shout rose clearer. A shot cut through the rush. A bullet bit the wood beneath his horse.

"Yah!" He dove over his saddle horn and kicked his horse to a run as a second shot sounded from somewhere on the ridge. Up the bank and across the open prairie, everything in him shouted to find cover and figure out how to take the ambushers down, but that was not his mission, and he was quite sure of one's identity already. His ride had been moved earlier because of Mackenzie's suspicions. All Benjamin had to do was identify the man as Norman Drake. He glanced behind.

No sign of the shooter, but horses stood on the horizon. A black like Drake's and. . . Benjamin veered his course just a little. No shots followed, but he would be out of range of any revolver and most rifles by now. He needed a closer look at the horses. A black and a bay, white splashed across the latter's face. His gut clenched. Again, he glanced to the ridge, but no one showed themselves. They were hiding somewhere among the tall grasses and brush. Going back would be handing them the cash. He turned toward Caylee, pushing his gelding to a breakneck gait.

Another horse appeared on the horizon, its rider small with blue skirts billowing. He veered in her direction, and hooves ate up the distance between them. "What are you doing out here?"

Instead of answering, Anna swung from her saddle and rushed to him with eyes brimming and red. He slid to the ground, and she threw her arms around him. "You're alive."

Her grip suggested an honest belief that he might not be. And after seeing her brother's horse... How much did she know?

"I was going to try to warn you, but I didn't know it would be you. I overheard them talking. Ernest and another fellow. About the money. And robbery." She buried her face against his chest.

He glanced behind to make sure he hadn't been followed, but even then he couldn't allow himself to return her embrace. He was on duty, and she was his only witness to a possible crime. "Let's get you back to Caylee. Then we'll talk."

Chapter 11

The sun kissed the horizon by the time they rode into Caylee. Neither of them spoke during the ride—not that their pace encouraged it. Benjamin kept them at a steady run, not trusting that Ernest or his partner wouldn't make another attempt. Anna could have been sent to slow him up in case they missed the first time.

No. He refused to believe that she would purposefully deceive him—except hadn't she already? He shook his head as he dropped from his horse and moved to assist Anna. She'd kept up with him all the way back to Caylee, and both their horses glistened with sweat, but there were other things to see to first.

"Can you go across the street and ask Hal to come?"

Anna glanced across the street and then at him. "Who?"

"Hal Rogers, your landlord at the livery."

Her eyes lit as the connection was made.

"Tell him to see to the horses." He waited until she hustled across the street before emptying his saddlebag and hauling the pouch of cash into his office. He tossed it onto one of the cots, draped a blanket over top, and locked the cell. Best he could do for the night.

Benjamin opened the door and looked to the fading sun. He'd like to leave someone here and ride after the bandits, but he'd have no light to track them by. Hopefully, they thought they'd retained their anonymity, and he could round them up tomorrow. Would Anna give him the evidence he needed against them?

As though sensing his thoughts or maybe just his gaze, Anna looked up. She walked a couple of steps ahead of Hal, her expression unreadable.

"Take them back to the stable with you, will you?" Benjamin called out to the livery owner. "We'll be over in a while." To Anna, he held out an open palm and motioned for her to join him inside. Her head dropped forward as she obeyed.

He closed the door, lit a couple lamps to hold the deepening shadows at bay, and then set a chair in the middle of the floor for her. "Have a seat."

"I think I'd rather stand," she murmured.

"Please." As much as he'd also like to pace as they discussed what she knew, sitting across from someone was much more effective during an interrogation. He lowered into his chair behind his desk and waited for her to settle. The lamplight danced across the contours of her face and lit highlights of gold in her hair. Maybe this wasn't the most effective strategy in this case. "Tell me what you heard."

She swallowed hard. "A man I've never seen before came to the cabin this afternoon. He and Ernest were talking out by the corral, but I could tell Ernest was upset, so I snuck out to listen."

Benjamin's chest constricted. He didn't like her taking that risk. What if she'd been seen? Would her brother have protected her from Drake? "Go on."

"Ernest was upset. Said he didn't like how much Mr. Mackenzie had been talking to you." Her brows pushed together. "Or that. . .he'd changed his plan?"

Benjamin nodded. "I wasn't supposed to go until tomorrow."

"The other man said they had nothing to worry about. Something about money and how easy it would be for them. . ." She met his gaze and moistened her lips. "To get it."

"All they had to do was shoot me off my horse while I was crossing the bridge or riding up the slope." It actually didn't make sense that they'd missed. Drake had a reputation as a marksman.

A miracle?

Anna stared at him, eyes wide and mirroring what he was starting to understand for himself—how close he had come to death.

"Is that it? All you heard?" he prompted.

She nodded.

He'd get her description of the other man later. It was time to dig deeper. Benjamin leaned his elbows on his desk. "Is this the first time your brother's been involved in a robbery?"

Her gaze dropped to the floor. She shook her head.

"When?"

Silence hung between them like a noose waiting for a villain. Her eyes slid closed. "Months ago. In Montana."

So that was why they had come north. Hadn't he suspected as much? Running from the law. "And murder?"

Her head snapped up, and she shook it vehemently. "He's never killed anyone. I know he hasn't. I know what he's done is wrong, but please, he's not evil." Unshed tears glistened in the low light. "He's my little brother."

"He's not little anymore." Quite the opposite. "But you've been trying to protect him, unconcerned about the harm he was causing others." His words came out edged, but couldn't she see her sweet little brother had attempted to shoot him?

Her mouth hung loose but not from shock. He wasn't daft enough to misread the pain etched in her face.

"Ernest. Not Frank Wilkins. What else do you need to tell me about your brother?" And herself. How many lies had she stacked between them?

"Ernest Köhler." Clutching the cross around her neck, she

cleared her throat and straightened her shoulders. "Wilkins is our mother's maiden name."

"Anna Köhler." He slumped into his chair, an unfamiliar pain swirling in his chest. "So you did lie to me."

Anna couldn't take it. Not the hurt in his eyes or everything horrible he must think of her now. She pushed to her feet, her head shaking. "I didn't lie. Not intentionally or directly."

He also stood, a scowl forming creases on his brow and shadowing his eyes. "You let me assume a lie. How is that different?"

"I kept my mouth closed to protect my brother. What would you expect me to do, announce to the local Mountie that my brother is wanted and running from the law? Is that what you would have done?" She looked him up and down. His perfect uniform, his squared shoulders, the look of betrayal in his eyes. "I suppose it is, isn't it? What does family or love mean when duty calls?"

Anna charged the door. She'd failed both him and her brother, and the shame of it burned through her along with a large dose of hurt. Apparently, he didn't care enough to even try to understand her actions.

His boots sounded on the wooden sidewalk behind her. "You're going to lecture me on love?"

She gritted her teeth and spun. "You think you don't need one? Or is it love you don't need?"

"It only seems to complicate my life." He threw up his hands. "There are always strings attached, someone wanting something from me."

A flame flared in her chest, and her breath trembled from her. "I wanted nothing from you. I tried over and over to push you away. You're the one who kept coming back, shoving your way into my life, my feelings. You were playing the hero, not just being a 'good neighbor.' You might stop and ask what *you* wanted from me."

The words escaped her before she became aware of the attention they had garnered from every other person on the street. Heat singed her cheeks, and she spun away before they made more of a scene. Her breaking heart was not for the entertainment of the community.

Anna jogged across the street toward the stables. She could see her horse standing in the large double doorway, the livery owner busy with the curry brush. "Where's my saddle?" She saw it even as she asked and grabbed it from the nearby stand. The man jumped out of the way, and she tossed it over the animal's back. She glanced behind to see Benjamin fighting with his keys and the front door of his office. She hurried with her straps, finishing as he reached her.

He looked as if he wanted to say something more, but so many eyes were still on them. He sent a frustrated glance over his shoulder at their audience as the muscles worked in his jaw.

"I don't think you should go home tonight." His voice came as a growl. "Not alone."

"I'm quite sure you have more important things to do, Constable, than act as my nanny, but I can't very well wait in town all evening." Anna pulled herself into the saddle. "Besides, I'm perfectly safe. He's my brother, remember?" She hadn't made it more than a few yards before new tears blurred her vision. She had no reason to be angry with him. She was the one in the wrong. But what was the chance that anything she could say would bridge the gulf she had dug between them? He would never see her the same, never trust her again, and, as much as it hurt, she couldn't blame him in the least.

By the time she reached home, the reality of the situation had settled through her. There would be no reconciliation. Ernest would be on the run if Benjamin didn't bring him to justice first. Either way, Anna had no place here anymore. Her little cabin nestled so sweetly in this valley would no longer hold anything for her. She had no employment other than keeping house for her brother. What was left for her but to return south of the border?

It was time to go home to Baltimore.

She put Cocoa out to pasture and started toward the cabin. Strange. From a distance, the door looked ajar. The sun sank quickly behind the mountains, leaving long shadows, and she suddenly regretted not heeding Benjamin and staying in town. She moved slowly, wishing Hannibal were by her side. Or his owner. That would be nice too.

She bit her lip as another tear slipped down her cheek. No, it was better he wasn't here. He'd already wasted too much time rescuing her.

The door was open a full foot. Anything could have pushed inside. And Marble could have escaped. A lantern would be nice, but it was in the house.

"Lord, protect me," she prayed as she inched toward the doorway. "Hello!" The soft echo of her voice sent a chill through her, but if a wild animal had sheltered inside, better to frighten it into action while she was still without. "Anybody?" Talking aloud made her feel foolish, but she was too frightened to stop. "Come out if you're in there."

Nothing but the rush of the wind over the hills. She stood to the side and pushed the door the rest of the way open. The moonlight cut a path across the floor. All was still. Everything as she'd left it. She stepped inside.

A black shadow landed with a thud beside her.

She jumped, a scream scratching her throat before her brain registered Marble rubbing against her leg. Anna released a shaky breath and hurried to the lantern and her stash of matches. She lit the room, searched the corners, and then slammed the door shut.

It rocked open again, the same as she'd found it. The latch

hadn't caught. But she had closed it well when she'd gone to find Benjamin, so someone must have been here since.

Heart pounding, Anna closed the door securely and then climbed to the loft. Ernest's bedroll and clothes were gone. Back down the ladder, she searched the room. The biscuits she'd baked that morning were also missing, replaced by a small piece of paper. Her hand trembled as she reached for it.

Bang, bang, bang thundered against wood. The door flew open behind her, and she spun to Benjamin, who stood with gun in hand.

"Are you hurt?"

"Why would I be hurt?"

"You screamed. I thought. . ." He glanced around the room, searching the shadows. Finally, his chest sank and his shoulders dropped.

"Ernest isn't here." She looked at the paper and scanned the short message. "But he was." She held out the note, unable to keep her hand steady.

Benjamin locked his revolver back in its holster and took the sheet from her. He read aloud. "'Anna, I ran into some trouble and have to leave, but know that what I did was for you. Please go home. Ernest.'"

Tears prickled her eyes, the rumble of Benjamin's voice bringing to life her brother's farewell. And his own. A numbing ache spread through her, and she sank into a chair.

"Home? Back to your family in Maryland?"

She nodded. Home. How displaced from this rolling prairie in the shadow of the Rockies. An ocean instead of grasslands as far as her eyes could see. Anna looked up at the man in his red coat, flat-brimmed Stetson now in his hand.

He handed her the letter. "Where do you think your brother will go?"

"I don't know." She had thought Caylee was as far as they'd need to run.

Benjamin cleared his throat and straightened. "I'll be riding out first thing in the morning to see what I can find. At some point, I'll have more questions for you."

She nodded again, not trusting her voice.

He stood in the doorway for another minute or so before he backed away. His voice mumbled just outside the door, and a moment later his dog trotted into the cabin. The door smacked closed in his wake, and Benjamin's boots whispered out his goodbye.

Anna sank to the floor and wrapped her arms around Hannibal's neck before letting the tears fall.

Chapter 12

Benjamin waited while the men concluded their business, shook hands, and parted ways, an armed guard of three men now overseeing the money's protection. Back in his office, he closed his eyes and allowed them to rest. He'd not slept last night after his trek to Anna's to make sure she was safe, replaying yesterday's events and her confession. He'd been an idiot to let down his guard. He'd always suspected something about her brother, and now he had the confirmation. But how to find him and his partner? How far would they go? And what had spooked them?

Unless they had seen Anna with him. Would she be safe?

"Here's your mail, Constable."

He jerked his eyes open and extended his hand to the mercantile owner, who also housed the post office. Usually, he didn't deliver, but Benjamin appreciated the gesture today. "Thanks." He took the single letter and glanced at the return address. His heart thudded. Mother. Had something changed, or was this her usual correspondence? The past few weeks seemed something of a blur now, and he was too tired to deal with anything more. He folded the missive and tucked it into his pocket before striding across the street for his horse. He'd go to the bridge where the shooting had taken place and begin his search from there. The descriptions of Köhler and Drake had already been telegrammed to the nearest posts, so he wasn't the only one looking.

The ride south did little to clear Benjamin's brain, especially as it kept circling back to Anna and every conversation they'd had. It all made perfect sense now. Her distrust and early attempts to keep him at arm's length. Her brother's coolness. But, try as he might, Benjamin couldn't fault her actions. Not if she truly believed her brother had changed. She'd come to the law with the truth when it mattered.

The gurgling rush of Willow Creek refocused his thoughts on his mission. Ernest and his companion had been hiding on the ridge. He followed it toward the west to where the grass and brush had been pushed down. A rifle lay near the edge. Benjamin dismounted and crouched near the weapon that could have easily ended his life. Now it lay abandoned. But why? He closed his eyes and thought back to his crossing of the bridge. The first shot had certainly been from a rifle, but the second had a different sound. Probably a revolver. And both had missed.

No answer presented itself, so he reached for the rifle—and froze. Droplets of blood smeared across the dark wood of the butt. He searched the grass and saw more stains. He stood, and his gaze snagged on what he had first assumed was a rock behind the low saskatoon bushes. His gut flip-flopped as he moved to stand over the body of Norman Drake.

"No." He gritted his teeth as he examined the man shot through the chest from behind. Anna's stricken face flashed through his mind, and his stomach soured more. How would he break it to her that being wanted for attempted robbery was the least of her brother's worries? Murder could get a man hung.

Benjamin rode hard back to Caylee and telegrammed the situation to the nearest post. Willow Creek was the border of two territories, so he would gladly turn over the removal of Drake's body to the neighboring NWMP post. His focus was to track down Anna's brother before someone else did and to make sure Ernest was brought in alive.

Benjamin picked up the trail easily enough near the old cabin Anna had somehow transformed into a home. How ungrateful a creature was her brother to put her through this?

But I did it for you.

The sentence in Ernest's note had rung strange last night when he'd read it, but now it pestered him with foreboding. What had Ernest meant? That he'd attempted the robbery for her? Or that he'd killed a man?

Benjamin rode away without disturbing the cabin. He wasn't prepared to tell her what more he'd discovered. Not yet. Instead, he followed Ernest's tracks north. Benjamin had figured he'd head that direction—south held nothing for him now. Though, if all he was wanted for was a robbery south of the border, he'd be safer facing those crimes.

While he rode, Benjamin played scenario after scenario through his head. Had Ernest and Drake fought over their plan? Over how they would divide the money? Or how they would get the money?

I did it for you.

The easiest way to get the cash from Benjamin was over his dead body. No witnesses. No having to hide away, a dozen Mounted Police itching to bring the killer to justice for gunning down one of their own. Had Ernest Köhler decided the cash wasn't worth killing for?

No, he'd shot Drake sure enough.

For you.

For the love of a sister who had come to care for a Mountie?

If that was true, how was Benjamin supposed to bring in a man who had saved his life? Even given the circumstances, a judge could rule either way, and Ernest's life would hang in the balance.

But Benjamin knew his duty.

What does family and love mean when duty calls?

Benjamin pushed Anna's words aside. She didn't understand. He rode hard, having lost Ernest's trail amid the well-beaten tracks left by the day-to-day trek toward Mackenzie land. If only he'd brought Hannibal with him, but leaving the dog with Anna brought more peace of mind. The direction made sense. Ernest would keep off the main roads but make his way north, probably as far as Calgary. Though, if wanted for murder, he might go a lot farther.

Dropping down into a coulee, Benjamin crossed the Highwood River and then searched the banks for fresh tracks. The ground was soft, and deep hoofmarks confirmed his suspicion. Ernest's mount had indeed crossed recently, and his trail was marked, leading into a cluster of willows and to a campsite. Must have made it this far the night before. How hard had he ridden today?

As Benjamin mounted, a twig snapped behind him. Then he heard the rustling of a branch. Hair rising on the back of his neck, he slid to the ground and put the horse between him and the sound. He'd been shot at enough for one week. "Köhler?"

"How'd you find me?"

Benjamin released the air from his lungs and peeked over his horse to where the large man stepped from the brush, revolver raised. "Thought you'd be a lot farther by now. Not that it'll do you much good. Every Mountie between here and Edmonton has your description."

"You suggesting I turn myself over to you? Not much on going to jail."

Benjamin kept eye contact while easing his revolver from its holster. "How long do you think you can keep running? You're wanted in two countries now."

Ernest took a step, gun leveled at Benjamin's head. "Anna was supposed to keep her mouth shut." He swore. "She had to get all tender-eyed over a lawman."

"You could have reformed while you had the chance." Benjamin brought his revolver up but kept it out of sight. He'd rather not shoot the man or be shot in return. "Maybe it's not too late."

Ernest barked out a laugh as bitter as it was sorrowful. "You know it's too late, Constable. I never killed a man before." He looked like he might lose his breakfast over the thought of it.

Benjamin lowered his gun and stepped around the back of his horse. "You saved my life, didn't you?"

The young man met his gaze.

"I doubt you intend to take it now."

Ernest stared down his sights at him, his hand not as steady as a moment ago. "Do you love her?"

Anna flashed across Benjamin's mind, and he felt the nod come on its own. "I do." More than he wanted to admit. Thoughts of her filled his chest with a tenderness he'd never experienced before.

Ernest released the revolver, and it thudded to the ground. Benjamin was holstering his own when the young man spun and sprinted into the trees. With a curse, Benjamin raced after him. A branch swung back, taking off his hat and possibly a little skin above his eyebrow. In the center of the thicket stood Ernest's bay. The horse shifted nervously as his owner raced to him and grabbed the rope to pull him free. The animal was already moving forward while Ernest took hold of the saddle horn.

With a sudden lunge, Benjamin threw himself forward and grabbed the larger man around the torso. They fell forward together under the horse, which thankfully sidestepped them without clipping anyone in the brain with his granite-like hooves.

Ernest rolled and plowed a fist into Benjamin's face. "Why couldn't you have stayed away like I told you to?"

A burst of pain and black splotched his vision. He scrambled for some distance and to regain his feet. "Would that have made it easier to let him shoot me?"

"Obviously." Ernest found his feet as well and grabbed for Benjamin's shoulders while jerking a knee toward his gut.

Benjamin caught the thrust with his arms and then jerked them up to ward off the fury of limbs that might as well be clubs. Almost six feet tall, Benjamin had never considered himself a small man, but suddenly he felt an awful lot like David in his Goliath-fighting years. He ducked another punch and tossed out one of his own that made contact with Ernest's jaw. No matter what he felt for the man's sister, he still had a job to do while keeping his own skin intact.

In a tussle, they again tumbled to the ground, where they grappled for the upper hand and to keep from getting walloped too badly. Anna's brother had a painful amount of strength behind his blows, but finally, panting and pouring blood from his nose, Benjamin got Ernest's arm pinned to his back and pressed a handcuff around his wrist. The larger man sagged against the ground, seemingly accepting his fate. He allowed Benjamin to shackle his second wrist.

"Thanks." He helped Ernest to his feet and walked him to his horse.

Ernest grunted his reply. "Do you figure they'll hang me?"

Benjamin supported the man as he climbed into his saddle and then took the reins to lead the horse. He had no guarantees. Not for Ernest or his sister. He couldn't help but wish he had never caught up with the man.

Anna sat outside of the empty NWMP post, nausea churning her insides. She'd been unable to stand the silence of the cabin any longer, but waiting in town did little for her nerves. A horse whinnied in the north, and her head swung in that direction. Just a silver-haired cowboy heading out of town.

She tapped her foot against the boardwalk, all she could do to remain in place as she scanned the horizon in every visible direction. Two forms approached from the west, the sun at their backs. She jumped to her feet, any question as to their identities quickly fading. The flat-brimmed Stetson set off a distinct profile, and not many men were the size of her brother.

Anna wrung her hands, uncertain what she felt beyond the strange haze of numbness and anxiety. She'd fought with how to pray all morning. For Benjamin's safety. For Ernest to turn himself in. . .or to escape? She focused on her brother, her feelings in even more of a tussle when it came to the scarlet-clad Mountie.

Her heart squeezed at the dried blood on Benjamin's face and the bruising around his left eye. Her brother seemed to have fared much better in their obvious scuffle.

"Why, Ernest? Why did you do it?"

He looked down at the ground and answered nothing while Benjamin led him inside the jail. She followed. "Please, may I speak with him?"

Benjamin looked to her brother, who shook his head. "Give him some time."

Insides in a tangle and heartsick, Anna watched as Benjamin locked the cell door behind her brother. The click sank through her, and she turned back outside. *Oh, Ernest.*

A few minutes passed before Benjamin joined her on the boardwalk. She felt a wince at the blue growing out from around his eye and the dried blood on his lip and the front of his uniform—crimson against the scarlet. The need to touch his brow and ask him if he was all right itched like a festering mosquito bite. But that was not her place anymore, nor would he appreciate her concern. Better to focus on her brother and his needs. "What's going to happen to him?"

"I don't know. If it had just been attempted robbery. . ." Benjamin shook his head. "Homicide changes everything."

Anna's head spun. "What? No one was killed."

Benjamin gave her a thin smile—more of a cringe. "Ernest

shot the man he was working with."

She felt for the side of the building, her legs losing strength. Murder? Ernest couldn't have. This was a mistake. "I don't believe it."

She felt Benjamin's hand warm her arm and wanted to lean into him, soak up his strength, while he told her everything would be all right, her brother would be safe. Safe from the law. Safe from Constable Cole. She clamped her eyes closed.

"I'll do everything in my power to help him."

Anna shook her head and stepped away. How could he, when it conflicted with everything he was, everything he stood for. The very things she loved about him held them apart.

Chapter 13

In the morning light, Benjamin stared at the thin strip of paper delivered to his hand minutes earlier. He sank to the edge of his desk.

YOUR FATHER PASSED AWAY LAST NIGHT *Stop* PLEASE COME HOME.

"Bad news?" Ernest asked from his cell.

"My father." An image rose in Benjamin's mind, but not the one he had locked in place for the past seven years. Not the hard-faced dictator, but the half-smiling man who had taken him fishing and patted his back when he'd excelled in his studies. "He's dead."

Vocalizing it only pressed the reality of the words deeper into his chest. His father was dead, and suddenly, instead of all the hurtful words that had passed between them and the arguments they'd had, all he could think of was the tales Papa had told by the fireplace during cold winter evenings before bed and the way he'd mess Benjamin's hair and tell him he'd done well.

How he craved that now.

"Were you close?"

He shook his head, but memories kept surfacing from where he'd buried them behind anger and hurt. The man who had taught him to seek God, reading out loud from the Bible every evening. Talks about God by the riverbank. "At least, not for a long time."

"Seems the way of it," Ernest murmured.

Benjamin reached into the pocket of his coat, fishing out the letter from his mother he had forgotten. He tore the edge of the envelope, heart squeezing, part of him not wishing to know what she had to say.

But the handwriting wasn't hers. Neither was it the strong, steady strokes of his father's pen. His own hand trembled as his father's must have.

Son,

Your mother's insistence has worn me down, as has the approach of the eternities. She has asked me to write what I would wish to tell you face-to-face if you were here. I know my time is short, and so is my hope of seeing you again. And so, I consider my final words to you. I know we did not agree upon your choice of vocation, and I fought you every step of the way, but over the past few months, your mother has forced me to listen to every letter you've written her. I admit, I am proud of the man you have become and the good you are doing out there.

Benjamin's vision blurred, and he lowered the paper. Regret pounded in his heart and clutched his insides. He should have returned. He should have been there to say goodbye—to hear these words from his father's mouth. And to offer forgiveness in return.

He withheld a blink, knowing it would dislodge the moisture pooling in his eyes. He pushed on his hat and moved toward the door. "I'll be back," he murmured on his way out. After securing the lock, Benjamin hurried around to the rear of the building, where there was less chance of being seen. He leaned into the log wall and closed his eyes. Tears tumbled down to his chin. "Oh, God. . ." *Why didn't I go back?* Why had he let stubbornness and anger keep him away for so long?

Why are you staying away?

The words came from beyond him but stirred his soul to remember a different Father, one he had also pushed away. "God, forgive me."

He continued his prayer in the shadows of the alley, silently pleading for forgiveness, peace, and an understanding about how to proceed. Finally, nothing was left to be said, and his face had dried. He filled his lungs and pulled his hat low on his brow. He had a half-dozen telegrams to send and arrangements to be made both for himself and his prisoner.

And Anna?

He ached to seek her forgiveness, to plead with her to understand what he had to do, but at the moment he had neither time nor the hope that she would want anything to do with him now that he had brought her brother to face justice. All he had left to offer her was an effort to help Ernest.

Wiping a hand down his face, he stepped again into the sunlight, which had climbed almost to its zenith, and stalked back into his office. Other than a glance to see Ernest reclined on his cot, Benjamin kept his focus on the papers he needed before again ducking out onto the street. He jogged to the telegraph office in the back of the mercantile. Thankfully, only one other person was in the store, a woman at the far end where they kept housewares.

"Afternoon, Constable," Robert Smith said as he maneuvered behind his desk. "I was sorry to hear about your father. Did you want to send a reply?"

"I do, but first I need to send one to Fort Calgary." He handed the telegraph operator the message he had written explaining the situation and asking for leave of absence for his father's funeral. If he left in the morning, he would probably be able to make it home for the service. For his mother's sake if nothing else.

The second telegram was to a sheriff in Montana, the name

given him by Ernest as the lawman who had pursued him a few months earlier. A long shot, but probably Ernest's best one. Benjamin prayed for the miracle it would take to make his crazy scheme work.

And finally, a telegram to his mother, saying he would come as soon as possible.

The bell on the front door jingled, and Benjamin glanced at Anna, whose head tipped down as she walked toward him. When she did look up, surprise opened her eyes. She blinked, and her step faltered. Her gaze dropped again to the letter she clutched.

Benjamin stepped aside and searched his foggy brain for something to say.

"Afternoon, Miss Wilkins," Smith greeted. "What can I do for you?"

"I have a letter to post." Her gaze brushed Benjamin before focusing fully on the man she addressed. "But I should correct you. My name is Köhler, not Wilkins."

"Oh? I could swear that was the name your brother gave me." His eyes grew large, and his gaze darted to Benjamin and then to the telegraph machine. "Köhler?" He turned a somber face to Anna. "I'm sorry." Smith shifted uncomfortably, obviously having put together everything he had just sent over the wire and how it concerned the woman standing in front of him. "Did you need anything else, Constable Cole?"

Benjamin started, his own thoughts quite distant from the purpose of his presence and that it was no longer required. "No. But please let me know the instant you hear back from anyone." He stepped out of Anna's way, and she brushed by him. As much as he ached to take her in his arms and hold her until all their troubles and pain faded, now was neither the time nor place. He tipped his hat and walked away.

Anna listened to Benjamin's footsteps as they retreated out the door, leaving nothing but the tinkling of a bell and her aching heart. He'd walked away without so much as a word. How he must hate her for her deception. She hurried to post the letter to her parents, a full confession of everything that had transpired and a plea for their prayers on Ernest's behalf. Long overdue.

A small trunk standing on end near the door of the mercantile caught her eye, and she asked for it to be set aside for her. If she was taking the train home, she did not have to resort to saddlebags to hold her dresses and any belongings she chose to take with her.

She started walking toward the North-West Mounted Police post but stalled halfway across the street. She wasn't ready to face Benjamin again so soon. The livery and smithy waited in the opposite direction—a much preferable option. Or at least much safer.

"Morning, miss. The constable told me you would probably come for your brother's horse," Hal Rogers said as she passed through the wide double doors. His eyes held a dozen questions, probably about her brother's arrest, but she had nothing to tell him.

"I actually plan to leave on the train as soon as things are settled with my brother and will not be able to take either of the horses with me. I'm looking for someone willing to buy them."

His eyes narrowed in a contemplative way. "What are you asking?"

"Let me know what you think is fair, though I might double-check with the constable on his opinion." Or not, but saying so might encourage a fairer deal.

He looked over to the stall housing Ernest's tall bay. "I think we can make arrangements. Where are you off to?"

"Baltimore. I'll be returning home."

He nodded, his brows pressing low. "Right unfortunate about your brother. Something always did seem off about him." His tone pressed for more.

He's not the villain you imagine. But she had no grounds upon which to argue that. She folded her arms tight across her abdomen. "I also have a cat. I wish I could take her, but I don't think she'll manage well on such a long journey."

He cocked a brow. "She a good mouser?"

"Yes, very good." Benjamin had chosen her the perfect companion.

"I'll let her have a warm place to sleep, then, and make sure she gets enough to eat."

"Thank you."

They concluded their business, and again Anna found herself facing the North-West Mounted Police post. One last task before going home. Shoulders back and head up, she knocked on the door and waited for Benjamin to appear. She allowed herself to really look at him this time. His chin wore the shadow of stubble, and his eyes were bloodshot, probably from lack of sleep. She hoped Ernest hadn't given him too much trouble.

"Anna." Was she mistaken, or did he still speak her name with a degree of tenderness?

"I came to check on Ernest." *And you*, truth be told. "Any news?"

He massaged his temples. "Not much. At this point, he'll probably be taken to Calgary and tried there."

"When?"

His head tipped forward. "I don't know. Soon."

He looked so forlorn, she wanted to slip her arms around him and hold tight. Assure him that she still loved him. . .

The thought dropped her back a step, and her heart thudded. She *loved* him, standing there in his scarlet uniform, doing his duty though it hurt her. She loved him not just in spite of it but because of it. She'd never met a truer man besides her father.

A shuffle from inside drew her attention past him to the shadow of her brother behind the barred door. "I need to speak with him."

Benjamin glanced at his prisoner.

She gripped his sleeve. "Please. Just for a few minutes."

His gaze lowered to where her hand touched his arm, and he stepped aside. Then he closed the door as he stepped outside. While she appreciated the privacy to speak with Ernest, it seemed another barrier between them.

Fortifying herself with a breath, Anna crossed the room, hands clasped tightly. There was no way to save her relationship with Benjamin, but she did need to know the truth. She stared at her not-so-little brother through the iron bars. "Oh, Ernest, what have you done? Is it true what he said? Did you kill that man?"

A short nod.

Even braced for it, the silent confession tore through her. "Why?"

Instead of answering, Ernest started to laugh, low and bitter.

"You can't treat this like some joke! It's not funny. You are about to be tried for murder."

"You're welcome, Sis."

She leveled a glare at him.

"I could have been free with enough money to set myself up on my own ranch. But no, you had to go falling for a lawman."

"What if I did? That has nothing to do with what you did. How could it?"

His head tipped to the side with a patronizing look. "Hank or Drake, or whoever he really was, was going to murder your Mountie. Not wound him. Not knock him off his horse. He was going to shoot him dead through the head and throw him in the river to buy us time. No witnesses. No worries."

Understanding lit her mind with its dreadful reality. "You killed him to save Benjamin's life."

"For all the good it did me," he murmured.

"Oh, Ernest." Her feelings slammed between gratitude and horror. She reached through the bars to touch his hand, but he drew away.

"And now I'll swing for it."

"No." There had to be another way. "Not if you explain it like that. You saved a Mountie's life. They've got to take that into consideration. They can give you jail time for attempted robbery. Surely that will be enough." But would it? The judge would have no one's word but the man on trial.

"Your Mountie doesn't seem convinced I stand much of a chance up here."

"We'll make them listen. I'll go home once everything is settled, but I'll be there with you, I'll make them listen. I won't—"

"No!" Ernest swore and then looked away, teeth gritted. "I don't want you here. You should have let me go a long time ago. Stop hanging on."

"But. . . You're my brother. I want to help."

"I know you do. But I can't live with you hovering around anymore, hoping I'll be the man you want me to be. I'm not him."

"Ernest, I—"

"No, Anna. I won't let you give up any more of your life for me. You should be married and raising babies, not hanging out here feeling responsible for me. You're not responsible. You need to let me go."

She shook her head, the ache in her chest growing sharp. "Just until the end of the trial. Let me stay that long."

"No." His chest sank, and he stepped back to her. He gripped her hands. "Please, go home. On the next train."

She shook her head. "I'm not ready." To let Ernest go. To let Benjamin go. She pressed her palm over the small golden cross at her neck. *What should I do, Lord?*

The short inscription on the pendant lit in her mind, a verse Mother had encouraged her to commit to memory as a youngster.

"I can do all things through Christ which strengtheneth me."

Oh Lord, help me trust. She gripped the cross and unhooked the chain from around her neck, then pressed it into her brother's hand. "I'll go only if you take this. Keep it safe."

A muscle ticked in his jaw. "Mother gave it to you." His voice was clipped.

"And now I'm giving it to you. It's gold, but its worth is far greater than that. It's a reminder, Ernest, that God lives and He cares for *you*. If you seek Him, you'll find Him waiting." She kissed his knuckles through the bars. "I'll not stop praying for you."

His head bobbed with a quick nod, and moisture glistened in his blue gaze, like the stormy ocean they had left behind.

"Goodbye, Sis."

"Goodbye." She forced herself to turn away, but it wasn't a goodbye at all. Nothing about this was *good*, and all of it struck her heart like stones against glass.

Hope of finding Benjamin waiting for her outside shattered under the strike of yet another invisible stone. He was gone. And soon she would be as well.

Chapter 14

At first light the next morning, Anna folded her nightgown and pressed it into the small trunk already holding the rest of her possessions. She looked around the small cabin, so bare now with everything stored away. Over the past two months, she had turned this mousetrap into a comfortable home, small as it was. Hard to walk away.

It's not the house that you'll miss.

As much as she wished to deny the sentiment, how could she? Everywhere she looked, Benjamin lingered in her thoughts. The smooth gliding hinges on the door. The neat stack of chopped firewood in the corner. The tight roof overhead. A piece of wood shimmied under the table to keep it from rocking. So many memories of him, conversations, laughing until her stomach hurt, the warmth of his hand. . .and kisses.

Tears rose in her eyes, but she swiped them away and closed the lid of her trunk. It was time to say goodbye and start a new chapter in her life.

Are you sure you're not running away?

Of course not. She was keeping her promise to her brother and putting her trust in God. There was nothing left for her here. She'd wanted to speak with Benjamin, but it seemed he had nothing to say to her.

Again tears pressed, but she simply hurried with the last of her preparations so she'd be ready when Mr. Rogers came for her.

Marble rubbed against her leg, and Anna pulled the cat into her arms. "Oh, my pretty, I wish I could take you with me." As it was, their journey together would be very brief. At the sound of axles and harnesses, Anna stepped to the door and waved to Mr. Rogers. He jumped down and loaded her trunk into the wagon before tying Cocoa to the tailgate. Anna climbed onto the high seat to watch, keeping Marble tucked on her lap.

The ride to town was uneventful. A whistle blared as the train pulled into the station only a short time before its scheduled departure. Hal unloaded her trunk and took Marble from her arms. A quick farewell. Anna arranged her ticket quickly, praying for a couple of extra minutes before she needed to board—enough time for one last goodbye.

Leaving her trunk with the ticket master, Anna hurried back to the police post and knocked her fist against the door.

Nothing from within.

The whistle pierced the air, warning passengers time was short. She knocked harder. "Please!"

Silence answered from the other side of the door. She tugged on the latch, but to no avail. Locked tight. Panic ignited her nerves. She couldn't leave like this. Anna hurried around the back, where she had seen a small, barred window. On the tips of her toes, she peered inside. Empty. How was that possible? Had Benjamin left with her brother already?

She dropped down and looked to the station. The train was northbound, its destination Calgary, to meet up with the main line that would take her to eastern Canada before one final train ride south to Baltimore.

Skirts lifted for the sake of haste, it was now more important than ever that she be on that train—or so she prayed. Anna searched the narrow platform and area surrounding the train, but there was no sign of a red-clad constable or Ernest. Collecting her trunk, she stepped aboard the single passenger car tailing a half-dozen cattle cars. A gush of relief fled her burning lungs.

Ernest walked up the aisle in her direction, hands shackled and followed by Constable Benjamin Cole. Her brother saw her right away and gave a rueful smile. Benjamin seemed oblivious until he motioned Ernest into a seat and was lowering to sit beside him. Benjamin jerked to his feet and watched her approach. She slipped into the bench across from them, dropping her small trunk on the seat beside her.

"What are you doing here?" Benjamin lowered back down, his gaze steady on her.

"I'm on my way home." Upon Ernest's insistence. Had her brother known? From the look of him, staring straight ahead, bland expression, it appeared Ernest didn't care.

"Home? I—I didn't think you'd be leaving already." Benjamin's brows pushed together as though a little shaken.

Hurt and hope struggled within. "Obviously, there is nothing holding me to Caylee any longer." The words came a little too sharply.

The muscle in his jaw tightened. "I guess not."

Anna averted her eyes, wishing she'd chosen a different seat far, far away. Heat rose behind her eyes, threatening her with the embarrassment of tears. When she dared glance back, Ernest caught her gaze and gave her a funny look. "What?" she mouthed.

He rolled his eyes.

Great. The last thing she wanted was her brother's silent lecture—especially since she had no idea what he meant by it. He was the reason she was on this train to begin with!

Benjamin's voice rumbled from beside her. "For some reason, I pictured you still here."

Would that change anything? The final blare of the whistle and the squeal of steel wheels against iron tracks drowned out any attempt at further conversation.

Minutes passed, and Anna found herself looking for another seat, somewhere she could cry without an audience.

Benjamin raised his voice above the din. "At least you should be pleased to know that my superiors have agreed to Montana's request for extradition."

She snapped her attention back to him. "What? How is that better? How did they find him?"

He gave a shrug, which easily answered the last question.

"You told them?"

Benjamin shifted to the edge of his seat and leaned into the aisle. "He'll only be tried for robbery in Montana. What will that give him, three to five years of prison? He'd get at least that here."

But maybe much longer or worse because a man was dead. She read the silence and the look in his eye clearly and managed a nod. "Thank you."

"I wish I could stay until the decision is final."

But he would be needed back in Caylee, of course. "I'm sure you've done what you can."

The racket of the train again filled the awkward tension between them, and Anna settled into her chair, turning her head to stare out the soot-stained window at the passing hills and valleys, the Rockies looming in the west. She would miss the mountains, but there would be no coming back. No reason to.

———

Benjamin had never felt so drawn to someone and yet so distant. Though she sat only a couple of feet from him. With her brother his prisoner and duty unbending, those feet might as well be thousands of miles. . .as they soon would be.

"You two are pathetic."

Benjamin glanced at Ernest. "Excuse me?"

"Pathetic. The both of you."

His defenses rose. "I have a job to do, and I need to respect your sister's feelings on that matter."

"Here I thought you knew her better than that." Ernest shook his head, his voice a low murmur. "I may as well have let Drake take his shot. Guarantee he wouldn't have missed."

The retort smacked Benjamin upside the head. Ernest was right as far as his sister's heartache was concerned. But was it in Benjamin's power to set things right? He looked over to see her glancing at the other passengers as though hunting for someone. A tickle of sweat at his temple encouraged the removal of his hat, and he turned it over in his hands while he considered his choice of words.

A chuckle from the man beside him grated. "You have no idea what to say to her, do you?"

Benjamin refused to reply—mostly because Ernest was right, though admitting it chafed.

"You had an easy enough time confessing to me that you love her. Have you said as much to her?"

"Not really the best time or place." Not for that depth of conversation. All he had to do was convince her to wait.

"Not sure you're going to get a better one," Ernest insisted.

Benjamin blew out his breath. What if this was his only chance to bare his soul to her? He shifted in his seat and glanced around. He wasn't much on audiences.

Ernest nudged his arm and then nodded toward his sister— who stood and made her way to a new bench several rows ahead.

"So much for that," his prisoner murmured in his ear.

"We have time," Benjamin growled.

"I suppose. Another hour to Calgary before she hurries to switch trains and is off to Baltimore."

An hour never seemed so short.

A cowpoke sat in the seat across, taking Anna's place.

"You can't sit there." The order was out before Benjamin could think better of it.

The man's eyes stretched a bit when he took in the scarlet

uniform and prisoner in wrist shackles. "Sorry, Constable. I figured when the seat opened up, it was preferable to listening to my friend's snores." He waved to where an older man's head flopped back in deep sleep, then started to stand.

"It's not that the seat is unavailable, it's. . ." Benjamin blew out his breath.

Ernest leaned past him. "You see that lovely young woman four rows up on the right? Blue dress, straw bonnet? Constable Cole here is very much hoping for a second chance to woo her, since his first attempt was a dismal failure."

The cowpoke shot Benjamin a questioning look, amusement just as evident. Yet how could he refute it? He forced a tight smile that only lasted until the man began to laugh. "Let me see if I can help." He winked and started toward Anna.

"Now look what you've done," Benjamin grumbled to Ernest.

"Someone needed to. Though with your luck, that fellow will win her over before you get your second chance. Personally, I think I'd prefer him as a brother-in-law."

"'Course you would." But the strangeness of the situation wasn't lost on him. If Benjamin was able to convince Anna to be his, her brother would become family. Maybe it was a good thing he had no brothers of his own, as one obviously couldn't be choosy.

"So much for that hope," Ernest muttered a minute later when Anna stood and shuffled past the cowpoke, who flashed a toothy grin their way. He still looked far too amused. Anna had left her trunk behind and stopped just in front of them, one hand bracing on the back of a seat for balance while the other came to her hip.

"I was told you had something to tell me, *Constable*." Her expression revealed little.

"Yes, I—" His hat slipped from his fingers, compelling him to retrieve it from the floor. He dropped it in the seat as he stood, trying not to notice the curious gazes shifting their way. "I. . ." His heart trembled in his chest. How to tell this amazing woman that he wanted her to be his—his partner, his friend, his wife. . .

Ernest groaned behind him. "He loves you, obviously."

"A strange thing to tell you but not me," Anna said to her brother, though her eyes grew uncertain as they shifted back to Benjamin. "Is that what you wanted to say?"

"Yes," Benjamin nodded, ready to remove all doubt. "I love you." There, he'd said it. Now what?

Ernest nudged him.

Ah, yes. "I wish this didn't have to come between us."

"My brother's mistakes are not your fault," she whispered so softly he almost didn't hear. "My mistakes, though, I do have to take responsibility for. I understand your anger."

"Surprise. It took me by surprise." He hardly remembered that part anymore. "Doesn't change anything."

"You could've fooled me." She bit her lip.

"Then I guess we're even." He tried to say it in jest, but her expression gave him concern. He reached for her hand, grateful when she slipped it into his. "The past two days. . .haven't been easy. But it's not your fault. Nothing is your fault."

"You never even told her your father died?" Ernest supplied, for which Benjamin would thank him. He wasn't sure if he'd be able to say the words and keep his emotions in check. Only now did he realize how much he ached to share that with her.

"Your father." The compassion in her voice was almost his undoing.

"I'll be headed to Ontario for the funeral."

"Oh, Benjamin, I'm so sorry."

He squeezed her hand, somehow drawing strength from her. Hope rose within him and pressed the air from his lungs. "Come with me."

"To the funeral?"

He nodded.

"And then?"

"There's a little white church where my father preached for the past forty-some years. I think we should get married there."

"Married?" Her mouth curved, those perfect lips of hers tempting despite the audience. "I'd like that."

"You know," Ernest said behind them, "if you sent a telegram from Calgary, the rest of the family would probably have time to meet you there. It would mean a lot to Mama."

Anna's tears spilled onto her cheeks as she beamed at her brother. "Thank you."

He leaned back in his chair, hopefully ready to stay quiet for a few minutes. While, in hindsight, Benjamin appreciated the help, the only thing left on his mind didn't require assistance. Well, except from Anna. Kisses always worked best between two.

He hardly even heard the murmurs of disapproval or the whoops and cheers on their behalf.

Chapter 15

One month later

Home at last. Anna smiled not just at the thought but at the deep feeling behind the sentiment. Finally, home again. With her husband. His wolf-like dog. And her cat.

She scratched Marble's head while the wagon jostled toward the whitewashed frame house that would serve them until Benjamin was given a new posting. He figured they had a year, maybe two.

"I'll warn you," he said from beside her, "the house could use a woman's touch. Mrs. Bryce moved most of their things with them when they were reposted last year. She didn't always follow her husband with the children, but Edmonton is an all right place for a family. Not like some locations up north."

Anna gave him a sideways look. "I don't think I'd like that—being left behind. I can come with you, can't I, anywhere you are sent?"

His mouth twitched a smile. "I sure hope so. Not sure I want to go back to my bachelor days anytime soon."

"And later?" She raised an eyebrow at him.

A laugh. He turned and kissed her. "Let me be more specific. Never. I *never* want to be without you. But I'd understand if you'd not want to be so displaced from civilization and comforts." He held her gaze, his own somber. "I want you to be happy."

"Then let me be very clear, *Constable*. Never. You never get to leave me or any children God gifts us with."

He seemed to relax as he focused back on the dual trail leading into the yard. Hannibal gave a happy yip from where he waited up ahead. "Children, huh? Won't that be something." A moment passed. "It was nice meeting some of your other siblings."

"To prove that we aren't all on the run from the law?"

He shrugged casually, but his smile slipped away. His gaze dropped to his breast pocket.

"Is there something you want to get off your chest?"

He chuckled but shook his head. "I hoped to give you a day to get settled."

"Before you tell me what, exactly?" Uneasiness turned her stomach, which had already felt far too unsettled the past few days. Probably from travel—though she hadn't discounted other possibilities.

Benjamin fingered his pocket. "A telegram was waiting for me in my office."

"Something I'm allowed to read?" Not all the correspondence for his occupation would be.

He nodded.

Anna reached across and slipped the thin paper from his pocket, lingering long enough to plant a kiss on his mouth. No matter what news awaited, together and with the Lord, they could face anything.

ERNEST KÖHLER SENTENCED TO THREE YEARS IN FEDERAL PENITENTIARY *Stop* HOPE YOU FIND RESULT SATISFACTORY.

"From the sheriff down south," Benjamin stated as though Anna couldn't guess. He'd kept her well-informed on the communications he'd had with the man about the trial proceedings and his attempt to speak on Ernest's behalf.

"Three years isn't so long." She clutched the paper and her husband's hand. "Maybe it will be enough time for him to stop and consider the course he was on. Maybe he'll be able to make some adjustments. . .and remember God."

"We'll pray for that." Benjamin squeezed her hand in return. "Who knows, maybe someday he and I will be able to be friends."

Anna leaned into his shoulder as he brought the wagon to a stop in front of the pretty house with white shiplap and curtains in the windows. Everything appeared tidy and comfortable—so different from the mousy hovel she had lived in with Ernest. While she wished her brother had a better future to look forward to, she was grateful they were done running from the law and that she had been quite thoroughly caught.

To keep from freezing in the great white north, **Angela K. Couch** cuddles under quilts with her laptop. Winning short story contests, being a semifinalist in ACFW's Genesis Contest, and a finalist in the 2016 International Digital Awards also helped warm her up. As a passionate believer in Christ, her faith permeates the stories she tells. Her martial arts training, experience with horses, and appreciation for good romance sneak in as well. When not writing, she stays fit (and toasty warm) by chasing after five munchkins.

Love along the Shores

BY CARA PUTMAN

DEDICATION

Readers, each story is just words until you interact with the characters and their journey. Thank you for investing your time in the world I've created. I hope you enjoy every word.

ACKNOWLEDGMENTS

It's such fun to be back in World War II with a homefront story that highlights what the war was like here. At the same time it was a challenge to sink back into the time period and make sure I captured the flavor of that era. Many thanks to Andrea Cox and Hannah Grindley for reading and commenting on the early versions of this novella. You encouraged me when I wondered if I was getting it right.

Prologue

L auren's eyes flew open with a start.
Pitch black.

It was all she could see.

What had awakened her from the deep sleep of a weary body?

Was Steven back? Her brother's boat, the *Southern Miss*, had been late arriving. Not unusual but worrisome, as the Battle of the Atlantic filled the newspapers. She wanted to believe the slip of the North Carolina Outer Banks she called home was safe, but was it?

What had awakened her?

Her thoughts felt muddled, and sleep teased at the edges.

A shriek from the other room sent her thrashing from the blankets wound around her legs as she tried to pull her thoughts together.

A tremor pulsed through her as her feet hit the cold floor.

Was that just her body vibrating to life?

A wail replaced the shriek even as the pitch echoed in her ears.

"Lauren?" Allison's voice punctured the darkness as Lauren pulled on the worn slippers she kept next to her bed.

In a couple of steps, Lauren had stumbled the few feet from

her bed, across the hall, and into the narrow space that Allison called her room. It was little more than three walls and a pallet, but it worked for her little sister, a cozy space Allie burrowed into for sleep when she wasn't wandering the dunes looking for the next sighting of the *Southern Miss*. Watching for Steven gave Allie a goal as she walked her beloved dunes in the hours between school and dusk. It didn't matter to the eleven-year-old that Steven could be erratic in his schedule as he labored along the Outer Banks working his crab traps in the small vessel.

It also didn't matter that it was easier to see the larger tankers like the *City of Atlanta*, which carried cargo up and down the East Coast between Newport News, Virginia, and the Caribbean. The old fishing boat had been a part of their family since her father had fished from it. Recently, Steven talked about joining the merchant marines like so many other men on the banks had, but if he left, she didn't know how they'd survive on the hardscrabble strip of dirt their family had called home for more than a century.

"Allie, shh. I'm here."

Thin arms wrapped around her as Lauren patted her shoulder. "What happened?"

"Nothing." But it couldn't be nothing since it had awakened them both. Not for the first time, Lauren wished they weren't alone in this little cottage at the edge of the village.

Bells began a low tolling, probably from the beachside chapel on the other end of Ocracoke. She froze, her heart racing inside her chest to the point it drowned out the echo of the bells.

That could only mean one thing.

A ship had gone down.

Now the race would begin to find and save those poor souls on board.

———

John Weary's Coast Guard dreams of glory had died with his assignment to desk duty at the Ocracoke Rescue Station. In an emergency, though, his nights could be interrupted, and he could catch glimpses of what he'd imagined his future held. On those nights, the bells would toll a warning that a rescue was needed, and in moments he'd join the others in running to the rescue cutters.

Right now, the Navy and Coast Guard were on edge. At least one ship had been torpedoed, the tanker sinking with only a handful of the crew surviving. The oil from its load was already lapping at the shores of the barrier islands. It was hard to keep a secret when the evidence of destruction discolored the sands of home.

His rest had been intermittent as the rumors a German wolf-pack prowled off the coast appeared in his dreams. Each time, the cutter he rode was too late to save the sailors on ship after ship attacked by the U-boats. It was the worst nightmare and kept him tossing and turning with each explosion. It didn't matter to his mind that so far no one had spotted the pack of submarines. His subconscious was poised and ready for an attack that mimicked those happening across the surface of the Atlantic.

Then the earth quaked. The sort of thing that didn't happen in this part of North Carolina.

He'd given up on sleep only to hear the call to the boats, and now he stood on the prow of a cutter, binoculars pressed against his face, as he scanned a quadrant of the sea while the Coast Guard cutter bobbed in and out of the swells. Seaman Andrew Stiles did the same on the opposite side of the boat. John didn't want to see something dark against the rolling waves. That would mean something or someone was present, but as a flash of light on the horizon caught his attention, he knew it didn't matter what he wanted. Because fires didn't just appear on the waves. They only existed when man intervened.

"Captain, to starboard. I see what looks like flames."

John felt the boat begin to turn that direction even before he'd finished speaking.

As the boat neared, he knew there wouldn't be sleep.

Not on this night.

Chapter 1

Friday, February 6

The faded red gingham curtains fluttered in the kitchen window as Lauren Randolph eyed the clock hanging above the timeworn table. She had two hours to finish getting the corn bread and fish ready.

Steven would leave in the morning, off to join the merchant marines, following in the footsteps of so many others like Jim Baum Gaskill. The trickle had started slowly with the declaration of war following Pearl Harbor but had picked up speed. In another month, Ocracoke and other islands would be emptied of men, a thought that left her unsettled as the tar and oil of wrecks continued to taint the shoreline.

Those who chose to make their homes on the islands were tough. You wouldn't choose the hardscrabble existence of fishing and crabbing if you didn't like the rugged isolation, but it had never felt lonely like this.

She straightened her shoulders and pushed away the dark thoughts. Today was for celebrating her slightly wild brother. Maybe the discipline of working on another's ship would give him structure he'd return with at the end of the war. The thought quirked her lips at the edges. *Order* and *structure* were not words anyone would use to describe her island brother. He might be twenty-five, but he showed no inclination of settling down and finding a rhythm to his days.

Allie bounced into the room, her navy blue, short-sleeve T-shirt bringing out the ocean's color in her eyes, her dirty-blond hair twisted into hasty braids that showed the attention the eleven-year-old gave to everything that wasn't her beloved outdoors. Her sister was a quick spit-and-shine girl, a perfect product of the island that was her home. "When will the people arrive?"

"Around six." Lauren nodded to the chair. "Put your sweater on."

"I'm not cold." Allie frowned and shoved her hands in her overalls' pockets. "They're getting here too late to play games."

"Steven wants to set a bonfire." She wasn't so sure that was a good idea with the talk of blackouts, but he insisted they were far from the risk of shining a light for any Germans out in Diamond Shoals from their side of the island. She could argue or she could hide the matches. She'd opted for the latter, knowing it would only delay him but might be enough if Steven became distracted by his friends. "Besides, we should have electricity."

Her sister's frown deepened. "That's a big maybe."

"What are you talking about?" Allie was too young to remember the days before the generators had arrived on the island. They were fortunate their cottage was on the edge of the village, or candles and lanterns would replace the single electric lights hanging from the center of each room. Lauren flipped the switch on the wall, still a bit awed by the ability to have light stream into the room. "This is magic right here, and we'll use it tonight."

A couple of hours later, the cottage was full and loud. Steven and his friends were all hurrying to speak over each other, telling tall tale after tall tale, Allie curled in a corner, eyes big and ears open as she took in all the words. Lauren didn't want to ruin the fun by reminding her that these were whoppers and not all should be believed. As the hot air filled the living area and pressed into the small kitchen, she grabbed her father's old coat and stepped outside. She needed a breath that wasn't heated by the exaggerated tales.

The whisper of the waves formed a soothing sound as they touched the sand before racing back to the channel. As she stood looking at the water, if she pivoted right, she could see the lights from the other homes in the village. Only darkness reached her as she looked left and toward the south. If she walked one mile to the east across the island, she'd look straight across the shoals to the Atlantic. There on most nights, one could watch the lights of the boats sailing up and down the coast on their paths from South America north and then south again.

The breeze off the water rustled the sea grass, and she took a long inhale.

She didn't mind Steven having all his friends over. . .not really. But she needed this moment before she could listen to their tall tales. She knew the truth behind many of the stories.

They were small-island folks who were facing the crowding of the world into their quiet lives. Radio had made the dingbatter world more present, but the events of the last two months were pressing ever more against their quiet lives.

The sound of shoes on the sandy dirt brought her head around, and she stilled as a man in uniform stepped next to her.

John Weary was the new Coast Guard officer on the island. His few months still made him a dingbatter who would one day belong if he stayed long enough. His gaze always seemed locked on the water, while he spent his days at a desk. Somehow he and Steven had connected in a way that surprised her. John was not a banker but the quintessential stranger. He still didn't understand when people let the brogue color their words. In fact, his nose would wrinkle and his shoulders hunch as he tried to follow a conversation at the post office or general store.

"Mind if I join you?" His deep voice rumbled through her in a way she didn't mind at all.

"The water is vast." He turned to her, and she barely saw the quizzical look. "There's plenty to share."

"Ah."

"Do we still confuse you?"

He shoved his hands in his pants pockets and set his jaw. "The *Oi*'s instead of *I*'s are beginning to make sense, but there are still times I feel like I'm listening to another language in a different country."

"Maybe you are." She purposely kept her words in standard English.

"Maybe." He bumped her shoulder, a light touch that sent a shiver through her. "Are you ready for Steven to leave?"

She wrapped her arms around her middle and blinked quickly. "I don't have a choice."

He seemed to hear the quiver she'd tried mightily to still, because he turned to face her. There was something solid and comforting about this man who didn't belong here.

———

This young woman was a mystery to him.

Since the moment he'd hit Ocracoke Island and the Coast Guard station for his position as the liaison officer with the Navy, it felt like he'd been fighting to gain his footing. The people were quiet and closed off to strangers, or dingbatters as they liked to call him. Steven had been an exception with his gregarious nature and quick friendship. But it was his quiet, contained sister who had caught John's attention. She had a core of strength that was reflected in her perfect posture and the small smile she often wore when he saw her.

Someone turned the radio up, and the sound of a swing band playing "Jitterbug Party" rolled from the house. Those notes morphed into a Glen Miller tune, "Moonlight Serenade." It was the perfect music for the evening, and Lauren began to sway next to him. She probably wasn't aware of the motion, but when he reached out a hand, she gave a shy smile and then accepted.

She felt so right tucked next to him, her petite height putting the top of her head at his chin, he didn't want the notes to end. When the music shifted to another song, they continued to sway. He'd never let himself think about what could be, instead being content to live alone. Now he wondered. Maybe there was more possible than a solitary life.

A throat cleared behind them, and Lauren startled as she pushed from the circle of his arms.

John swallowed a growl as he stepped back and looked up to find Steven leaning against the door, arms crossed and a crooked grin on his face.

"I knew you were about this." The words didn't sound angry but amused.

Lauren squeaked and then made another move away, creating more space that made him feel empty. "Steven, this isn't anything."

"It's all right. Oi kind of like the idea of you with John while I'm away."

"I don't need you thinking about me while you're gone." A hiccup interrupted her words. Did that mean tears were on the way? "Just stay safe. . ." Another hiccup. "And come back to us." With those words, she spun and headed across the sandy yard toward the beach.

John waited a moment for Steven to follow, but he didn't. "Should one of us go after her?"

Steven shrugged and then pushed off the door and approached him. "She'll be fine." He stopped next to John and squared off. "While Oi may like the idea of you watching over my sister, if anything happens to her, I will find you."

John held up his hands and took a step back. "I'm not that kind of guy."

"Sure. That's what they all say, but you are a man with a man's needs." Steven seemed to puff up even more as he took another step forward. "She is my responsibility. One I take seriously."

A woman's laughter spilled from the house, and then she stumbled out the door. "Steven? Where'd you go?"

"Right here, Rachel, my love." He winked at John before slugging him in the arm. "Be careful with her, but watch her for me. I trust you with her and Allie."

"I don't know why. I've only been here a few months."

"Long enough for me to take your measure. You're a better man than Oi." He grinned then turned toward the woman. "Ready to leave?"

She giggled again, stepped forward, and linked her arm with his. "But it's your party. There's a bunch of people in there still wanting to say goodbye."

"Then let's get to it." He led her back to the cottage, and laughter rolled out as he spread jokes and good cheer.

Steven Randolph was an interesting man and very different from his quiet sister. He tended to be the life of the party, but with an underlying edge of hardness that went further than being a product of the barrier island life. He seemed to see more than most, almost around corners, which made John wonder what he thought would happen when he was with the merchant marines. The islanders weren't fully privy to the information John knew through his work with the Coast Guard, yet they all knew Germans sat off the coast hidden in the submersible U-boats. It was a reality that couldn't be avoided, as the beaches were coated with the oil and tar and other debris of the destroyed tankers.

A few boats so far, but who knew how many it would be as the new phase of the Battle of the Atlantic touched their small corner of the world.

Those were the thoughts he wrestled with as he waited for the petite beauty of the island to return.

Chapter 2

Lauren clutched her father's oversized jacket around her shoulders as she trailed Allie down the beach. A wind blew off the sea, pools of oil leaching into the sand at the water's edge. Pristine beaches were a fading memory as the lifeblood of yet another merchant ship lapped on top of the waves caressing the sand. The blackened sand was tainted by the oil spilled when the ship had exploded. She wasn't supposed to know it was another wreck, not when the Navy remained silent.

In the weeks since Steven left, the rumors another ship had been torpedoed added to the evidence that lapped at the edges of the beach. The fires burned late at night or in the earliest morning hours, just visible at the horizon. An orange ball appeared where only the velvety darkness of the sea should be.

The evidence rocked her nascent belief they were safe on the secluded barrier island. It also had her sending up whispered prayers for protection for Steven at all hours of the day and night.

She wrapped her arms tighter around her middle, fighting the cold that came as much from the inside as from the bitter wind. The last weeks had been empty without Steven bouncing in and out at will. His presence brought a light and silliness that she missed as she tried to figure what to do now that he was gone and the reserve of money he left behind melted away with the purchases she had to make so she and Allie could survive.

The air felt still and heavy, the laughing gulls deep into their migration this time of year.

She needed to stop feeling sorry for herself. They weren't the only ones on the island confronted with men gone, women left behind.

She stilled as a figure walked toward her. In a minute, she could see it was a man in a Coast Guard uniform. More of them had arrived at the station on the northern edge of the ditch. Anymore, she didn't know who the next dingbatter would be, but something loosened inside her when she realized she knew this one. John Weary's steps lengthened when he spotted her, and then he stopped in front of her.

"Hello, Lauren. Cold day for a walk." There was warmth in his gaze, and, unbidden, she wished he would take her in his arms like he had when they'd danced on the lawn.

She fought the smile that wanted to erupt at his words, feeling heat in her cheeks. "You're out in it."

"A quick patrol."

"Opposite side of the village from your station."

"Yes, but I'll loop across and up the side closest to the shoals and ocean." Soberness tinged his words, and she swallowed. "My Jeep is that way."

Silence settled between them, and she tried to look anywhere but at him, yet her attention kept sliding to him. Something in her had shifted as they'd danced, but there was no sign it had affected him. There was a deep kindness about him, yet she didn't want him checking on her just because of Steven. "You don't need to find me every day. It's a tiny island. If anything happens to me or Allie, you'll hear at the post office or we'll have to come to the station to be transported to the mainland."

He edged back a step, and she felt the distance. "I don't mind, Miss Randolph."

She hated when he did that. Used her formal name when the island wasn't that formal. "Lauren."

"What?"

"Lauren's my name, as you well know."

The edges of his eyes crinkled slightly, and she found she didn't mind if she amused him. "Thank you."

She shifted to the side to watch the waves on the beach. Their music didn't soothe as it usually did. He moved next to her, hands hanging easily at his sides. He was taller than she and fit in a way she wouldn't expect from someone who spent time at a desk. Yet here he was in the middle of the day checking on her. A sudden fear struck her. "You've heard nothing. . ."

"From Steven? No." He studied her intently as if wishing to communicate something. Why wouldn't he just say it? "My grandma always liked to say that no news is good news."

"Not always."

"No. But we don't have any reason to think it's not for him."

"He never was one to write before." She bit her lower lip between her teeth to keep from saying more.

"At least you know which ship he's on."

It was a small comfort. Something to watch for in the papers and the rumors. "Any other wrecks?" She hated how her chin trembled as she asked. Maybe he'd think it was just the cold.

The softening around his eyes warned he saw through her. "You know I can't say."

"But you're here not just to check on me." She knew it was true, and not just because of the tar soiling the beach. "You were walking rather than driving the Jeep to the cottage."

"Yes." He sighed, and she felt him turn to study her, but she kept her own focus on the waves. "Make sure your lights aren't visible at night."

"I doubt that one bulb in a room will make much light outside."

"You'd be surprised. Think about the night of Steven's party. It's important to keep anyone watching guessing about where the beach is."

"All right." She'd seen the notice at the post office. "We'll do our part."

"And if you see anything. . ." He let the words dribble off.

"I'll find you. I have work to do." He'd know the words were a lie, but she walked away before he could remind her just how alone she and Allie were in the cottage at the edge of the village. She needed to keep the fear pressed away, since there was nothing she could do to change the reality of their circumstances. The weight of the obligation and responsibility pressed on her continuously without the reminder.

———

John let Lauren leave. His job was a tricky one of not sharing the truth of what happened on the waves. The Navy refused to acknowledge what was happening off the coast of North Carolina, but the people who lived here could see the evidence with their own eyes. Once Lauren was at the cottage, he returned to his quick walk along the beach. It had been a bloody month on the sea. The *Jacob Jones*, one of two Navy destroyers sent to protect the East Coast waterways, was one of the most recent to sink, with all but 11 of the 190 souls lost. Those few had been picked up by a Coast Guard ship, and he'd heard the stories secondhand from Andrew and others who'd been on that boat.

He felt the tension radiate through him as he fought the sand, looking for debris that wasn't. It wouldn't be the first time a body had washed ashore, and he didn't want an Islander to be the first to find it. Other Coasties were walking the shoreline in other places. Without paved roads, it was often easier to walk at a certain point. Maybe they should use some of the island's wild ponies for patrol.

An hour later, he returned to the Coast Guard station on the northwestern side of the island. He nodded at the men scrubbing down a cutter at the end of one of the piers then continued through the doors.

When he reached his small office, he hung his cap and then his coat on its peg next to the door. The room wasn't overly warm, but it was better than being out in the biting wind. Fifty degrees felt warmer away from the water.

A stack of envelopes sat on his desk, and he worked his way through the pile. Of note was a packet from headquarters in New York. As he read through it, he grimaced. The Navy was considering adding a post at the Ocracoke Station. That would mean many more bodies in their barracks that were part of the main building. The life station wouldn't house anyone.

Then he read further and saw that the Army was also sending mobile defense forces, and he was tasked with coordinating housing for those being sent to Ocracoke. He stood and walked to the window. It faced the harbor, and he could make out many of the cottages and homes that circled the water. The Pamlico Inn might house some, but the Navy would likely want its space for officers when they arrived.

Would the various townspeople be willing to house one or two of the arriving mobile defense forces in their homes?

He didn't know the residents well enough yet to make a guess. While they were friendly, they also drew a clear distinction between those who grew up on the island and those who didn't.

What he knew was something had to change. The *City of Atlanta* had been the first of many boats. On that one, forty-three souls were feared perished. By the time rescuers had reached it, many of the men had disappeared or floated beyond human help on the surface. That scene had played out six times in February in the area known as the Diamond Shoals off the coast of North Carolina.

The United States Navy had to figure out a way to stop the attacks, but John wasn't sure it would happen before many more ships were lost as they attempted to slip up the coast with cargo bound for the big cities or to join the convoys headed across the northern Atlantic.

A rap at the door pulled him from his thoughts. He turned toward his desk and stilled as Andrew approached, a slump to his shoulders and sag that wasn't normal for him. "You okay?"

"Sure." Then he shook his head. "No, the images of our recovering bodies from wrecks for transport to Hatteras Station won't leave my mind."

John blew out a breath. It was war, but civilians were the ones being killed and recovered. "I'm sorry."

"Nothing we can do but carry on." Andrew looked pressed down from the burden of what he'd been part of. "I knew recovery was one role for the Coast Guard, but it's not what I expected."

"I know what you mean." John sank into his chair and steepled his hands on top of the desk. "Did you learn anything while you were at Hatteras? Any help coming to patrol the waters around here?"

"Nothing new. Just the same rumor that the Navy is on the way." Andrew snorted. "I know we're part of them now, but I'll believe the Navy's coming when I see the evidence."

"Don't forget the destroyers."

"Two." Andrew shook his head then ran a hand over his cropped hair. "Wait, they reduced the promise. Make that one destroyer. That's not enough to do anything to protect the boats trying to slip up the coast. I want to get one of those U-boats. Someone has to be the first to take one out. I think it should be us."

"Could be." Andrew studied him, and John refused to squirm under the scrutiny.

Andrew shook his head. "You don't know what it's like out

there. Since the destroyer was taken out, we all know we could have a periscope focused on us anytime we're out at night."

John knew his words were accurate. "I want to be on the cutters."

"But you aren't." Andrew took a deep breath and then rolled his shoulders. "Now's not a bad time to be stuck here." He glanced around the small office with its desk, chairs, and filing cabinets. "Someone has to keep the records so we get paid. Might as well be you."

As they continued to talk for a few minutes, John couldn't shake those words. *Might as well be you.* But it wasn't what he wanted. He wanted to do his part, and this desk duty didn't feel like enough. Maybe once the base was up and going, he'd get his chance.

Until then, he had work to do getting housing for the arriving folks.

"Best get to it."

Andrew made a face. "What, mate?"

"Better get back to the paperwork. It won't complete itself."

"All right." Andrew stood then waited until John met his gaze. "No hard feelings?"

"No, we're good."

They might be good, but life would be better when he was on the boat next to his friend.

Chapter 3

The truth stared Lauren in the face as she ignored Allie's boisterous singing and studied the notebook where she logged the family's accounts.

She and Allie would be out of ready cash at the end of March if Steven didn't send more. It put her in a quandary. She had to find a way to make money because she couldn't wait for something Steven might or might not do. By the time she knew he was late, her bills would be delinquent. She couldn't do that to those on the island who provided the items and services they needed, especially when they too were hitting the time of the year when their pantries were getting lean. She wouldn't think of how lean their own pantry was getting, especially when there weren't many options for income.

The chair she pulled out from the table teetered before she settled on it. She slumped at the battered table that had served her family for at least fifty years. Her family was such a part of the island, but unless you fished or crabbed, there weren't many options for income. After her parents had died when she was sixteen, she'd barely finished the schooling that was available, and her options felt so limited. Steven never felt the need for more knowledge when their dad had trained him to run the family fishing boat. Lauren thirsted for knowledge, but she'd exhausted the supply of books in the tiny library on the island. There was never enough extra to spend on frivolous items like books when Lavender Cottage required the repairs and maintenance of an island home.

Now she felt the lack of opportunities and learning keenly.

What did she have to offer anyone?

She couldn't teach school.

She probably couldn't get hired at the Coast Guard station even if there was a job available. That reality didn't change the starkness of the numbers.

Something had to change. But what?

John had received another missive with instructions to find housing for those coming to the island by Monday morning. If even half the anticipated number came, he was in trouble. He had less than forty-eight hours to pull off a miracle on an island that didn't boast more than two small hotels. This wasn't one of the more popular barrier islands that was prepared for outsiders to spend their summers escaping the city heat with sea breezes.

There were a couple of ways to find housing he hadn't tried yet. Drop in at the post office, library, and general store. Sunday he could also check around at church with anyone he missed at the other locations. Surely he could locate residents at each who would be willing to turn over a bedroom for a little bit of cash. The island had such limited ways for people to earn income, and with so many men gone, the women left behind might welcome the money.

If only their homes weren't so small. It would be tight quarters for everyone.

He understood why the Coast Guard was tasked to help

the mobile defense forces find housing, but the powers that be hadn't considered the practicalities of the matter. There were only so many homes on the island. Maybe if he promised to supply some food for the newcomers, it would help open rooms.

He slapped his cap on his head, left his office, and headed out the door. He ignored those he passed in the hall, wishing he could pass the search on to some other sop while he climbed on the next cutter like the *Icarus* and took off in search of U-boats. He'd studied how to lay a diamond formation of depth charges like the others at the academy. Yet his classmates were junior officers on boats while he'd been sent here to see to the needs of the Army and its mobile defense men and women. Hard to find the valor in that.

John paused as he walked past the latest cutter pulled up to a pier and waved at the sailor cleaning the deck. The man's blue pants were soaked to the knees, but he didn't seem to mind even though there was a cold bite to the salty wind coming off the Pamlico Sound.

And also that every man should eat and drink, and enjoy the good of all his labour, it is the gift of God. The words from Ecclesiastes 3 ran through his mind. His labor was good even if it wasn't exactly what he wanted, so he could find contentment where he was, but it was a struggle. A real battle in the moments, if he was honest. He firmed his resolve to stay focused on that even when it was hard to find value in pushing papers around a desk when so many were risking it all in Africa and the Pacific. Then there was the buildup across the Atlantic.

He gave himself a mental shake. He wouldn't find housing for those arriving on Monday if he stood in place. The sun hid behind a cloud, and he started walking again.

It didn't take long to walk along the dirt road past the small structures. Many looked like they were intentionally built low to the island to provide a stubby profile when storms blew across the narrow island. It wasn't a bad strategy. He'd heard the stories of more than one storm that tried to blow everything west into the harbor and channel.

When he reached the post office, he paused and squared his shoulders before opening the door with a firm smile, ready to greet the postmistress and whoever else waited inside as she sorted the mail delivery. He glanced at his watch to confirm the boat should have arrived with its delivery in the last hour, so his timing was good to run into residents.

He paused halfway in the door when he spotted the dark-haired beauty Lauren Randolph in the building. Her younger sister, Allie, was with her, twirling in place as she watched a blue ribbon she held float out around her.

Lauren turned at the sound of the bell over the door, and her smile widened, a slight crinkle forming at the corner of her eyes.

———

Twenty minutes after Allie arrived home from school, the two walked back to town, clasped hands swinging between them, Allie skipping along the dirt road. The scrubby live oaks encroached on the path, their height cut by the salt-heavy water. Most of the island couldn't support trees except for the small area around the village. Myrtles grew in random locations behind the beaches and protecting dunes. It was a rugged spit of land that reflected the lives of those who called it home. They had to have a sturdiness to survive on a narrow island that bore the brunt of the wind and waves protecting the coastal areas of the state. Still, it was home, and Lauren didn't want to live anywhere else.

She enjoyed the moments of silence, listening to the birds that rested in the trees. The moment felt almost perfect, as perfect as it could be with worries trying to crowd back in.

"Can we stop at the library?" Allie tugged hard on her hand, pulling Lauren to a stumbling stop.

"Ouch." She rubbed her shoulder where her sister had tried

to pull her arm loose. "I suppose." It had been a while since she'd claimed a new book from the compact but jammed library. The smallest in North Carolina, it still managed to host more than four hundred books. "Let's check the post office first. Then we can see if there are any books for us."

Allie let go and raced the last block to the post office, a swirl kicking up with each step. The days had been dry, and rain would be welcome to knock down the dust.

When Lauren entered the building, Elizabeth Parker, the new postmaster, leaned over the narrow counter as Allie spun the knobs on one of the 125 postboxes lining the two-sided wall. Elizabeth's hands were filled with mail ready to be slotted into the boxes after the afternoon's delivery of the post. The petite woman reached up to slide an envelope into a box on the top row. Watching her work was like watching a choreographed dance. "Have you heard the rumor?"

"Which one would that be?" Lauren asked.

"One of the services is sending some people to patrol the coast. I heard several women are arriving on the island and need places to stay. They can't bunk with the guys at the station. Have room?"

Lauren glanced over to where Allie was sliding the small key into the box and then twisting the dial right and then left.

Elizabeth caught Lauren's gaze and grinned as she pulled an envelope from the open-ended side of the box nearest her. "I had a feeling I'd see you today." She waved the envelope in front of Allie. "This is for your brother."

There was a sound at the door, but Lauren didn't turn to see who it might be, because Allie's face collapsed as she began to sniffle. Her face wrinkled, and Lauren feared her sister was ready to dissolve into tears.

At a complete loss, Lauren studied her sister. She had taken to high-strung emotions that were exhausting to monitor and manage. "Allie, what could be wrong and cause you to cry here?"

"I miss Steven." Her voice rose on a wail.

"Why tears now?" She'd barely seen her sister show she noticed her brother wasn't a minute from returning.

"Because Mr. John is here and Steven should be here too. He should get the letter. Not us." Giant tears trailed down Allie's spotted cheeks. Whatever she'd done on her walk from school was speckling her face.

Lauren looked away, feeling helpless and adrift blended with a deep discomfort as her sister created such a public display.

There was something apologetic in John's eyes as he stood straighter and tipped his cap to her and then to Elizabeth. "Good afternoon, ladies. I'm sorry I'm making you sad, Allie."

"Not your fault. Steven should have stayed." Allie sniffled and then wiped her arm under her nose.

Lauren let it go because right now parenting her sister was overwhelming her limited knowledge. She looked to Elizabeth. "Does this get easier?"

The woman's mouth pursed while her eyes twinkled, reflecting her enjoyment of the scenario. "Not at all. 'Twouldn't be fun if it did."

John snorted then walked the two steps to stand beside her at the small counter. "Am I interrupting anything?"

"Not yet." It was a good thing Lauren knew Elizabeth was happily married, or she'd assume the woman was flirting with the officer. "I was just telling Miss Randolph about your housing needs. If she's willing, the Randolph cottage could be a solution for a woman or two."

Lauren glanced down at the floor, calculating what would be needed. "Do you know anything about them?"

He considered her before he gave a slow shake of his head. "I'm afraid not. Not even names."

"How much are you paying for their room and board?"

"Five dollars a week per person."

The ten dollars wasn't a lot, but it was more than she had right now, especially in the in-between of waiting for Steven to send funds.

John hurried on, seemingly taking her quiet as disinterest. "We will also provide limited rations, and they will eat some meals at the station." He shifted to the side and met her gaze. "It would be a help to me. I have ten women, maybe more, to find lodgings for by Monday."

"I can't take ten but should be able to find space for two."

Elizabeth leaned over the counter, chin propped on her clasped hands as she watched them.

"Would you like us to finish our conversation outside?" John asked.

The woman shook her head. "Not at all. This is the most fun I've had in here for a while. Better than a picture show in the big town."

Lauren bit back a giggle when John groaned. Nice to know he didn't like being the center of attention. She'd have to remember that for when it would be a helpful distraction, though once Steven came home, she wouldn't see him as much. She'd still bump into him, but he wouldn't feel the need to watch over her and Allie.

John shifted his stance as if to block Elizabeth and her unwanted attention. "I would like to give you time to consider, but I'm afraid I can't. The women transfer from Hatteras Station first thing Monday."

"What do you think, Allie?"

Allie shrugged, the gingham edge of her dress bouncing above her knees. "It might be nice. Maybe they'll like to cook."

Elizabeth burst out laughing. "From the mouths of babes."

"I'm not a babe." Allie planted her hands on her hips and frowned ferociously. "I'm so tired of being treated like a kid." She stamped her foot, negating her adamant words.

Elizabeth covered her smile even as she met Lauren's gaze with a hint of concern. "I'm sorry if it feels like I talked down to you. But I think it could be nice too. That's why I'm willing to house one in the room at the back. She couldn't take meals here, but if most meals are eaten at the station, it should work."

Something that might be relief lightened John's stance. "That would be a great help. Thank you." He returned his attention to Lauren. "Lauren?"

"I think we can accommodate your need for two of the women, particularly if they will have some assistance with food." She grabbed Allie's hand. "Do you have anything else for us, Elizabeth?"

"Not from the mail."

"Thank you." Lauren started toward the door but stopped as Allie tugged hard on her hand.

"Not yet, Lauren." Allie tipped her head in the direction of the postmaster. "Ask her."

"That's right." Lauren whispered a prayer before she asked the question she needed to know the answer to even as she hesitated to ask. "Have you seen or heard anything from the boys on the *Caribsea*?"

Elizabeth straightened and rubbed the back of her neck as she considered. "No. Haven't heard anything. The boys don't think about us waiting to hear from them. Remember, no news is good news."

"I'm really starting to hate that phrase," Lauren muttered under her breath.

Chapter 4

The postmistress pounced on him before John could do anything other than let the door close behind Lauren.

"You take care with that family."

Her words didn't make sense. "What?"

"They do not need one more piece of hurt. Those girls have already endured too much."

John considered pushing for information. A part of him understood that there was much about Lauren he didn't know, but he was curious. She was a woman of strength who, according to Steven, hadn't flinched when he announced he was leaving. Maybe she'd expected it, with so many others leaving, but she had kept her chin up and smiled even as he noted a hint of worry in the faint lines around her eyes. "I will take that into account. I hope you know I would never intentionally hurt another."

"I don't know you well enough to judge, but intention and reality can be two very different concepts, young man." She returned to her sorting, and he turned to leave, but her voice stopped him. "You won't find a better woman, I don't care where you are. Life has been hard for her, but she hasn't allowed it to make her hard." She slid another letter into its home. "I'm not sure how she's done it, but I greatly admire her." Another letter snicked into its slot. "You can bring my young woman over first thing Monday. I'll be here and have the place ready by ten."

The rest of the late afternoon and early evening passed with additional stops at places on the island like the general store and Pamlico Inn. What men were left around would often gather at the inn in the evenings for a round of cards and jawing. Right on the water, it was an easy stop for the sailors at the end of the day. The smell of fish and beer assaulted him as he entered, reminding him why he never saw women going into the inn. It had earned its reputation as a men's establishment and one that was losing its guests to the military.

Maybe it would make a good spot for an officers' mess if the Navy did more than talk about coming to the island. John filed the idea away and shook hands with the owner. "How's your son?"

Mr. Gaskill shrugged and stepped behind the narrow bar. "Haven't heard much lately. Would you like anything?"

John shook his head as he took in the handful of older men sitting at a couple of tables. "We've got some folks coming with the Army's mobile defense. They need places, especially for the women. Anyone have an extra room?"

The men looked at each other, but before they could start joking, John raised his hands as if to staunch the words. "These women are likely enlisted, though I'm not certain. They'll be working hard and need good places to sleep. . .alone."

One of the older men guffawed. "Want to spoil our fun?"

Another elbowed him. "Think she's like your daughter, Angus."

The man rolled his eyes and slouched in his seat. "You know Oi ain't had a girl for years, ever since she ran to the mainland." He leaned farther in the chair until he'd tipped back on two legs. "Can't help ye. Now, if you have a couple strapping men who'd like to fish. . ."

Several others nodded their agreement.

"Oi could use the help meself," a smaller but sturdy man agreed. "With all the young men gone, there's too much work for the likes of us."

"You're not concerned about the wrecks?"

"You mean the Germans?" The short man shook his head. "Oi've already patched me walls from the cracks."

Another man pushed to his feet and took an empty glass to the bar. "I think a German boat came up under me the other night."

John stiffened. "Where were you?"

"A few miles offshore. On the edge of the shoals. I turned tail and hurried here lickety-split."

"Could you point it out on the map?"

"Not likely. I was trawling back and forth looking for fish, but they weren't interested."

John made a note to press for more details when the others weren't listening too closely. "I think I'll head out. Thanks for your time."

The owner swiped the empty glass and set it underneath the bar. "Next time buy a drink and stay a bit."

John shrugged noncommittally and then left with a wave toward the crew. The man with the trawler pushed from the bar and followed him out. John paused for him to catch up. "Anything more you can tell me?"

"Warn them Navy boys that the ships shouldn't be moving about at night. Crazy how one minute it was just me on the ocean and then next I could feel something larger."

"You sure it wasn't a tanker or something similar?"

"Certain. You work the ocean for a lifetime, you come to know many of the boats."

"Let me know if you see anything else."

"Sure. I'll try to be more attentive to location."

"Thanks."

The man tipped an imaginary hat at John and returned to the Pamlico.

Sunday, March 1

The morning sky was crystalline blue as Lauren and Allie walked down the road to the chapel that sat on the beach. Two curved windows flanked the door, and a small steeple topped with a cross pointed to the sky from the top of the structure. A short cross also topped the narrow portico over the door. The pews were half-filled with the women and children who had been her neighbors all through her growing-up years. It still felt odd to have only a handful of basses contribute to the hymns as the congregation sang. Pastor Thomas Hutchins, a man in his forties, led the group of islanders assembled in the sanctuary in a prayer for the boys in the military and Merchant Marines. In his sermon, he expounded on how much God cared for them if He cared so well for the birds, but Lauren found her attention straying. She needed Him to care for Allie and her, and maybe the arrival of boarders was part of that.

Allie leaned over, a red ribbon tied to the end of one of her braids tickling Lauren's arm. "You're supposed to pay attention."

Lauren bit back a smile at the intense words.

"What? It's what you always tell me."

Lauren held a finger to her mouth to quiet Allie, and her sister stuck her tongue out before crossing her arms with a huff. Mrs. Owens frowned across the aisle, and Lauren sighed. She'd likely get a lecture about controlling her sister after the sermon. She didn't need anyone reminding her how hard it was to raise an eleven-year-old when she was only nineteen.

"Before everyone leaves, we have an announcement." Pastor Hutchins's words focused her attention. Then the thin man with a flop of gray hair brushed over his bald dome swept an arm as if welcoming someone in the front row. "Chief Petty Officer."

A man stood in his Coast Guard dress whites. When he

turned around, he stilled as his gaze landed on her. There was a faint murmur as if everyone else wanted him to get to the announcement as much as Lauren did. She smiled at John. Maybe it would help him unfreeze, and it seemed to work, because after a slight shimmy to his shoulders, he took a step back and then made a plea for help finding housing.

Lauren looked around those in the pews as her fingers toyed with her necklace. Working her fingers along the simple gold cross eased her panic as she considered all she should do to make their cottage ready. The cross had been a gift from her dad's old friend, Ernest Köhler, and touching it reminded her of his favorite verse, Philippians 4:13. The verse inscribed on the cross's surface was a reminder that she could do all things with Christ's help.

"The government could use your help if you have a spare bedroom and a willingness to host someone."

"How long?" Alma Lawrence, the schoolteacher, piped up from her spot in the second row.

John grimaced but quickly settled back into his neutral expression. "I don't know for sure. However, if things change in your ability to offer a room in the future, I will work with you to find an alternative arrangement for the boarder."

A few other questions were asked. Then John sat, and Pastor Hutchins closed the service with a benediction. Miss Lawrence and several others approached John, and Lauren was glad to see his excitement at finding volunteers, though she guessed the pay didn't make them truly volunteers.

Allie tugged at her arm. "Can we go?"

"I need to ask John a question, but you may go speak with your friends." Before Lauren could give her any more instructions, Allie shot out of the pew and slipped between two older women and down the aisle.

Mrs. Parker edged toward her in the other pew. "An enlightening sermon."

"Yes." Lauren scrambled to think of an insightful comment to add. Her panic must have shown because Mrs. Parker laughed and patted her arm.

"I would expect you were distracted by a handsome man in uniform."

Heat climbed Lauren's neck, and she wished her skin were its darker summer color. "Of course not."

"You'll hear no recrimination from me. He's handsome and kind. I think the second is more important."

"Of course."

"Steven didn't ask him to look in on you because he wanted you to be managed, you know." There was a serious glint underlying the light words. "Your brother cares deeply."

"Then I wish he'd send his pay along." She mashed her lips together before she spilled more secrets.

"Are you running low on funds?"

"We'll be all right." Especially now that she'd receive something from the government.

Mrs. Parker studied her another moment before nodding. "Times are tight, but I'll keep my ears open. Work may become available."

"I'm a hard worker."

"I know." The woman squeezed her arm then started moving farther down the pew. "Let me know if you need anything."

The walk to the cottage wasn't long. It was only after they walked a few minutes that Lauren remembered she hadn't asked John her question. She groaned then grimaced as Allie darted across the road. "You really should be careful. There are more vehicles each week."

"Who needs a car here?" Allie spun with her arms flung wide. "Give us a pony and a boat, and everyone can get anywhere."

"True, but we don't have a pony."

"I know." Allie pushed her lower lip out. "We should. Then

we could go anywhere."

"Let's check on the *Southern Miss*, and then we'll need to clean."

Allie raced across the road, past the cottage, and down toward the beach and pier. The Ocracoke Lighthouse stood sentinel behind them, a short structure that hadn't been lit for a couple of weeks. The boat was a smaller fishing vessel that had been in their family since her grandpa had turned it over to her dad. Then it had passed to Steven, and while she'd considered taking up the fishing when she realized how tight money was, the continued debris from the wrecks kept her off the water. What if she stumbled on a wreck before anyone else? She shuddered at the thought.

It only took a few minutes to ensure the faithful boat was tied tightly to the mooring and hadn't sprung any leaks. Then the two made their way to the cottage for a quick bite of lunch. After changing clothes, it was time to get to work making a place for the guests who would arrive the next day.

The cottage wasn't large, with the living area the first space. The couch was a little worn, but her grandmother's sailboat quilt provided a nice splash of color with red and blue calico forming the triangle boats against a muslin that had faded to cream and blue sea. It contrasted with the doilies on the arms and the net hung on the wall. If she continued through, she'd run into the kitchen and off that the small bath. To the left of the living space were two rooms that could be used as bedrooms. Up a steep set of stairs was the tiny second floor with Lauren's room and the garret space Allie had claimed as her own.

Lauren set to work cleaning the room that Steven used. The room held a twin bed, dresser, and not much else. She found an old milk crate that she put his clothing from the dresser into. She set his personal items from the top of the three-drawer dresser on the clothes and then carried the box up to her room, where she tucked it into a corner out of the way. As she worked, she prayed for the woman who would live in the space. A quick dusting and then she opened the window to air out the room. If it were spring, she'd find some wildflowers or dune grass to place in a jar on top of the dresser, but there was nothing at the beginning of March that could warm the room.

This was the best she could do, and she hoped it was enough.

Then she stared at the closed door next to Steven's room. It didn't make sense, but the thought of someone staying in her parents' room gave her pause.

Her parents had slept in that room until they died in the accident three years earlier, and she was still getting used to the idea that neither would stride up the path to their door. Her mother would fill the table with food while her dad told tales as he filled his belly with fish from his catch.

Allie came in from airing the sheets, and Lauren set to work.

The room was wasting, and there was someone coming tomorrow who needed it. She would do her part. Even if it meant eradicating the lingering presence of her parents.

Chapter 5

Monday, March 2

All day the Coast Guard pier stayed busy with arriving cutters dropping off the mobile defense personnel. John had the tables inside the mess filled with men completing the requisite paperwork they hadn't brought with them. While he wasn't responsible for their day-to-day work, he did need to know who to contact if something went wrong and a system for tracking where each would be billeted. Fortunately, the Hatteras Station cutter filled with its charming load of women wouldn't arrive until midafternoon.

A few hours later, John was on hand to welcome the new arrivals. A couple looked green after their hour ride from the other island. They'd started in places like Elizabeth City, and it was a long journey to someone who was used to land travel.

"You may stack your luggage over there." After they did, he led them to the tables and chairs that had been pushed from their formal rows as the day wore on. "Have a seat, ladies. You'll find a small stack of paperwork and a pencil at each place."

The racket of chairs scraping against the floor dulled the quiet voices, and then a quieter air filled the room as the women set to work completing paperwork. What kind of women were in this group? He hoped they were ready to get started. With several of the men who had worked near him in the administration building receiving orders to other postings at a variety of stations, the help was welcome so long as they focused and didn't get distracted by the boredom of life on the small spit of land.

Soon he was matching the women with their new homes and sending various seamen to take them to their new quarters. When he looked up again, only the two he'd decided should live at the Randolph cottage remained.

He led them outside and to his Jeep, hoping he'd selected the right women for Lauren. They might provide companionship but didn't need to demand things from her. He'd noticed an air of strain around her and hoped this would help rather than burden.

Betty Scott was a petite woman with her hair in a swirl at the base of her neck. She wore a plain yet smart outfit. She'd barely said two words but seemed pleasant, with intelligent eyes that seemed to take in everything. Her companion, Rachel Roberts, was the opposite. She must have been more local because he'd seen her with Steven on occasion. A tall, thin woman, she babbled as if the threat of silence was unimaginable. She looked and acted a bit like Katherine Hepburn.

"So, Officer Weary, what should we expect while we're on the island?" Miss Roberts couldn't keep her hands folded and still. Instead, they flapped like birds ready to take flight. A gust of wind blew through the windows of the Jeep, and Miss Roberts squealed as she reached up to capture her hat.

Miss Scott smiled as she shook her head and patted her hat, which hadn't moved a fraction of an inch. "I told you to use a stick pin."

Miss Roberts stuck her tongue out, and John was grateful he could turn off the dirt road onto the narrow path to the Randolph cottage.

"This is a bit out of the way." Miss Scott's eyes were big as she took in the cottage and scraggly scrub brush that flanked the house before melting into a low dune.

"Everything's relatively close. It should only be a fifteen- to twenty-minute walk to headquarters. The island is fifteen miles long from tip to tip and about half a mile wide in some places, but the village is small. As you can see, we aren't far."

Miss Roberts inhaled sharply. "This is where you want me to stay?"

"Yes. I think you are familiar with the Randolphs."

A flash of emotion tightened her expression, and then her face returned to its soft lines. "Some."

She made no move to exit the vehicle, and Miss Scott eyed her. "Anything I should know?"

"No. Lauren is fine." Miss Roberts swallowed and smoothed the front of her dress. "Her brother is at sea." She looked slightly green as she said the words.

John didn't rush them out of the Jeep but instead took a moment to let the peace of this spit of ground sink in. While on the edge of the village, with the way the dunes sheltered it, the cottage felt like it was alone in a gentle way. The waves lapped against the beach just over the dune, creating a peaceful backdrop even as the sun blazed from behind the clouds.

"Are we going to stare at it all day?" Miss Scott smiled but looked uneasy as her shoulders hunched and her gaze skittered around the space.

The front door to the cottage opened, and Lauren stepped onto the front stoop, her simple blue dress highlighting the sea in her eyes. He opened the door and climbed from the Jeep as she wrapped her arms around her middle as if protecting herself from the unknown these women represented.

———

Two women about her age stepped from the Jeep, one with a bound and the other with the attention to placement that indicated a background in refinement. How would they fit with Allie? She hadn't considered the impact her enthusiastic sister would have on her guests.

She rubbed vigorously against the goose bumps that had erupted on her arms. "Welcome to Lavender Cottage."

The petite blond carefully picked her way along the dirt path. "Thank you for making space for us."

"I'm glad to help." And she was. Down deep. In the part that wasn't nervous about welcoming dingbatters into her home. "It's small, but you're welcome."

The taller woman strode past the other and stuck out her hand that wasn't clutching a suitcase. "I'm Rachel. It's a treat to meet you." Her bright gaze took in the area around the house.

Why was she acting like they'd never met before? "It's nice to see you again."

Rachel ran her hand down her skirt, and Lauren noticed a slight tremble. Rachel opened her mouth but didn't say anything.

Miss Scott seemed to notice the awkwardness and rushed to fill it. "There's so much sand."

"It is an island." Lauren tried to soften her words, but truly, what had the woman expected? A high-class hotel? "I think you'll find it's peaceful and a nice place to call home for however long you stay."

"Oh, we'll be here as long as Uncle Sam wants, right, Officer?" She grinned, her red lips the perfect bow, as she looped her free arm through John's.

Something slithered through Lauren, something she did not want to analyze. What did it matter to her that another woman was connecting with John? He had done nothing to indicate he noticed her as more than his friend's sister. "If you'll come with me."

John followed them inside, and she was glad she'd gotten up early to make sure the space was as clean and welcoming as it could be. For the women, of course. It had nothing to do with John. Though she felt every place he turned, and wondered how he saw her home. She'd never cared before, but now she did.

She rubbed the back of her neck and sighed.

This was a terrible idea.

Truly, what was she thinking to let him bring anyone here? She tried to imagine the space the way these strangers would see it. Did it reflect her grandmother, who had first lived in the house and crocheted the doilies that covered the arms of the love seat and armchair? Did they notice the love stitched into the quilt that reflected the oceans and boats that occupied generations of the family? What about the undersized table her father had made from driftwood that stood in front of the couch with a few of the books her mother had treasured resting on its top? On the wall behind the couch, she'd hung a fishing net that one of her uncles had made knot by knot. Each piece told a page of the story of her family. It would feel like a trivial story to any of these people who lived off the island, but to her it was home and comforting.

"You will each have a bedroom through those doors." She gestured to the matching doors.

"I'll take the one on the right." Rachel moved to take Steven's room, and Lauren wondered if she knew it was his. Rachel opened the door and set her suitcase inside the room. "It's quaint."

A nice way to say small. "Thank you."

The petite woman opened the other door and set her case inside the slightly larger room then turned to Lauren. "I'm Betty Scott. This will be a nice place to land at the end of the workday. Thank you for making room for us."

"You're welcome." Lauren cocked her head as she observed her new roommates. "I hope this is a place you can relax. I understand you'll take many of your meals at the station, but the kitchen is just there. My sister and I share a space upstairs. The bathroom is on the other side of the kitchen." Maybe an unusual configuration, but the cottage hadn't been built with a bathroom when her grandpa constructed it fifty years earlier.

"I'll be leaving you, ladies." John edged toward the front door, but Rachel hurried to grab his arm.

"Oh no you don't. We're ready to get to work, aren't we, Betty?"

"There's no reason we can't start."

John's feet shifted as if he wanted to escape, and Lauren tried not to laugh at his agitation.

He glanced at his watch. "I suppose I can take you back to the station if you prefer. I thought you might want to rest and get settled."

"Did you see the suitcases we brought in? Nothing to them."

"That may be, ladies, but the day ends at five for civilians, and it's four now."

Lauren stiffened and edged toward the kitchen. He was going to leave her with them? Of course he was, but still, she hadn't expected it to be quite so abrupt. "Of course they'll stay here. Tomorrow is early enough to start their work."

"Oh, we can't wait to get started." Rachel smiled sweetly at John as she tightened her grip. "And I bet he has work for you as well. He seemed surprised there weren't more of us on the boat when we arrived."

John grimaced and eased free of Rachel. "I'll collect you at oh-eight-hundred in the morning to make sure you know where the station is, and then you'll be on your own after that." He tipped his cap then turned to the door, pausing only long enough to say, "Could I have a word, Miss Randolph?"

She eased past the two women, feeling the edges of her home shrink as they filled space that was usually empty, and followed him to the stoop. He closed the door behind her and then gestured to the path. "Walk with me?"

"All right."

He seemed awfully formal and stiff as he clasped his hands behind his back and strode down the path to his car, head tipped as if scanning for something.

"John?"

He stopped and turned to her. "Are you sure you'll be all right with them?"

"Yes. Miss Scott seems nice, and I've met Rachel a couple of times." Though the girl seemed on edge, Lauren had no reason to think they wouldn't get along. "It's doing our part, and I need the money."

"You know I'll help."

"Yes, but you shouldn't have to. Steven will send money, and we'll be fine until then with the bit from the military for housing."

"If you need extra food or anything, send word." He rubbed the back of his head. "There might be work at the station too."

She waited until he truly looked at her. "John, I don't want your charity." No, what she wanted was for him to see her, really see her. But if he couldn't, she didn't want him to feel obligated. "You don't need to take care of Steven's little sisters. Allie and I will be fine."

And they would be. She'd make sure of it.

Chapter 6

John needed to leave, but he couldn't, not before he said something to clear up Lauren's misunderstanding. "I don't see you as his little sister." He reached for her hand, but she grabbed the cross at her neck, telling him as surely as any words could that she was nervous.

"What do you mean?" Her jaw tightening was the next signal his words bothered her.

He cleared his throat. "Never mind." This had been a bad, not fully formed idea. Time to retreat while he still had some dignity.

She lowered her arm. "You can't say something like that and then stop."

"You're right." He took a deep breath, eased his shoulders, and unclenched his hands. "I'd like to spend more time with you. . .and not because of Steven." He felt heat begin in his neck and hoped he could keep it from spreading. A cool breeze off the water would be well timed.

"Really?" There was a note of hesitation layered with something else, and she turned slightly away.

John reached out and touched her cheek, noting the electricity that zinged through him as her eyes closed. "Really."

She leaned into his touch but then glanced toward the window. "We likely have an audience."

"Maybe." He wanted to let the moment stretch until he was

sure she noted his sincerity. "I don't say things like this to other women, Lauren. Only you."

A soft color flooded her cheeks, and he smiled. He wasn't the only one feeling the moment.

"Right now isn't good." Her eyes opened, and her smile was small. "Let me get the women settled, and we can talk later."

"All right." He stepped away and slapped his cap on. "Think about it."

She bit her lower lip and nodded. "All right."

"I'll return in the morning to give the women a ride."

"Thank you." She pivoted and headed inside then stopped and gave him a quick wave.

He rubbed his neck and caught the flutter of the curtain at the window at the top of the cottage. Was that Allie? He raised a hand in a wave in case it was then climbed into his Jeep. His thoughts kept returning to Lauren on the short drive. She hadn't said no, and he was grateful.

When he entered the station, it buzzed with activity. Andrew hurried over and led him to a corner. "We've received a report of spies."

John frowned as he shifted from thoughts of Steven's sister to this new area of concern. "What?"

"Two people came by all upset. They claim there are strangers on the island skulking about."

"Sure—the new folks for the defense work."

"We tried to tell them that, but they expect action." Andrew shrugged and put his hands into his pockets. "What should we do?"

"You've been waiting on me?"

"Yep. You're our liaison with the Navy."

"That doesn't make me the highest-ranking officer."

"No, but you were the one to check in the newcomers. Maybe you'll recognize who they're describing."

"Doubt that." He pulled his cap off and ran a hand through his hair before shoving it on again. "Lead on."

The tables and chairs were returned to their orderly rows, and someone he recognized vaguely from the general store sat at a table, arms crossed over a stomach that bulged over his belt. The man struggled to his feet and stuck out his hand. "Amos Garfield."

"Pleasure to meet you, Mr. Garfield. I'm Officer John Weary."

"Amos is fine."

"What can I do for you?"

"I saw a man who doesn't belong on the island." The man stuck his thumbs through his belt loops and rocked back on his heels like he'd said something monumental.

When he didn't say anything more, John caught Andrew's tight smile and then focused again on the man. "Can you explain what was concerning about that?"

The man snorted. "I know you're a dingbatter, but you might have noticed this is a narrow spit of an island. The only way on and off is by boat. People don't just show up. They take the ferry or they come by one of your boats. Occasionally, we get fishers or others who pilot their own boats. Those folks are easy to spot. They don't fit, but they've got a purpose."

"Sure. I've seen what you mean." Those were the three basic groups. "What made this person different?"

"He was taking notes. Going places visitors don't go."

"We did receive a bunch of new folks who will be here for a while courtesy of the Army."

"And we got more of you Coasties and even Navy." He rocked back again. "This is different. The man wasn't from here."

"You've already mentioned that."

The man blew out a breath. "He had an accent."

As far as John was concerned, many of those who'd spent their lives on Ocracoke had a brogue. He spotted Andrew's shrug from over the man's shoulder. "Can you describe him?"

Amos rattled off a standard definition. "About so high." A gesture that put the man anywhere between five six and six feet. "Dark hair, pale skin, mustache. Dressed like a mainlander. Takes lots of notes."

"I'll circulate the description and have the petty officers and seamen keep a lookout."

"That's all I ask." The man turned and gestured from Andrew to John. "That ain't so hard." Then he stomped out.

Andrew moved to stand beside John. "I know three men on the island who fit that description."

"Nah. The mustache is distinctive as is the note taking."

"Chances are it's someone working with the Navy. I've heard talk of a Navy base here."

"I've heard the same." Though he wasn't sure where they'd cram it. "I'd expect them to check in here first."

"Maybe they did when you were working with the new-comers." Andrew's stomach growled, and he looked toward the kitchen. "Well, I'm ready to get some grub before patrol."

"I'll be there in a minute. Want to write down the description."

"You don't think there's anyone, do you?"

"I don't know." As 1941 had turned to 1942, he hadn't expected U-boats to torpedo along the North Carolina coast. War changed everything.

———

Tuesday, March 3

The next day, Lauren dropped into the *Southern Miss* after a quick lunch. Life was simple on the small island.

Allie had school. Lauren had chores and a few chickens. Together they had church.

That was it.

A life stripped to the bare essentials.

After steering into the Pamlico Sound, she cut the engine and let the boat float as she lay on the narrow bench. The boat reeked of fish and salt, and she tried to ignore the stench and focus instead on the warmth of the sun on her face. *Father, what do You have for me? Do You see Steven? Is he all right on his boat? When will he come back to us?*

Her heart raced as the questions pulsed through her.

How would she provide for Allie? What was she supposed to do while Steven was gone?

She took a steadying breath and then another.

Right now she knew God saw them all, even Steven, wherever his boat was. Who had better hands to place her brother in than God? She spent some time praying rather than fretting about what she couldn't change or control. Praying settled her mind and spirit and helped her let go of the fear that she didn't have the resources to do all that had been placed on her when Steven left.

She would focus on what she did know. She and Allie were safe, and having the boarders provided some income until Steven sent money. She fought a yawn as the rocking of the boat and the kiss of the sun worked their magic. "Time to get up or I'll fry and Allie will worry."

After allowing herself another couple of minutes, Lauren eased to her feet and moved back to the pilothouse. She made it to the cottage with a few minutes to spare.

The small structure was tidy but weather beaten. The shingles needed to be repainted as the faded blue curled around the edges where it had been applied several summers before. It was a losing fight against the wear and tear of the salty air. The flower boxes at the two front windows would be filled with red geraniums and provide a splash of color in the summer, but they were barren now. The garden plot to the side of the cottage flourished in the summer when she could keep the rabbits at bay long enough to harvest the lettuce and peas first. She couldn't wait for the tomato plants to grow alongside beans and peas. She didn't enjoy canning, but the vegetables would help carry them through another year. She needed to do what she could to maintain their self-sufficiency.

Lauren walked into the kitchen and grabbed a mason jar from the drying rack. After filling it with water, she made her way through the living area to the front stoop. She sank onto the step and took a sip while she waited for Allie to fly up the path from school.

Supper was a simple but quiet affair. Betty and Rachel were settling in and kept up steady conversation about the happenings at the station. Lauren had baked some potatoes and set them out with butter and thinly sliced cheese. It was filling if not exciting.

"What I wouldn't give for a slab of bacon." Rachel rubbed her stomach while Allie watched her with rapt attention. "There's nothing like that salty goodness to doctor up a boring spud."

Betty frowned at her compatriot then rolled her fork over the top of her potato. "Thanks for feeding us when you weren't prepared to." She glanced around the kitchen with its stove. "I'm sure we can help." She frowned. "Do you have an icebox?"

"No."

"Electricity?"

"Most of the time."

"But there's electricity at the station."

"Generator." She shrugged. It had to be. "The island is compact, so we make do with two generators that serve the cottages in and close to the village. This cottage is basically the last, but sometimes it gets disrupted."

"You don't have your own generator?"

"We don't really need it. And the expense is too much for us." These women needed to understand they had just journeyed to the outer limits of the United States. They weren't in a big city with all the amenities. It was a quiet and peaceful place, but it was not modern. At all. That was part of its charm.

But as she considered her new roommates, she wasn't sure they found it charming in the least.

They accepted the simple meal of potatoes with grace, but Lauren had a feeling it wouldn't be long before they'd miss the variety they were used to. Instead of listening to the voice in her head screaming that they would be quick to tell John all her shortcomings, she tried to focus on their banter with Allie.

Her sister had quickly warmed to the two. She'd led Betty around the cottage, pointing out all her favorite things, and the young woman had humored her with grace. Maybe it would be okay, and they'd get along for the duration.

Wednesday, March 4

The next morning, Rachel raced through the kitchen to the bathroom as Lauren was making a simple breakfast of oatmeal. She wished she had bananas or something else to slice into it. At least she had cream.

She pulled the oats off the stove and turned off the burner before following Rachel. "You okay?"

"Fine." The word sounded like it was ground out between clenched teeth.

"Sure?"

"Yes." Rachel groaned and then retched.

Lauren backed away. "I can get you a wet towel."

"Please leave."

"All right." Maybe Rachel was someone who wanted to be left alone at times like this. Lauren hurried to the stove while keeping an ear tuned to the bathroom and praying for the young woman.

A couple of minutes later, the door opened, and Rachel eased from the bathroom.

Betty breezed by. "Oh good. I really need a few minutes to get ready before Officer Weary returns."

Rachel, pale and wan, staggered to the table and sank onto a chair.

"Is there anything I can do?" Lauren grabbed a towel and wrapped the last few ice cubes from the bottom of the freezer in it. She made a note to pick up more ice from the ice-house. "Here."

Rachel placed it at her neck. "Thank you."

Lauren sat across the table and studied her. "How can I help?"

"Force your brother to come home."

"What?"

"He got me into this mess."

Lauren's jaw slacked, and she studied the young woman she barely knew. "What do you mean?"

"I think I'm pregnant."

The door to the bathroom opened, and Betty stepped out. "Well, that's a fine kettle of fish."

Rachel lurched to her feet and dashed back to the bathroom while Lauren tried to understand.

Chapter 7

The stars never looked more numerous or brighter than when John Weary stood on the deck of a ship. Tonight he'd caught a ride on the cutter, the *Daedalus*. Some of its regular crew were sick, and he'd hopped on at the last minute to give a hand on its shakedown cruise before it headed out for convoy duty along the coast. This short jaunt would be more excitement than he would see in months managing the paperwork at the Ocracoke Island station. Paper cuts hadn't been his anticipated danger when he signed up for the Coast Guard and attended officer training.

Paper cuts or no, the week had gone quickly as he made sure all the paperwork was complete for the Army and started to liaise with the Navy as plans ramped up to build a base next to the Coast Guard station. At the same time, he'd done a bit of investigating on the stranger. No one he'd talked to had seen anyone who looked like the mystery man Amos Garfield had reported, though each time John stepped into the general store or ran into him anywhere, the man was quick to ask for an update. There were too many new people on the island to determine if someone nefarious had slipped in as well.

There wasn't much of worth on the island that would make it a prime location for spying. If anyone had been here, they'd likely moved on to the mainland.

With all the chaos, John was grateful to have a night at sea even if it meant he wouldn't sleep.

He turned his face to the salt-laced breeze coming off the waves and kept his knees soft to stabilize himself as the cutter rocked on the waves. Without a visible horizon, it was easy to lose the sense of stability and one's stomach to the rocking.

With its low profile, the ship slipped along the waves, displacing little as it patrolled the waters. In a month, it would guard convoys as the ships raced along the East Coast in an effort to avoid the German wolfpacks that sank tons of cargo, ships, and crews. John wanted to be on the boat when it left. He wanted to do more than push paper. Somehow he had to convince his commanding officer he was more valuable sailing the ocean than surfing his desk.

If he were on the ship, maybe he'd be responsible for the deck and keeping a close watch for U-boats that were hard to detect with the naked eye. Instead, he imagined what it would be like to be on duty every night as the boats formed up in a convoy's rows and stretched across a section of Atlantic that required eagle eyes to keep the supplies and men safe.

He longed to be part of the network of sonar and radar that formed the core of the defensive approach of the convoys. The planes had a wider range and better chance of locating the small subs than the cutters as long as they were within their 400-mile range, but the ships and crew did what they could to locate and eliminate the risk of wolfpacks.

Nights that had repeated since January 22 emphasized how impotent the Coast Guard was to end the threat. They had to get better. Each day more ships went down. That meant lost lives and sunken cargo. Both were crucial for the Allies to survive the war.

He contributed less than his share from his safe perch on Ocracoke station. You'd think Uncle Sam would want to extract its money's worth after training him, but not so far. He tried to be patient, to tamp down the need to contribute in meaningful ways, but he wasn't wired to sit on the sidelines and watch others put their lives at risk day after day. Not when any boat in any convoy could be targeted by a German torpedo at any moment.

His gaze trailed to the constellations, which lit the sky with pinpoints of light. For prior generations, those stars had guided ships across the sea. They still played a critical role in navigation when the newest gadgets failed.

"John, see what I see?" Andrew yelled to be heard over the waves.

John scanned the horizon, trying to pierce the dark on dark to see anything. "Where?"

His friend pointed to the east. "I make out something darker. Two o'clock against the horizon." He handed the glasses over. "See if you spot it."

Tucking the binoculars against his eyes, John tried to see what had caught Andrew's attention. He knew from fishing off small cutters together that his friend had eyes like a hawk and could decipher shapes and images from dark smudges. If he saw something, it likely existed, but what was it? Would the cutter turn to explore the sighting? "I don't see anything."

Andrew took the binoculars back and walked to the conn tower, where he relayed the message to the captain. The sailor called to the radar room. "See anything on radar?"

The line crackled with a response. "There looks to be something a mile to the northeast."

"Submerged?"

"Negative. Doesn't appear to be a sub." There was a pause as if the sailor waited for another sweep or two of the radar. "Too small for that. Maybe a fishing vessel."

Even with some training on sonar, John was surprised with what the experts could see in the sweeping circles. He watched as the captain turned the wheel. In a few moments, the rumble of the screws picking up speed vibrated against his feet, and soon the vessel was moving toward the new heading. The engines eased back as they approached the spot.

John moved next to Andrew. "Do you still see it?"

Andrew stayed quiet as he swept the horizon in a slow arc. If he went too fast, he'd miss the speck of dark in the search. The ocean was massive, the waves chaotic, a boat tiny, especially if it was a fishing vessel. After a minute, he lowered his binoculars and pointed. "There. It's still listing, but I don't see any crew."

That could mean anything. A captain sleeping or sick. Possibly injured. "What will you do?"

"Probably send a craft over. Captain's call."

A buzz of organized activity ignited with the words—a drill put to practice by the need to see what was on the ship. John had heard stories of the Coast Guard boarding boats during prohibition, but this was more likely a lifesaving mission.

The lifeboat was lowered, and ten minutes later, the men who went out returned. When they reboarded the *Daedalus*, Andrew strode to John. "It's empty, but we've lashed it to take back to shore."

John nodded. "Any information on the boat? Anything we can use to identify its owner?"

"Just the name on the side. Something *Miss*." He shrugged. "The cabin's barely big enough to shelter from rain. Don't think whoever owns it would live on it."

"All right." Guess the captain could worry about that when they reached the station. "Good thing we were headed back." He squinted to see the outline in the dark. Did he know that outline? He shook his head at the craziness of the idea. Too many boats looked the same, but Steven Randolph had a boat about that size. Nah, it was a stretch to think he could see enough detail in the middle of the night on the wave-tossed sea.

"The challenge will be figuring out whose boat it is." Once they got to the station, they could look up the name, potentially find it in the Coast Guard registrations. If not, it would be a trickier process.

"Don't suppose it was registered with us." Andrew let the binoculars fall against his shirt.

"I can search the paperwork back at Ocracoke and check with Hatteras if my records are bare."

But if that boat belonged to Steven, it meant there was a problem because the boat had been stolen. The alternative wasn't something he would consider now. "You're sure no one's on board?"

"Whoever was on that boat isn't there now."

Wednesday, March 11

After straightening the cottage, Lauren headed into the village and the general store. She needed a few things to cook for Betty and Rachel. Four of them ate more than when it was just Allie and her, even if poor Rachel still struggled with morning nausea. While she wasn't sure what to think of Rachel's claim that Steven was the father of her baby, she didn't want to add to her suffering. However, the question added a layer of tension to the house when everyone was home.

She needed Steven to come home and handle this situation, because she didn't know the right thing to do. Was he the reason Rachel was in this situation?

What Lauren could do was try to help Rachel since she now lived at Lavender Cottage. And when Steven came home they'd sort out the rest.

Adding variety to the meals seemed like a small way to help. She needed to find something that didn't send the woman running to the bathroom.

Fortunately, evenings were better than mornings, but Rachel needed more than potatoes and Spam. They all did. Lauren smiled at Amos Garfield as she stepped into the series of rooms and grabbed a basket from the stack by the door. Items seemed to crawl to the ceiling in a hodgepodge that had felt fun as a child but was disorienting the first few times she shopped there. Soon she'd figured out that he added new items where there was space rather than where it made sense.

"How are you, Mr. Garfield?"

He snorted then looked to the left and right before leaning forward on the counter. "Seen anyone strange about?"

She stopped in front of the simple display of canned goods, considering the limited options. "No, sir."

The man harrumphed and wagged a finger at her. "Be careful walking around. There are strangers on the island, and they don't belong."

"Thank you for the warning." She hurriedly grabbed a few items and then paid. "Anyone in particular concern you?"

"Man with a mustache. There are too many dingbatters. Makes it hard."

"It is different."

"And they aren't visitors. Aren't coming in and buying things."

"It's not exactly vacation season."

He grunted then handed her a bag with the cans. "Watch yourself."

"I will." She held up the bag. "Thank you."

As she walked back along the shore toward the cabin, she considered his words. Were they so used to the same people that anyone new was suspicious, or was there something to be genuinely concerned about?

Everything was unsettling and in turmoil. She rubbed her forehead where it pounded. *Father, give me wisdom, and protect*

Allie and me. We don't have anyone to turn to.

John's image came to mind, and she felt a spark of warmth and hope. He was a good man and seemed to enjoy time with her. If only it was because he wanted to be with her and not that she was his assignment.

Yes, he would help if needed, but he wasn't close. Yet, if she was honest, she didn't really need anyone around. There had been nights before that her dad and Steven spent on the boat. The difference was the presence of German boats off the coast. The U-boats were there. Somewhere. Hidden and deadly.

She shivered.

She didn't want to live in fear but be aware. There was a difference. One was wise and the other limiting. She had to find the right balance of being wise as a serpent and innocent as a dove so she could protect Allie and not live paralyzed by the what-could-happens.

She walked around the house to the kitchen entrance. Something caught her attention. Something was wrong. Different. Not right.

She set the bag on the stoop and then made a slow turn. Nothing seemed out of place until her gaze took in the pier.

Wait.

Maybe Mr. Garfield wasn't crazy, because something important was missing from the pier.

Where was the *Southern Miss?*

Chapter 8

When the *Daedalus* returned to Ocracoke, John slipped into his room at the barracks for a few hours of shut-eye. Before he was rested, the sunlight filtered through a crack in the curtains and cut across his face. Guess it was time to get up despite the late night.

After making his bed and straightening the small space, he headed to the mess for a quick bite that turned into a meeting when a Navy officer sat next to him.

The man extended his hand. "Lieutenant Warren Dules with the Civil Engineering Corps."

"Lieutenant John Weary." He studied Dules, taking in the one stripe on his pin and the khaki uniform. "How can I help you?"

"Navy's sent me here to find the spot on the spit of land to add a Navy outpost."

"I'd heard rumors."

"Well, they're no longer rumors. We want to start construction as soon as possible to get an outpost started for striking back at the U-boats." He took a swig of black coffee. "I understand you're the liaison officer."

"Yes."

"Then I need you to help me figure out the best place and way to get this all set up."

"What exactly do you need?"

"We're going to take your little compound here and enlarge it while also adding a communications station on the other side of the island facing the shoals." He set down his mug. "That's all I can say now, other than Uncle Sam will purchase some land and you can help smooth the path."

"I will help where I can." What else could he say? "I've only been here six months, so I'm still getting to know the islanders."

"There can't be that many here. You've had plenty of time."

"All a matter of perspective." John flipped a clump of now cold scrambled eggs with his fork. "It's an insular community that takes care of its own. We just asked them to take in some of the Army's mobile defense forces."

"Once the Navy's up and running, they likely won't need to do that. We can start with a barracks when we scoop out the harbor."

"They call it the creek around here. And I think it was dredged already."

"See." Warren slapped him on the back forcefully enough to make John glad he hadn't picked up his mug of coffee. "This is exactly why I need your help. We'll make a good team." He glanced at his watch and then pushed away. "I've got a meeting with a boat to check the harbor. I'll make sure it's deep enough for Navy ships to get in here."

John watched the man leave, mind spinning with what he'd learned. The plans were bigger than he'd expected and would change the dynamic of the island around the Pamlico Sound closest to Hatteras Island. When he reached his small office, the desk piled with files and the matching filing cabinets looked untouched. It was too bad someone hadn't come in overnight and completed all the lingering paperwork. With the work he'd do as liaison with the Navy on the expanded base, the files would multiply.

He sank to the chair and rubbed the back of his neck as he considered where to start.

Best place was on the boat from last night. He'd knock that out and get down to the items covering his to-do list. What was the name on the ship?

A quick walk to the pier, and his concerns multiplied.

The boat was the Randolphs' *Southern Miss*. He'd do a quick search to make sure there wasn't another one registered with that name. Steven had left the boat secured to their small pier, and each time John had been at the cottage, he'd made sure it was still firmly tethered to its post. So how did the boat get to the middle of the ocean far from land? Mechanics had inspected the boat, and nothing seemed wrong with it that Steven hadn't complained about the last time they bumped into each other.

Had Lauren noticed? If so, she had to be worried, but John didn't want to raise fears that might be unfounded. Sometimes boats slipped their moorings and washed from a pier.

Or maybe Amos Garfield at the general store was on to something and someone had stolen the boat. If so, where was the person when the boat was found?

A crazy thought raced through his mind. Had someone used the ship to rendezvous with a U-boat? Was that even possible?

He pushed back from his desk and walked to the window, where he could watch the small boat bob alongside the dock. It seemed like a stretch, but the Navy liaison might know.

The village of Ocracoke sat on the narrow spit of barrier island with no more than six hundred residents. That meant there weren't many places for people to gather beyond the post office, general store, and church. Add in Mae's Diner, and it was the definition of a blink-and-miss-it town, only instead of requiring a drive, it could be walked in minutes.

It would take more time before he felt comfortable on this isolated island. The only way to get on or off was by boat or plane.

He was used to places like Norfolk, Virginia, and the edges of this village pressed in against him. Most people were closed to those who hadn't grown up on the island, making Steven one of the few he could call a friend. At least with the Coast Guard, he had easy access to cutters and could go to the Hatteras station as needed.

A quick walk around didn't reveal Lieutenant Dules, so maybe a walk to the post office would clear his head and help him focus on what needed to be done next. John dug his hands into the pockets of his winter coat and hunched his shoulders against the cold wind coming off the water. Silver Lake Drive was fairly empty as he walked from the Coast Guard station and around the creek.

The seagulls cawed as they spiraled in the sky, and one landed on the edge of the road and cocked its head.

"No lunch to share today." Not that he ever did. Such dirty creatures, but someone must feed the birds, since they seemed to know when to appear for the next free meal.

As he approached the post office, he watched for the mysterious man Amos had seen. If John was right, it was too late to find him if he existed. The post office door opened, and a young woman barged out and collided with him. He absorbed her weight with an *oomph* as several envelopes flew from her grasp. Her fingers curled around his arm as she bobbled. One envelope sailed into a puddle of water, and she groaned as she brushed hair from her face.

Dark hair waved, held ineffectively by some sort of pink ribbon. A flash of something flew across her expression, and he took a step back.

"Lauren. I'm so sorry. Are you all right?" He steadied her, doing a quick assessment to make sure she appeared unharmed.

"It was my fault." She quickly stooped to pick up the envelopes and shook the wet one as she held it away from her body.

A sigh slipped from her as she looked at the others and held it separately. "I should have been more careful coming out." A cloud crossed her brow.

———

She'd been on her way to the Coast Guard station after the post office to report the missing boat. "Something's happened to the *Southern Miss.*"

His eyebrows jumped above eyes the color of a stormy sea even as there was a slight relaxing of his shoulders. Why was she noticing now how much she liked getting lost in them? "I know."

"What do you mean you know? I just noticed it was gone."

He pulled his bucket hat from his head and held it in front of him, studying it as if it held some sacred answer.

"John, what's going on?" She felt her pulse pick up as he delayed. "You're making me nervous."

"Have you noticed anything different around the cottage?"

"No. It's just Allie, Rachel, Betty, and me."

"You haven't heard or noticed anything strange?"

"No." She wanted to stomp her foot as he continued to question her without answering her simple question. She did not lose her temper. She couldn't now, not when she needed to find out what he knew. "John. You know something. You said as much, so tell me what you know."

"I'm not sure I can."

She released a sigh as the wind snaked down her jacket and made her shiver. "Please. I'll fill in the blanks otherwise and probably get them wrong." She froze as a crazy thought flitted through her mind. "Could it be Amos's strange man? Do we have a spy on the island? One who steals boats?"

"I don't know. Maybe. Let's go inside, where you can sit and be out of the wind while we talk."

"The post office is really too small to sit."

"We'll find a way, and you're shivering. I want to get you inside."

"You know Elizabeth Parker will listen."

"I imagine she's already found a way to take in everything we've said. The walls aren't that thick."

Lauren laughed, and he opened the door, a smile answering her amusement. Why couldn't she pull her gaze away? What would it be like to be held in his arms and captured by his kiss? She swallowed hard. What was wrong with her? She needed to learn what John knew and reclaim the *Southern Miss*, not reimagine a scene from one of the books she'd read.

He continued to hold the door and watched her with a quirk to his head. "You all right?"

"Yes, just nervous. Let's get this over with. I need to know what you know and get my boat back before Allie arrives home from school and finds I'm not there."

———

John loved listening to the musical lilt of her words. Her accent wasn't as heavy as some of the older residents he'd interacted with on the island, but he could listen to her longer if he didn't need to get her out of the cold and figure out what had happened. "You just noticed the boat was gone?"

"Y'all coming in or just letting winter in?" Mrs. Parker did not sound happy.

"Sorry, ma'am." He closed the door and stared at Lauren. "So?"

She shoved the envelopes in her coat pocket and then crossed her arms. "Yes, an hour ago maybe."

How could she have not noticed sooner? She matched his frown, but he couldn't shake the idea that someone, possibly a spy, had been that close to her cottage. "Never mind the post office. Let's go to the station, where I have something to show you." Maybe the movement would warm her up, since the sun wasn't hiding behind clouds.

She sashayed past him, the motion not fitting with the thick pants and heavy coat she wore. Still, he schooled his mind to stay focused on how she could help him solve the mystery regarding the boat.

Distances were short on Ocracoke, with it being half a mile from the post office to the station. The road curved along the edge of Silver Lake Harbor, which had been dredged in preparation for the Navy ships in the months before he arrived on the island. With the way the tides and storms came in, it would likely require similar effort every five to ten years to keep the harbor ready for boats bigger than sailboats or the smallest class of Coast Guard cutters. The cottages they walked past had the battered look of dwellings that had borne the brunt of saltwater-laced breezes, the wood siding discolored and rough.

She didn't say anything, and he didn't feel the need to fill the silence. Not when he didn't know with certainty what would confront her at the dock. She wrinkled her nose as they edged closer to the Pamlico Sound and the odor of the oil confronted them.

She followed him with two steps for each of his. He slowed his pace so she didn't have to run. "Sorry about that."

"What's wrong, John? This isn't like you."

"We found your boat."

"Really? That's great news. I was afraid it was gone for good. Steven would kill me."

"Sure, I'm glad we found it, but the crazy thing is where we found it."

They curved around the creek toward the station. Lauren pulled him to a stop. "If you don't just spit it out, I'm going to assume something happened, like a spy snagging it."

"There's no reason to think that's the case." He sighed and started walking again in the direction of the ship. "But we do have a small mystery."

She followed him double time again. "Slow down and explain

what kind of mystery you mean."

"We found the *Southern Miss* miles from shore. On the other side of the island."

She stopped with a gasp. "How?"

Chapter 9

As they neared the station, the two-story, white-shingled structure topped with a red roof stood in sharp contrast to the blue sky and sea behind it. A long deck extended from the back of the building into the Pamlico Sound with multiple docks for various Coast Guard cutters and smaller Navy vessels. While the Navy planned to add to the barracks and hospital, the administrative building wasn't that impressive compared to other stations. However, contrasted to the other buildings on the island, it was a landmark for the village alongside the lighthouse.

John's office was tucked on the second story in a back corner, so he walked her past the porch that stretched along the front of the building and through the front door. Her shoes clapped across the battered wood floors as he led her to the staircase and up. He felt her right behind him as he kept a steady pace, and she wasn't breathing hard when they reached the top.

"My office is down this way."

"Why aren't you showing me the boat?"

It was a good question. "Guess we should have started there." He pivoted and headed down the stairs, taking her along the hall and out the back door. She was silent as she moved next to him on the dock. "It's on the last pier."

"All right."

The wind off the creek threatened to blow them from the pier and into the water. He widened his stance when they reached the end and pointed at the small vessel. "Is that your *Southern Miss*?"

———

Lauren bit her lower lip and mimicked his wide stance as the pier swayed slightly in the wind. A chunk of hair blew into her mouth, and she pulled it out as she studied the boat she knew so well. Without asking permission, she climbed down the ladder and boarded the boat.

"What are you doing?" He didn't look happy as he followed her onto the boat.

"There's an easy way to confirm this is ours." She walked into the small wheelhouse and reached beneath the ledge. A moment later, she handed a pilot book to him. "You'll find Dad's name and then Steven's on the inside cover. Steven stashed it where it would be protected from the water."

He took the book and flipped through it. "This is a start. Do you have the logbook?"

"It should be under here too." She reached back underneath and pulled out the logbook. She handed it over with a sigh. "Where did you find the boat?"

"About ten miles from here. Slightly closer to here than Hatteras."

"That doesn't make sense."

"I know."

Lauren studied the *Southern Miss*. It looked fairly dilapidated, like so much around Lavender Cottage. She remembered how things had been before her parents died, but she and Steven had been overwhelmed with surviving since then. The burden of upkeep led to neglect, and it had spread to the boat. Steven had never cared as much about the fishing, always with a look in his eyes to the horizon and what could be over the line. The lack of care had accelerated with his departure because she couldn't keep up on her own, even as she longed for things to be neat and orderly. She wanted John to see her as competent and capable. Instead, allowing the *Southern Miss* to drift away and not noticing. . . "How could it drift so far?"

"It couldn't. Not and go around the island like it did. Maybe drifting to the mainland would be possible, but not to the shoals." Jonathan crossed his arms as he studied the boat.

"It's at least twenty miles to the mainland."

"And doesn't require the fiction of drifting around the miles of island."

"It's only eight miles."

"But it's sixteen miles from end to end. Either way, that's a long distance to drift without a captain."

She nodded because he was right. Nothing made sense other than the fact someone had stolen it. "Then it could be a spy?"

"Maybe." His jaw worked back and forth as he considered. "It seems far-fetched but. . ."

"Amos saw someone." She shivered and rubbed her arms.

"Maybe. Let's get you warmed up inside."

"In a minute." She thought through everything they'd conjectured as she scanned the boat. Nothing seemed amiss or out of place other than its location. "Why our boat?"

"Maybe whoever it was realized there was only you and Allie. Maybe he assumed you wouldn't notice for a while, and if you did, you wouldn't say or do anything."

"Maybe." She bit her lower lip and wrapped her arms around her waist. "It feels so invasive."

"At least we found the boat."

"True." She shivered again.

He sighed and took a step toward the station. "Let's get you some coffee. Then I'll help you get the boat back to your place."

"I can pilot it."

"I know, but I'll feel better inspecting the mooring."

"All right." They climbed from the boat, and she followed him inside, trying to make the pieces fit. "Why take the boat?" she asked again. She watched John pour a mug and then accepted it from him.

"I don't know." He held up a pitcher. "Cream?"

"Do you have sugar?"

"Yes." He stepped behind the counter and pulled out a little canister. Then he handed her a spoon.

"Thank you. Do you think the government will really ration food?" She let the sugar drizzle across the top of the coffee, trying to imagine what it would taste like without.

He filled a second mug and took a sip of the midnight-black brew. "That's above my pay grade, but I've heard whispers."

"So what do we do about the boat?"

"Warm you up, and then I'll go back with you to your house. When we look around, maybe we'll see something."

Once on board the *Southern Miss*, Lauren turned the wheel to ease from the pier and into the ditch and then the sound for the trip back to the cottage. She'd felt a restlessness stirring inside for a while. The need to do something beyond care for Allie and cook for Steven. He'd hesitated to let her help him work on the boat because he'd said it was too big a risk if something went wrong. With their parents gone, Allie needed one of them to be okay. But Lauren had felt a worrying concern that there was something he was doing that he didn't want her to know about. Something he wanted to keep hidden. Was it the depths of his relationship with Rachel? It would make sense he'd hide that.

John gave her room, standing behind her but not interfering as they reached her pier.

She pulled alongside the Lavender Cottage dock, and John helped her inspect the pier and mooring, yet nothing seemed amiss. Everything was as it should be with no unaccounted for footprints or anything else out of place except her boat. John double-checked the mooring then started up the path toward the cottage.

"I don't see anything." Anything else he wanted to say was cut off as Allie came barreling from the house and into him.

"John! I've missed you." She wrapped her thin arms around him and squeezed.

Lauren hid a smile as John looked at her and then down before returning the hug. He mouthed *Anything wrong?* and she shook her head. "You all good, kid?"

"I'm just so glad you found the *Southern Miss*. When I saw that man take it, I was so mad."

Lauren gaped at her sister. "Why didn't you say anything?"

"You were busy, and then I forgot."

John knelt in front of her. "When did you see the man on your boat?"

"I don't know." She swayed from side to side for a moment. "Maybe Monday after school."

John met Lauren's gaze. "So when we found it this morning..."

"He would have had plenty of time to move it and get off." Lauren put her hands on Allie's shoulders and waited for Allie to look up. "What did the man look like?"

"I wanted it to be Steven, but it wasn't. He was too wide." She shrugged. "By the time I could see his face, he was too far away."

An hour later, Allie was tucked into her bed and alcove, leaving Lauren to stand at the window and watch. She opened the door and stepped onto the small, covered porch. The darkness pressed against the space, and she wished there was someone close who would tell her Steven was okay.

Instead, the quiet of the waves pressed against her, the darkness reminding her how very alone she was here on the strip of beach she called home.

She clutched the cross necklace she always wore. It reminded her she wasn't alone. . .even when the night whispered she couldn't be more so.

After John returned to the station, his mind spun with the implications of what Allie had seen. He hadn't pressed her when she looked ready to cry. He wasn't equipped to manage the tears of a child, no matter how much he loved her family.

He froze on that word.

Love.

Did he love the Randolphs? Sure. But when he thought more deeply about it, there was one who captured his attention with her dark hair and fierce determination. She encapsulated that Shakespeare quote "Though she be but little she is fierce." He wasn't sure she saw it in herself even as she lived it in the way she handled adding women to the household, the boat disappearing, and daily life on the rough island.

He needed to decide what he was going to do about his rising interest in this strong woman. Or if he was going to do anything at all. Leaving things as they were felt cowardly. Maybe there was someone in her life, someone who'd left with most of the men.

He should probably know and could ask Steven if he was here.

Regardless, she deserved to be treated with the utmost respect and care, something she probably hadn't experienced enough of.

The following day was a routine one until Andrew ran into his office.

"Get to the dock, Weary."

"What?"

"Another boat's been torpedoed. A freighter picked up survivors, and we're being sent to help with recovery. Navy's sending other ships out from Virginia Beach and Hatteras to look for the U-boat."

John rubbed his eyes and pushed up. "All right."

"Ten minutes."

How had another ship been torpedoed? The attacks had to be stopped, but so far nothing was working. He'd heard of a couple of Navy destroyers racing out to find the U-boats and being completely ineffective. The strategy had to shift, but it wasn't his role right now.

When he reached the *Daedalus*, it was prepped, and they set out. The cruise was quiet, everyone alert. So far, boats had been attacked only at night. The working theory was the U-boats had to surface to shoot the torpedoes. Still, extra men were posted along the deck to watch for any sign of the enemy. After an hour on the water, the *Daedalus* rendezvoused with the *Norlindo*. The number of survivors was small, only seven men.

Once they were settled in the hold, John sat across from a couple of the survivors. The men looked tense and worn but had been picked up relatively quickly. "What ship were you on?"

"The *Caribsea*." The man spoke the word softly, like a prayer, as he clutched his mug of coffee.

John stilled. That was Steven's boat. "Did others get off?"

"No, we're it of the twenty-eight crew."

"Any warning?"

"No. We were drifting at five knots because the captain had been told by the Navy to approach Cape Hatteras only in the daylight." The sailor scrubbed his face with trembling hands. "Those were good men."

"How long did it take to sink?"

The men glanced at each other. "Maybe two minutes. It was so fast, we couldn't make it to the lifeboats."

"The explosion. . ." The quieter man shuddered. "Those poor souls."

"We were the lucky ones."

John nodded, keeping to himself that one of his friends had been on that ship.

How would he tell Lauren? She needed to know, and he was the best one to tell her. The thought gutted him because he knew how it would impact her and Allie.

Their lives were about to change again.

Chapter 10

Thursday, March 12

Lauren looked out the kitchen window and froze when she spotted John Weary walking back and forth along the edge of the shore near their pier. What was he doing here?

Her heart dropped in her chest. If it was a good visit, he wouldn't hesitate out there. Instead, he would march up the short walk and knock, and Allie would let him in with childish exuberance. *Father?* It was all she could breathe before she squared her shoulders, lifted her chin, and walked out the back door.

He must have heard her because he stopped pacing and turned to her.

The sadness coating his face halted her on the worn path.

"John? What's wrong?"

He took a step in her direction and reached out as if to pull her close. In that moment, she wanted, needed him, to do that.

"Please."

"Come sit with me." He took her hand and led her to the end of the pier.

"Why here?" She didn't have a coat, grateful the sun warmed the air.

"Allie shouldn't hear." He swallowed, and his Adam's apple moved.

"Steven." She breathed her brother's name as a grim certainty gripped her.

John closed his eyes and then helped her to sit on the edge of the pier. Only when their legs hung off the side did he turn back to her. "There's been another explosion."

"The *Caribsea*."

"Yes."

She swallowed hard against the tears that threatened. "Tell me."

"We picked up survivors late this afternoon. They'd been picked up by a freighter."

"Steven wasn't with them."

"No."

"And you don't think he's out on the shoals waiting to be found."

His jaw tightened as he shook his head. "It doesn't sound likely. I'm so sorry." He tugged her closer, and she sank against him. His hand rubbed her back, and she couldn't stop the tears. "I'm so sorry." His words crooned over and over in her ear as she cried against his coat.

When she had no more tears, she stayed in the safety of his arms. The heaviness in her chest made it feel as if the reverberations of the *Caribsea* explosion vibrated through her. "How will I tell Allie?"

"I don't know."

She should pull away, create space, but if she did, she would have to acknowledge how very alone she was. And there was comfort in the safety of his arms. Right where she was.

It truly was just her and Allie. . .and maybe this man who had come to tell her the awful news. She pressed back. "I should find Allie."

He didn't immediately release her. "I'll come with you."

"You don't need to." She took a breath then slowly released it.

A horrible thought entered her mind. "Rachel."

John cocked his head as he considered her. "What?"

She bit her lip, imagining what she would need to tell her brother's girlfriend. "Nothing. She'll be devastated, I think."

John closed his eyes. "Right. They were together."

"You knew?"

"Saw them on several occasions. I can tell her tomorrow so you don't have to. She may already know since she's been at the station."

"I hadn't thought of that." Lauren wiped her cheeks. "Can you help me up?"

John scrambled to his feet then reached down and eased her up.

"Thank you." Lauren glanced around. "Where's your Jeep?"

"I walked over." He shoved his hands into his coat pockets as if to keep from reaching for her again. "I needed the time to pray and figure out how to tell you."

"I'm going to be realistic, but maybe he'll be okay. The fact the others didn't see more survivors doesn't mean he couldn't still be alive." John started to open his mouth, but she stopped him with a raised hand. "I know it's a vain hope, but I have to let myself believe at least for a couple days."

This wasn't the first time the ocean had swallowed one of the island's own, and it wouldn't be the last. Not when its history traced back to Blackbeard and his band of pirates. The sea's stamp on the island and its residents was long and integrated into the fabric of daily life.

She would remember that and not the way John watched her with pity as she turned and walked away.

⌒

Dinner was a quiet one as Lauren tried to find the right moment to mention the strong possibility that Steven was dead.

How exactly was one supposed to launch a conversation like

this? *I'm not sure how to tell you, but your brother and your boyfriend likely died on another boat the Germans torpedoed, but we aren't supposed to know that's what's happening.* The whole thing was preposterous.

Betty eyed her over the chicken noodle soup with biscuits. "Everything all right, Lauren?"

"Sure." She swallowed and looked up from her bowl to find three sets of skeptical eyes focused on her. All right, this would be the moment.

"I know." Rachel grinned. "You're mooning over the handsome Lieutenant Weary. Good thing Steven claimed me first, or I just might compete with you for his affections."

"What? Why would you say that?"

"You looked heartsick when he left. Is he getting stationed somewhere else? I bet he has interests for a boat station."

Lauren felt light-headed and fought for balance. "You can't mean that."

"Sure. He hops a ride on every boat he can. At least that's what I've seen."

Betty nodded. "He does good work with all the paperwork, but you can tell by the way he watches the sea that he wishes he was there."

"He can't." Surely he would have said something. But then she thought about it. Why would he? There were no promises between them. Just a friendship that seemed to spark with the prospect of more from time to time.

But that wasn't true. She wanted so much more with him.

He was a man who knew the greater world but had found a way to fit into their quieter life on the island. He knew so much yet never made her feel less qualified because she didn't have the same experiences as someone who lived on the mainland. Instead, he seemed to appreciate the unique experience she'd had living on the tiny island.

Betty reached across the small table and took her hand. "Are you all right, Lauren?"

Rachel looked concerned as well. "You can't be thinking about something serious with John, can you?"

"I don't know." She shook her head and then eased her hand from Betty's grasp. She forced a smile and stood. "Of course not. I'm fine. Just tired, I guess."

"We'll get the dishes tonight, won't we, Rachel?"

"You don't need to. I mean, you both worked all day."

"No, we need to do things around here to help you out. It's the least we can do to thank you for letting us live with you." Betty stood and added Allie's empty plate to hers. "We've got this tonight. You go take a walk or read upstairs, and we can talk another time about the chores we should take on to make sure we're carrying our weight."

"Betty is right. Sorry we didn't do this before." Rachel collected the silverware and moved to the sink. "Allie, do you want to wash or dry?"

"I have to help?"

"Sure you do." Betty leaned close to the girl. "Someday you want to get married and have your own house, right?"

Allie wrinkled her nose. "Maybe?"

Betty laughed and tugged one of Allie's braids. "Well, it's important to know how to care for a home. It's a lot of work, and it isn't fair to your sister to leave all of it to her."

"But I have homework."

Rachel grinned as she set everything in the sink. "That's important, but not the only kind of work."

Lauren grabbed her dad's jacket and went outside where she sank on the step. *Father, do You see us? What am I supposed to do?*

There was no immediate answer, but asking felt like shifting the burden from her shoulders to His. He was much better able to deal with the questions and ambiguity than she was. Now to leave the burdens and questions with Him. To trust in His concern for her and Allie.

A bird flapped to alight on a branch of the small myrtle. The bird eyed her, and she watched it. *Look at the birds of the air, for they neither sow nor reap nor gather into barns; yet your heavenly Father feeds them. Are you not of more value than they?* The verse from Matthew filled her mind, and with it came a peace that sank deep into her soul.

Even with the unknowns related to Steven, she could rest in knowing that God saw and cared. And for today that was what she would cling to.

Chapter 11

Saturday, March 14

When Lauren woke up on Saturday, she knew she needed to be realistic. Steven wasn't coming back. Still, she couldn't ignore the part of her that fought against that knowledge.

After a quiet breakfast, she gathered her coat and Allie. "Let's go for a walk."

Her sister looked at her quizzically then nodded. "Okay."

Rather than walking with her, Allie spun circles and sprinted ahead only to dash back at a pace that felt twice her usual intensity. As they crossed the road that ran along the eastern side of the island, Allie froze. "Will you tell me why we're here?"

"Why?"

"We usually walk on our side of the island."

"Maybe I wanted a change."

"If that's what you wanted, we'd leave. Nothing ever changes here."

Lauren couldn't fight a smile at her sister's words, even as she knew time was running out. "Let's walk a bit farther."

As they walked, Lauren watched for anything along the beach that might look like driftwood but was instead a body or debris from one of the wrecks. What would she do if debris from the *Caribsea* washed up? Her younger sister did not need to see that on this or another one of her rambles along the dunes and beaches.

Instead, she needed to focus on surviving the tragedy of the *Caribsea* and then find a way to move forward in the raw beauty of the island. There was a future for her and Allie—it was just hard to imagine at the moment.

The waves crashing against driftwood provided a syncopated drum beat as Allie bent down, picked up a stick, and then poked around in the sand.

"What did you find, Sandbug?"

Her shoulders barely lifted as she worked. "I don't know." She poked again then lifted her face, sea-blue gaze colliding with Lauren's. "I want to find a crab."

Lauren watched. "It's too cold for the crabs to come out."

"That's why I came to them with the stick." She bore down and then twisted before plopping on the sand. "Where's Steven?" Her chin trembled as she bit her lower lip.

Lauren squatted beside her younger sister. "I don't know." She needed to admit just how much she didn't know. "See the waves coming in?"

Allie nodded, her blond braids bouncing.

"They are pushing hard, and when a boat, especially a smaller one like Steven's, is trying to get home, sometimes the waves push it the other direction."

Allie frowned at her. "I understand that." She pointed back toward their cottage. "We live by the water."

"Of course we do. But I need to tell you, there was an accident on his boat." Lauren swallowed hard against a sudden lump.

Allie's eyes widened. "Is he okay?"

"I don't know." Lauren smoothed one of Allie's braids then pushed to standing. "I'm worried too." The words slipped out, and she fought to keep her face neutral even as she felt tears clouding her eyes.

"You are?"

"Absolutely. The accident happened a few days ago, and Steven hasn't made it home."

Allie looked away, and Lauren wasn't certain she was seeing anything specific. "Do you think he's alive?"

"I hope so, but I don't know." The heaviness in her heart made words hard to speak. She wanted to give Allie hope but couldn't lie to her. "Only God knows exactly where Steven is."

"Did other people come from his boat?"

"Yes." The word hurt to say, especially as the light dimmed in Allie's eyes.

Allie took a step away and watched the waves in silence. Then she turned to Lauren with a forced smile. "Do you think we'll see a pony if we keep walking?"

The change in topic was quick, and Lauren wouldn't force her to dwell on Steven. There was time for that later. They'd already experienced so much loss. Instead, she followed Allie's lead. "There aren't as many as there used to be, since many were moved a few years ago." The wild ponies were descended from those who survived shipwrecks back when the Spanish were first exploring the coast. The hardy ponies weren't as common a sight since a big push to move them four years earlier.

"I would love to see one." There was a wistful tone to the words. Allie had been very young when they were relocated. Then she sighed and pushed to her feet. "I'm ready to go home."

"All right." Lauren reached for Allie, comforted by the warmth of the mittened hand even as her gaze continued to scan the horizon.

"We need to pray for Steven."

"You're right." Lauren only prayed it wasn't too late for the prayers to alter the outcome.

⌣

When John arrived back at the station, he went in search of Andrew. If anyone could help him search the beach for Steven's body, it would be his friend. They probably had three hours at most before Andrew had to report to duty if he had a night patrol. That should give them sufficient time to do an initial search. His misplaced hope had turned into a recovery mission. He couldn't let someone else find his friend's body if it washed up to shore. That grim chore should fall to someone who'd done it before.

Half an hour later, John piloted the boat while Andrew scoured the coastline with his binoculars. Andrew's legs were in a wide stance to provide balance as he kept a steady sweep moving along the horizon to the beach and back.

"Dial it down a bit."

John eased off the speed until the cutter was barely moving. "See anything?"

"Not sure. There's some driftwood I want to scan carefully."

John turned off the engine and came to stand next to Andrew. He could see the collection of wood on the edge of the beach several hundred feet from where they rocked. "Want me to go closer?"

"Maybe." Andrew frowned, and he had the look of a yellow lab on point with a bird. "I think you should."

John hurried to the small pilothouse and, after restarting the boat, turned the wheel to ease it toward the beach, being careful to stay far enough back to keep from grounding it. The water was only five feet deep in most of the area around the island, so he had to keep a constant watch for sandbars. "I think this is as close as I can get."

Silence answered him as Andrew focused on the driftwood. He lowered his glasses and turned to John. "We need to go ashore."

John lowered the anchor, and they hopped over the side of the boat, sloshing through water that started at their waist, the ocean cold enough to suck the warmth from his body in an instant. "That'll steal your breath."

"Yep." Andrew pressed through the water with a singular focus, aiming for the beach and driftwood.

John followed him onto the shore, shivering as the water dripped from his legs. The sand clung to his ruined shoes, and he knew the saltwater would shrink them the moment he pulled them off. He sloshed to the pile of wood, pace quickening when he saw it wasn't a log.

———

Allie had wandered ahead, and Lauren let her, knowing the area she was in shouldn't have wreck debris. Maybe she needed the time to process the reality of another loss. She could see the results of her sister, birds spiraling in the air overhead, before she spotted her.

"Steven!" The shrill call had Lauren's shoulders rising toward her ears, then she took off running to catch up with her sister. When she crested the dune, Allie barreled into Lauren. "Where is he?" Her head turned from side to side as she searched for him with a frantic air.

Lauren sighed as her heart clenched. "He's not coming back."

Allie frowned, and her skin paled. "But I found something."

"What?" *Please, don't let it be his body.*

"Over here." Allie reluctantly stepped forward, gripping Lauren's hand tightly.

As she walked, Lauren prayed for wisdom and grace. She was ill-equipped to walk her sister through the uncertainty of a shipwreck. Her heart stilled and then took off as she spotted what Allie had found.

The flotation device clearly had *Caribsea* painted on it as it bounced in the waves at the edge of the beach. She walked to water and leaned over to grab it. "How did that get to this side of the island?"

"It means he's not coming back, doesn't it?"

"Yes." Though a part of Lauren's mind wanted to scream that if it had reached here, maybe her brother had been clinging to it and made it home too. She pushed the far-fetched thought aside. Surely he would have been spotted by a boat rather than drifting aimlessly around the long island to arrive at this point.

"Why?" Allie's voice held a plaintive sound that cracked the last reserves Lauren had.

"I don't know." Lauren fought the tears that surged for release. They'd both lost so much, it wasn't fair to have one more person taken from them.

Allie walked away, then back and forth, as if she couldn't figure out how to process the emotion. "We should take it to John." She resolutely walked to the life ring. "I'll carry it."

When they reached the cottage, Lauren felt stripped of energy. She needed a minute before she walked to the station to find John. Allie was right. He was exactly who she wanted next to her as she navigated this new loss.

Lauren sank onto the back-door step and then patted next to her. Moments like this she longed for the wisdom and help of a mother or aunt. She didn't know how to give Allie the words and comfort she needed, but she didn't have the luxury of waiting for someone else to provide that. Her sister had only stopped asking about their parents a couple of months earlier. Now this. There was nothing fair or right in an additional loss. Allie sank beside her, shoulders slumped and chin quivering, as Lauren slid an arm around her and edged closer.

"I'm sorry we don't know where he is. But we have to accept that he's not coming back." She swallowed hard against the reality that the ocean wouldn't release him as it had released the life ring. "And I will stay here with you. You know that, right?"

Allie sniffled and turned into Lauren's shoulder. "I miss him."

"Me too." She held her sister as she cried, wishing there was someone to hold her.

Chapter 12

Sunday, March 15

The task of bringing a body to the station had become too common. The images hadn't left John all night, and now as he walked into the church, he longed to divert his focus in other places. He nodded hello to several people, but his heart was looking for one person. When he spotted her dark hair, he changed his direction. There was a space next to her, and he edged toward it. "Mind if I join you?"

A faint smile tipped her lips, but it didn't reach her eyes. "Please."

As he settled next to her, he felt a slight tremor. "Everything all right?"

"No. Allie found something on the beach yesterday."

His heart sank as he took in her too-pale face. He kept his voice low and steady. "What did she find?"

"A life ring with *Caribsea* painted on it. I put it on the *Southern Miss* but couldn't make myself leave for the longest time." She seemed to curl into herself, as if subconsciously trying to shield herself. "I'm sorry I didn't bring it sooner. I just couldn't accept the truth."

He wanted to take her in his arms and let her know that she

wasn't alone. That he saw her and cared about her pain. Instead, he allowed their shoulders to touch as she stared toward the altar. He'd only known Steven for a matter of months, but the man's death would leave a larger-than-life-sized hole. "I'm sorry this is happening."

She nodded, and he caught the tremble of her chin from his periphery. "I know we aren't the only family losing loved ones right now."

"That doesn't make your loss insignificant." She sighed and leaned against him, and he wished there was more he could do beyond acknowledge that her pain was real and Steven should still be here. "I wish I could take this away."

She sniffled, and he felt her arms come around him. "You can't." She shuddered, and he brushed his hand in a sooth-ing motion on her back. "I'll be okay. Seeing the life ring just made it real."

"We found a body on the other side of the island."

She pulled away enough to look up at him. "It wasn't. . . ?"

"No. Another soul." He blinked hard as he met her gaze then looked away. Pastor Hutchins's wife took a seat on the piano bench and began to play the notes of a hymn. "Can I walk you home?"

Lauren nodded and then slipped her hand in his.

After the service, Allie raced out of the church, and Lauren followed at a more sedate pace. John paused to speak to a few islanders, and she noted the way he knew each of them.

Her thoughts strayed to what he'd told her about his week.

What must it be like to be a part of recovering the victims of a wreck? Lauren could be glad she hadn't seen a body, but if the wrecks continued at the pace they had been, her luck could run out. They reached the cottage, and she paused on the stoop. "Would you like to come in for something to drink?"

"Sure."

"If I had something better than Spam, I'd offer to make lunch."

A grin split his face. "That's all right. I'll get real meat at the station."

"Sounds like you should invite me to lunch then."

He chuckled, and she liked the way it lit him from the inside. "Another time."

"Sure." Once they were inside, she filled the kettle with water and turned on the gas beneath a burner to heat the water. She needed something to warm her from the inside. Betty had gone to the mainland for the weekend, making the cottage feel more like it had before taking on the boarders.

John seemed to notice that she'd slipped away in her thoughts. "You all right?"

"I will be." Eventually. She pulled two mugs from the shelf as she decided what to share. "Just thinking about all the changes this year."

A minute later, Rachel stepped from her room. Her face looked wan as she eased to a chair.

Lauren felt a flash of concern as she studied the young woman. "You all right?"

"Good as I am these days. I thought extra sleep would help with the nausea." She grimaced. "It didn't do as much as I'd hoped." She swallowed and then focused on John. "Do you know when the *Caribsea* will return? I need to talk to Steven."

John's gaze darted to Lauren's as his shoulders edged up. "You haven't told her?"

Obviously not or Rachel wouldn't have asked the question. Still, Lauren schooled her features as she gave a small shake of her head. "I didn't want to until I was sure."

"Tell me what?" What little color had been in Rachel's face receded.

John didn't want to be the one to tell her, but she needed

to know what had happened. "Steven's ship sank, and he didn't make it," he said as gently as he could.

"What do you mean? Steven didn't make it?" She pushed back the chair and stood, a hand pressed against her stomach. "What am I going to do?"

John glanced between the young women. "The *Caribsea* sank a few days ago. No one has been rescued since the night of the eleventh."

"There's no chance?"

Lauren walked over to Rachel and took her cold hands. "No. We have to accept he's gone." Her last words were whispered as she pushed them past the lump in her throat. "I wish the answer was different."

Rachel stiffened as if she braced against the news. "I think I need to be alone."

After she closed the door to her room, John took Lauren in his arms again. "You're all going to be okay."

"We will survive." She let herself relax into the moment. This man was good and true, and he would be there when she needed him. Tension built at her temples, and she took a deep breath that she released slowly. "I'll need to find a job, but that will come."

"There's always work at the station." John's words were quick, but she didn't want to rely on them.

"Maybe. But I don't have many skills."

"You're smart and kind. Both are key when it comes to working with others." He settled his chin on the top of her head, and she never wanted to move as she let his words soak into her heart.

"God sees us, and He's not surprised by this tragedy. I just wish He would have spared Steven." She eased back from John. "Do we have a funeral when there's no body? A memorial?"

"You can give it time. What's best for Allie?"

Oh, she loved this man. Lauren froze as the words hit her. She didn't know when he had become that important to her, but she knew it was true. He had shown his depth and character. But she didn't want him to feel obligated to her. She needed to feel chosen because he saw and cared for her, not because she was part of a problem he needed to solve. She wanted to show him she could handle the new challenges on her own, that she was capable of solving the new problems confronting her.

Yes, she might need help, but she was also going to need to stand on her own.

What if he did go to sea?

She had to learn to rely on herself, so if that happened, she was ready and prepared.

———

One moment everything felt right and secure. The next something changed. John felt Lauren move away in more ways than just the physical distance she created. "Did I do something wrong? I thought you liked. . .this. . .us." He gestured between them, frustrated by the lack of the right words.

"I do, but I need to figure out what's happening and how I'm going to handle it."

"But you don't have to do that alone."

"I do. What about when you get assigned to a boat like you want? What am I supposed to do then?"

"What do you mean?" How did she know that was his goal?

"It's been your goal all along."

"Maybe my goal has changed." The words resonated in a way he didn't anticipate.

"Then I guess we'll see what happens."

"That's not very encouraging."

"It's the best I can do right now." She sighed as she rubbed her temples. He wanted to step up and rub the tension away but kept his hands fisted at his sides. "I need you to know I can handle life. I need to know I can do that." Her gaze searched his as if pleading for understanding. "This is hard, but I have to figure this out."

"And I'm supposed to watch and wait?"

"Maybe?" She rubbed her gold cross, as if gaining strength from it. "I need a bit of time." She sighed. "There are so many changes happening, it's a lot to sort all at once."

He heard her and tried not to internalize the words as rejection. She was asking for time, not asking him to leave. "I don't want you to be alone."

"I'm not. I have Allie." She gave him a half-hearted smile. "And there's everyone on the island. We take care of our own."

"Will I see you at the station or church?"

She nodded. "And around." She reached over and took his hand, her small one soft in his. "I need all the friends I can get."

His thoughts raced. "Okay." He stepped back and lightly tugged his hand free. "Then I'll head out. There's plenty of work for me at the station."

"Thank you."

He walked out the front door, not allowing himself to look over his shoulder. The walk through the village gave him time to consider her request. While he'd promised Steven to watch out for her and Allie, it had become much more than fulfilling a promise. He loved this woman and needed to do what he could to convince her the way he saw her and felt about her was real.

He thought back over her words. She'd really been requesting the opportunity to stand on her own two feet. He could respect that. He wouldn't want to be dependent on someone else if there was an alternative. Maybe she needed that independence before they moved forward. At the same time, his thoughts returned to her statement about him getting on a boat.

After losing her father and Steven to the sea, he could

understand her reluctance to be involved with a sailor. Yet he worked for the Coast Guard. He couldn't guarantee he would never be moved to a ship even if he gave up his pursuit of a placement.

That conundrum filled his mind as he worked through the leave and transfer requests that had piled on his desk while unraveling the mystery of the *Southern Miss* and the sinking of the *Caribsea*. Could he find the value in spending his days in the Coast Guard on such tasks?

Based on Lauren's words, he'd need to.

That would require a shift from seeing the real value in serving with his life at risk. Instead, he'd have to find meaning in providing the unseen backbone that supported those serving in the front.

That thought followed him through the next days as he worked with the Navy liaison to create a site map for the expanded base. It seemed new Coasties arrived every day along with Navy, all needing to be processed. That would only ramp up as the creek was dredged again to deepen it for a new class of Navy boat as well as the construction of the base and radar station. The Navy had already reached an agreement for the radar spot.

Then the liaison officer told him that the Navy was exploring spreading mines in the shoals on the east side of the island, and there was plenty of work for him to do coordinating and planning. Might he need some help to manage that process? He considered the men currently working around the station. Most were great with their hands and the sea, but not so much with the bookwork that filled John's days. While Lauren claimed she didn't have the right education to work in a setting like that, he'd heard Steven tease her about reading all the books at the library, a claim she hadn't denied as soft color filled her cheeks.

There was a solution, and he'd help her find it.

Maybe in the process she'd see how much he cared for her.

It gave him a goal worth pursuing. One he'd relish. And maybe in the process he'd find his place in this war and in the Coast Guard.

Chapter 13

The weeks passed, and with each, Lauren focused on helping Allie and Rachel handle the reality that Steven was gone. Betty had stepped in to help keep the house clean and food prepared as the other two women in the cottage walked in the veil of grief. Lauren didn't think she could have managed helping Rachel and Allie while also processing her grief without Betty taking on so much of the work around the cottage.

The future was so unclear.

Rachel had begun to show the smallest evidence of her pregnancy, and that meant there were decisions that needed to be made about what happened next. Somehow Rachel would have to provide for her baby since there weren't extra funds. Lauren lay awake many nights as scenarios spun through her mind like a constellation of questions and concerns. She needed to help Rachel, but right now she wasn't sure how she'd provide for Allie.

Through it all, John was a constant presence. He was always there but never in a way that pressured. Instead, he kept her informed of the happenings at the station, dropping nuggets about jobs, but Lauren kept looking for another option. She didn't want to demonstrate to him just how much she didn't know.

But as she strolled on the island, she saw its character was shifting. When she walked south on the island, she often saw Coasties riding patrol along the beach. As the calendar neared May, it wasn't clear the patrols made much difference as more boats sank in April. The beach was littered with debris and stank of the tar and oil. All of it left her wanting her island back to its prewar condition.

Like it or not, this was the way the island was now.

Then in early May, she opened the door to find John and a Navy officer walking up the path to the cottage. She ran a hand to smooth the hair that escaped her ponytail and then wiped her hands along the sides of her skirt. "John."

He tipped his hat in her direction with a smile that warmed her more than the spring sun before quickly sobering as he turned to the man next to him. "Lauren, I don't know if you've met Navy Lieutenant Warren Dules."

The man extended his hand with a nod. "Ma'am."

"Miss. Doesn't matter." She smiled as the lieutenant shook her hand. "What brings y'all out this way?"

"May we come inside?" The man's baritone was formal, and she glanced at John, who shrugged but didn't meet her gaze.

"Of course." She walked them back to the kitchen table. "Can I get you something to drink?"

"That'd be nice." The man pulled a chair from the table and sat.

"Lauren, you sit, and I'll grab it." John motioned her to a chair, but that only made her more on edge.

"I've got it. Thanks." A moment later, she set tea in front of them. "No sugar, I'm afraid."

"Rationing has us all being more mindful."

"It hasn't even started yet, but I may be hoarding it." She took a sip and then focused on the lieutenant. "How can I help you, sir?"

"You may have seen the Navy is expanding the station."

"I've heard rumors." The post office grapevine remained active.

The man took a sip of his tea then placed his hands on the table in front of him and leaned in. "I'm going to be direct. We need your property."

Lauren felt the world tilt and placed a hand on each side of her chair to ground herself. "What do you mean?"

"The Navy is prepared to purchase your land at a fair price, but we need it."

"We're across the creek from the station. There are other properties closer."

"And we're negotiating with them as well. Yours is in a good position for monitoring this side of the harbor."

"Why would you need to?" She glanced at John, wanting him to help her. "This is all my sister and I have. It's all that's left of our family. I can't just sell it."

"We are in a war."

At his words, she stiffened. "I am well aware, as my brother died on the *Caribsea*."

John finally reacted. He shifted into the table and the conversation. "Dules, will you give us a minute?"

The man looked like he was going to argue then nodded and stood. "I'll be in the other room."

Lauren felt tears filling her eyes, and that only added to her lack of control. "I can't sell."

"I know." John took her hands in his, finally connecting with her for the first time since they'd arrived. "Warren is a good man doing his job, but he doesn't understand everything that's happened. He has the big job of getting this base running as fast as possible. That doesn't leave a lot of time for softening words and phrases."

"Do I have to sell?" She could barely push the words out as every fiber of her body fought against the idea. Her breath came in gulps, yet her lungs didn't fill.

He let go of her hands and pulled her close, making soothing circles on her back. "Take slow breaths." He gave a slow release. "Follow me."

As she worked to time her breathing with his, some of the panic subsided. Whether it was the breathing or being encircled by his arms, it didn't matter. He was bringing peace to her. "Thank you." She closed her eyes and felt the moment. "What do I do?"

"Listen to what Lieutenant Dules offers. Then choose what you want to do. If it's a good offer, you can sell and leave the island. You'd have the funds to start over somewhere else. Or choose to stay and trust God will open another door."

"You want me to leave." The thought had the panicked edge returning. "I won't be able to find a job. Allie and I have never lived anywhere else. This is home."

"Then you don't need to leave." He pulled back, and when she couldn't look at him, he gently tipped her chin up. "You have a choice. Before we arrived, you didn't. Now you can decide what's right for you and Allie."

"I can't decide this on my own." It felt too big and too overwhelming.

"You don't have to. God is always with you and will lead you. I'm here too." His clear gaze never wavered. "I'm not going anywhere."

Questions filled her gaze. "You're not trying to get assigned to a boat?"

"Not anymore. You're where I want to be. I've been thinking and praying a lot, and I realized I'm good at managing all this paperwork. Not everyone can say that. There's a contentment that comes with knowing I'm using my skills in a way that matters." He grinned and felt the peace that had been with him since he withdrew the transfer paperwork. He was right where he wanted to be and contributing in the best way.

"Okay." She cleared her throat and swiped at the tears that

had slid down her cheeks. "Lieutenant Dules?"

The man reappeared in the doorway. "Ma'am?"

"I'm ready to hear what you have to say. However, I have to be honest and tell you that I find it hard to imagine leaving."

John settled back as Warren walked her through the Navy's offer. As he listened, he wondered what the right answer would be. He couldn't picture her anywhere but the island, but that didn't mean this wasn't God giving her a bigger opportunity. She *was* this island with her quiet, slightly rough-edged beauty. It was a reflection of the rugged place she called home. A simple yet hard life.

Twenty minutes later, the two men walked back to the Jeep for the short drive to the station.

Warren leaned an elbow on the window and took his cap off. "How'd that go?"

"I'm not sure she'll sell."

"I doubt she will. I had to try." Warren turned to look out the side. "There's something about these people. You offer them a chance to get off this island and an easier life, and they stay."

"It's their home." John slowed as he neared the post office and then passed the library. "If this was where you grew up, you'd be reluctant to leave."

"Nah. This is a hard place."

John pulled into the parking slot, and Warren hopped out. "Thanks for the ride, John." He closed the door then leaned back in the open window. "I need that land, which means as the liaison, I need your help getting it."

John met his gaze and didn't flinch. "Not doing that. She's a capable woman and can decide what's best for her and her sister."

Warren stared him down. "Think about your allegiances."

"Always."

"Then I'll see you at chow."

As the man strode away, John had the sense he wouldn't

easily give up. As far as John could tell, the Navy didn't have to build anywhere near Lauren's cottage. He'd back her up even if that meant making Warren angry.

———

Lauren spent hours walking and praying that week. The Navy's offer felt like a lot of money. But it didn't change the fact that she had nowhere to go and the cost of leaving all she'd ever known would be more than she was willing to pay even with the generous offer from the military. Things like roots were worth more than cash. While this island might feel constraining to some, to her it was all she'd known.

Step away? She couldn't do it. This was home and always would be. She would not be the reason Allie lost anything more. Even if it meant Lauren had to choose to be alone for the sake of her sister. It was a sacrifice she was willing to make as many times as necessary until Allie was old enough to decide her own future.

School would be out soon, and Lauren was still looking for work. Maybe it was time to swallow her pride and ask John for help. He would be finely tuned to the needs the Coast Guard and Navy had at the station.

As she walked through the village, she said hello to Amos Garfield as he swept the steps of the general store. Activity increased as she neared the station, and for the first time, she had to check in at a central desk and wait for John to come down to her. His step quickened when he spotted her, and a smile warmed his face.

He stopped in front of her, arms relaxed at his sides. "Lauren, is everything all right?"

"Yes." She noted all the people moving about the entryway and then glanced outside. "Could we talk for a few minutes?"

"Sure." He opened the door and waited for her to precede him before walking alongside her. "Want to sit at the picnic table?" He pointed toward one sitting in the shade of the building.

"Is it new?"

"Installed this week."

"Looks perfect." It was tucked slightly out of the way and would give them the privacy for her to ask for his help.

After they sat next to each other, he settled his hands on the tabletop and angled her direction. "What's going on?"

Lauren lifted her face to the breeze and felt it cool her skin. Then she sighed and turned toward him. "I need help with a job."

"You know I'm ready to connect you." He left unspoken the *and have been.*

"I know." She deflated at what she had to admit. "I wanted to stand on my own. Figure out how we were going to do this. The Navy's offer was good, but it's not right for us. Allie is a child of the island. I can't move her without changing her. And I can't find a job here. There just aren't any."

"Except at the station, where I need smart women."

"I'm not smart, John."

"You are. Smart is more than sitting in a classroom, though I bet you did fine there. It's understanding people and working hard. You do both."

She glanced at John without turning her head his direction. Her shoulder felt warm from where they touched, and she didn't need the added distraction of catching his eye.

Her sister had already lost so much and at an age that could devastate anyone. Her parents' surprise child was the light of their lives until the day they took the ferry to the mainland and didn't return. Steven had been twenty-five to her sixteen, and they had both borne up under the grief because what else was there to do. Allie had only been nine, and her life had changed the most. Lauren still felt ill-equipped to guide her sister along the paths of childhood.

"I'll do anything if it will allow me to stay here with Allie."

He turned and took her hands, demolishing the small wall

she'd tried to erect. He seemed determined to break through all her defenses and show her how wonderful he was. "No one will force you to move. I promise."

As he said the words, she believed him to her deepest core.

"Thank you." She couldn't look away if she wanted to.

John seemed to feel the same as he leaned closer, so gently, and then, as he searched her face, came within a whisper of her lips. "I want to kiss you, but I won't if you don't agree."

She felt the smile start in her soul and then whisper its way out. "I agree."

And then his lips touched hers, sweet and light, and she knew she wasn't alone. Not anymore.

Chapter 14

Saturday, May 8

A new rhythm was coming to Lauren's days with her job at the station. John had been right. This was a job that fit her perfectly and allowed her to earn enough to sustain her small family, especially when combined with the income from housing Betty and Rachel. Rachel was making plans for what came next, but that was a journey she had to make on her own. Lauren could only be there to provide a safe place in the interim. In fact, Lauren thought there might be a sailor or two who was smitten with the young woman. The question was what Rachel would decide.

All Lauren knew for certain was that the baby growing inside her friend would be loved. And she would do her part to make sure the child always knew that so long as Rachel allowed her to be a part of the child's life.

Lauren had also told Lieutenant Dules that she couldn't sell. She and Allie needed the consistency the cottage gave them.

With that decision made, life felt more settled even though she couldn't see the future clearly.

Allie had begged Lauren to take the *Southern Miss* out on the water, and she'd taken that as a good sign, since her sister had barely been able to look at it since John returned it. So she found herself steering the boat along the Pamlico Sound toward the station. She wouldn't take it on the ocean side of the island, but they could enjoy the sun on their faces and wind in their hair for a bit.

"Can John come?" Allie knelt on the bench across the middle and propped her elbows on the side.

Lauren adjusted their direction to take them toward the station's pier. "We can see. I don't know what his plans are today."

Knowing him as she had come to, he was likely working at his desk. The paperwork never eased despite having her help and another clerk. It was amazing to her the amount of paper required to pay the Coasties. If there was a way to make a process complicated, the military seemed to have it included in its processes.

"Help me grab the pier."

Allie reached over, but before she could do more than toss her blond braids behind her, a Coastie had hurried over to help.

"Can I be of assistance, ma'am?" His smile revealed a small gap between his front teeth.

"Thank you." Lauren turned off the engine and tossed the Coastie the rope. He caught it easily and made short work of wrapping it around the pillar. Then he offered a hand, and Lauren and Allie scrambled out of the boat.

"What brings you to the station?"

"Looking for Lieutenant Weary. Have you seen him?"

"Yes, ma'am. He was in the mess working on a book a while ago."

"We'll head there then. Thank you for your help."

He tipped his hat toward her, but she felt his gaze on her as she led Allie to the station. It was quieter than it was during the week, but with the war, it never emptied completely. There was constant monitoring of the shoals and other areas as the hunt continued for U-boats. She had access to more information now that she worked with John, though he'd sworn her to silence. The Allies had yet to knock out one of the U-boats that trolled the area, and the result was consistent. At least fifteen boats had been torpedoed in April along the North Carolina coast. The loss of supplies and men was immense. It was just one reason she'd stay safely on the mainland side of the island.

When they entered the mess, John was bent over a table. She could imagine he was working on rows of numbers, something he took particular care and pride in. Allie took off toward him before Lauren could remind her to be quiet.

"John! We're here, and we want you to come with us."

His head snapped up, and it took a moment for his attention to focus on Allie. "Allie, what brings you here?" His attention shifted to Lauren, and she felt the heat of his gaze in a way that warmed her through. Right here with this man was where she wanted to be.

Something shifted in Lauren's face as he sank into her gaze. He could get lost in those eyes and never want to come out.

Allie cleared her throat. "Are y'all okay?"

Lauren gave a half laugh then took a step back. "We didn't want to intrude, but we've got the *Southern Miss* at the pier and wondered if you'd like to enjoy the water with us. It's a beautiful afternoon."

"Please?" Allie leaned into the table and batted her eyelashes at him with what she probably imagined was a pretty pout.

John fought the strong urge to laugh and instead closed the account book he was working on. "Sounds like a welcome break. Let me run this up to my office. Give me five minutes?"

Allie huffed, and Lauren elbowed her. "Okay."

Lauren mouthed *sorry.* "Take your time. We'll get a glass of water, right, Allie?"

———

Thirty minutes later, he pulled the boat to a stop and dropped the anchor. The water was calm, and the gentle rocking of the waves soothing. "I could get used to this."

"Spending time with us?" Lauren's words held a hint of longing, and he wanted to pull her toward him and never let go.

Instead, he grinned and sank on to the bench closest to the pilothouse. "Well, that too." He leaned his head back and let the sun warm his face. "It's peaceful out here."

"Yes." Lauren's voice was quiet.

"You could let people rent the boat for short tours in the sound."

"It's a thought." She sounded skeptical, but he'd learned she often needed a bit of time to think an idea through and reach a decision. All he wanted to do was give her options.

Allie moved from her bench to come sit by him, the boat rocking more heavily as she did so. She wasn't as comfortable on the boat as he would have expected, but maybe the summer would change that.

Quiet eased over the boat, the sound of the waves and the occasional seagull providing background music. Allie leaned against him, and in a few minutes he realized she'd fallen asleep. Her easy trust surprised him. "Has she been sleeping well?"

Lauren nodded, her eyes softening as she watched her sister. "The water usually has this effect on her."

John noted the gold cross. "You often wear that."

She glanced down, and her fingers gripped it. "This?"

"Yes."

"It's been in my family for generations. It's amazing none of us have lost it, but it's a reminder that God's love is faithful in every season and in every reason. Even when we can't see Him clearly." Her voice trailed off, and she followed a seagull riding an air current. "I keep reminding myself that God cares for us so much more than He cares for that bird. Yet Matthew tells us He cares deeply for the bird and its needs."

"He does."

She turned her attention back to him with a smile. "You're one way God has demonstrated that to me."

Her words made John pause. "Why do you say that?"

"He brought you to Ocracoke out of all the places the Coast Guard could have sent you. Then you and Steven became friends. And you decided to adopt me and Allie too." She swallowed hard. "When I feel alone, God reminds me that you're here as well as other people on the island. We aren't alone. Thank you."

John knew he should head the boat back, but Allie was still peaceful. As he looked at her and then Lauren, he couldn't stay silent. "I want to be there for you forever, if you'll have me, Lauren. I know there's a lot that is uncertain in this life right now, but one thing I am certain of is that you are an amazing woman, and I would feel the loss if I walked away without you next to me."

Lauren's mouth hung open, and tears filled her eyes.

"I didn't mean to make you cry."

"You didn't." She swiped at her cheeks. "I've just wanted to say the same thing. I know you won't stay on the island when the Coast Guard moves you. But if I'm with you, I know Allie and I will be fine. We can always come home when we need a break, but I want to make my home wherever you are."

She eased forward and wrapped her arms around his neck, careful not to disturb Allie, and then she kissed him with a sweetness filled with promises of what the future could hold.

Author's Note

There reaches a point in each author's research where we have to release finding the perfect answer and write. I wish I could share all the resources I relied on when writing this novella. I learned so much about living on the Barrier Islands during 1942. But even with *all* the research, there are certain details I simply couldn't find. At that point, I had to fill in the gaps as best I could and write the story. I hope you enjoy it!

One change I made is that when the *Caribsea* was sunk, the survivors were taken to the Little Creek Coast Guard Station, not Ocracoke. I changed this so that John could be a larger part of the process. Regardless of where they were taken, the Coast Guard up and down the coast were a key part of the Battle of the Atlantic as it played out along the North Carolina coast.

If you'd like to learn more, I highly recommend the following resource: *U-Boats off the Outer Banks: Shadows in the Moonlight*. Written by Jim Bunch, it does a wonderful job pulling together what happened in the first seven months of 1942. While most of the fighting occurred in other parts of the world, during this season of time, the Atlantic coast was under siege.

I truly hope you enjoyed this step back in time through Lauren and John's story.

Since the time **Cara Putman** could read Nancy Drew, she wanted to write mysteries. In 2005, she attended a book signing at a local Christian bookstore. The rest, as they say, is history. There she met Colleen Coble, and since then she's been writing award-winning books with the count currently at thirty-six published and more in the works. In addition to writing, she is a mom of four, attorney, clinical professor at a Big Ten university, and all around crazy woman. Crazy about God, her husband, and her kids. Cara graduated with honors from the University of Nebraska-Lincoln (Go Huskers!), George Mason Law School, and Purdue University's MBA program.

JOIN US ONLINE!

Christian Fiction for Women

Christian Fiction for Women is your online home for the latest in Christian fiction.

Check us out online for:

- Giveaways
- Recipes
- Info about Upcoming Releases
- Book Trailers
- News and More!

Find Christian Fiction for Women at Your Favorite Social Media Site:

 Search "Christian Fiction for Women"

 @fictionforwomen